I0741084

BONDFIRE

a Tale of
LOVE

BETRAYAL and a

Dangerous
GAME

CAROLYN R. GREEN

ACKNOWLEDGMENT

First, I give thanks to God for granting me the opportunity to fulfill a lifelong dream of becoming a published author.

A special thanks to my children, Toriano and Sheneetra, and my daughter-in-law, Robyn, for supporting and encouraging me to pursue my goals and dreams.

To Inez Warren, Ericka Stewart, and Pamela Holt for pushing me to write, even when I didn't feel like it. Your motivation encouraged me to keep telling the story.

Finally, to Azaida Media for taking a chance on me and helping me accomplish this dream!

DEDICATION

This book is dedicated to

the memory of my late mother,

Mrs. Arbra Green,

who always pushed and

believed in me.

She never gave up on me,

even when I was willing

to give up on myself.

Table of Contents

1

TISH

Today is the beginning of the rest of my life. Sam, who is the love of my life, is coming home after serving an eighteen year sentence in a federal corrections facility. We can finally begin our lives together. No more long trips just to visit him for only a few hours, and no more fifteen minute phone calls. I wish my family and friends were happy for me, but they all think that he is not the man for me because I am college educated with a successful career.

My friend Carol hates him with a passion; but I can truly say that she always listens when I talk or complain about Sam. When I am done, she talks bad about him and offers to kick his ass or get rid of him for me. On the other hand, my friend, Lisa, has a million things to say and she is always interjecting her opinions and negativity into my relationship with Sam.

Sam and I have been dating since I was eighteen years old and I love him with all of my heart and soul. He makes me so happy and he makes me feel like a queen. He is the only man that has ever made me feel like I am the most beautiful girl in the world. Those are the reasons why I waited on him and held him down while he was in prison. There's my man looking good, tall, dark and handsome. As he exits the last security gate, he yells out, "Tish!" He approaches me with a big smile on his face, grabs me and then starts kissing me. Suddenly I feel a rush of emotion and want to drop my panties at the gate. However, I remember that I am a lady, and I will act as such. We have the rest of our lives to make passionate love, even though I have not had sex with another man during his eighteen year sentence. I have been faithful to my soul mate.

During our eight hour drive back to Memphis, we cannot keep our

hands off one another. The sight of him makes me horny. I unzip his pants and pleasure him with the stroke of my tongue while he is driving. We soon pull over on the side of the interstate and commence to making love like rabbits, but it only lasts for two minutes. I hope that is only because it has been awhile, and not a glimpse of what may possibly be the standard for years to come. We continue on our journey and the time is now approaching 2:00 a.m. We are almost back in Memphis, so I decide to reveal a few surprises to Sam that will help us better plan for our future together.

"Babe, I signed the lease on our new condo downtown, and the view of the river is breathtaking. Also, I know you will need transportation as you begin to seek employment; so, I have a new Chevy Impala waiting for you. And lastly, I am taking you on a shopping spree because it is a requirement that my man look good!"

"Tish, that's wonderful! I don't know what I would do without you."

I gently kiss him on the cheek and then snuggle close to him for the remainder of the trip. The next day, Sam immediately lands a job as a detailer at Enterprise Car Rental. He is not happy with it, but it will suffice until something better comes along. I assured him that he does not have to worry because I have his back. However, after a week on the job, Sam begins to complain. He is thinking about quitting because he feels that the pay is not enough in comparison to the amount of work he has to do. He also suggests that I should pick up a second, part-time job so that we will not struggle financially. After giving it some thought, I finally agree. I will do anything for the love of my life!

LISA

It is the beginning of what I anticipate to be a great school year, and the ending of a fantastic summer. I am ready to greet my third graders and challenge them to have the most awesome school year ever! Preparing for the new school year is one of my favorite times of the year. Although I have

spent a lot of money on books and bulletin board decorations; when I see my youngsters and the smiles on their faces, it makes it all worth it.

I completed my education specialist degree and passed the administrator's exam. I also have all of the credentials that are required to be a Principal. However, I probably will never leave the classroom because that is where my heart and passion thrive.

It is the end of the week and I have a date for the first time in a while. It's a real date and not a booty call. I met a gorgeous, tall, big, bald, sexy, caramel-colored man at the gas station. We exchanged numbers and have since had long phone conversations like teenagers. He finally asked me out, and I said yes. We have a lot in common, despite the fact that he is six years younger than I. However, he is very mature and quite successful. He just may be a keeper. I have not told my besties, Tish and Carol, about him because I don't want to get excited about a man, only to be let down again. Carol will be excited about the news, but Tish most likely will be a hater as usual. If the date goes well, I will tell my girls all about him afterwards.

As it turned out, Mike was such a gentleman during our date. He opened doors, pulled out chairs, and even ordered for me. Chivalry is still alive and well! He treated me to a romantic dinner at The Pier on the riverfront, which is a five-star restaurant. We had engaging conversation; and while waiting for our dinner, he serenaded me with a song. The tone of his voice was both awesome and seductive. After dinner, we went on a carriage ride, and then took a boat ride on the Memphis Queen. We ended our night with a simple kiss on the cheek.

I think I like him. For once, it feels so good to meet a nice man with a successful career; and one that is not immediately trying to get me into bed. Mike has been like a breath of fresh air. Ever since our first date, he calls me every morning before work and we talk during my drive. He sends me sweet text messages throughout the day and he has flowers delivered to my job once each week. But most important, he is intellectually stimulating. Where

has this man been all of my life?

Wow! It's quitting time already. I chuckle at the irony of that because an educator's job is never done. I leave just in time to listen to Stan Bell's "Drive at Five" radio show. Today, he is showcasing Prince. "Still waiting" comes on and all I can think about is the only sexual contact that Mike and I have had is a kiss on the cheek. But, he is romantic, attentive, and a gentleman. He gives me anything my heart desires and more, especially in regards to material things. I do not want to mess this new relationship up by pressing the issue of sex, but he is so fine. I desire him! Although I have many questions and concerns, I refuse to mess up a good thing or scare him away. For now, I am just going to go with the flow. In the meantime, whenever I become hot and bothered, I will just visit my "Bedroom Kandi" sex toy collection. No harm, no foul!

CAROL

It is the beginning of the semester, and I get to meet a new group of freshmen from all over the U.S. and abroad. It is also the beginning of fall...the season I love! This fall is very unique because my son will be entering his senior year at Tennessee State University, and my daughter will be a freshman at the University of Tennessee at Chattanooga. I am very proud of my children. Both of them are excellent academic achievers, and it feels so good to be a single mother who has raised great children. They beat the odds! I really tried to be a great mother by keeping them focused on their academics and involving them in extracurricular activities. Actually, I kept them so busy that I neglected to notice that I no longer had a life of my own. My life has mainly comprised of taking care of my children, caring for my mother, and working a full-time job. Oh, I almost forgot about Carl!

Carl and I have been together for fifteen years, and He is eleven years my senior. He has been there for me and my family, and he practically raised my children as his own. We have taken family vacations together, and

he has been there for all of their "firsts". Before Carl and I got together, he had been married with three children. Although they later divorced, he remained active in his children's lives. He is an excellent provider, listener, romantic at times, and a freak in his prime. Unfortunately, he has one fault that is just not bearable. He is a man whore who thinks that he is slick.

Carl and I are at a crossroad in our relationship. Now that I am aging and have matured, I think more about marriage. I have never thought of myself as being a wife, but somehow I am entertaining the idea. Every time I mention the word marriage or drop the slightest hint to Carl, he acts like it is kryptonite. He asks "why do you want to change things? Our relationship is solid. If it's not broke, don't fix it!" So I now have some decisions to make regarding my future; and those decisions may lead to me and Carl parting ways.

I have invested an extensive amount of time into this relationship. When Carl and I began dating, he dressed like a farmer and a Mississippi pimp. He would wear big straw hats, collar shirts buttoned up to his neck, long shorts and long white socks that stopped at his knees. On our first date, he wore a red suit with red shoes and a wide brim red hat. I wanted to pass out in the driveway in an attempt to get out of the date. Reluctantly, I went on the date anyway. However the entire time, I prayed that I would not see anyone that I knew.

After the date, I called Lisa, one of my besties, to give her all of the details. She said, "Girl, he is a good, stable man. You can get pass that and teach him how to dress." She also reminded me of how handsome he truly is. Carl is six feet tall, dark-skinned and muscular with salt and pepper colored hair. He looks quite distinguished. Anyway, I took Lisa's advice and took Carl for a makeover. Now he seems to think that he is Tyson Bedford when it comes to his dress and appearance.

Overall, our relationship has been good, but I desire better. I have been playing house with him all of these years, and now I want a marriage license.

Playing house and wearing this five carat rock no longer works for me. However, I am struggling internally due to unanswered questions, such as, "Do I want to start over with someone new?" "Will I meet someone who has the same goals and aspirations?" "Where will I begin to look for a new man?" Although Carl is a blue collar guy, he has always supported my career and my educational goals. We have always been on one accord in everything... except the topic of marriage. The word marriage is tearing us apart!

TISH

It has been two months since Sam and I reunited; however I hardly see him or get to spend time with him. I am working two jobs to prevent us from falling into financial ruin. Sam spends his days job seeking. As for nights, I wish I knew where he was spending some of those. Sometimes it seems like as fast as I make the money, it disappears. Every job that Sam lands, he quits after a few weeks because he says the work is back breaking. Nevertheless, I believe that he will soon find employment that he enjoys.

Tonight is our date night! Nowadays, we have to plan to spend time together. I want to go out to dinner at Bonefish Grill, but Sam said that it is not in the budget. I feel that I deserve a night out for dinner as hard as I have been working. ANYWHO! We will have a romantic dinner at home and then watch a DVD. Honestly, it does not matter. The important thing is that we will spend some quality time with each other.

Before we begin date night, Sam's parole officer will stop by for a visit. So, I have been up since 4:00a.m. cleaning and prepping for today's events. Due to my work schedule, I barely have time to clean or cook; and Sam wants the house spic and span to impress his parole officer. In addition to the dinner I have to prepare, Sam wants me to serve finger foods for his meeting. He told me to take care of the meals and to leave everything else to him. Regardless, all of that will have to wait until after I get home from

work. Oh yeah, and after I make a detour by Victoria Secrets so that I can turn up the heat on Sam tonight. Today is going to be a long day. Lord, help me to endure!

Except for the discussion about Sam's current job situation, the meeting with his parole officer went well. Sam says that as long as he pays his parole fees and checks in with his parole officer as required, it doesn't matter if he has not landed the job he wants. I totally agree with him. As long as he has me on his side, he will survive. I will take care of his needs and wants because that is what a good woman does...stands by her man!

Dinner is complete and the menu includes meatloaf, baked potatoes, turnip greens, cornbread, and for dessert, carrot soufflé. That is his favorite meal. The table has been set for two with candle lights. We eat, talk, laugh, and just enjoy the moment. By the time we finish dinner, it is evident that we have drunk two bottles of Moscato. Sam then decides to blindfold me. He takes my hand and begins leading me to who knows where. All he keeps saying is, "just trust me." When he finally removes the blindfold, I see a path of rose petals, a glass of wine, and candle lights surrounding the jacuzzi. I cannot stop the tears from flowing. It is refreshing and reassuring to know that he loves me and that I am appreciated. Next, he undresses me, leads me to the Jacuzzi and tells me to get in. After I submerge myself beneath the bubbles, he begins bathing me. He slowly caresses my body and kisses my ear. Oh my!! I am so turned on. I try to grab him but he will not allow it. He is in full control. Finally, he joins me in the Jacuzzi, spreads my legs, and enters me with all twelve inches. For forty-five minutes, the only words I can say are damn, Sam, and yes!

We finish the night with a movie while snuggling on the couch. I am so in love with this man! Just when I think we are about to go for round number two, he kisses me on the forehead and hits me with the statement, "Baby, I need four thousand dollars to pay off a gambling debt." He sure knows how to ruin the perfect night.

LISA

I have taken the day off from work to enjoy a day at the spa. My spa day is complimentary of my new suitor, Mike. I am getting the works: manicure pedicure, full body massage, and a bikini wax. I so need this day of relaxation. My suitor knows just what a lady needs. He is trying to win my heart and he is doing a great job. In the social media world, I would call that #Winning and #Romantic.

I am so excited! After a beautiful day of being pampered, I am now headed to enjoy a night out with my girls, Carol and Tish. Can you say, "Wasted!" My mouth is just watering for a gigantic strawberry margarita with extra shots of tequila from the Happy Mexican restaurant. Plus, I have so much to tell them about my new romance with Mike. I will also get a chance to hear what they have been up to, especially Tish. I rarely hear from her since Sam returned. Whenever I call her, sometimes she answers and sometimes she doesn't. When she does decide to answer, she only talks for a minute before saying she will call me back...but never does. On the contrary, Carol and I talk at least three times a week, but she does not yet know about Mike.

"Hi, Ladies", I said as I approached them in the waiting area. I've missed you girls. Tish, I see you have lost a few pounds. You look great! Carol, I love the hair and your make up is flawless as always."

"Thank you", said Tish with a big grin on her face. "I have lost a few pounds. Sam has been good for me. Since he's been home, I have joined the gym. He wants me to lose one hundred pounds. So that, along with my two jobs and my wifely duties, keeps me on the move".

"What wifely duties?" Carol quickly asks. "I don't see a ring, nor have I witnessed a marriage ceremony."

Carol, I cook, clean and keep my man's sexual appetite satisfied. You may need to try it sometimes. Maybe Carl will embrace the idea if you try it."

"Heifer, you are crazy!" Carol shockingly exclaims. "First of all, Sam does not work. He needs to cook, clean and have his dick at attention when you get ready. Secondly, Carl and I both clean, cook and work. It's called a partnership in case you've forgotten. And third, he provides seventy percent of the household finances."

"Alright Ladies, calm down and enjoy your margaritas", Lisa says with a confused look on her face. After taking a few sips of her drink, Lisa then asks, "Seriously though, Sam isn't working? I know for certain that I saw him driving a new impala about a week ago."

"Where did you see my Boo?" Tish asks.

"At the Crescent Club having lunch with a group of guys. He didn't tell you that he saw me?"

"No!" It must have slipped his mind" said Tish. "I bought him a new impala so that he could look for a job, and have transportation to and from work once employed. He found a job, but the pay is not comparable for the amount of work he has to do."

"So in other words, he quits a job as soon as he gets one? He can't spend eighteen years in prison and then get out expecting to make twenty dollars an hour. He has to work his way up, or start his own business. Isn't that right, Carol?"

"See! That is why I have not been talking to you bitches. The only thing both of you do is talk negatively about him; especially you, Lisa".

"Girl, bye! The truth hurts; but if you like it, I support you. I really hope for your sanity that he gets it together. But, I need to know one thing. How is the sex? Do you ride it every night? He should have plenty of testosterone built up!"

"Don't worry about our sex life! However, if you just need to know, it's great and there are no complaints!"

"Un huh" said Lisa, seemingly unconvinced.

"So Carol, how is yours with Carl these days?"

"Well, I really wish he would admit that he needs Viagra or something. But, with Donovan, it's awesome! It's the thrill of the sneak!"

"I remember when you would not look at another man before Carl cheated; but look at you now", said Lisa.

"I am older and wiser, now. I didn't look at other men because I thought Carl wouldn't look at or touch another woman. I did a one-eighty turn around when I hooked up with him. However, things change and people change. Enough about us, Ms. Lisa! Who in the hell got you glowing?" Lisa starts to laugh hysterically at my question which was not that funny; so I know there is something she has not told us.

"I met a man and he seems to be awesome, thus far. He's a pure gentleman! Chivalry still exists within this man. He opens doors, pulls out chairs and sends flowers. Let's see, what else? Hmmm! Oh, boat rides, carriage rides, sweet texts all day every day, wake up calls, drive home calls and good night calls. Also, we have dinner at least four times a week at the finest restaurants", Lisa proudly exclaimed.

"Damn girl", said Carol. "I am so happy for you! Come over here and give me a hug."

Tish, who is now on the edge of her seat, asks, "How is the package? A man doing all of that is either gay, the package is small or he is married! I'm just saying."

"Here comes the hater. Why can't he just be the man of her dreams? At least we know that he works! He does work, right, Lisa?"

"Yes!" He is an IT manager at Federal Express. But, you know what? He is really a gentleman. As far as sex, we have only kissed, and that's perfectly fine with me. I am following his lead and will see where it goes."

"Whatever" says Tish. He sounds gay to me."

"Well, he has my friend glowing and smiling; so that is good enough for me!" Then Carol blurts, "Details, honey, details...describe the physique!"

"He is tall, bald and caramel-colored with big sexy eyes and a salt and

pepper haired beard. Actually Carol, he is more your type."

"How ironic is that? I am with a man that's more your type, and now you have found my type. Waiter! Can we have another round of margaritas?" "Ladies, let's toast to happiness, love, and employed men!"

"Watch it, Carol!" commands Tish. "That's why Carl needs Viagra!"

Then Carol, not missing a beat, says, "I'll take Viagra for one hundred, Alex!", and we all laugh.

"Ladies, I have enjoyed this evening with you, but now I must go. I have to be home by nine so that I can give Mike my undivided attention. He doesn't like to share me. I have to be in bed and solely focused on him when he calls."

"Be careful, Lisa. Call me, later."

"I will."

As Lisa exits the restaurant, Tish says, "Carol, you can call me a hater all you like, but something is not right with her new beau!"

"Hursh, Tish! Something ain't right with Sam either!"

2

CAROL

Fall break has finally arrived...yippee!!!   Carl and I are traveling to Montego Bay, Jamaica and I am really looking forward to this vacation. It may help to rekindle the fire that I once had for him. Lord knows I am just going through the motions right now. Most times I just pretend to be asleep when he wants sex. Whenever I do give in to it, I have to think of Donovan to get through those few minutes. The sad part is that he believes he is God's gift and has the nerve to want it every night.

We just arrived at the resort and it is immaculate. Our room has an ocean view. The sunset is exquisite with gorgeous orange and red hues. After getting settled, Carl and I decide to sit on the balcony and drink a glass of wine. I must admit that it is rather romantic sitting on the balcony while enjoying the view. Maybe this trip is what we needed.   The scene is so peaceful and serene. We can hear the sounds of the waves as they roll inland. Carl suddenly turns toward me with an interesting look on his face.

"Carol, I really do love you despite what you may think."

"Same here. I have never doubted your love for me."

"Do you think that our love will survive this storm?"

I take a quick glance at the ocean and then say, "For the first time in fifteen years, I can truly say with all honesty that I don't know."

"Why?" Carl asks while looking stunned.

"Because I feel that we are at a crossroad and neither one of us is willing to give in to the other. Honestly, I don't think I ask for much. But those things that I do ask of you, I expect. At one point in this relationship, I knew that I could count on you to do the right thing. Compromise was easy for us, and you wanted seemed to really care about my needs."

"Hmmmm". "We already have everything. I give you everything that you ask for. I am always home with you when I am not working. I don't understand why you are letting the issue of marriage, a piece of paper tear us apart. Technically, we are married."

"Let's agree to disagree for now and enjoy the remainder of the night."

"Okay, but we need to finish this conversation and shrink this elephant." Feeling a little annoyed, I let out a huge sigh and simply say, "This view is beautiful and serene."

The itinerary for this trip is rigorous, and we need to select the activities to attend. Tonight, we are going to a beach party and I am ready to dance the night away. This will lighten the atmosphere between Carl and me. Now let's see, what shall I wear? Every piece of garment in my luggage has tags. I have been shopping ever since we decided to take this trip. I guess I will wear this royal blue bathing suit with a gold wrap and royal blue flip flops. I have lost fifty pounds and I look fierce in this ensemble.

As Carl and I arrive at the party, reggae music is playing. I notice a huge selection of food, the cash bar, and lots of people partying and enjoying life. Reggae music and drinks make a great recipe for all night grooving.

Day two is busy. We are going snorkeling and taking a tour of the island. And on tonight, we will attend a formal gala. Carl wants to continue the conversation that we began on yesterday, but I keep avoiding it. The only words that I want to hear from him are "Will you marry me?" Any other words are irrelevant at this point.

While Carl is in the shower, I start getting dressed for our excursions. Suddenly, the telephone in our room rings and I wonder who could be calling our room? Whoever it is should know to call our cell phones, especially if it is important. The phone keeps ringing and now someone is texting my cell phone. I look at my phone and see that the text message is from Donovan. It says, "Pick up the phone or I will just knock on the door." What the hell? I hurriedly go to answer the room phone.

"Hello."

"Hi baby", says Donovan loudly.

"What are you doing?" I ask while trying to make sure that Carl does not hear me.

"I am on vacation with a friend. I knew you and Carl were here, so I decided to reach out. Besides, I've missed you and want to see you."

"Are you crazy?"

"Yes! Crazy about you! Will you all be attending the gala on tonight?"

"Why?"

"We will be there. I just wanted to know if I needed to ask Carl for one dance with you."

"You cannot be serious."

"Oh, I am very serious. You are a strong, smart woman, and I know you can handle an uncomfortable situation."

I laugh and say, "Keep your distance. Do you understand me?"

"I plan on being up close and very personal. See you tonight."

As I hang up the phone, Carl exits the shower and asks, "Who was that on the phone?" Thinking quickly, I lie and say, "No one important, just the front desk." I cannot believe that Donavan would pull a stunt like this. How could he follow me to another country? Most of all, how could he flaunt another woman in my face? He knows the rules; and until now, he has played by them well. I am furious!!! Nevertheless, I got this because I am the queen of games. I am going to enjoy our day of excursions and put my game face on for tonight.

Today was great! Carl and I really enjoyed this time together. It somewhat felt like old times. It is amazing what a change of scenery can do for the soul. Consequently, I still have that Donovan situation which has subconsciously been on my mind all day. I am glad that I did not see him anywhere we went today. I guess I will take a quick nap before our next event.

It is time to get dressed for the gala and my stomach is bubbling with nerves because I do not know what will happen tonight. Regardless, I must remain in control. Carl is already dressed and is looking rather debonair in his black tuxedo. To compliment the tuxedo, he is wearing a royal blue bow tie which also matches my royal blue dress. My dress is sleeveless with rhinestones and a long split. We are dressed to impress!

The gala we are attending is a very elegant affair. The monies raised will be donated to charity. Carl and I have been here for an hour and we are really enjoying ourselves. DAMN! I spoke to soon. Here comes Donovan with her. I immediately feel contempt for her which is very wrong of me. Donovan is looking so handsome. He is literally Terrence Howard's look alike.

"Good evening, Carol."

"Well, hello Donovan. I did not expect to see anyone familiar from the states. This is my man, Carl. Carl, this is Donovan. We worked together many years ago for the city.

"Hi man", Carl says as they shake hands.

"Carol, this is Regina, My lady."

"Pleasure to meet you", I say with a fake smile.

"Do you all have a table? If not, you are welcome to join us."
Carl just always has to be Mr. Nice Guy. This is so awkward.

"We will be honored to join you. I must say that seeing a familiar face in a foreign land is a pleasant coincidence."

Donovan now has this smug look on his face. I want to slap him, but he will never know just how angry I am. He is sitting next to me so that he can slowly taunt me.

"Aww, I like this song. Carl, Regina does not dance. Do you mind if I have a dance with Carol?"

"How do you know that Carol dances?"

"Oh, back in the day when we worked together for the city, she would

always throw down at the Christmas Party."

Still trying to avoid him, I say "Donovan, I don't feel like dancing at the moment."

"Go ahead Babe. It's a slow groove."

"Regina, do you mind?"

"Not at all! Be my guest."

Donovan takes my hand and leads me to the dance floor. We slow dance to Luther Vandross' "If Only For One Night". God, he feels good. My emotions are all over the place.

"In case you did not know, had you refused this dance, I would have caused a scene."

"No you would not have. How dare you flaunt another woman in my face and show up on my vacation?"

"The same way that you leave me to go home to a man that no longer satisfies you, without consideration for my feelings. So, I decided to turn up the heat."

"What heat?" I am not bothered, nor concerned with her. Besides, you knew what the rules and stipulations were when we started this."

"What if I no longer want to play by your rules? I think it's time for me to make some rules of my own. It's my name that you scream when you are in my bed, not his!"

"Stop acting like a little bitch!"

"Naw!" I am acting like the man that I am, and the one that you love. You just won't admit it."

"This dance is over."

"I don't think so. You are going to accept this key that I am placing in your bra; and when this gala is over, you will meet me in room 2001."

"Oh, hell no! You must be out of your mind. You expect for me to leave my man in bed and sneak to another room to be with you? What about Miss Thing?"

"You will be there. I will be expecting you at 1:00a.m. If you are not there, Carl will receive a message at the front desk about your infidelity. Besides, I know you want to. Don't worry about Regina, I got her under control."

"That is impossible! He will notice that I am gone at that hour of the night and will have questions that I will not have answers for."

"Then, I suggest you put that brilliant mind of yours to work. Thanks for the dance, my love!"

As Donovan and I return to our table, he turns to Carl and says,

"Thanks for allowing me to borrow such a beautiful woman."

"No problem, Man."

"Regina, I am jet lagged. I think we should leave and turn in early."

"I'm okay with that. Good night you two. Nice meeting you."

"So soon?" asks Carl. "Well get some rest and have a goodnight!"

"Night" I simply say, careful to show no emotion.

Carl has gotten full of crown royal and he is ready to dance all night. He is also getting frisky. My mind is running a mile a second. I must keep Carl entertained and come up with a plan to meet Donovan later. I am mentally exhausted. However I think the best plan is to make sure that Carl keeps drinking. He will eventually get so drunk that he will pass out as soon as his head hits the pillow. Oh there's the waiter. "Waiter! Keep the drinks coming please."

Well, my plan worked. Carl is done for the night. I quickly undress him down to his boxers, then quietly leave for room 2001. What have I gotten myself into? I nervously use my key to open the door. When I enter the room, Donovan is lying on the bed wearing red silk boxers and sipping on a glass of wine.

"I knew you wouldn't let me down."

"That's because I am being black mailed. I feel used."

"Oh, please. Relax girl" he says as he pours me a glass of wine.

He then invites me to have a seat on the bed. After a few minutes of small talk, he gently grabs me by my waist and pulls me toward him. He starts kissing me passionately, and I can feel my clothes coming off, piece by piece. I manage to whisper, "we shouldn't do this" as his hand slowly moves up my inner thigh. He ignores me and continues focusing on my body. I feel the tip of his tongue in my ear as he caresses me. Soon after, he gently starts sucking my breast, and then the stroke of his tongue glides around and over my nipples. As his tongue slowly moves down my abs, I feel my clit starting to tingle. I faintly plead for him to stop because I am enjoying the moment too much. I say to him "This is not the time, nor the right place"; but he continues to ignore me because he knows that I don't really mean it. He then places his finger over my lips and continues to slowly move his tongue into my navel. I want him so bad, but I still try to refuse to give in. He keeps moving farther south until finally he inserts his tongue into my Vijay-jay. I no longer can resist. DAMN! The man has skills.

TISH

It has been four days and Sam has not slept in our bed. He is upset with me because I have not given him four thousand dollars to pay off his gambling debt. He has been coming in at three in the morning and sleeping on the couch. I am going to give him the money, but I first had to get approved for a loan by the credit union because I did not want to dip into my savings. I am furious with him on so many levels. However, I have to remember that he is re-entering society and that I have to practice patience. In the meantime, I cannot afford any more financial surprises until he gets a stable job. I have friends who are in hiring positions, but Sam says he does not want any handouts.

My Mom and my besties have been talking down about Sam, but he is trying. I refuse to give up on him after all of this time. I have mentioned to him that returning to school may be an option, but he says it is not an option

for him. He said that if he does not find satisfactory employment soon, then he would like to buy or start up several laundromat businesses. I am not sure how he plans to do that, but at least he has a vision.

On another note, today is my birthday! For the past eighteen years, I have celebrated my birthday with my besties. This year I am going to celebrate the blessing of another year with Sam. I am about to explode with anticipation because I know that he is going to make this the best day ever. Today will also be great for him because I am going to surprise him with the money that he needs.

Lisa and Carol wanted to take me to my favorite spot. However, I refused to go with them because I didn't want to miss whatever Sam has planned for me; especially since he texted me and requested that I come straight home from work. When I walk into the house, I see four dozen roses, a blue teddy bear, and a balloon that reads "Happy Birthday". Aww, I feel so special!"

"Happy Birthday, Babe! I love you and thanks for all that you do. I know that sometimes I act ungrateful, but that comes with being my lady."

"Oh Sam! Thanks for making a girl's 40th birthday feel so special."

"Anything for my special girl. There is more. I am taking you out for dinner."

"Okay. I have a surprise for you as well."

"Well, come on, let's go. I'll drive."

As we get into the car, it dawns on me that this is the first time that I have been taken for a ride in the Impala. I have no idea where Sam is taking me, but I am happy just knowing I will be celebrating with him. After about ten minutes, Sam starts to complain about his back.

"Babe my back has started hurting. Can we get dinner to go?"

"No, I don't mind. I am okay with having dinner at home."

"Cool! I will just pull in line right here."

"Welcome to Chick-fil-a. May I take your order?"

"Yes you may. I would like two Chick-fil-a meals with a large sweet tea and large lemonade."

"So my birthday dinner is Chick-fil-a, Sam?"

"What's wrong with Chick-fil-a?" he asks with a confused look.

"Not only are you taking me out to Chick-fil-a; but to add insult to injury, the drive thru? Are you ashamed of me or something?"

"Tish, you are being very disrespectful and unappreciative. I am going out of my way to spend money on you and to make your day special; but this is the thanks I get!"

"Thanks?! Really, Sam? You did not answer my question. Are you ashamed of me?"

"No! If I were ashamed of you, I would not be with you. But honestly speaking, your face is gorgeous, but you do need to lose about one hundred pounds."

"Take me home Sam! Here is your money." I am boiling with anger and disappointment. This has turned out to be the worst birthday ever. When we arrive back at home, I go straight to bed and hope that I will forget that this day ever happened.

LISA

Mike has invited me to join him on a weekend getaway to the cabins in Gatlinburg, Tennessee. I do not know whether or not to accept his invitation. Our relationship is fairly new, so I do not want to convey the wrong message. We have been dating for three months and still no sex; only kisses. Maybe this trip is his idea of moving to the next level. Being the man that he is, I am sure that he wants our first time to be special. I have imagined what our first time will be like a thousand times over.

I am enjoying the view during our drive. The mountains and trees are beautiful during the fall. I think this trip will be great for us. I do not know the itinerary, so I will just follow Mike's lead.

"Our first stop is going to be in Nashville so that we can do some shopping at Opry Mills Mall."

"I love that mall. My friends and I take a girl's trip to Opry Mills at least twice a year."

"Oh really? Well, that can now become our thing to do."

"Sure! Why not?"

"What are your favorite stores?"

"Michael Khors, Coach, Saks Fifth Avenue, Steve Madden and Old Navy. Oh, I can't forget about Bath and Body Works."

"Well, today I am going to buy you something from each store."

"Wow, Mike. That is not necessary."

"I know; but I need my lady to allow me to do nice things for her. I know that I don't have to, but I want to."

We arrive at Opry Mills Mall and it is packed as usual. So far, I have seen about four people from home that I know.

"I see that you are familiar with quite a few men."

"Not really. Two of those guys went to college with me, and the other two were my frats."

"The two frats were a little too friendly, and I didn't like it one bit."

"There is no harm. That is how we greet each other. You are Greek, so you of all people should know and understand how it works."

"Yeah, I do."

"I am committed to you and only you. I am dating you and only you. Before you, I had not dated in a long time."

"If I grabbed you right now and pushed you against the wall and starting kissing you passionately, what would you do?"

"I would embrace you and kiss you back."

"That is a great answer and good to know. I get impulsive sometimes. And so that you know, I like public display of affection. I want everyone to know that you belong to me."

While laughing, I say "I love a man with authority!"

"Let's wrap up this shopping so that we can get back on the road."

I have so many bags. I hope it all fits in the car. Mike spent so much money on me and I feel so guilty. In addition to all of the clothes, he bought me two purses with matching wallets from Michael Khors and Coach; and eight bags of lotions, body washes, body sprays, candles, soaps, and oils from Bath and Body Works. He told me that money is not an issue, and to get whatever my heart desired. Well, he now knows that I have a shopping addiction, and he seems not to mind enabling it. Yes, he is in there!!! DAMN! I forgot to get some shoes!

"Wow, this was a long ride, but it was also beautiful Mike."

"Yes, the drive was awesome and I have enjoyed having you in my presence. It did not seem as long to me though. Probably because we talked and sang all the way."

"Thank you for this trip. It will allow us an opportunity to get to know each other better."

"You have passed the test, my dear."

"What test?"

"The test of being in the same space together for a long time without encountering any friction. This weekend is going to be a breeze."

Mike unlocks the door to the cabin and we both walk inside and take a look around.

"This cabin is gorgeous! I love the fireplace in the bedroom suite."

"I am glad to know you love it. I have owned this place for about three years. This is only the second time that I have used it."

"Wow! I appreciate you sharing this adventure with me."

"I am honored that I have found a lady worthy to share it with."

"Oh Mike! You are going to make me cry."

"If you cry, I will wipe your tears away. Get comfortable while I bring our things inside. Afterward, I will start a fire in the fireplace. And oh yeah,

the chef is going to prepare a five course meal for us".

"Is this dinner formal? What shall I wear?

"I have a dress, shoes, and jewelry already waiting for you.

"Wow! You have thought of everything."

"I told you that I was going to take good care of you."

"Indeed, you did."

"This is only the beginning, love."

While Mike is making the fire, I go into the bathroom to shower and he has a surprise waiting for me. There are rose petals, lighted candles, with a glass of wine on the tub. Also, the water is steamy and there is a note that reads "enjoy your bubble bath and dinner will begin at 7:00 p.m." It is now 5:30p.m., so that gives me an hour and a half to get ready.

As I enter the dining area, Mike seems to light up at my appearance.

"Damn girl! You look good, and you are wearing that dress. I knew that dress would complement your curves and the shoes would make those big legs look beautiful."

"Thank you! You are making me blush."

"That is what a real man does for his woman...spoil her."

"Well, spoil me, baby!"

"While we are waiting on the chef, may I have this dance?"

"Yes, you may!" We begin to dance to Luther Vandross' "Wait for Love" which is very appropriate for the moment. Soon after, the chef enters and says, "Excuse me. Dinner is served."

The whole evening has been so refreshing, and I am basking in the care and attention that Mike is giving me.

"Dinner was magnificent!"

"Thank you, Ma'am. I am stuffed."

"So am I." Mike takes my hand and leads me to the couch. We both take a seat on the couch by the fireplace and talk for hours as we sip through three bottles of wine.

"Wow! It's late. Time passes fast when you are in the company of a beautiful, intellectual, woman."

"It does; and even more so when you are enjoying the company.

"Let's move this party to the suite. Is that okay with you?"

"Sure!"

Mike places his arm on my shoulder as we walk into the bedroom. I hug him back and he starts to nibble on the back of my ear lobe. He stops me at the door and slowly kisses my neck as he unzips my dress. My dress falls to the floor and he begins to kiss me on my shoulders and moves his tongue slowly to the small of my back; straight down the middle. He whispers in my ear and says "model that lingerie for me". I oblige. As I prance around the room and model the lingerie, Mike moves to the bed and takes off his shirt with all eyes on me. DAMN! He is fine!

"Come here, woman!" I slowly walk over to him and gaze into his eyes. I am so mesmerized. It is almost like a drug. I then straddle his legs, sit on his lap and place my arms around his neck. I kiss him on his lips over and over again. He unsnaps and removes my bra, then gently grabs my breasts and licks my nipples in a circular motion. My body responds accordingly and I start to feel very sensuous. I push his upper body backwards onto the bed and unzip his pants, then pull them down to the floor. Before I could do anything else, he grabs me and flips me over onto the bed, where he slowly proceeds to remove my panties with his mouth. His lips and tongue stroke me in places I never knew would arouse me. I then flip him over onto his back and grab his erect penis. It's thick and hard just the way I like it. I begin licking the head in a circular motion, and then I place the tip of my tongue in the hole. I slowly move my tongue up his body until I reach his nipples. I suck them like a baby searching for milk. Mike then flips me over, looks into my eyes and slowly inserts his hard penis into my soak and wet vijay-jay. He slowly begins making love to me, going deeper inside of me with every thrust. During our time of passion, I have multiple orgasms.

This man has taken me to ecstasy. Suddenly, he screams my name, "Lisa! Girl, I love you! You are mine for life!" I knew that our first time would be special and worth the wait. It is too early in this relationship to declare that I love him but I am in strong like.

"Good morning, love" Mike says as he kisses me on the forehead.

"Good Morning!"

"I had the chef make breakfast. No need to get up, you will be having breakfast in bed. Your wish is my command."

"Thank you, Honey. You are so good to me."

"I am just serving my queen."

"What are the plans for today?"

"I want to keep you in bed and make love to you all day. But, I don't want you to think that is the only reason that I brought you here."

"Never! I like that plan."

"Oh you do, huh? Well, we are going zip lining, white water rafting, and touring Dollywood."

"Sounds exciting! I am going to embrace every moment of this trip.

Mike did an excellent job planning our getaway. It wasn't too much or too little. Everything was planned just right. Unfortunately, our time away has come to an end. This weekend has been both exhilarating and romantic; and Mike says that this is only the beginning. I get to scratch two items off my bucket list (zip lining and white water rafting). However, the most important take away from this weekend is that I got laid . . . and it was GREAT!!!

CAROL

DAMN! DAMN! DAMN! It is 6:00a.m. and I am still in room 2001! I cannot believe I fell asleep in Donovan's room. So much happened last night and I am both mentally and physically exhausted. I pray that Carl is still asleep. If he is awake, all hell will break loose.

"Donovan, this is all your damn fault."

He laughs and says "Yeah, I did knock you out didn't I?"

"There is nothing amusing about this situation! What are you going to do about her?"

"Don't worry about her! Her name is Regina, and I did you a favor."

"I have to go! I am furious with you!" I grab my clothes and quickly get dressed, then rush out the door slamming it as hard as I can.

He yells, "I love you too! See you tonight; same time, same place."

What am I going to do? I will stop by the breakfast bar to get a cup of coffee to calm my nerves. DAMN! I smell like Donovan's cologne. I cannot enter our room smelling like him. What if Carl woke up in the middle of the night and realized that I was gone? This is ugly! I have to think fast! I now know the true meaning of the song "Careless" by Johnny Taylor. I finally get to my room and slowly enter. Great . . . Carl is in the shower.

"Carol! Is that you?"

"Yes, Honey." I have to get out of these clothes before he smells Donovan's cologne. I take off my clothes as fast as I can and put them in a plastic bag inside of the closet.

"Where have you been?"

"I could not sleep, so I went down for coffee to clear my mind."

"I have been awake since 5:00a.m. I turned over and you were not there. Your side of the bed had not been slept in. So again, where have you been?"

"I told you that I could not sleep. I never got in bed. I logged on the laptop, checked and answered a few emails, then played around on social media. Afterwards, I still was not sleepy, so I went down stairs and stayed until now."

"Why didn't you wake me up?"

"You needed to sleep that crown off."

"Did you eat breakfast yet?"

"No, I just drank coffee."

"Come and go to breakfast with me."

"Baby, I am finally sleepy; so I am going to take a nap before it's time to go on our excursions."

"Okay. Well your former co-worker called the room and asked if we would like to join them for breakfast. What is his name again?"

"Who? Donovan?"

"Yeah. That's him! I told him that we would go.

"Well, you go right ahead and enjoy yourself. I am going to sleep."

Donovan is really on one. I want to text or call him to tell him a thing or two. But, he is so out of control that he may show Carl the text. Besides, I am exhausted. I will just deal with him later. While Carl is gone, I have to take a shower. That was a close call. I have to regain control of this situation. Up to this point, Donovan had not been a problem. I call the plays not him. Usually he is my escape to serenity, not my stressor.

This is our last day in Montego Bay. I just want to lay by the pool and relax. However, Carl wants to spend the day doing more excursions. Fortunately, I convinced him into only doing a half day. The other half will be relaxation. I want to inquire about his breakfast with Donovan and Regina, but I am scared and nervous. The curiosity is killing me, so I am going to ask anyway.

"So, how was breakfast?"

"Interesting."

"How so?"

"Donovan talks too much and his girl laughs at everything that he says. What kind of work did you say he does for the city?"

"He is a police officer in the organized crime unit. So, what did you guys talk about? Guy stuff like football, things we do for fun, work, women."

"Oh, I see."

"I know that you do not want to talk about our conflict, but we need to

handle it before we leave this island."

"There really is not much to talk about. You have two choices. You can say those words that I want to hear, or not say them."

"That sounds more like an ultimatum to me. You know that I don't take to those too well.

"I would not dare try to manipulate you with an ultimatum. I have two choices, too. I can stay with you even if you don't say those words to me, or I can agree to disagree and move on."

"So, it's that simple with you, huh?"

"Damn skippy! I don't want you to do anything you don't want to do or feel pressured to do."

"Well, I feel pressured; and it hurts me to know that you are willing to throw away fifteen years over a few words and a piece of paper."

"It hurts me that you have strong me along for fifteen years! But as of today, you have until my birthday to make a decision.

"You cannot be serious."

"This conversation is over. Let's enjoy this final day in paradise."

"Now, I can agree with you on that."

"Carl, why is this so hard for you?"

"It is not hard. I just want to do it in my own time.

"Time is not really on your side. I'm just saying."

"Who keeps texting your phone? We are on vacation."

"That was smooth how you changed the conversation. It is the kids checking on us. They saw the pictures that I posted on Facebook and Instagram."

It is Donovan who keeps texting me. At this very moment, I do not care if Carl accidentally finds out. If I'm never going to be his wife, then why should I care about him finding out? I was feeling guilty about my rendezvous with Donovan; but now, not so much. This foolishness with Carl is one of the reasons why I fell into Donovan's arms. The other reason is

because Carl cheated on me while I was being a faithful saint. I know that two wrongs don't make a right; but at times, revenge is sweet. I had the option to shoot his ass for cheating on me; but instead, I found the comfort of another man.

The evening has come quickly and I need to start packing to prepare for our return to the states. I'll go ahead and finish doing that now because I have a late rendezvous with Donovan. I am curious as to why he insisted on the beach as the meeting place. I have already prepared my half-truth of an excuse if Carl has questions about me leaving the room later. I wonder what Donovan will say to Regina. She probably does not ask questions, and I'm sure that is why he chose her. She reminds me of Tish.

"I am done packing, so I am going for a walk to clear my head."

"I will come with you."

"No thanks. I want to be alone in my thoughts."

"Where are you planning on walking to?"

"Wherever my feet lead me."

"It is not safe for a woman to walk alone in an unfamiliar country."

"They have security and I have my phone; so I will be fine. See ya!" Finally, I am free from Carl. When I arrive at the beach, Donovan is already there waiting.

"Hi, Beautiful."

"You know that I am upset with you on so many levels. First, you showed up on my vacation. Second, you brought another woman. Third, you blackmailed me into spending the night with you. And lastly, you invited my fiancé to breakfast knowing good and damn well that I had just left you and needed to sneak back in. Really Donovan?! What is wrong with you?"

"There is nothing wrong with me. I am just going for what I want. I know we have rules that we play by; however, I want more. It is sweet that you are jealous of Regina. But for the record, she is my cousin."

"I am not jealous. And do you really expect me to believe that she is your cousin?"

"Have I ever lied to you?"

"Not that I can recall right now. But I am sure that you have. All men lie and cheat at some point."

It's a shame that he is changing such a beautiful, strong woman into a bitter woman. Come on and let's just relax for a few minutes. The moon is big, yellow and glowing; and the temperature is perfect. Close your eyes. Now take my hand and listen to the waves."

I take his hand and follow as he leads me. We arrive at a blanket with pillows and a picnic basket. After sitting down, he fills two glasses with wine. It is a romantic scene and I am not concerned that we are on a sneak. He is looking quite handsome, too. He is dressed in white linen and looking like Terrance Howard. For over an hour, we talk, laugh, hug and kiss. I soon forget how furious I am with him. He then puts his hand in his pocket and says that he has something for me.

"Did you get what you wanted out of this trip from Carl?"

"Not really."

"Give me your hand and close your eyes."

"For what?"

"For once woman will you just let go of control and trust me?"

I give him my hand and close my eyes.

"Now open your eyes."

I open my eyes and he is on one knee ready to place a ring on my finger. My mouth is wide open; and for the first time in my life, I am speechless.

"Carol, I know that you are in a long term committed relationship. I feel that two years is a long time as well. I love you and I can't imagine spending my life with anyone but you. Will you give me the honor of being my wife?"

"Donovan! What are you doing?!"

"You don't have to give me an answer tonight. You don't have to say

yes right now. Just please don't say no!"

"Donovan! This ring is beautiful! You know that I can't wear this ring or take it home."

"Yes, you can. Take your time and think about it."
Donovan places the ring in my hand and closes my hand. I got the proposal that I have been waiting for all of my life. However, it is not from the man that I have given up so much for and shared so much with. I do care for Donovan, but I am at a crossroad with Carl. I am filled with so many emotions as tears roll down my face. Donovan wipes them away and kisses me on the forehead.

"Donovan, you have put a lot of thought into this. How long have you been planning this?"

"Ever since you told me that you guys were going on vacation here."

"Donovan! I am at a loss for words."

"In some situations, silence is the best answer."
He gathers the blanket and the picnic basket. As we head back to the resort, we hold each other's hand and stroll down the beach in total silence.

3

LISA

In excitement, I yell "It is FRIDAY!" in my Sir Charles voice. I am meeting my besties Carol and Tish for drinks at Happy Mexican. We have so much to catch up on. Although Mike is not happy that I chose to hang out with them instead of him, I plan to enjoy myself. He has not called or texted me all day. On yesterday, I had to give him the time and location of where we planned to meet. He says that committed women should not be hanging out drinking. They should be with their men. But, I need a break from him. I have been spending every second of my free time with him. Either he is at my house, or I am at his house. When we are apart, we are always talking on the phone. The only time that I have alone is my time at work. He even showers with me. I love him and appreciate the attention, but damn!!!

CAROL

Just got paid. It's Friday night. Yes! Tonight I get to kick it with my girls Lisa and Tish. I have so much to tell them. I have decisions to make and ultimatums to be resolved, including a proposal from a man that I have been dating for two years. Montego Bay was interesting! I now see Donovan in a different light and not just a man who sexes me. He has won my heart. However, Carl is still walking around like we don't have any issues to resolve. All I can think about twenty-four seven is that romantic proposal and Donovan's patience for an answer. I keep the ring given to me by Donovan in my purse. I find myself taking it out and staring at it. I love Carl, but I am not getting any younger. When my birthday arrives, If Carl does not say those words that I have been waiting to hear, I don't know if I will truly be able to walk away.

TISH

I am still pissed at Sam for ruining my birthday. I should have celebrated with my girls instead of with Sam. But that's okay. I know my besties are going to make up for it on tonight; although I am dreading having to listen to the trash talking that is about to happen. I know I cannot defend Sam this time. Hell, I just may join in with them. He still does not have a job, but he is working on a business plan to open four laundromats. At least I have one good thing to share about Sam. I wish that I did not love him so much.

"Hey! I am so glad to see y'all! I am ready to hear all about Montego Bay and Gatlinburg."

"Naw", says Carol. "We are starting with your birthday highlights. Let us get pissed off first, so that we can try to end on a good note."

"Yeah! Carol and I already know that Sam did something stupid."

"How do you know?"

"Well, if he had done something extravagant, you would have already called and told us about it. Plus, when I texted you at 8:oop.m. and asked if you were happy, you texted back "in bed". I knew then that something happened. So I called Carol and then we called you on three-way, but you didn't answer. So tell us, what did the fool do this time?"

"Wait, Lisa! Let's order drinks before she starts because I'm sure we are going to need them."

We all laugh and then place our orders with the waitress. Soon after we receive our orders, Lisa quickly says, "Okay Tish, let's hear it!"

"It started out romantic. I was excited to spend my birthday with my man for the first time in eighteen years. He texted me to say come straight home after work. When I walked in, he greeted me with a blue teddy bear, four dozen roses, and a birthday balloon."

"That was sweet."

"Lisa, stop interrupting!" said Carol.

"After telling me how much he loved and appreciated me; we then leave to go to dinner. Guess where this bastard took me?"

Lisa and Carol both say in unison, "Where?"

"Chick-fil-a . . .the drive thru at that!"

"Aw hell nawl" they both say in unison again.

"What the Fuck?" yells Lisa.

"Yes! I was furious, and I still am. Eventually I will get over it, but it will definitely be a while."

"You are a better woman than me! That is all that I am going to say! Please let me cook his ass that pie!"

After Lisa and I laugh at Carol, I say to them, "There is a little more. I asked him if he were ashamed of me."

"What did he say?" Carol asks.

"He said, "no"; but that I need to lose a hundred pounds."

"Now I am ready to kick his ass!" said Carol as she slams her drink down on the table.

"I have never felt so disappointed in him and so low of myself. I'm sorry for crying now, but the emotional impact has finally hit me."

"Tish, you do too much for him; and you have stood by him too long for him to pull a stunt like this. It's time for you to move on from this no good, trifling ass man", said Lisa as she and Carol try to comfort me. Although hurtful, it felt good to finally talk about it. I cannot tell them everything that is going on; but my heart is a little lighter.

"He better hope and pray I don't see him anywhere!"

"Carol, please stay out of it! Enough about me! What about your trips? Lisa, you go first."

"Okay, if you insist. Ladies, Mike is like something out of a fairy tale book. First, we stopped in Nashville and went shopping at Opry Mills Mall. He inquired about all of my favorite stores and bought me so much stuff. He spent about three thousand dollars. Baby, he has a black visa card!"

"DAMN, girl! So, did you have sex?"

"Shut up, Carol and let me finish! The cabin that he owns is so beautiful and elegant. He has owned it for three years and has only used it twice. He said that until he met me, no one has been worthy enough to share it with."

"Aww" said Tish.

"He hired a personal chef, and he had already bought me a dinner dress and jewelry. Ladies, that man made love to me like no man ever before. I had orgasm after orgasm. He took his time with me, and it was so worth the wait!"

"Hot Damn!!! You got some!

"Carol, I crave him every day. We do it four days a week, three times a day. Honestly, I could have him three times a day seven days a week; but he has this schedule thing going on."

"What kind of foolishness is that? Sex on a schedule?! What kind of man are you rolling with?" asks Carol.

"A working man. I knew the hate would come soon!"

"Does he know that you want it all day every day?'

"Yes! But I am cool with the schedule."

"He must have another woman on the other nights", Tish says.

"No! We spend all of our free time together. If I am not at his house, he is at mines."

"Well something is not right!"

"It amazes me how you can see something wrong with someone else's man, but cannot see that Sam is trifling!"

"Whatever!" says Tish.

"At least the man works, wines and dines her, which is more than you can say about Sam."

Looking annoyed, Tish says "Carol that is why Carl will not marry you!"

"Well bitch, if he doesn't, I got a proposal on standby."

"Say What?"

"Sure you do" says Tish.

"BAM!" Carol says as she holds up the engagement ring as proof. "Donovan showed up in Montego Bay with another woman that turned out to be his cousin."

"Shut up! Let us see that rock!"

"When I found out he was in Montego Bay, my first thought was that he came just to taunt me, which initially he did."

"She probably bought that ring herself."

"Tish, please!!! You are the only one buying your own gifts because Sam is living off of your money."

"Girl, keep talking. Forget about Tish."

"He called the room, showed up at the gala, and asked Carl could he dance with me."

"What did you do?"

"I danced with him because I was too afraid not to. He is out of control. Before we left the dance floor, he slipped a hotel key in my bra and blackmailed me into joining him later in another room."

"How did you pull that off?"

"I got Carl drunk. The next morning, Donovan invited us to breakfast. I was too exhausted to go, so Carl went to breakfast with him and his cousin. I had just made it to the room and it was a close call."

"So, how did the proposal play out?"

"On our last night there, I told Carl that I was going for a walk to have some alone time before our departure. Instead, I met Donovan on the beach. He had a picnic basket filled with different cheeses, a blanket, two glasses, and a bottle of wine. Then he proposed."

"So, what are you going to do?"

"I have no idea. Donovan has won my heart after that stunt."

"Girl, I am so happy for you, but conflicted at the same time." Lisa says as she hugs me.

"Welcome to my life!"

"Tish, has Sam found work?"

"No, but he is developing a business plan to open four laundromats."

"On whose dime? Yours? I need another round of margaritas."

"Sam can never do anything right in your eyes. Can he Carol?"

"My eyes don't matter. You know my line; if you like it, I love it!"

"Well Ladies, I have to get home to Mike because he wants me home by ten. He says committed women do not keep late hours."

"Huh?"

"I have a great idea! I think it's time for me and Carol to meet Mike. Then next month, you all can reunite with Sam."

"Okay" says Carol. Let's have a date night with the men. I will take care of the details."

"That sounds wonderful! I have to go now. He has already called my phone ten times, and now he is texting."

"Later, girl!"

"Carol, you may think low of Sam, but I am telling you now that Mike ain't right."

"You just make sure that Sam shows up next month so that I can tell him a thing or two."

"Girl, Sam will be fine. Leave my man alone."

"You need to leave him. You have that scenario correct."

"I'm out! Till next time."

LISA

Shoot! I am going to be late getting home. Let me hurry to my car. As I turn the corner to walk towards my car, I suddenly see Mike.

"Mike?! What are you doing here?"

"Why are you not answering your phone and returning texts?"

"My phone was in my purse."

"You were supposed to be on your way home fifteen minutes ago in

order to make it there by 10:00p.m."

"Sorry! I lost track of time."

"It better not happen again."

Dang! I knew it. Mike is serious about that 10:00p.m. curfew. Oh well, I hope Tish didn't see us; but I'm almost certain she did. Damn!

TISH

Sam and I are barely speaking since my birthday fiasco. He thinks that I am being selfish. I think that he does not appreciate me. I sacrifice a lot for him. Now he wants me to get another bank loan in addition to the four thousand dollars he needs for the business startup. He has it all figured out, but his plan includes more responsibilities for me. My days are already filled with me working two jobs, cleaning, and cooking. Now he expects me to manage the business and do the bookkeeping. He claims that if the businesses prove to be successful, then I can quit my second job.

I am stressed! Today I am going to do a little retail therapy to maintain my sanity. I want to take Carol and Lisa with me, but they will stress me out more by bad mouthing Sam. I want to go lay on my mother's lap, cry, and tell her everything. But I do not want to hear those words, "I told you so." Before I leave for retail therapy, my first priority is to do our laundry. I really wish Sam would do chores around the house. Sheesh!!!

What is this in Sam's pants pocket? Why would he have an ultrasound picture of a baby in his pocket? He better not have some floozy pregnant. That would mean that he is having unprotected sex with someone other than me. God, I cannot take another blow to my stomach. Maybe this is why he comes in at three and four in the morning. He sleeps on the couch; and whenever we make love, it is quick and straight to the point. Hell some nights he does not come home at all. For now, I am going to forget what I found. When I get back, hopefully he will be at home, then I can confront him.

I have been so busy working, paying bills, and taking care of Sam until I have totally neglected myself. This is the first time that I have spent any money on myself. I am buying whatever my heart desires, and I am treating myself to a seafood dinner. It feels good to focus on me and only me for a few hours. Sam has been calling my phone and sending inappropriate text messages which call me out of my name. I refuse to allow him to ruin this day for me. I will deal with him later. However, I am disturbed by the last text that I received from him. It reads "you are a low down, dirty bitch and a user." I find that both ironic and amusing. Nevertheless, I will not entertain his antics. He is just seeking attention.

Despite all of Sam's drama, today was a great day. I spent a lot of money on me that I will probably regret later, but it felt good. Sam is going to be upset because I spent all of the overflow money shopping. As I pull into my parking spot, I see his car; and he is sitting on the patio. I guess he has been watching and waiting for me to drive up. I will still ignore him and remain silent for now. My mom told me a long time ago that if you ignore ignorance, it will go away.

"I see you've been out spending money that we don't have. How can we start a business if you're spending it all? I know all of these damn bags are not in the budget. So, I suggest that you take all of this stuff back!"

"That is not going to happen. This is the first time that I have spent money on myself since you've been back."

"I don't see any bags for me."

"There are no bags for you! Let my hair go! You're hurting me!"

"You are feeling yourself tonight. You better recognize who is the boss of this house and this relationship!"

"Sam! You may boss that floozy around that's carrying your baby; but you are not my boss! I am the bread winner here. Therefore, I have all the say in how my money is spent!"

"What floozy? And, what baby?"

"This baby! This ultrasound belongs to Bianca Jones!"

"Crazy woman! That is my cousin!"

I begin to cry and say, Sure Sam! You think I'm stupid, but I'm not! Why would you have your cousin's ultrasound in your pocket?"

"I took her to a doctor's appointment a few days ago and she accidently left it in the car. I put it in my pocket so it wouldn't get damaged in the car. I called and told her that. She told me to put it up for her.

"Why is it that I have never heard of this cousin named Bianca? I know your family!"

"You do not know all of my family, just like I don't know all of your family. Hell, I don't know all of my own family!"

"You are sleeping with somebody because you are never here and you have become so distant. Not to mention that you have been coming home at three and four in the morning, and sleeping on the couch!"

"I sleep on the couch and stay away from home because I'm hurt! You made me feel like I was less than a man when I tried to make your day special!"

"I need you to call Bianca, and put her on speaker phone so that I can hear her say that she is your cousin!"

"I am not going to call that girl to satisfy your insecurities. If you would lose some weight, then maybe that would help!

"My weight has nothing to do with you screwing around, getting her pregnant, and lying to my face!"

"What do you want from me?"

"After all of this time, if you don't know, why bother?"

"Every time you go and hang out with Lisa and Carol, you come back acting like you run something! If you keep it up, I am going to stop that monthly meeting!"

"I am going to bed!" Tomorrow is a new day! I cannot stomach another minute of Sam and his bullshit!

LISA

Mike's parents are coming to visit for the holiday and it is making him crazy. His craziness is stressing me out. He wants everything perfect, from dinner to their entire stay. He has prepared a to-do list for both of us, and it consumes a lot of time. In addition to all the papers that I have not graded, I have to complete this list by the end of the week. He says that his mom is OCD, and his dad will complain about the smallest thing. He makes me rehearse how I should act, talk, and respond to his parents. He told his parents that I was his perfect, ideal woman, and perfect is what they will be expecting.

My parents are disappointed that I will not be spending Thanksgiving with them; but Mom understands. However, Dad is another story. He has been pressuring me to introduce him to Mike, but I make up an excuse each time. Dad is very territorial when it comes to me; and honestly, I am afraid of what may happen when they meet. Mike is territorial as well, so I am not ready to face the power struggle. Every relationship where I allowed the guy to meet my dad has ended in a disaster. Each time I felt good about a man or thought that he was the man for me, my dad would find something wrong. The sad part is that he would be right. I love Mike and I am afraid of the prophecy that my dad has in store. Whatever my dad has to say, I do not want to hear it. In his eyes, no man will ever be good enough for his baby girl. I know that the time will come for my family to meet Mike, but it will not be anytime soon.

It is three days until Thanksgiving. Mike's parents will arrive day after tomorrow. I will begin cooking the desserts tonight and I hope to do well with him mom's recipes. I wanted to create and serve my own menu for Thanksgiving dinner; but Mike had his mom put the menu together, along with the recipes. I finished the decorations on yesterday and Mike approved them. The decorations were the only area where I was able to provide input. I wonder will a life with him always consist of pleasing his parents.

Today is the day that Mike's parents will arrive. I am so nervous and stressed! At least I will get a little alone time while they are here because Mike and I will be staying at our own homes. His parents do not believe in co-habitation before marriage. Anyway, Mike called about ten minutes ago to say that he was at the airport picking up his parents. Lord, give me strength to get through the next few days, and please let his parents like me.

"Lisa! We are here! Hey Babe. These are my parents, Mr. Gerald Hampton and Mrs. Paula Hampton. Mom and Dad, this is Lisa Collins."

"It's a pleasure to meet you Mr. and Mrs. Hampton."

"Nice to finally meet you", says Mr. Hampton.

"Hi Darling", says Mrs. Hampton.

"Lisa, please show them into the living room while I put their coats and luggage away."

"Sure. This way, please."

I escort the Hamptons into the living room. Mr. Hampton seems much more laid back and nothing like Mike described. Mrs. Hampton seems uppity and looks down her nose at others. But, I am not going to judge the book by its cover. I am going to get to know her first. She begins a small talk conversation with me by asking me questions regarding my career.

"Lisa, Mike tells us that you are an elementary school teacher. How long have you been teaching?"

"I have been teaching third grade for ten years."

"Do you inspire to do more than teach? I believe Mike told me that you have your administrator's license, but you have no desire to use it."

"Yes, ma'am. That is correct."

"I see. Well, in order to be great, one must step outside of their comfort zone. I was a registered nurse for fifteen years and I went back to school to pursue a degree in administration. Now, I am the Director of one of the leading hospitals using cutting edge technology."

"Yes Ma'am, I understand."

"Mom, don't harass her and run her off. I really love her!"

Mike's father suddenly changes the discussion to lighten the mood.

"Ms. Lisa, my son really cares for you. The reason I know that is because you are only the second woman that he has allowed us to meet and interact with. Welcome to the family!"

Mike's mother continues to be a total bitch!

"The verdict is still out for me. She has done a lovely job decorating for Thanksgiving though. I will give my approval after tomorrow's dinner".

"Mom!!!" Mike yells with a disgusted look on his face.

"Thank you Mr. Hampton. Thank you as well Mrs. Hampton. "I am going to retreat to the kitchen and continue cooking." As I rise to leave the room, I think to myself and conclude that Mike's mom is a certified bitch!

"Honey, I will be there in a minute."

"There's no need for you to do that Mike. Just spend some quality time with your parents. I have everything under control".

Soon after, Mike comes into the kitchen to assure me that I am doing great; although it surely does not seem like it. It seems as if I am walking on egg shells. I have been in the kitchen all day and night, however I am finally about to wrap things up. Mike took his parents out for dinner to give me a little sigh of relief. The only thing that I will need to prepare on tomorrow is the turkey, the ham, and the cornbread dressing. Upon their returning, Mrs. Hampton retires to bed. Mike and Mr. Hampton are in the living room laughing, talking, drinking, and having a good time. I over hear a conversation between the two of them that was not meant for my ears.

"Lisa is a good girl. You have to tell her about Shelia and the girls."

"I know Dad. But, I am so afraid of losing her."

"You should have shared that with her as soon as the relationship got serious."

"I have been waiting for the perfect moment to tell her. Every time that I vow to tell her, I lose my nerves."

"There will never be a perfect time! You just have to be honest with her. I think she will understand."

"Do you think she will forgive me for waiting to tell her?"

"That girl loves you! However, she is going to be upset that you kept that information from her. Put yourself in her position and think how you would feel if she had kept something important from you. Nevertheless, I think you both will be able to work through it."

Damn! Who in the hell is Shelia and the girls? Mike has been keeping secrets. Have I broken up a happy home? I knew that he was too good to be true. I am in love with a cheater. This is bad!! He should have told me up front and allowed me to make the decision of dating a married mad. I feel like a fool! When this holiday is over, we are done! I am going to disappear and he is never going to hear from me again!

Thanksgiving Day is finally here. The day begins with Mike, his parents, and I watching the Macy's Thanksgiving Day Parade. I am putting the finishing touches on dinner and trying to put on a happy face to mask the anger that I feel for Mike. Impressing his mom no longer matters to me. My mind is racing with the questions, "Should I confront him or not?" "Should I allow him the opportunity to tell me and explain?" Last night I cried a million tears.

Dinner is served. Mike and his dad are full of conversations while his mom and I eat in silence. She is too busy licking her fingers. Apparently, I did well. Finally, Mrs. Hampton breaks her silence.

"Lisa, I'm very impressed! The turkey was a little dry, but we'll work on that. Also, next time add a little more sugar to the sweet potato pies."

"Yes Ma'am. Thank you." Mike grabs my hand, but I pull back!

"What's wrong dear? I have given you the stamp of approval! Your eyes are puffy. It looks like you have been crying or have been up all night."

"She is tired. She put a lot of work and time into making sure everything went perfect."

"Mike! She can speak for herself. Is everything okay, honey?"

"Sure. I am just exhausted." No, everything is not okay! I should have put ex-lax in their son's food so that he could feel as miserable as I do.

"Well Lisa, Gerald and I are going to clean the kitchen and allow you to get some rest. You and Mike go sit, relax, and watch TV. We will take care of the rest. You have done well!"

"Thank you! But, that is not necessary. I will get the kitchen later."

"We insist!" adds Mr. Hampton.

"Come on baby. She is not one to argue with." Mike tries to hold my hand, but I resist, again. He then forcefully hugs my neck and asks, "What is wrong with you trying to defy my affection in front of my parents?"

"I do not want your affection!"

"Whatever your problem is, I suggest that you put it away until my parents leave. Now, come on in the living room with me!"

Mike and I retire to the living room and sit close on the couch. I do not want him anywhere near me. He tries to kiss me on my forehead but I turn away. He grabs my arm really tight.

"Lisa! What is your problem?"

"Shelia and the girls are my problem!" Mike looks at me with surprise and guilt in his eyes. You have been lying to me?"

"Technically, I did not lie to you. I just never told you about them; and it is not what you think! I promise that I will explain everything when the weekend is over."

"Can we please wait until then?"

"I guess I can wait, especially after all of the time and effort that I have put into this weekend."

"Thank you! I love you!"

I am so hurt right now but I do owe it to myself to hear what he has to say. MEN!!!

CAROL

My favorite holidays are upon us. I love Thanksgiving and Christmas. Next is New Year's and then my birthday. The children are coming home for Thanksgiving and everyone will gather at our house for Thanksgiving dinner. My daughter, Tera, is always the first to arrive. She is my cooking partner. I have passed the sweet potato pies and all of the desserts to her, and she is good at it. She is almost as good as me. My son Tony always arrives the night before Thanksgiving due to work. Carl's daughter will arrive on Thanksgiving morning.

Carl and I have to put on a big front so that the family will not pick up on the tension between us. I want to tell them everything, but Carl thinks that we should leave them out of our business. It is hard for me to front because my facial expressions are worth a thousand words. Tera knows me like a book and will probably pick up on the vibe. Carl's time is winding down. He has less than a month and a half to say those four words to me. I guess, in order to keep a happy face, I will focus my attention on Donovan's romantic proposal. I am meeting him for a few minutes while I am out running errands.

"Hi beautiful. I've missed you!"

"Hi love! I missed you more!" Donovan and I hug, kiss, and caress each other for about five minutes.

"How long do we have?"

"About two hours!"

"What if I want more time?" Donovan asks.

"I would give you more if I didn't have to finish shopping for Thanksgiving dinner."

"I will let you off this time. Oh by the way, I will be in New Orleans this weekend to attend the Classic."

"You are out of control!" I say to him while laughing. "Please do not say that you are in the same hotel as us!"

"I tried but there were no rooms available. I am across the street."

"What am I going to do with you?"

"Love and marry me! Come here so I can slow dance with you."

Donovan and I slow dance to the Temptations "This is My Promise". He knows that this is one of my favorite songs. He is so romantic! Gosh!!! This moment in time not only feels good, but it also feels right! After dancing, he leads me to his bathroom where the shower water is running, and it is steamy. He undresses me and leads me into the shower and we make love in the shower. Our love making produces more steam that the hot water. My time with him just gets better with time.

Now that I have satisfied my craving for Donovan, it is time to focus on Thanksgiving. All of the children are now home. It is just like old times. I really enjoy having the house full again. Tera and I have been up all night cooking. Tony and Carl have been sampling all of the foods, and eating the cake and pie batter. Later today, Carl's family and my family will be joining us for a good old fashion family gathering for the holidays. Although Carl and I are not happy, I am going to pull it together and enjoy this day. Besides, my meeting with Donovan on yesterday will keep me going for a while. Then on tomorrow morning, we will leave for our annual family trip to New Orleans for the Bayou Classic.

As we gather for dinner, we keep the tradition of having everyone at the table give thanks. We have a feast and that is definitely something that we all are thankful for. The women and children outnumber the men as usual. We eat, drink, talk, laugh, and enjoy family. After dinner, the women clear the table and clean the kitchen. The children go outside to exert their energy, and all of the men retreat to the family room to watch the Dallas Cowboys play football. After cleaning, the ladies join the men to cheer our team on to victory. Thanksgiving turned out to be a beautiful time with family.

The time has come for our trip to New Orleans. We left early this

morning and have now arrived in the Big Easy! It is about to be one big party weekend. I love this event. I get the opportunity to see my college roommates, suitemates, sorority sisters, fraternity brothers, and classmates. The Classic weekend is one of the largest gatherings of African Americans in the state of Louisiana. I love my school SU (Southern University), and I am a Jaguar for life. I return every year. It is a family tradition that I have passed on to my children. Now that they are adults, I don't have to babysit them. We all can go our separate ways.

We have all checked into our hotel, the Chateau Sonesta located in the French Quarter. This hotel is very elegant and we arrived early enough to get a room with a balcony view that overlooks Bourbon Street. That is a plus! We can enjoy the fun without being a part of the crowded street. Oops! Donovan has sent four text messages notifying me that he has arrived in the Big Easy. He is registered across the street at the Ritz Carlton. I will try to make time for him, but it is going to be a challenge with all that is going on. I have so many people to see and events to attend in such a small window of time. Getting away from Carl will not be a problem. The only event that he attends is the game. The remainder of the time, he will be sitting on the balcony drinking Crown Royal. My only concern is not running into my children.

I am headed out to meet up with my fraternity brothers and sorority sisters. We are meeting up at the dome for the battle of the bands and the Greek show. As I exit the hotel lobby, I see Donovan standing out front.

"Hey beautiful!"

"Hi handsome!"

"I just wanted to lay eyes on you before you got busy."

"Aren't you a sweet heart? Who are your friends?"

"Oh, those are my co-workers, Michael and John."

"Well, don't get into any trouble. There is a lot of temptation available during this weekend."

"Where is Carl?"

"You know he is in the room. He is probably sitting on the balcony with a drink in his hand."

"Will it be okay for me to walk over to the dome with you?"

"Sure!"

"Before I forget, here is your ticket to the House of Blues. We will be attending a Wynton Marsalis concert on tomorrow night."

"Wow! How did you get these? Tickets to the House of Blues are hard to come by. Wait a minute! How did you know I would go with you?"

"You'll find a way; and you will be spending the night with me."

"Damn! You drive a hard bargain. I still have to be careful."

"Girl, it's so busy and so many people here that we can almost do whatever we want."

"Okay. I'll see you tomorrow." He is so thoughtful. He knows that I love jazz. Donovan is winning!!!

One night down, now on to day number two! Today is the big game . . . Southern University versus Grambling State. Carl wants to leave early so that we can get a little tailgating in. The problem is that I am tired from last night. After the battle of the bands and the Greek show, I went for drinks with my Greek family. I just got in three hours ago.

"Come on woman, you should have come in at a decent hour."

"I'm good. I never get much sleep during the classic weekend anyway. You are the one that is old and can't hang."

"I know my limitations."

"Your limitations are growing more and more."

"I was thinking that maybe after the game, we could go down to the riverfront and the casino."

"I don't think that will be possible. Besides, you know the casino is really not my thing."

"Why?"

"I have to get a little sleep. Also, I have that Greek formal event tonight.

"Oh! I did not know about that. When did that start? I didn't see it on the schedule of events."

"It was added at the last minute."

"Well, that shouldn't last all night. How about we go afterwards?"

"You can go ahead. Depending on the time it ends, I will text you. If you are still there, then I may join you if I am not too exhausted."

"Well, I think you should make time."

"I will try, love." Now all of a sudden he wants to do something extra. Usually after the game, all he wants to do is sit on the balcony and drink. As he leaves the room, I lie down for a quick nap.   Shoot! I overslept! Let me hurry and get ready. I shower, quickly get dressed and then dart out the door to meet Donovan so that we can go to the concert. He is looking good, dressed in a black suit with a gold tie ensemble. Ironically, I chose to wear a black dress.

"I see that we have ESP."

We both laugh as he says, "You look stunning in that dress!"

"You look mighty dapper yourself."

"Let's go make everyone in the room jealous."

As we depart for the House of Blues, I see Carl. I quickly grab Donovan's arm and say, "Quick, duck into this building. I just saw Carl."

"Where?"

"Across the street! You cannot miss that white hair."

"Where is he going?"

"He mentioned the casino and the riverwalk. He wants me to meet him later."

"Too bad, you will not be going."

"Damn, that was close! I really think he saw us."

"Personally, I really don't care; only for your sake. If he did see us, then maybe he will be angry enough to walk away, and then I can finally have

what I want!"

We wait a few more minutes to give Carl time to disappear. After checking to make sure he is out of sight, we proceed to the concert venue.

It's 11:30p.m. and the concert has just ended. Donovan and I decide to have one more drink before heading back to his hotel. While walking back, we engage in small talk and take in all of the action happening on the streets. It is lit as usual and the atmosphere is quite festive. As we approach Donovan's hotel, he hands me his room key and tells me to go on up so that we do not walk in together. I oblige because it is a good idea. About 15 minutes later, Donovan enters the room accompanied by a room service attendant. He has ordered food and wine for the both of us. He tips the attendant as he leaves and then locks the door.

"I was beginning to wonder what was taking you so long to come up."

"Well, it's been several hours since we both have eaten, so I thought I should order something light for us to snack on. Being that it's late, I got a couple of salads. Is that okay?"

"Sure love! That was very thoughtful of you."

"Well, you know I try. However, I must say that all day I've had something else in mind to eat ."

I watch as he pours us both some wine and say, "Oh really? What did you have in mind?"

He turns toward me with a smile, hands me my glass and says, "You'll find out soon enough."

"Donovan! You are so naughty!" We both laugh as we begin to eat our food.

After we finish eating and talking for a bit, I decide to take a shower while Donovan clears away our mess. As I exit the bathroom, Donovan decides to shower also. It would have been lovely for him to join me. But oh well, maybe another time. While he is in the shower, I pour myself another glass of wine, slip on some lingerie and then lie across the bed. It's been a

long day, but I am feeling pretty good.

Donovan finishes showering and comes out of the bathroom wearing only a towel. The mere site of his upper torso causes an arousal within me, but I play it cool. He puts on some music, pours himself more wine and then places the bottle on the nightstand by the bed.

As I start to sit up in the bed, Donovan quickly says, "No, keep relaxing. I'm about to join you."

"Well come on and join me then."

"On second thought, go ahead and get up so I can get a better view of that lingerie."

"Oh, so you want to see it? For a minute, I thought you didn't really notice."

"Babe, I notice more than you realize. And right now, you are looking very hot and sexy to me!"

On that note, I get up and do a slow turn in front of him. Feeling the groove, I start swaying to the music while making erotic gestures. Donovan stands up and drops his towel to the floor, then gestures for me to come closer; but I don't. He then sits back down on the bed, spreads his legs and leans back on his elbows. I continue to dance in front of him as I watch his penis slowly rise and become fully erect. He whispers for me to come closer. I slowly oblige, but stop just short of reaching him. As I turn my back to him, I bend over and grab my ankles. Donovan then gets into a slight squat behind me. As he slowly stands, I feel his hard penis gently gliding up my inner thigh. I am now very wet and tingling on the inside. After he turns me around and embraces me, we engage in passionate kissing as we make our way over to the bed. After I sit down, he kneels on the floor and spreads my legs wide open. His hands softly glide up my legs and then my thighs. When he reaches my vagina, he gently massages my clit as I try to contain myself. Suddenly he buries his head between my legs and I feel his tongue licking and stroking my vijay-jay inside and out. The strong, fondling vibrations of

his tongue pleasure me greatly and cause me to start contracting. Sensing my reactions, Donovan inserts his penis into me and begins to make love to me like never before. He's in no hurry as he slowly thrusts in and out, going deeper with every thrust. I scream his name as he hits my g-spot, and then his repetitions get faster and faster. I feel like I am about to explode. While staying in motion, he licks and tongues my nipples. His thrusts and gyrations are giving me life! Suddenly we both climax and let out a scream. I can hardly breathe as I enjoy the release.   This man has just rocked my world for sure!

It's almost 5:15a.m. and I am headed to my room to get ready for the trip home. The concert was awesome; and the night with Donovan was super awesome! Actually, the entire weekend has been epic. But now it is time to get back to reality and I hope Carl is asleep. I unlock the door and walk in.

"Where the hell have you been? I saw you!"

"Saw me where? What was I doing?"

"You were on Bourbon Street flashing your breasts!" I start laughing uncontrollably.

"What is so damn funny?", asks Carl.

As I gain my composure, I say "Nothing! I'm sorry. I have been with my Greek family and Bourbon Street was not on our agenda. You must have drunk too much!"

That was a hilarious and exhilarating moment . . . I really thought that I had been caught!

TISH

Thanksgiving Day is tomorrow. I am going to spend the entire weekend at my mom's house so that I do not have to deal with Sam. However, he will have Thanksgiving dinner with us against my better judgment. Unfortunately, I cannot let my mom know that he and I are having major problems. He is ruining me financially, refuses to work, and has a baby on

the way that he keeps denying. I cannot stand him right now, but I still love him. I believe that our love will carry us through this rough patch, and we will be a power couple soon.

"Tish, have you had your shower?"

"Why, Sam?"

"Just answer the question!"

"Yes, earlier today."

"Well, I am horny and feeling frisky."

"What does that have to do with me taking a shower?"

"Before we have sex, I need you to take a shower. Go on before I lose the mood!"

It has been weeks since he's touched me. So if taking an extra shower will help him get intimate with me again, off to the shower I go. I have some new body washes and lotion fragrances that I have not used. Now, I have a reason. I also have some new lingerie that I bought on my shopping spree. I think Sam will love it. Maybe tonight, will be the night that we get our spark back in the bedroom.

I step into the bedroom modeling my new lingerie for Sam. He has set the mood while I was in shower. Teddy Pendergrass' "Turn of the Lights" is playing in the background. Candles are lit around the room. Sam is lying in bed looking sexy as ever with his penis at attention. I move close to the bed. He takes my hand and places it on his penis. I begin to stroke it up and down just to tease him. I have a surprise for him that is going to blow his mind.

"Close your eyes, Sam." After he closes his eyes. I spread whip cream on his nipples and down the middle of his stomach to his penis.

"Damn girl! That's cold! What are you doing?"

"Just keep your eyes closed and trust me." I slowly lick the whip cream off of his body.

"Mmmm. Ahhh shit! What has gotten into you?"

I finally reach his penis and give him a blow job unlike any he has ever experienced from me before. He is hollering so loud. I know that the neighbors hear him. He grabs me and sits me on his face. Before long, we are in a sixty-nine position. He rips my lingerie off and makes love to me passionately. He has not made love to me like this since our first date night. I look at the clock and it is an hour later. That was GREAT!!!

"Now that's the Tish I remember!"

As we both laugh, he cuddles with me and kisses me. Maybe it has been me all of this time. I have not been taking care of my man in the bedroom. That is why he cheated on me. I just needed to turn up the heat.

"You are finally complete. Now you are meeting all of my needs. Keep up the good work, Tish."

"Does that mean that you are moving back into the bedroom?"

"Yes, my love."

"Is that why you cheated on me and got that girl pregnant?"

"You mean allegedly cheated on you and got someone pregnant. I told you that she is my cousin on my dad's side of the family. I moved out of the bedroom because you did not do it for me anymore."

"Sam, I work two jobs in addition to doing all of the cooking and house chores."

"A real woman can do it all, whether she is tired or not. She is going to keep her man happy!"

"You are a cave man."

"It is a man's world. The only thing that I need you to do is to work on losing that one hundred pounds. The lingerie is cool, but it is kind of hard to see the thong. I'm just saying!"

Again, Sam knows how to build me up just to tear me back down. But, if he wants me to lose this weight, I am now more motivated than ever.

It's Thanksgiving Day and I am feeling so good! I got my man's affection and attention once again. I am excited to see my mom and my family. I

cannot wait to taste my grandma's homemade caramel cake. Oh, I forgot that I am supposedly starting my diet. It will have to wait until after the holidays. Sam will be upset, but as long as I am going to the gym and trying, he will be fine.

Thanksgiving Day has been awesome! It was full of joy, laughs, and fun with family. I even enjoyed Sam being around. My world finally feels complete and content. I did not get to enjoy food, though, because Sam was watching me like a hawk. Every piece of food that I picked up, he shook his head no. My family is probably wondering what the heck is going on. Sam has demanded that I not bring any leftovers home. He says that from now on, I am eating healthy.

"Tish, I am going over to my mom's house for a couple of hours."

"Ok. I will see you on Sunday."

"Sunday?!"

"Yes, Sunday. Remember, I am spending the weekend here so that mom and I can catch some black Friday sales."

"No! That is too long! You need to be home by Saturday at noon and that is the final word."

"But Sam, I promised her that we would spend the entire weekend together. What am I supposed to tell her?"

"The truth! Your man wants you home. She has a husband, so she will understand. Don't mess up our happy home!" Sam demands as he leaves. So, in order to keep the peace in my household, I will be home by noon on Saturday.

LISA

Mike has a lot of explaining to do. I am so hurt that he has been lying to me. I blame myself for letting my guard down so quickly. For the first time, I have allowed a man to lead me in a relationship, and look where it has gotten me. Tonight, I do not want a fancy dinner or romance, just the truth.

"Mike, I want the truth."

"Lisa, you know that I love you with all of my heart, right?"

"I have doubts Mike, because you did not trust me with the truth."

"I wanted to protect your heart. That is what a man does, he protects the one he loves."

"Who is Shelia and the girls?"

"She is my wife. Well my soon-to-be ex-wife. She lives in Charlotte, North Carolina and she is raising our two daughters, Meagan and Sydney. We have been going through this divorce for three years because the only thing that we can agree on is joint custody of the girls."

"How old are the girls?"

"Meagan is seven and Sydney is four. I love my girls.

"Why is the divorce taking so long?"

"Money! In our ten years together, we accumulated a lot of property, businesses, and money together. Luckily, I came from money and there was a pre-nuptial for those finances.

"Are you providing for the girls financially? Do you communicate with them?"

"Yes! I send a three thousand dollar check home each month. I can show you my bank statements if you need proof. Plus, I skype with them every morning after I arrive at work."

"Why didn't you feel like you could trust me with this information?"

"Lisa, when I met you, I had gotten so tired of fighting with her over this that I had started to consider reconciliation. But then, we happened, and I am not sorry for that."

"So, am I the reason that your girls have an absent father?" I do not know if I can live with that."

"Lisa, I have not lived in the house with them for three years. I transferred my job here because Shelia and I could not live in the same household or city."

"But you were having second thoughts, right?"

"Only because of money. She and I both would have been miserable, and that would be unhealthy for my girls."

"After all of this time, you are telling me that she will not agree on any settlement?"

"Yes because she wants it all! Each time my attorney presents an offer, her attorney sends it back denied. Look Lisa, I love you and I am not going to allow you to get away."

"May I see a picture of your girls?"

"Sure" he says as he takes a picture from his wallet. "Sydney is on the left and Meagan is on the right.   Nobody visits me here but you; so there is no need to have any pictures up because I keep them close to me in my wallet and in my heart."

"Mike, they are beautiful! Is Shelia Latino?"

"Yes she is, and thank you. I know this a lot to consume at one time. Please forgive me for keeping this a secret."

"I need some time Mike. I have a lot of thinking to do. So, I think that we should take a break until I can emotionally work through all of this. I mean you have girls. Will they like me?   How are they going to feel about you having another woman in their lives? Shelia may not appreciate you bringing her babies around another woman."

"I know it's complicated. But we can get through this, Lisa! Can we agree to mutually attend therapy sessions to help us?"

"Just give me a few days to digest all of this. I love you, but I just need a little time."

"I don't know if I can be without you. Does that mean that we will not talk or what?"

"No, we will check in with each other. But there will be no spending the night together.

"I guess I will have to accept that stipulation for now."

I am so mad that he did not trust me with this. I wonder if he would

have told me had I not over heard his conversation with his father. The fact that I love him with all of my heart infuriates me more. This goes against everything that I stand for. Two of my stipulations regarding men are "no children" and "no baby mama drama". I do not date married men. I did not ask for any of this . . . Mike volunteered me. I have a lot of decisions to make. I need my bestie, Carol! I will text her to see if we can go out for drinks tonight. Lord, help me to make the right decision and give me discernment in this situation! MEN! UGH!!!

4

LISA

I am on my way to meet Carol for lots and lots of drinks. I need someone to talk to who is rational. Carol is that go to person. She will help me rationalize every detail. I want to include Tish; but unfortunately, I cannot because she has been looking for faults with Mike since day one.

"Hi Chica! What is wrong? You sounded distraught. I know it has to be bad because you are already drinking.

"Girl, it's Mike! He is married with children!" I blurt out while crying.

"Oh honey! I am so sorry. How do you know?"

"His parents were visiting for Thanksgiving and I overheard a conversation between Mike and his dad."

"Okay. How is that possible? You guys spend so much time together. Also, he spends money on you like there is no end! A man with a family cannot spend time and money like that on another woman."

"She lives in Charlotte, North Carolina. Her name is Shelia and they have two girls, Meagan and Sydney. The heifer is Latino and the girls are gorgeous!" Can you believe he kept that shit from me?!

"Are they teenagers?"

"No. They are seven and four."

"This does not make any sense. Did he explain? What did he have to say for himself?"

"He said that they have been going through a divorce for three years and he pays child support every month. They accumulated a lot of money and assets together; but they can't agree on a settlement because she wants it all. The only thing they agree on is joint custody of the kids."

"Money can tie up a divorce for years. Do you love him?"

"I do with all of my heart and soul! I am mad at myself for letting my guard down. I am more furious with him for not trusting me enough to tell me. I told him that we need to take a break from each other so that I can have some time to sort things out."

"That is a lot to take in! You will definitely have to do some soul searching and praying."

"You and only you can decide whether or not this is the life and man that you want."

"You know that I do not like men with children, married men, or baby mama drama. Dammit! Mike has all three!"

"Well, I support you no matter what you decide. If you love him, so will I. If you hate him and never speak to him again, so will I."

"He assured me over and over again that he loves me; and that he wanted to tell me, but he kept losing his nerve. I do not doubt his love for me, but I will not be a part of anyone's game."

"Well, make a list of his good traits and his bad traits. If the good outweighs the bad, then he may be worth sticking this out."

"He can be a little controlling at times, but I can handle that. However, I do not like being lied to or played for a fool."

"Well, let me make you laugh. Carl said that he saw me on Bourbon Street flashing my breasts!" We both start to laugh uncontrollably. When he said that he saw me, I actually thought he saw me and Donovan walking to the House of Blues."

"Wait! Donovan went to New Orleans?"

"Yes Ma'am! He took me to a Wynton Marsalis concert!"

"Girl, you are crazy! How in the hell did you pull that off?"

"The only thing that Carl usually does is attend the game and then either sit in the room or on the balcony and drink; although this time he did try to turn left on me. He wanted to go to the casino and the riverwalk, but I played it to the right."

"So, what are you going to do about Carl and Donovan?"

"I don't have a clue! If Carl does not propose to me, he can get his shit and kick rocks! As for Donovan, time will tell. But these days, Donovan is winning!"

"Well, Mike is cut off from the pocket book! I communicate with him, but that's it. I still crave the hell out of him; but until I figure things out, it will be me and the toys. Dammit!"

"I will drink to that! On another note, have you heard from Tish?"

"No!"

"Neither have I. I guess I will try to call her on tomorrow. So, can we still do the couple's night? I was thinking about hosting a little Christmas party at my house with just drinks, finger foods, and music."

"I will let you know."

"Cool."

"It just hit me that if I stay with Mike, I will be an instant step-mother! Now that shit really does scare me."

"Girl, let's order more drinks. It will help us figure things out"

"Wait a minute, Carol! Who will you bring to date night?" Lisa asks as she laughs.

"Girl, you play too much!"

CAROL

I just retrieved our mail from the mailbox and there is a letter addressed to me; however there is no return address. I open it and see a typed letter and a picture of Carl's SUV. The letter reads "when your man sometimes claims to be working overtime, he is lying. He is actually with me. Just Look at the picture! The sun rises in the east and he comes over to my house and spends the night. He leaves by 5:00a.m. to make it seem as though he just left work."

What trick is he messing with that is bold enough to send a letter to my

house? This is upsetting, but I think I am going to sit on this information for a while. It is going to be hard for me not to say anything. He has less than a month before I kick him out on his ass anyway. This is the second time that his old ass has cheated on me; and I am done! However, I am not going to say anything just yet. My attitude will be so awful that I will not be able to stand myself. I may just invite Donovan to the Christmas party. The old me would have been waiting on him in the drive way with a gun, ready to let bullets rip. I feel so violated! Ugh!

"Carol! What's for dinner?"

"Your five fingers! Get to licking!"

"Haha! That is funny; but seriously, what did you cook?"

"Not a damn thing!"

"Did you not go to the grocery store either?"

"Nope! Is there a problem?"

"Yeah! I'm hungry!"

"Well I suggest you go get some take out because Susie Homemaker is on strike. I ate earlier."

"So you did not think to bring me anything to eat?"

"Not at all. Now I have to go somewhere. See you later!" That is as nice as I can be to him right now. Besides, Donovan texted and asked me to meet him. He is working on I-40 today; so I am on my way to grace him with my presence."

"Hi Beautiful! Come give me a big ole hug."

"Hi Baby!"

"I know meeting me here on the interstate is not ideal, but I am scheduled for a lot of shifts before my vacation starts next week. I just had to see you."

"I will meet you anywhere these days! You have really stepped your game up this time. Everyone who passes by us is going to think that I am in trouble."

"This is a search!"

"Baby, you can search me anytime!"

"Assume the position, girl!"

"Whatever you say! What if Carl drives by and sees us?"

"Then he sees what he sees. Today, I really don't care! So what did he do? Do I need to pull him over and give him some tickets?"

"That's a conversation for another day, but you can give him as many tickets as your heart desires."

"I got you, Baby. I see you wore my ring for me today. Thank you."

"It's so beautiful! I can't wear it every day, but I keep it in my purse and stare at it every opportunity I get."

"I love you, girl."

"Ditto! I have to get going so I can get to work on time. The good news is I will no longer be teaching night classes for a while."

"Be careful! Just know that if you need me, I will be right there!"

Carl thinks that he is slick as usual. Tomorrow night, I may just show up at DuPont to see if he is really working or not. Depending on who is working, his crew will tell me whatever I ask because they cannot stand him. He needs to leave tonight because the sight of him presently sickens me. He knows that something is up because he keeps trying to talk to me and be overly nice.

"Why did you trade in your ring Carol?"

Oh snap! I forgot to take off Donovan's ring and put Carl's back on. "I did not trade in my ring."

"That is not the ring I bought you, so where is it?"

"It's in my purse where it will remain until you come correct!"

"Oh okay. So it's like that? Show me the ring!"

"It's right here, still safe and secure. And furthermore, you have no idea how it will be."

"Is that a threat?"

"Honey, I am a lady. I do not make threats. It's a promise . . . my promise to you."

"I see you want to play games? So, when did you buy that ring?"

"Who says that I bought it? You should not assume things, Dear."

"I do not care for your attitude these past few days. Are you messing off with another man?"

"I find it funny that you are accusing me of cheating. I have never cheated on you!"

"So you say. All I know is that your attitude is bad. You've stopped cooking, and some of your time is unaccounted for. To top it off, you currently smell like a man's cologne, and it is not mines!"

"Fool! I work around men all day long. I greet them with hugs and sometimes their cologne is so strong that it leaves a scent on everyone."

"You got an answer for everything; but don't let me find out otherwise."

"Whatever! You just make sure that you are really at work whenever you claim to be working those twelve to sixteen hour shifts. Don't let me find out that you are not!"

"When you go to the bank, the proof is in the paycheck. You spend so much until you don't even notice. All you do is swipe! Today, you better swipe some groceries up in here. I don't say much, but you know how I feel about groceries in the house."

"I'll think about it. Maybe I will, maybe I won't."

TISH

Today Sam is presenting his business plan to the bank for a small business loan. Against my better judgment, I am putting my name on this loan. I could draw down some of my 401k, but if it doesn't work out, I can never get that money back. He has one shot at this business thing; and if it does not work out, nine to five it will be. Something has to work out for him because I am tired of working two jobs. I am trying to hold my man down;

but he has one year to get it together, or I am done with him.

I am so tired mentally as well as physically. I can only tell Carol and Lisa so much because of their feelings toward Sam. Some days I feel like my head is going to twist around on my body. I just hope that Sam does not make me regret this financial sacrifice and my investment in him. I wanted to ask Lisa and Carol to invest with me, and possibly enlist some other investors. However, I know the answer to that before parting my lips. Sometimes, it is hard defending and standing by the one you love.

Surprisingly, we got approved for two Laundromat businesses instead of four. Sam wanted to start with four, but there is nothing wrong with starting small and expanding later. We have enough for equipment and more. The first one will open on the first of January; and the second one will open on the first of February. It looks like the New Year is going to be full of changes and prosperity. Look at my man! I knew he possessed the skills deep within to be successful. This calls for a celebration. I am taking us out for dinner at Ruth Chris' Steakhouse tonight.

"Thank you, baby for believing in me."

"That's what a real woman does. She supports her man."

"I will not let you down! You'll see. I am so excited for us. Let's toast to securing our future!" As we clink our glasses together, I say, "I will drink to that. I cannot wait to share the news."

"I'm sure, especially with your judgmental ass friends."

"Sam, do you know those people over there who keep staring at us?"

"Where?"

"They are seated to your right and my left."

"No. I have never laid eyes on them before in my life."

"Maybe they are staring because we are having too much fun."

"I don't know, but that is possible. I waived and they waived back. Are you sure that you have never met them?"

"Yes Tish, I'm sure. Now stop focusing on them and focus on your man

doing big things."

"If feels good to share this moment with you without arguing."

"Yes it does. I finally feel complete."

"Good. I have something else to share with you."

"What is it? Is it good news?"

"I think so. It is kind of a miracle. I missed my menstrual cycle. So I took a home pregnancy test and it was positive!"

"You cannot be serious!"

"I have a doctor's appointment on Monday."

"Tish! I thought you said that you could not have children."

"That is what my doctor has been telling me all of this time."

"Tish, we cannot have a baby right now. If the doctor confirms that you are pregnant, you will have to abort. I am sorry. I would love to have a child with you, but the timing is awful."

"Sam! How could you suggest something like that to me? I am keeping my baby with or without you!"

"Do you hear yourself and how selfish you sound?"

"Me?! I am far from selfish. You are an insensitive bastard!"

"I should have worn condoms."

"I do not believe what I am hearing from you!"

"Neither of us have time. That is all I am saying. You work two jobs and I have to focus on making this business work. Besides, you are an older woman and the pregnancy will be high risk. Not to mention the risk of the baby possibly having down syndrome. It will create problems that we do not need."

"I can't talk to you anymore. I am ready to go home. Check please!"

"Tish! You cannot have a baby right now and that is the final say on that subject."

It is a long, quiet ride home, and I am crying and furious! As I look at the side view mirror, I notice a red BMW following us. It appears to be

the same guys from the restaurant. Maybe it's just a coincidence and they live in the same area. I am not talking to Sam so I will just keep it to myself. Why did I have to love the most insensitive, selfish man in the world?

I just left my doctor's appointment. He confirmed that I am eight weeks pregnant and that I have a STD. I get one blow after another while dealing with Sam. Regardless, I am keeping my baby. Let me get myself prepared to tell him when I arrive home.

"Hi Sam. The doctor confirmed that I am eight weeks pregnant; and that I have a STD."

"Who did you get it from? What do you have?"

"How dare you try to turn this around on me? In eighteen years, you are the only man that I've given my love to. You need to go to the doctor; and tell that nasty trick that you slept with that she needs to go, too!"

"When are you going to schedule your abortion?"

"I am keeping my baby with or without you!"

"No you are not! You just lost ten pounds. If you have a baby at your age, you will never lose weight. There are too many risk factors regarding your health and a baby."

"Go to hell. Sam!"

This is supposed to be the happiest time in my life. This baby is a miracle, and I cannot celebrate and enjoy the news because of this trifling man that I chose.

LISA

Mike and I have been checking in with each other daily and we talk each night. We continue to talk out our problems, which is helping to release the tension. I guess the old saying is true that communication is the key. I am still hurt and upset, but now I'm a little more sympathetic. If I fully allow him back in, he will have to work extremely harder than before. He wants us to attend therapy, but I am not sure how I feel about that yet. I think he

should just give it all to her and start over. I have a successful career and so does he. However, I know that letting go of what you have sacrificed and worked hard for is easier said than done. Their portfolio is very hefty; so I guess I would fight for it too, if the shoe was on my foot.

Mike is a good guy overall. No man is perfect. I have to decide whether or not I am willing to deal with the baggage. He should have told me everything from the beginning, but I kind of understand his reasoning. I just do not agree with it. He has been pleading with me to incorporate one night a week that we can spend together, but I am not ready; although I do miss sleeping in his arms. I agreed to go to dinner with him tonight, but nothing else. I am meeting him at the Butcher Shop which is one of my favorite dining spots. He really thinks that he knows me.

"Hi Babe. You look great! It seems like I have not seen you in a lifetime. Come here and give me a hug."

"Hi. I sort of missed you, too." Damn! He smells good, feels good, and looks good!

"How was your day?"

"I cannot complain. How was your day?"

"It was incomplete until now."

"You are so damn charming!"

"I am just trying to keep my girl's heart."

"Your points have increased by one point five."

"Oh! Do I get points for the card and flowers I send each day?"

"No. That is required of you."

"Dang, Baby! You are a firecracker, but I still love you."

"Do you still love her?"

"As a person and as the mother of my girls, yes. As a wife and lover, hell no! I feel that a cordial relationship is required for the sake of the girls. If you choose to let me back in one hundred percent, I will go out of my way to assure you that I love you and not her."

"What is the custody agreement? How often will the girls be here?"

"I get them for all school breaks in the spring and summer, and we will alternate the holidays."

"That is pretty fair."

"Lisa, I want us all to get along and have a healthy relationship. We are all educated, reasonable adults. If we are going to be together, we must all be accepting."

"I agree, Mike. But please remember that you have all of the baggage that I've never considered tolerating. However, here I am thinking about it."

"I know baby. I feel like what we have and what we share together is worth you taking a chance on us. When you are ready, I want to introduce you to Shelia, and then the three of us will have a sit down with the girls."

"You would do that?"

"If you were to tell me right now that you are ready to meet her, then we would get on the first flight out. I know that I messed up by keeping Shelia and the girls a secret, but I am going to make things right from this point on."

"I hear you. But know that I have my eyes on you! Let's enjoy the remainder of the dinner. No more talk about our issues."

"I will drink to that! I love you."

"I love you back. There's one more thing that I just have to ask."

"What?"

"Have you considered giving Shelia everything and starting over?"

"At times I do; just so that I can bring this thing to an end. I think that giving her seventy percent of it all is pretty damn fair. I want my girls to have the best and live a good life."

"I was just curious. Seventy percent is very fair. If she knows that you have totally moved on, it may get ugly."

"She knows! I have told her that we need to get this settled so that we can get on with our lives."

"Well, I just don't know, Mike. I want to try one of these therapy sessions that you are recommending."

"Okay, cool! Will you go with me to Charlotte next week? We are meeting with the attorneys and the mediator. I want you there."

"No. I want you to finish your business with Shelia. After all of that is settled, then maybe I will go to Charlotte."

"Okay. That's fair."

My date with Mike was nice. It felt good to be in his arms for a hot minute. I think I may take a chance on him, but with my eyes, ears, and antennas wide open. He almost got a chance to spend the night. I will give in to that demand after he returns from Charlotte. I really want to have a conversation with Shelia. I have been so tempted to look her up or get her number from Mike's phone. However, that would be deceitful and I would be doing the same thing that has me furious with Mike. But, if I have a private investigator look her up, technically that wouldn't be the same. It would be a third party giving me information. If I am going to have a future with Mike, I need to know everything about him. I am going to have an investigator look into all aspects of his life. I will never allow him to surprise me with details about his life again. I will already know. I see it as an investment in my future, or possibly saving me from a lifetime of heartache.

I have always had issues with trusting men. The couple of times that I have trusted one, it turned out bad each time. I started out trusting Mike and he had a secret. Although, he is working hard to earn my trust again, it is hard for me to allow the brick wall to come down. After this investigation is complete, I will make a final decision on Mike. In the meantime, the verdict is still out, and I am going to continue to enjoy the royal treatment that he keeps giving me.

CAROL

Lisa and Tish both have agreed to our monthly outing which will include

the men in our lives. We girls are bonded for life, so it is time to bring the men together. I am the only one with a long standing relationship. I guess Tish's relationship or whatever the hell it is with Sam has been long standing, but he has not been around. I wonder does that fool know how to act civilized. I have decided on hosting a little Christmas affair at my home. It will be nothing big . . . just us three couples enjoying food, drinks, music, and conversation. I will call it "drinks and conversations". The only individual that probably won't have a conversation is Sam.

TISH

I have to fake happiness at this damn "drinks and conversation" affair that Carol is hosting. There are some good things happening for me and Sam. Unfortunately though, in the mist of the good things, there is still plenty of drama. There is no way I can just sit there and listen to Carol and Lisa talk about their perfect little make believe lives and I not share our news about the baby. Sam is going to get mad as hell when I announce my pregnancy on tonight. Maybe if others know besides us, he won't push the abortion issue. I wanted to call Carol and Lisa as soon as the doctor confirmed it, but I couldn't. If they knew what Sam wanted me to do, they would hang him by his balls, especially Carol's crazy ass. She would probably have special food and drinks just for Sam. Knowing her, she would be waiting on him at the door with her favorite fist to the nose jabber. On the flip side, the up and coming business venture is on schedule and both of my jobs are going great. I am just so stressed! I have been going to the doctor daily to keep my blood pressure monitored. It was 160/120 when I checked it this morning! Maybe releasing this news will help me feel a little relief. At least I will be around my girls who will be happy for me and ready to welcome this baby into this world.

LISA

I agreed to introduce Mike to Tish and Carol on tonight. Carol knows about our issues and she has been supportive. However, I have not told Tish. I probably will never tell Tish. Her man is a piece of poop and it is her desire that every man in America is too. I was hoping that my investigator would have gotten back to me by now. Unfortunately, he has not. I am waiting patiently! Mike is extremely excited to meet my friends. He said that he has felt like "my little secret". So now he thinks that he is in there! Unfortunately for him, the verdict remains open. He leaves for Charlotte on tomorrow and I hope he comes back as a divorced man. I have been wondering whether or not to give him a night of romance before he leaves. I have punished myself long enough. Besides, Shelia may begin to look good to him and he may forget what they are going through for the moment. After the social tonight, I am going to make sure that I stay on Mike's mind.

CAROL

My guest will be arriving soon. The food and drinks are ready. The house is full of holiday cheer. Everyone who knows me knows that Christmas is my favorite holiday. I always decorate two large Christmas trees, a small tree, the fireplace, the staircase banister and the entire house with Christmas cheer. I cannot wait to meet Lisa's new beau, Mike. However, that damn Sam is another story. Tonight, I am going to let go of the horrible feelings that I have towards him. Besides, I can direct those feelings toward Carl. I hope he gets drunk and tells on himself. Oh, there's the doorbell. It's Mike and Lisa.

"Hi Lisa. And this must be the famous Mike?"

"Yes, Carol. This is Mike."

"Well hi Mike. The pleasure is all mines. You guys make yourself at home. This is Carl."

"What's up man?" Carl says as he shakes Mike's hand. "Welcome to the

madness. It's nice to meet the mystery man who stole my girl's heart."

"That would be me. But no, I am excited to meet Lisa's best friend. Hell I am just glad to meet someone in her circle."

"Carol, I keep trying to tell him that our circle is small."

"That's true, Mike. A small circle keeps down drama and confusion."

"So Mike, where do you work?"

"I am an IT manager at FedEx. I've been there for fifteen years. What do you do?"

"I am a Chemical Specialist at DuPont. I have been with them for twenty eight years."

"Oh wow! I want to be like you! You're close to retirement."

"Keep working and living. You will get there."

"Girl, I love this. They are getting along."

"True. So far, so good." As I complete the finishing touches, the doorbell rings again. It has to be Sam and Tish.

"Hi girl. Sam."

"Hi Carol, it's been a long time."

"Not long enough."

"Carol! It's too early for that. Can we get out of the cold first?"

"I apologize for my rudeness."

"Do not make apologies that you really don't mean."

"You are right. I take it back!"

"Mike, this is our other bestie, Tish, and her man Sam."

"Pleasure to meet you both."

"So, you are the mystery man in the flesh!"

"It is I in the flesh."

"Carl, do you remember Sam?"

"Vaguely; but hi man. I have heard a lot about you."

"Good things, I hope."

"No comment." Everyone then laughs.

"There is plenty of food and drinks; so eat and drink as much as you would like. I do not want any leftovers. Please enjoy."

"Sam, how has life been for you lately?"

"It has been great! Tish has been very supportive."

"Where do work?" Damn, Mike just has to ask.

"Nine to five has never been my thing. On the first of January, I will be opening one of two laundromats. The second one will open on the first of February."

"Man that is awesome. Congratulations!"

"Yeah man. I like to see black men owning their own businesses."

"I knew my man could do it."

Lisa and I give each other the eye because we know that Tish is the financial support for this business venture he's bragging about. No wonder we have not heard from her. Hell, she is stressed!

"I have more news!" Tish says ecstatically.

Sam clears his throat and says, "Dear, can I see you in the kitchen?"

"No you cannot."

"What the hell is going on between the two of you? Tish, you already know to keep negative energy out of my house!"

"Nothing. Tish and I agreed to hold this news until later."

"No! You decided that. I did not agree on anything."

"Tish, I am warning you!"

"Out with it or drop it" Lisa says as she grows anxious.

"We are going to drop it!" Sam yells.

"I am nine weeks pregnant! There, I said it."

The room suddenly gets quiet and everyone appears to be in shock. Sam appears to be so furious that he is changing colors from black to blue black. I must try to smooth things over.

"Congratulations! But I thought that you could never have children." At this point, Lisa's emotional ass is crying.

"I am going to be a Godmother again. It's a miracle!" yells Lisa.

"A miracle it is."

Carl knows that Sam does not want to hear it, but he speaks anyway.

"Congrats, man!"

"Yeah."

Mike, who has no clue, starts giving a mini speech. "Congrats, man! Being a father is one of the most important roles a man can have."

"I agree" says Carl.

"Tish, it's time for us to go!"

"No! We just got here! I want to enjoy and celebrate all that God has blessed me with. I want to enjoy my girls."

"I was not asking!"

Becoming very annoyed at how Sam is treating her, I say "Wait a damn minute!"

Carl then chimes in and says to me, "Carol, mind your business."

"She is my business!"

Sam, who has decided to be brave enough to talk to me with his chest out, says "What are you going to do?"

Without missing a beat, Carl says, "Look man, you are in the wrong house for that! I got her, but you do not part your lips to address her in that tone. You go through me!"

"Calm down guys!" Lisa says. "There's an underlying issue here."

"It sure is! He wants me to abort my precious gift from God!"

"That's because the timing is off!" Sam screams.

Feeling enraged, I blurt out, "I want to fuck him up!" I am upset because of the way Sam is treating her. And on top of that, he wants her to abort her baby. While I am trying to take up for her, the heifer flips on me.

"Carol, shut up!"

"Bitch, I am trying to defend you! What kind of man asks a woman to abort her baby? You are the bread winner not him. It is your body and your

decision! I can't stand that trifling bastard."

"Carol, don't worry about my man and do not talk to him like that! You should be worrying about your love triangle!"

"What is she talking about?" Carl curiously asks.

I think to myself I know this cow didn't just betray me. Thinking quickly, I say "She is miserable because she is pregnant with a baby that her so called man doesn't want! So, she has to try to take the attention off of herself."

Lisa tries to diffuse the situation by saying "Tish, you need to channel your anger towards the right person; and that is Sam!"

"Lisa, do not make me go in on you! I saw Mike stalking you in the parking lot at our last meeting. He probably beat that ass. He is controlling and you better get out while you can!"

"Tish, I am going to ignore you because I know you are hurt and need someone to lash out at."

"Sam and Tish, I think it's time for both of you to leave. Tish, don't ever call my phone again."

"Carol, you don't mean that" Lisa says with a surprised look.

"I think you know me well enough to know that I mean what I say."

"Come on Tish, We out!" Sam then walks toward the door.

"Yeah, we out!" yells Tish. "Make sure that you keep your boy toy in line so that he doesn't travel across seas to propose again!"

"What is she talking about?! Carl asks again.

"Nothing, Carl! Misery loves company!"

"It better not be what I am thinking!"

Mike, who has been taking everything in, suddenly turns to Lisa and asks, "Did you tell your friends that I am controlling?"

"No, Mike!"

Carl, whose eyes are now red, turns to me and says, "Carol, you have got some explaining to do!"

This night has been a total disaster thanks to Tish! All I tried to do was defend her and she ends up turning on me! I am so pissed! How dare she put everyone else's business out in the open? It's not our fault that she is in that jacked up situation. I thought she knew better, but I guess loyalty means nothing to her. That's okay though. I got her number. We are done!

5

CAROL

I cannot believe my friend of over thirty years would betray me like that. She knows how I feel about loyalty. I was trying to defend her and that is the thanks that I got! That friendship is over. I am hurt, but it is what it is. Lisa thinks that we should reach out to her because of what she is going through. She was not too distraught to mess up my relationship. Lisa and I have been great friends to Tish. We have put up with her condescending ways. As a friend, we accepted her for who she was and loved her like a sister. This time she went too far.

I had to sleep with one eye open last night because Carl was enraged. He told me that when he gets home from work, I had better have a good damn explanation. All I can do is deny, deny, deny! I know that he is going to drill me like a prosecutor trying to get a conviction. If Tish wasn't pregnant, I would wait outside of her house, catch her while she is going to her car, and give her something her parents never gave her, which is a good ass kicking! Lisa may forgive and forget about Tish's betrayal, but I will not! I will forgive in time because it is my Christian duty, but I will never forget that she tried to ruin my relationship with Carl.

My strategy in dealing with Carl will be to have a good explanation for every question, and then confront him with the letter that I received. I can turn this entire fiasco around and say that he is suspicious of me cheating when he is really the one cheating. Ha! He just does not know what he has coming.

"You think that I am naïve, old, and stupid. But I am wise. I have not lived fifty years and gotten all of this gray hair for nothing. I allow you to think that you run this relationship. I allow you to do as you please most of

the time, and I don't say a word. But just because I am old, country, and don't say much doesn't mean that I don't know or suspect things. I bring the money home and you give me an allowance. Hell, you don't even have to spend your paycheck! I pay the bills and supply all of your needs, as well as your wants. You get a new car every two years, and you take no less than four trips a year. Pretty much whatever your heart desires, I oblige! So with all of that being said, I know damn well that Donovan was not and is not your boy toy that Tish mentioned; because my intelligent, educated woman would not dare take a dumb ass risk like that! That would be too close for comfort. However, if that is the case, then I have truly underestimated you. I will go as far as to say maybe you are in over your head. What do you have to say for yourself?"

"I told you that Tish is miserable in her relationship and she wants company! Donovan is a former co-worker that I know from my MPD days."

"So you are telling me that your former co-worker just so happened to be in Montego Bay during the same time as us? Not only was he there, but he inserted himself into our company!"

"Yes, that is true. However, it was a mere coincidence. Do you think that I would be bold enough to have an affair in your face like that? No! If I were cheating, I promise you that you would never know."

"I don't think that you are that bold! However, I do think that he is. He is a police officer and most of them are cocky risk takers. I think he is out of control and that you were blind-sided by his antics. I also think that he gave you the fuel and energy to act out because I am taking my time to propose to you. Oh, not to mention, he stopped me for speeding and served me with a ticket!"

"Carl, I think you know me well enough to know that I do not need fuel to act out. I am a damn natural! Besides, if you were actually speeding, then that is why you received a ticket."

"You keep playing with me and I am trying to hold my peace and

stay calm. I find it ironic that the man I met in Jamaica is the same one to give me a ticket. Not to mention how often I see him in some of the same places that I frequent."

""Carl, I am done with this conversation. I explained to you how I know him and that is the truth!"

"So how can you explain smelling like his cologne? Oh yeah, you told me. You encounter men all day at work, right?"

"You know what? You are the cheater not me! Your floozy sent this in the mail addressed to me. Now what do you have to say? Oh, you're stuck, huh? The real cheater is always the one to make false accusations against the innocent party."

"I am not cheating and I do not know anything about this letter! I seriously doubt that you are innocent! Besides, we are discussing you and your infidelity!"

"No infidelities here, Boo! You are speculating on hearsay. But I have proof! Ha!"

"Well, your boy toy probably sent that letter. You got him all turned out; so much so that he followed you to another country, knowing that you were there with your man!"

"Apparently, you are doing something good for some two-bit floozy that she wants me to know! She is going to get you kicked out on your ass! This is just disrespectful and I feel violated that your trick knows our address!"

"Your boy toy is the police. Need I say more? But I will tell you this; you better get a handle on this situation before I turn his ass into Internal Affairs!"

"That is between you and him. It has nothing to do with me. As a matter of fact, you are just paranoid because you are the cheater! That explains why whenever we have sex, you don't have any gas left. If you are going to cheat, go get you some viagra. Then maybe I will stay awake!"

"You are a piece of work! Don't get hurt! You think I won't touch you,

but that mouthpiece of yours is deadly."

"Is that a threat? You do know that I am still connected with the police department, right?"

"I'm leaving to go back to work!"

"Yeah! You do that! You are probably on your way over to her house, trick!" He knows that he cannot win an argument with me; although he now has me thinking. Is Donovan capable of sending a letter to make me believe that Carl is cheating?

TISH

I have messed up! I have ruined my lifetime friendships with my two besties. Lisa will get over it as long as I apologize, but Carol is pretty much a done deal. Sam has me so crazy and my life is so stressed. Some nights I wish I would go to sleep and never wake up. The two people that I could always count on are not speaking to me. Sam is not speaking to me either, nor does he come home. He is still upset because I want to have this little miracle inside of me. I have always wanted to be a mother even though I was told that I would never give birth. Now that I have been granted this blessing, I have to keep it. Why can't he understand that? I am now forced to decide between holding on to my man or having this baby. I deserve this one thing after all that I have done for him. I have placed all of my needs and wants on hold. I just want to be happy. Is that asking for too much? I have the greatest news in the world and I cannot even share it with my mom yet. She is going to be a grandma! I am going to be a Mom!

Maybe on my drive to work an eighteen wheeler will swipe me, or maybe I will fall asleep at the wheel and crash into a pole. At least that way I will no longer have to worry about Sam who is the center of all my stress and problems. I texted Lisa, but never got a response. I really need to talk to someone. Whenever I text Sam, all he does is text back "is it done?" I feel as though I am dreaming; and one day, I am going to wake up from a very bad

dream. Shoot! Here comes more misery. Sam just walked in.

"Hi Sam."

"Yeah."

"Why are you so cold? I am having this baby whether you decide to be a part of our lives or not. One monkey don't stop no show!"

"It is not that I don't want to be apart. I just don't have time. If you will be honest with yourself, neither do you."

"By the time the baby arrives, the business will be well on its way; so that shouldn't be an issue."

"I plan to open more than two businesses, Tish. Two is just the beginning. This is a dream come true for me."

"Yeah, but with my money!"

"Oh, so that is how you are going to play me, by bringing up your money as a reminder? You want a baby as payback? Is that it?"

"No! I want this baby because I love you and it is a part of you. This baby represents something beautiful that we made together."

"Our main focus needs to be money! No distractions! It's your choice! I've told you how I feel and how I think you should handle this situation. Do not expect any emotional support or doctor's visits from me. You will get none of that from me."

"It will be just the same as everything else. I expect nothing!"

"What does that supposed to mean?" Let's face some cold hard facts. One, you are obese. Two, you are over the age of thirty-five. Both of those factors can cause a high-risk pregnancy or a baby with birth defects.

"Well those are risks that I am willing to take!"

"I will not leave you, but you are on your own. I'm out! I got business to handle."

"Will you be home tonight?"

"Maybe I will, maybe I won't."

"Wow! Really, Sam?" Well I guess another lonely night it is with

me, the TV, and pimento spread on a smoked sausage. Damn, I guess the cravings have kicked in. I hope Sam inherits all of my morning sickness. So far I have not experienced any. I pray that it stays that way.

I can't sleep for some reason. More than likely my depression is resurfacing due to all of the current events going on in my life. It looks like it is going to be a long night. I guess I will take this opportunity to go through the mail and pay some bills. I open a letter addressed to Sam, but there is no name in the return address. The letter says "Sam you had better do the right thing. If you decide to ignore your responsibilities, there will be consequences." Who has it in for Sam? He probably doesn't know about this letter. I know if I question him about it, I most likely won't get any answers. What kind of responsibilities are they referring to? What has he gotten himself into now?

I need my besties. I am going to try and apologize to them and correct my mistake. I never meant to hurt either of them. I was just being me. They know me and that I meant no harm. I was just lashing out. I have to make them understand, especially Carol. I pray that she and Carl are just fine.

LISA

Tish has lost her mind. She turned on me and Carol. She practically revealed that Carol is cheating on Carl, and ruffled Mike's feathers in the process. I had to convince Mike that I had not been speaking negatively about him to my friends. I had to put some mean head game on Mike to make him forget about Tish's rampage. Besides, I missed him and I wanted to make sure that he keeps me on his mind while he is gone.

My investigator still has little to report on Mike. He says that so far everything checks out, but he is going to do more research. I am prepared for whatever he finds, good or bad. Mike has checked in with me several times. I just want him to get this divorce over with so that I will no longer

feel like an adulterer. If he comes back divorced and the investigator does not find anything that I can't live with, then I will introduce him to my parents. I want to invite him to Christmas dinner, but we will see.

Today is one of those days that I dislike my job. I have two parent conferences. I get to hear parents make excuses for why their child is not performing on grade level and defend their bad behavior. The sad thing is that I have been trying to meet with one of the parents since the beginning of the school year. The Principal made a decision to not allow the student to attend class until a parent comes in for a conference. This is very troubling. My first conference will begin first thing in the morning, which means that my day will be interesting.

My first conference was way more interesting than I could have ever imagined. As I enter the office to escort the parent, I immediately become speechless. One of the parents is with Sam and she is pregnant! He is stunned to see me and I am for damn sure stunned to see him. But I am a professional, so I can handle this.

"Hi, Ms. Jones. I am Ms. Collins.

"Nice to meet you. This is my boyfriend, Sam."

"Hi Sam. I am surprised to meet you. Are you Kerry's father?"

"Pleasure to meet you, ma'am."

"No, he is the father of the baby that I am carrying."

"Oh! Well congratulations! How many months are you?"

"Six months. I am due March twenty-first."

I can sell Sam's ass for two pennies. However, I must admit he is smooth. I want to shine some light on his deceit so bad. I cannot wait to end this conference and call Carol. I want to feel sorry for Tish, but I can't. Especially after the fiasco she created at the social. Part of me wants to beat the hell out of Sam because I know how Tish has stood by his side and provided for him several years. He has the nerve to drive this woman around in the car that Tish is making payments on. I have even seen her

pick Kerry up from school in the car. I had no idea that it was Sam's car. This is a small world! That explains why he doesn't want a baby with Tish. It puzzles me that Tish is educated with a successful career and financially stable; but he prefers to have a baby with a woman like Ms. Jones, who did not finish high school. The reason I know that is because she told me. I do not understand his logic. Carol and I must go out for drinks tonight. I will text her now. I hope she's available because this has to be a face to face news break.

Mike called to inform me that he has returned from Charlotte. He has invited me to dinner. I will have to get with Carol on tomorrow. That will be better for her anyway. I hope that Mike has finalized the divorce. It will be a milestone in our relationship if he has. I feel as though we've hit a brick wall in our relationship, but have yet to find a way around it. At least I do not have the problems that Tish has. Sam is such a low life. You would think by him spending all of that time in lock up that he would return to her with some sort of gratitude. I know Mike has issues, but sheesh!

Mike is picking me up because he wants us to ride together. I think he is trying to set me up to spend the night with him. If I do not hear the words "my divorce is final", then there will be no overnight stays. The only reason it happened before he left was because I was making a chess move.

"Hi gorgeous! I've missed you!"

"Hi Babe! I missed you more!"

"How was your day?"

"Very interesting. But I cannot talk about it until I talk to Carol."

"Wow! That bad, huh? You are supposed to share those kind of days with me while I rub your feet."

"Not that kind of day. I found out some information regarding a mutual friend."

"Oh, I see. Girl gossip."

"Basically. So, how was your trip?"

"Great! Shelia and I finally agreed on a seventy-thirty split."

"Oh Mike! That is wonderful!"

"Yeah! A sigh of relief! Both attorneys convinced her that if she did not agree, it could take another three years. It is a step toward closing a chapter in my life. Her attorney told her that if the battle continues, the majority of her share will go to legal fees by the time an agreement is reached; which means she will get far less than seventy percent."

"I am so happy for you; and even happier for us!"

"I should receive the final decree by the end of the month."

"Dinner is on me tonight. For the first time since I found out that you were married, I feel really good about our relationship!"

"I am glad, Lisa! I really love you and want you in my life. I am so glad that you did not just walk out on me. I told her about you and that I want us to sit down for a talk. Then, I want to introduce you to the girls."

"Mike, you are really a good man. I hope they like me , and hopefully we can build a great relationship together."

"They are going to love you. I told Shelia that at no point will she talk ill about you or me to them. We are going to approach this like adults."

"When will all of this take place?"

"I am thinking Spring break. This will give the dust time to settle on the final divorce decree; and it will give me time to talk to the girls."

"Great! I love you Michael Hampton! Let's toast! To our future!"

"To our future!"

I love him more tonight than ever. A man handling his business is such a turn on. Tonight, I am going to rock his world. At this point, nothing else matters. The investigator still has not gotten back to me; but as for now, I do not care if he finds anything.

LISA

I am in route to meet Carol for drinks. I have got some things to tell her.

We have not talked since the social that Tish ruined; so we have a lot of caching up to do. Tish has been blowing my phone up. She has been texting how sorry she is and that she wants to make things right. I just don't know how she can right now. There may be hope later. If what I found out about Sam is only half of what he is putting her through, then I will give her a small window of sympathy. It won't be enough to allow her back in though. Her anger should have been directed towards Sam, and not me and Carol.

CAROL

Lisa said she has something important to tell me and that it could only be conveyed in person. I have not spoken to her since Tish lost her damn mind, so we have a lot to discuss. I need to tell her about my show down with Carl and get advice on how to proceed with Donovan. It is going to be a drunk, wasted girl's night for us. Ugh! Tish has the audacity to be texting and calling my phone right now. We do not have anything to discuss. She claims that she wants to make it right. She and I will never be right again.

"Oh, there's Lisa. "Hey girl! I ordered us two pictures of margaritas with four extra shots of tequila!"

"Wow! It sounds serious!"

"More like juicy! Sit down because I am about to blow you away!"

"What in the hell is going on?"

"Okay. Yesterday morning I had a scheduled parent conference, which is nothing unusual. But when I went to the office to escort the parent, Ms. Jones, to my classroom, guess who was with her?"

"Who?"

"Sam!"

"Shut the hell up! You mean Tish's Sam?"

"Yes! In the flesh, and there is more!"

"What happened? Did he act like he didn't know you?"

"Honey! She introduced him as her boyfriend. So I told him that I was

surprised to meet him; and he said it was a pleasure to meet me!"

"GIRL, STOP! God does not like ugly!"

At this point, we both are laughing hysterically. "Wait girl, there is more! Ms. Jones is pregnant! So I asked him if he was Kerry's father; but she chimed in and said "no, he is the father of the baby I'm carrying.""

"Aww hell nawl! He's got a baby on the way by another woman and trying to make Tish have an abortion?"

"Yes Ma'am! From the minute he saw me, you could have bought his ass for two pennies! He kept his cool though. "The woman did not finish high school. Get this, I have been seeing her pick the little boy up from school in Sam's car that Tish bought!"

"How do you know that she is a high school dropout?"

"She told me so at parent night."

"Well, I am not sorry to say that I don't feel sorry for Tish. If you ask me, she and Sam deserve each other. I have been a good, loyal friend to her. Here I am trying to defend her ass against him, and then she turns on me. I will forgive her because I am a Christian, but I will never forget."

"Same here. She was texting me until I blocked her."

"Me Too! Whenever she leaves a message, I do not listen. I delete it immediately! I meant what I said to her, do not call my phone. But now that I think about it, he is putting her through so much. She is probably losing her mind."

"Well now that he has finally alienated her from us, I am sure that he's ecstatic. He has her exactly where he wants her, alone with no support system."

"You are right! It's sad to see her work two jobs and take care of him. And you know she signed for him to get the money for those laundromats!"

"No doubt! Well, she will be okay."

"Yeah, I guess! I was able to smooth things over with Mike. How did you do with Carl?"

"Girl, he is no fool! But, I had a strategy in my back pocket. Deny! Deny! Deny! I turned the entire situation around towards him. I saved a letter that came to the house which indicated that he was cheating on me. When I confronted him with it, he claimed that Donovan probably sent it because he has been stalking him."

"What the hell?"

"Yeah. He said Donovan pulled him over for speeding and gave him a ticket; and that Donovan seems to frequent all the spots where he hangs out. When Tish dropped the dime, he started putting a lot of things together. However, I stood my ground! Hell, he was furious. I could see the rage in his eyes and was afraid to sleep that night. I had to sleep with one eye open. For the first time in fifteen years, I can truly say that I thought he was going to hit me!"

"It's your mouth!"

"Yep! But he did put something on my mind about Donovan possibly sending that letter. I will eventually get to the bottom of it all. I am going to find out whether or not Carl is really cheating, and whether or not Donovan sent that letter."

"I have the number for a good investigator that I am using to research Mike's past."

"Girl, I don't need an investigator. I am the investigator! Wait! You are having Mike investigated?"

"Yes! I do not want any more surprises. Even though I feel like he is being totally honest with me now, I can't be too careful."

"Girl, you could have hired me! You know I am good at being nosey and finding out information. How is the divorce thing going?"

"They finally reached an agreement. He returned last night and we went to celebrate. I will meet Shelia and the girls during spring break. He has already told Shelia about me; and now he wants us all to meet, talk, and have a face-to-face discussion with the girls."

"A black man handling his business . . . I love it!"

"Yes! It such a turn on! I am taking him to Christmas dinner to meet mom and dad."

"Uhh oh! It has gotten serious I see."

"Well the verdict is still out until I receive the report from the investigator."

"I like Mike. Everything will be fine. We must have another couple's night."

"Does that mean that you and Carl are okay?"

"Well, either way, I will have a man! I was really leaning towards Donovan; but if he is stalking Carl and sending letters, then that may change things. You know Carl isn't going anywhere, I will have to put him out."

"Yeah, he is a laid back man!"

"He claims that he allows me to run our relationship. Girl, I am a boss!" But right now, I have to go do a drive by at Carl's job, and then meet Donovan. So I will talk to you later!"

"See ya, girl!"

6

CAROL

Carl and I had our show down and I think that I won! He is no fool! I got my eye on him, though. If he is cheating, I will find out. That is the advantage of having On-Star. I can track his whereabouts. I have not seen Donovan since the showdown. I need to confront him about a couple of concerns such as the speeding ticket and the stalking. I won't mention the letter at this point. I have to inform him of what Carl knows and how he found out. I guess the old clichés are true, "if you don't want anything told, keep it to yourself" and "what's done in the dark will come to the light."

Carl's deadline is a few weeks away. I am anticipating what he will do. I drive by his job at least three times a week to see if he is really working overnight. I also call the job rather than his cell phone at random times to see if he is actually there. So far, he has been there. I have tightened the ropes on him a little. He is working tonight, so I promised Donovan I would come see him. I miss him and I can't wait to feel his touch. I know this relationship with him is wrong. It has gotten way out of hand, but I can't help how I feel about him. I am still wearing his ring. I wonder does he ever think about the possibility of me choosing to stay with Carl. I am so torn. At this point, I don't know who I will choose. It is obvious that I still love Carl; but does Carl love me enough to do right by me?

I can always count on Donovan to have the mood right! I have a surprise for him. I am wearing my trench coat with only my lingerie underneath, and those red five-inch pumps that he loves. I am going to put on a show for him! As I walk up, he opens the door.

"Hi, my love. Come here and give a hug. I just want to hold you in my arms. I've missed you!"

As we embrace and kiss passionately, I manage to say "Oh, I've missed you too, baby."

"You are looking sexy, and I see that you are wearing my favorite shoes. What do you have on under this coat?"

"It's a surprise just for you!"

"Do I have you for the entire night?"

"Yes! You sure do!"

R. Kelley's "12-Play" is playing in the background. Donovan unties the belt on my coat and sees that I am only wearing red lingerie. "Damn girl! You smell good. Is that a new perfume?"

"No, it's the same one I usually wear." I then push Donovan to the couch and begin to strip for him. I have his full attention. As I slowly strip, he strokes his penis. I walk over to him, kneel down, and pleasure him with my tongue as if his penis is a lollypop. He strokes my hair gently.

"Girl, you already have me looking for you in the daytime with a flashlight. You keep this up, and I'll....Ohh! Mmmm. Oohhhh! Damn!"

"You what?"

"I just love you! Come here!"

Donovan motions for me to sit on his penis. For the next hour, I ride him like a cowgirl in a rodeo. Our thrusts are strong and intense; so intense that Donovan has put bite marks all over my breasts. But hell, it feels so good until I don't even care. I will deal with hiding them later. I am sure that he did it on purpose.

After we finish making love, I lay in his arms for the next five minutes. There is total silence in the room. He kisses my forehead. As lovely as this moment is, I have to begin the talk with him.

"Donovan, I have something to ask you and something to tell you."

"What is it?"

"Which one do you want to hear first?"

"You can begin wherever you like."

"Okay. I had a little Christmas social at my house last week. "My friend, Tish, decided to drop a dime to Carl about us."

"What happened? What did he say?

"Basically, Tish and Sam have major issues. She shared some news with us and he got mad because he didn't want her to share it. I jumped in to defend her and she turned on me. In front of everyone, she told me to worry about my love triangle and my boy toy, meaning you, so that you do not follow me overseas to propose. That statement was the nail in the coffin."

"What?! Your friend said that?"

"Yes! But I kept it cool and calm as usual. Carl then said that I had some explaining to do. I responded by saying that she is miserable and wants company. The next day, Carl and I had a blowout, and I ended up turning the entire situation around on him. But he is no fool and he is on to us. Luckily, I had received a letter in the mail from an unknown party which he was not aware of. In short, the letter said that Carl was cheating on me; and that he's not really working when he claims to be working overnight because he is spending the nights with her. I never said anything about it until now. I used it to accuse him of cheating."

"Damn baby! You are good."

"I try! He also said that you are stalking him and that you gave him a speeding ticket."

"The speeding ticket is true. The stalking part is not. He and I joked about the ticket because he was trying to talk his way out of it."

"Well this has gotten sticky. I wish that we all could live together in the same house and have threesomes every night."

"Girl stop! I already hate sharing you now. If I had to see that, I would probably find a way to make Carl disappear."

We both laugh. "He went on to say that you are often at the same places he frequents, that you are out of control, and that you are probably the one who sent that letter."

"Me? I sent the letter? That is hilarious!"

"I thought so, too; but you have been showing up out of town."

"I may show up, but a letter is not my style."

"Hmm, okay. So what do you have to say about these passion marks you purposely left on me?"

"I was caught in the moment. Hey, with those on your breasts, I know he won't get any soon."

He won't for a few days, at least until the marks leave. I don't want to spend any more of my night talking about him. Let's take a shower together."

"You are not afraid of Carl and his suspicions?"

"Hell no! If you are, I got you! I will do anything for you."

"Let's go take that shower!"

He grabs my hand and leads me into the hot running water. I am turned on again. Carl Who? We make love again in the shower. Oh my! I am taking a day off work on tomorrow to recuperate from this night. Carl will be home because he worked overnight.

"Honey, I am taking the day off. Can I crash here? Carl will be home all day sleeping."

"Of course, you can."

"Can you go to my car to get my overnight bag?"

"Yes. You were already packed?"

"No, I always keep a bag in the trunk of my car emergencies."

"You can stay with me as long as you need. I am on vacation for the remainder of the year. I will make you breakfast and serve it to you in bed."

"That is not necessary."

"I know, but I want to."

Donovan is really a wonderful man. Trying to love two ain't easy!

TISH

I just left my doctor's appointment and my blood pressure is extremely high. The doctor has placed me on a restrictive diet. I don't think my eating habits are the cause. I believe that Sam and the situation with my besties are the causes. I have continued to call and text them, but to no avail. It has never taken us this long to make up, especially Lisa. However Carol is a different story.

I am taking my mom out for lunch today to give her the news about the baby. Sam is not supporting me, nor do I have Lisa and Carol anymore. However, I can always count on my mom. I am her only child and she spoils me. She will be excited and happy for me. The past couple of weeks have been lonely for me. I want my life to return to its previous state.

I have been thinking about my baby a lot. Will the sex of the baby be a boy or a girl? Who will the baby look like, me or Sam? Will he or she be intelligent and make good grades in school? Will I be a good mother? Will Sam ever accept him or her? One thing I know for certain is other than my mom, I will have someone to love me unconditionally.

When I returned home from my appointment, a note was taped to the door. It read "you cannot and will not continue to ignore me. I am out!" It has to be for Sam. Who the hell has he pissed off this time? It is always some drama with him. I am going to leave it so that the individual who needs to see it will. Speaking of Sam, he is driving up now. He has not been home in a week. I am so sick of this.

"Hi baby."

"Don't hi baby me. I have not seen you in a week! Where in the hell have you been?"

"Out of town."

"You go out of town and don't give me the courtesy of a phone call or text to let me know that?!"

"It was last minute. But hey, I am back."

"I think you forgot that you are living off my dime."

"Not for long! When my business takes off, I am going to give you back every penny."

"Yeah, right! A note is taped on the door for you." He reads the note and laughs. "Do I need to be afraid?"

"Naw. You are cool."

"I went to the doctor today. My blood pressure is high and the doctor placed me on a restrictive diet."

"Is that right? Well maybe something good will come out of this pregnancy after all. You will lose weight. Neither here nor there, I don't want to talk about your pregnancy. 'I told you to get rid of it because you were going to encounter problems."

"Sam, you cannot ignore this pregnancy!"

"Watch me!"

"So are you going to ignore this baby after he or she arrives, too?"

"Saved by the doorbell. What's up man?"

"Hey, I have been trying to contact you."

"What's up? I have been busy trying to rebuild my life."

"I knew something was up with you because I know that you would not just forget about me back at the joint."

"Why are you here at my door?"

"I just had to see you, man. You took care of my books when you first got out; then all of a sudden, the money stopped. I wanted to say something to you at Ruth Chris', but you were with a woman."

"How did you find out where I lived?"

"I followed you that night. You said that you had me when I got out; so here I am! I have left two notes for you."

"Sam! Who is that at the door?"

"An old childhood friend. Look man, you gotta go! I'll call you later!"

"Sam! Don't make me come back! You better get at me, mane."

"Hi! I am Tish. Excuse Sam's rudeness. Are you going to introduce us Sam? It is good to finally meet one of Sam's home boys."

"Tish, this is Fred. Fred, this is my girl, Tish. You know, the one who has been holding me down."

"My pleasure, Tish."

"Sam, stop being rude and invite him in."

"He was just leaving...weren't you, Fred?"

"Yeah! I just wanted to let ole Sam know that I was back in town."

"Well, don't be a stranger! You are welcomed to stop by anytime."

"I think that I will take you up on that offer."

"Bye now."

"Later!"

"He seems nice; but a little soft to be a friend of yours."

"He's cool. I used to take care of him. I was like his big brother."

"That's funny. I never heard you mention him before."

"We just reconnected."

"Oh, I see."

"Have you and the witches made up?"

"No! I think I really messed up this time."

"You don't need them. I am all that you need."

"I miss them, so I will keep trying."

"Why? I am glad they're gone, and I hope they never come back!"

"Enough about them. What about our baby?"

"Your baby; and I am not talking about that. If you continue to mention that baby, I am leaving and will stay gone for two weeks."

"Bastard!"

Maybe I should just abort the baby. My life revolves around making him happy. So why not do one more thing that pleases him. It seems that he will never accept him or her. I wish he would stay gone. It seems like I am more at peace when he is not around. At least my mom is excited that she is going

to be a grandma. I did not fill her in on how Sam is acting. I feel like just leaving this condo to Sam and moving back in with my mom. The truth is that I can't. I have to see this through because I have invested so much of my time and my money into Sam. I cannot help but continue to believe that he will come to his senses.

SAM

Fred is out of his damn mind stalking me and showing up at my crib! I do not do dudes anymore. He wants to hook up one more time. He says that he just wants one more time. The truth is if I give in to him once, he will want more. I have two kids on the way. I am all man. I have to find a way to get him off of my back. If all he wanted was money, I could handle that quickly. But he wants me to fuck him again. I can't bring myself to do it to a man now that I am on the outside.

LISA

Christmas dinner with my mom and Dad was better than ever. My dad actually likes Mike. For the first hour, he gave him a hard time, but Mike did not blink or back down. He always said that a real, honest man can stare another man in the face and welcome a challenge. That is exactly what Mike did.   He earned my dad's respect. He made my mom and my siblings melt like butter.   My sisters have claimed him to be their brother-in-law. However, I think that they are moving a little fast. I love Mike, but I believe in lengthy dating and a long engagement before saying the words "I do". We have a long way to go before we get there.

In five days, Carol, Carl, Mike, and I are going to invade the "Big Apple". We are going to New York City for New Year's Eve and to celebrate Carol's birthday. Too bad Tish and Sam will not be attending. I am sure that she still has her tickets. She and Sam just may show up anyway. She has still been calling; but for some reason, I just haven't allowed myself to respond. I

usually would have given in by now; but there is just something about that kind of betrayal that I just cannot come to terms with. I love her, but that does not mean I have to allow her back in. I wish her well because she is going to need it.

Mike is taking me shopping today for our New York trip. I am looking forward to that, especially since he is buying. I have not spent any money on shopping since Mike and I became official. Not many women can say that about their man. New York is frigid cold this time of the year. The only article of clothing that I am concerned with is a mink fur coat. I have always wanted one, but could never bring myself to spend that amount of money. Spending that kind of money on a fur coat is a waste of money when you live in the south. I probably would only get to wear it once or twice a year; and some winters, I might not get to wear it at all. But since Mike is buying, I am accepting.

The investigator has finally completed his research on Mike. I have been trying to decide if I should wait until we return from New York to get the results. I am so nervous because I do not know what to expect. I have a lot of emotions regarding this. However, I know I did the right thing and that it is for the best. So there is actually no need to wait. I am going to set up an appointment for tomorrow afternoon. I have butter flies in my stomach.

Well, the investigator found out that Mike played professional football for the Washington Redskins. His career was quite promising. It came to an abrupt end because he was accused of domestic violence on four occasions against Shelia, but he was never convicted on any of the charges. One of the affidavits stated that he assaulted her on the grounds of a restaurant because she did not make her curfew, which I find interesting. Another affidavit states that he beat her because she did not wear the proper attire that he bought for her to wear to the Espy awards. In his file, it shows that he has been attending counseling and therapy sessions for about two years now. He is very wealthy. Interesting stuff! I don't know what I will do with this

information, but I needed to know for my own sake. I believe in second chances. Maybe he had an abusive nature at one time, and now he is seeking therapy to deal with it. I would never judge him or anyone based on their past because people can change. I can only judge him by how he treats me, and he treats me damn good. Even though I have experienced a few episodes of him being controlling, he has never once been violent with me.

Consequently, once again he has failed to share information with me; and I can't say anything to him regarding what I know. If I do, he will know that I have been looking into his past. He may feel like I don't trust him, and may possibly feel violated. Although I am now aware, I am still going to take a chance on him. For the first time, I am following my heart and not my head. I will get out if the relationship becomes abusive. Oh well, it's time to hit the mall. He is outside waiting on me.

"Hi beautiful lady! Are you ready to go on an afternoon of shopping and then to dinner?"

"Always! How has your day been thus far?"

"Relaxed. I've been thinking of you."

"Aww! You are so thoughtful. That is why I love you!"

"Your dad invited me to play golf with him this weekend."

"You can't go! We will be in New York."

"Yeah, I know. I told him. He said that we can play at a later date."

"I am glad that he likes you. That is very rare for him. You better not mess up!"

"I promise you that I am going to try to be the best boyfriend, husband, son-in-law ever!"

"Whoaaa! Slow down cowboy. Just focus on the boyfriend role for now."

"Girl, we are at an age where we know what we want. I know that I want you for a lifetime. My father told me as a boy to claim whatever it is that I want. Do you love me?"

"Of course, I love you. I think of you twenty-four seven."

"When you have lost as much as I have being foolish, you learn to cherish the small moments, as well as the ones you love; taking no one and nothing for granted. You can have everything you ever wanted one minute; and in the blink of an eye, it can all be taken from you."

"Sounds like a man who has learned from his mistakes."

"I have a second chance with a good woman and I am taking full advantage of it."

"I know sometimes it seems as if I have my heart closed, but I can only give you so much at a time. I am careful because I have come across some trifling brothers in the past."

"I know! I am a patient man. Speaking of patience, when can we get back to spending all of our nights together? This one night a week thing is not working for me. It is making me a little crazy."

"I think we should gradually increase the overnight stays. How about two nights a week until spring break?"

"That is better than one. I don't like it, but I am a team player."

Mike and I spent countless hours shopping and ended the night with dinner. It is obvious that he loves me and I love him. I am not going to allow his past to affect our relationship. I am looking forward to a future with him. Besides, I know Tae Kwon Do. I will kick Mike's ass if he tries me. I have a few secrets of my own.

CAROL

Today is the day! Carl and I leave for New York City to celebrate New Year's Eve and my birthday. Being in Times Square on New Year's Eve has been a wish of mine for a lifetime. Carl bought the plane tickets and arranged everything back in March. The next five days are going to be grand. However, it may be the end for me and Carl. His deadline will end on the fourth of January, which will be our last night in New York. I have to

stand on my promise to let him go if he does not say those words that I have been longing to hear.

My relationship with Donovan has been great. I have been spending at least three nights a week with him. Since Carl has been working sixteen hour shifts, Donovan has been demanding my time. I must say, I do enjoy his company. However, I have lost my damn mind. It's a miracle that I have not gotten caught. Ever since Carl found out, I have been acting like he doesn't exist. I feel a little guilty, but I cannot leave Donovan. He's like an addiction that I have to satisfy. Donovan has been asking me about plans for my birthday, but I have not and will not tell him about New York. That would be a disaster. Just as sure as I tell him, he will show up; and I can't deal with that right now. I just want to enjoy this trip. I told him that I was not going to make a big deal of my birthday this year. He keeps insisting on making it special and said that he has a surprise for me. I am going to make a quick detour by his house before we leave for New York. As soon as I knock on the door, he immediately opens it.

"Hi Sweetheart."

"Hi Beautiful. Come in."

"I can only stay for a couple of hours. Carl is off work for the next week, and he has been questioning me a lot about my whereabouts."

"He will be okay."

"You are out of control."

"You should not have put that whip on me!"

"Whatever!" I say laughingly.

"Today, I just want to sit on the couch, hold you in my arms, cuddle, watch a movie, eat popcorn, and drink wine."

"Okay. I'm cool with that plan."

"Oh! I have something for you. It's an early birthday present. I know what you said, but I want to do this for you . . . for us. Here!"

"Oh my! Two tickets to Paradise Island, Bahamas! Donovan, you

did not have to do this. I am speechless!”

“I know. We will leave January tenth and return on January sixteenth. Please accept!”

“How will I pull this off with Carl? Work will not be a problem.”

“I am hoping that by the time we are scheduled to leave, that he will be out of the picture. I am counting down the days to the deadline. I hope this date will be the beginning of the rest of our lives.”

“Donovan, have you ever considered that he just may propose?”

“Yes! But I know that I am the better man. If he was being the man that you needed him to be, I would never have gotten in this deep. I love you and I know that you love me.”

“You do realize that if he proposes to me, I am going to say yes?”

“Are you really sure that you will? Honey, I am not convinced!”

“Donovan, I will not throw away fifteen years. I have invested a lot of time and heartache into him, in addition to all of the finances and assets that we have accumulated together.”

“Carol, you are torn because you love us both, and I get that. One thing I do know is that Carl is stubborn. He is not going to do it. He is not taking you serious.”

“Well, I will know in a few days.”

“Time will tell. So, are we going or not? No matter what happens with Carl, say that you will go.”

“Okay! I will go!”

“Enough Carl talk. Let’s enjoy this time we have together.”

“Agreed!”

Damn! I almost lost track of time. I always get lost in the moment with Donovan. Both Carl and Lisa are blowing up my phone with calls and texts. As I speed home, I decide to call Carl and endure this battle before we actually leave for New York.

“Woman! Where in the hell are you? We have to be at the airport in

forty-five minutes! I've been calling you and so has Lisa."

"Baby, I am so sorry! My phone died. I was out doing some last minute things for my sister. You know how that goes. I will be there in five minutes."

"Un huh. I have already put our luggage in the car. All you have to do is park and get in the car."

"Okay, cool."

"You know you got some explaining to do!"

"Don't start Carl! You will not ruin these next few days for me with your insecurities."

"I better not see anyone that I recognize on this trip!"

"Bye!" I hang up from Carl and now Lisa is calling with the drama.

"Girl! We have been calling you! Carl has been calling me."

"Hell, I know! I just hung up with him. I was with Donovan and lost track of time. I am pulling into the garage and we are leaving for the airport now."

"You are slipping! We are already at the airport. We will talk in New York. See you when you get here."

Carl has a terrifying look on his face. "I'm sorry for being late."

"So it took you three hours to take care of things for your sister? What all did she need for you to do?"

"The usual . . . the bank, Wal-Mart, pay bills, etc."

"Sure. So if I call her right now, can she verify what you just said?"

"Indeed she will. I will call her for you."

"You think you are a damn genius! But if Donovan shows up in New York City, they are going to find the two of you floating in the Hudson!"

I laugh at Carl and say, "Donovan has you spooked and paranoid! Why would he show up in New York? I have not seen nor heard from him since Montego Bay. I keep trying to tell you that I don't know him like that!"

"Sure you haven't." Where were you last Thursday night? I tried

calling the house, your cell phone, and I called Lisa. The next morning when I got in from work, I called your phone again and didn't get an answer. Then I called your job and they informed me that you had taken the day off. You weren't at the house and I couldn't get in touch with you. So again, where were you?"

"I spent the day at the spa. I needed a break from work and life."

"You couldn't give me the common courtesy of a phone call or text to inform me of your plans? I may have wanted to spend that time with you, or there could have been an emergency."

"I just wanted to be left alone. Let it go already, Damn!"

"That's your favorite line these days."

"Look! I don't want to argue. I just want to enjoy you, New York, and my birthday!"

"So do I! But you keep playing with me and so does Donovan. You tell him that I am a grown ass man and I don't play! The two of you will be a story on an episode of SVU or Criminal Minds if you keep fucking with me."

"I have always loved your sense of humor" I say, even though I know he's not joking.

We have arrived! New York is beautiful and crowded as ever. We have a suite at the Plaza. Carl did an excellent job on the accommodations. He paid for Lisa and Mike's stay as well. Too bad Tish messed up. She could have come. I tried to cancel her accommodations, but was not successful. Carl paid for a package deal; so cancelling hers would also have cancelled ours. She is still calling, and I still refuse to respond. I have to find some time to be alone with Lisa so that I can tell her about Donovan's latest escapade. I am really in a real life love triangle.

"Carl, Lisa and I are going downstairs for coffee and some girl talk."

"Okay. I will grab Mike and we will go do some guy stuff. Enjoy!"

"Okay. See you later." Lisa and I meet for a little girl time at the Starbucks next door.

"Girl, what is wrong with you? Lately, Carl has been blowing my phone up looking for your ass. The least you can do is let me know so that I can be prepared to lie, or not answer at all!"

"I don't know, Lisa. Donovan is like an addiction for me now. Hell, it's almost like a voodoo spell!"

"Well, you better get it together quick because Carl is on to you two thanks to Tish."

"I know. That bitch tried me! But Lisa, Donovan has paid for us a trip to Paradise Island, Bahamas that leaves on the tenth of January. It is a birthday gift. I tried to turn it down; but he made me accept it, no matter what Carl decides to do."

"Carol! You are in a web. I know you love them both. What are you going to do?"

"If Carl asks, then I am going to say yes. If he doesn't, then he has to go. It's just that simple. I have to stand firm on my ultimatum no matter how much I love him. It's been too damn long!"

"You are going to let fifteen years go just like that?"

"I have no choice. I may take him back later; but initially, he will have to go because I need to show him that I mean business."

"Okay. So if he asks you to marry him and you say yes, what will you do about Donovan?"

"I will still go on the trip with Donovan. I'll tell Carl that I have to attend a conference.."

"Carol! You will have to break ties with him. That will just be too risky. You will be leading him on, and that is not a safe thing to do."

"I really don't want to let him go. Honestly, I want both of them!"

"Carol! Snap out of it! That is impossible! You are losing control of this situation!"

"Girl, men do this kind of shit everyday! Why can't women?"

"Because women can handle being played better than men. Men dish

it, but they can't handle it."

"That's true. Carl is threatening to kill us both!"

"Damn! Well, I really believe he will! So be careful."

"Let's head back so we can begin this New York night life!"

It is cold as heck out here. We have two more hours before the ball drops and my face is numb. We have been out here for twelve hours; but I would not exchange this experience for anything. We have been drinking hot chocolate with Hennessy all day. So, we are good and drunk. We have been dancing to music performances from many different artists. This is a once in a lifetime experience. Finally, the countdown has begun. Ten! Nine! Eight! Seven! Six! Five! Four! Three! Two! One! Happy New Year! Times Square is in Chaos. Carl and I kiss.

"Happy New Year, Baby!"

"Happy New Year, Carl!" Lisa and I start screaming Happy New Year to any and everybody while we continue to dance to the music.

Today is our last day in New York. This has been the best New Year's and birthday ever. We are going sightseeing today, and Carl said he wants to end the evening with a carriage ride through Central Park. New York is so glamorous and exciting. I did not get to see it all, so I must return to visit this great city again. The Broadway production of "A Raisin in the Sun" is a must see. As we enjoy the carriage ride through Central Park, I suddenly realize that this is really the only time that He and I have been alone, other than when we were in our room.

"Carol, did you enjoy this trip?"

"Yes, I did! Thank you for everything! I love you!"

"I know! I love you, too!"

"Sometimes, you really surprise me! Your surprises are what made me fall in love with you."

"Well, your youthful, ambitious, I can do anything, I don't need a man attitude is what made me fall in love with you!" We both share a laugh; then

Carl says, "Carol, are you really ready to marry me?"

"Is that a proposal?"

"Does this ten carat ring seal the deal?"

"Ohhh Carl! You came through?!"

"I decided on when I would propose back in March as I planned this trip. That's why I never flinched when you gave me your ultimatum."

"You sneaky devil! Hell yeah, I will marry you!"

"You set the date and time, and I will be there. I love you, girl!"

"I love you, too!" I then think to myself, "now what in the hell am I going to do?"

7

TISH

I am so glad that the holidays are over. Usually it is my favorite time to the year, but this year it was depressing. I am still feuding with Carol and Lisa. Carol did not include me in her birthday plans. My life sucks! On a good note, our first laundromat opened on yesterday. The grand opening was a huge success. For the first time since Sam got out of prison, I feel like he is being productive.

During my last visit to the doctor, he informed me that I must quit my second job. It requires that I stand a lot, and that has put too much stress on my body and the baby. I have not mentioned this to Sam yet. Whenever I mention the words pregnancy or baby, he goes into fits of rage. His lack of concern only adds to the stress. Instead of quitting, I think I will take a leave of absence. I like teaching at the college level and have been thinking about transitioning my career from social work to a full professorship. This second job is my shoo-in.

I have been praying and believing for Carol and Lisa's forgiveness, but I don't think God is listening. I really need the love and support that they give me. Without it, I feel abandoned. Fred, who is a friend of Sam's, has been stopping by to visit a lot lately. I told him to stop by anytime, and he has taken full advantage of the invite. I will not complain though. Since Carol and Lisa are gone, he has become a good listener.

Fred needs a job and wants to work for Sam at the laundromat. He has asked me to convince Sam to hire him. I plan to advocate for him because everyone needs help at some point in life. Sam has had my help, so he should pass it on and help someone as well; but he is such a selfish bastard. In order to convince him to hire Fred, I will have to use the fact that it was

my money he used as leverage in order to start the business. Since he asked me to cook his favorite meal to celebrate the grand opening, I will take advantage of his good mood to tell him about my second job, and to put in a good word for Fred.

"Our future is looking very bright, Tish! I want to say thank you for giving me a chance to prove myself. I feel really good about the direction in which our lives are headed."

"You are welcome. It sounds strange to hear the words *our future* coming from your vocal chords."

"What! Did you think that I would forget about you? The one who stood by me when no one else would? I know that I can be an ass, but damn!"

"Sam, you are all over the place. I never know which Sam is going to show up."

"Your opinion of me is at an all-time low!"

"Stop acting like you care about what I think! As long as I do what you want and play by your rules, life is grand. As soon as I need attention, you do what you do best . . . disappear!"

"That is not true, Tish! I do the best that I can. You knew the type of man I was and how I rolled from the very beginning. I have always told you that you can either accept it or move on. No pressure!"

"Moving on is easier said than done. Why don't you just leave and never return?"

"Never!" What can I do to get you back to the quiet, loving Tish?"

"I thought that you would never ask. I have a demand of you, and it is not up for debate. I need for you to pay it forward!"

"Okay. Pay it forward to whom?"

"Fred. He just needs a second chance at life, and you are going to give it to him."

"Hell to the no!"

"Hell to the yes! It is my money and my name on the bank loan. Hire

him! He told me that he was the laundry guy while he was in prison. He also said that he can perform maintenance on the equipment. It's a done deal! He is going to start work on Monday."

"You do not know him, Tish! He is a master manipulator and he may rob us blind! You are naïve and have no clue about life in the streets."

"I am not understanding, Sam. He is your childhood friend and he needs a job. There is an opening at the laundromat, so what is the problem? He is asking for a job. He is not trying to rob or steal. I see a man trying to earn a living, and you as his friend can help him."

"Tish, you cannot help everyone! Fred is that guy that you cannot help. Trust me, he will want more!"

"All he wants is a job to provide a living for himself. That is the problem with us as a race of people. We are selfish, self-absorbed, and quick to forget about others when we make it. If one person who has become successful would reach back and pull one more person up with them, we would have some serious power."

"I hear you! I am all for helping my people, but not Fred. I do not appreciate him coming around you playing on your good heart. You stay away from him! If he comes over here again and I am not here, you better not answer the door. He has no business around my crib or my woman when I am not around!"

"Sam, I have other things to talk about. You will hire him and he will begin on Monday. That is final! As an equal partner in this business, he is now an employee. Do you understand me?"

"Damn! Yes!"

"Also, I am going to take a leave of absence from my second job per the doctor's orders. Standing for long periods of time is putting a strain on my body and on the pregnancy."

"When? We need that money until the second laundromat opens next month. I knew that baby would be a problem. I told your fat ass!"

"I was wondering when the real Sam was going to show up!"

"You don't listen and you are selfish! A baby is not a part of the plan at this point."

"Well, it is on the way, so deal with it! Fred thinks this baby is a wonderful thing. He does not know me and he is showing more support than you. My last day is the end of the month."

"I better not see him around here or hear of him being here ever again! Do I make myself clear? Do you hear me, Tish?"

SAM

That punk Fred got the game all wrong. He is not running any show by trying to go through Tish's gullible ass to get to me. I am going over there to let him know once and for all who is running this damn show!

"Dude! I will kill you! You are toying with my life and I do not play about that!" I grab his neck without thinking.

"I was wondering when I would get your attention. Besides, you know I like it rough."

"This is not a game! We are not on the inside anymore. I am a man and so are you. I only sleep with women!"

"Well, when there were no women, I kept your needs met and vice versa, three times a day! You know you miss this mouth and ass!"

"Stay the hell away from me, my woman, my house, and my baby!"

"Oh so now you want to claim the baby? Yeah, Tish told me all about you and how you feel about the baby. Poor girl! Half of the time, you are out doing God knows what with God knows who!"

"What do you want from me?" Fred then grabs my crouch.

"All ten inches anytime I want!"

"It's not going to happen! Tish has forced me to hire you. I have no control over that. But trust me, I will be looking for a reason to get rid of your ass every second of the day. As for my dick, I control that and it was

not made for men. Women only bruh!"

"That's what you're saying now. You can't tell me that you don't miss this!"

Fred unzips my pants and wraps his mouth over my dick. We struggle for a minute, but he knows all of my pleasure spots. I try to resist, but I fail. My dick gets harder and harder until I cum. I'm all in now and I want more. Fred continues to suck my dick until I start getting hard again. I push him off and turn him around. I gently insert my dick into his tight ass and it feels so damn good, just like I remember. I fuck him until I reach a climax like I've never experienced before. Shit! I feel good and dirty at the same time.

"I knew you still wanted me. I am a man that still likes women too; but we are who we are!"

"Go to hell, Fred!"

"I will see you Monday at 8:00a.m. Boss, Mr. Loverman! Remember, I have full access to get that dick anytime I want it."

"Don't make me put your ass in one of those dryers."

Damn! This is some sick shit! Tish has no idea about what she has forced me into. I must find a way to deal with Fred once and for all!

CAROL

I am in a weave of a web. Carl made the deadline by proposing to me in Central Park. Tomorrow, I leave for Paradise Island for birthday bash number two with Donovan. I have to lie to Carl in order to keep my promise to Donovan. I am faced with telling Donovan that Carl proposed, and that I accepted. I honestly don't know how he is going to handle it. I am torn between two men. Both of them are really great guys, and I don't want to live without either of them. I guess one can say that I want my cake and want to eat it too. Whoever said that you cannot love two is a liar. Donovan was only supposed to be a boy toy; but somewhere in time, both of us caught feelings for each other. I have been with Carl for fifteen years, and I refuse

to allow the man I groomed to be with another woman. Life is something! I have waited a long time to be a married woman. Now, I am faced with two men and two proposals.

I have been contemplating telling Donovan about the proposal before we leave. The consequence of my selfishness is that I do not want to ruin what may be our last rendezvous together.   He is so excited to make this trip happen for me, and I am looking forward to going. Lisa said that I am playing a dangerous game and that I should back out of going because she is afraid for my safety. I am in total agreement with her, but my heart won't let me. I told her that she is over analyzing things; and that both men love me and would never do anything to hurt me. Donovan knew all of the factors involved, yet he chose to stay in it. I never lied to him about my relationship with Carl or my feelings for both of them.

Carl is still suspicious of everything that I say or do. I want the nonchalant no questions asked Carl to return. I am exhausted from all of the excuses and lies that I have to remember. When I told him about going to this conference, he tried to make plans to go. Luckily for me, he could not get time off from work due to being short-staffed. That would have been a disaster because I would have been left with no choice but to tell Donovan that I could no longer go with him. Carl wants to know my schedule for this trip, but I keep putting him off. I told him that I would check in with him as soon as I got some free time. He has gone as far as offering to drive me to the airport. I persistently told him no!   I am going to drive myself and park at the airport; so that when I return, I can leave without having to wait for anyone. He is really working my nerves.

Our flight leaves at 10:45a.m. We fly into Miami and then cruise to Paradise Island. Let the fun begin! The Atlantis Hotel is gorgeous, and we have a penthouse suite. He did very well booking the accommodations!

"Hey beautiful, how did I do so far?"

"Great! I am impressed!"

"I'm glad you like it. I spared no expense for my favorite girl."

"Aww, thank you, honey."

"Today we are getting massages and relaxing in our suite. But tonight, I have something very special planned."

"What do you have up your sleeve?"

"You will have to wait and see! I have also arranged for you a manicure and a pedicure. We have a reservation for the sauna as well. Today is just total relaxation!"

"All of the things that I need! You thought of everything."

"I just want to pamper my baby. The best is yet to come."

I am enjoying this day of pampering and relaxation. Maybe with all of the relaxation, he will take the news well. I really have to come clean with Donovan. Every time I attempt to bring up the conversation, he cuts me off and says, "No Carl talk for the next five days!" I want to enjoy Donovan and focus on him, but it is so hard. He said that if Carl's name does not come up, then he does not exist. But the truth is that he does exist! However, the way he made love to me in that hot, steamy sauna made me forget Carl for the moment.

Donovan informed me that the attire for this evening is formal and that we will be leaving the resort for dinner. I am a little confused as to why we are leaving because the resort has everything we need and more. He told me to trust him and allow him to lead me, so I am putting my life in his hands. A limo is waiting for us as we exit the building. The driver takes us to a very elegant yacht. As we board, there is a butler waiting to greet us, and he is holding two glasses of wine.

"Welcome to the Martinique."

"Thank you!"

"Please come this way to be seated."

The ambiance is beautiful and quite romantic. The moon is full, and its yellowish hues are glowing against the glistening water. There is a table set

for two with smooth jazz playing in the background. The moment is perfect! We are then served a five course meal. We eat, drink, and dance as we gaze in each other's eyes.

"Happy Birthday, my love. I have a little something for you."

"Sweetheart, you have already done enough."

"You keep saying that. But will you please allow me to spoil you?" He then hands me a box.

"No. You shouldn't have."

"Open it, please."

"Oh my God!" Inside is a Pandora bracelet that chronicles our relationship. It is beautiful!"

"A beautiful gift for a beautiful woman, both inside and outside." My eyes swell with tears.

"Donovan, I cannot accept this. I have to tell you something."

"Whatever it is, I don't want to hear it." he says as he wipes away my tears. "Let's just sit on this deck and enjoy the beauty of God's light. I bought it for you and I will not take it back."

We sit on the deck of the Martinique for countless hours talking, cuddling, and holding hands. Once again, I have gotten caught up in the moment with Donovan and have forgotten to check in with Carl. Damn! Damn! Damn! My first priority in the morning will be to break free from Donovan so that I can check-in with Carl. I know that he is worried because we have not spoken since I landed in Miami. I have to handle this no matter what Donovan says.

It's 6:ooa.m. and Donovan is already awake. Since he doesn't want to hear Carl's name, I will have to go somewhere else to make the call.

"Hey Baby! I am going downstairs to the gym to get on the treadmill for about an hour."

"You are on vacation. Besides, you look good already."

"I still have to maintain. I've worked too hard to get where I am, so I

don't want to fall off of the wagon."

"Always know that I will love you no matter what. I thought that I was providing you a good workout!" he says while patting me on my butt.

"Yeah right! I will be back in an hour!"

"Okay love."

I need Carl to answer his phone immediately. He's probably sitting on top of the phone by now.

"Hey Baby! I was trying to catch you before you went to sleep."

"Don't baby me! I have been worried sick about you! I couldn't call the hotel or the airline because I didn't have any information."

"I'm sorry! The schedule has been rigorous and hectic. We have been in meetings from sun up to sun down. By the time I get back to my room, shower, and relax, it is too late to call you."

"It is never too late to call. The kids are losing their minds too! Your phone goes straight to voicemail."

"The reception in this hotel is horrible. I have to go outside in order to make calls. Just call them and let them know that I am fine please."

"Okay. Enjoy your conference. You better call me tonight!"

"Okay!"

"Love you!"

"Love you back!"

Whew! I got that over with, now off to the gym I go. Sometimes when I work out, I can think more clearly. Maybe this me time will help me decide how best to let Donovan know about my engagement to Carl, and the fact that I will not be able to see him anymore. I pray for strength and the power to let him go.

We have two more days left in paradise. We are going to spend part of the day visiting the beautiful underground aquarium here at the resort. Then we will relax by the pool later. Hopefully, we will have time to hit up the casino. Staying busy will keep me occupied so that I can't dwell on my

break up with Donovan.

"I love this aquarium! It's amazing to see all of the different types of fish that exist."

"Yes, it is" I say. You know I have a huge fascination with water."

"Water is peaceful and relaxing."

"Yes, very serene. Let's sit here for a while and take in the scenery."

"Okay."

"Honey, listen to me! Carl proposed to me with a ten carat ring."

"I figured as much. When?"

"On my birthday while we were in New York."

"Did you accept?"

"Yes. I have been trying to tell you, but you kept cutting me off."

"I did not want to hear it. As a matter of fact, I do not care. You are here in paradise with me. You are in the comfort of my arms; not his arms, but my arms!"

"I have to give you back the ring and the bracelet. It breaks my heart to know that I have to give you up."

"You don't have to give it back, the ring nor the bracelet. For the record, you are not leaving me or giving me up."

"But honey, that's not fair to Carl or you!"

"I feel that I have a say in this decision. I am not leaving and you are not going anywhere."

"Donovan! I am exhausted from all of the lies and excuses."

"You are not lying to me. It is Carl whom you are lying to. So who do you really love?"

"You promised me two years ago that if our relationship came to this, you would not fight it. Please don't make this more difficult for me than it already is."

"Two years ago, I did not know that I would grow to love you as much as I do. You cannot expect for me to turn my feelings off like a water faucet.

That's not going to happen! You are fooling yourself if you think that you can. The only reason that you are staying with him is out of obligation. You have been with him all of these years and you have gotten comfortable."

"That may be the case. I have invested a lot of time into that relationship and we have accumulated a lot of assets together. He has done what I've asked of him. We have built an entire life together. I cannot just walk away!"

"You do not have to. Just know that I am never leaving. You are stuck with me! You can make it easy or it can be hard. The choice is yours. I love you and you love me. No one else matters! If you have a wedding with Carl, I will show up and object. Just know that!"

"You cannot be serious! Please don't act this way."

"I am serious as a heart attack. So put your big girl panties on and deal with this bed that you've made. This is the end of this conversation. We have a day and a half left and I do not want to hear nothing about a break up; and I better not hear Carl's name!"

I sigh and say "Dammit!"

"I love you, too!"

Donovan is crazy and in denial. I cannot see him anymore. He believes that I am going to continue seeing him. If I try to leave him, he will make my life a living hell, especially Carl's!

LISA

I had a blast with Carol in New York City. That trip is one for the history book. I will never forget the fun that we had and I am so excited for her! After fifteen years, Carl finally proposed to her. She is currently in the Bahamas with her side piece saying goodbye to him, so that she and Carl can start fresh. I am ready to be a maid of honor and help her plan the wedding. The best part of being a maid of honor is planning the bachelorette party. We are going to have male strippers and exotic dancers. My girl's last night

as a single woman is going to a big bang!

It is a New Year. I am looking forward to March so that I can satisfy my curiosity about Shelia and her relationship with Mike. I am also anxious to meet the girls, and to begin developing a relationship with them. I do not have children, but I hope that I will do a good job with them. I have come to the realization that I have to share Mike with four other women, including his mother. Mike insists that he, Shelia, and I form a strong, sincere bond for sake of the girls. The fact that they live out of state will allow me time to prepare myself mentally. Most girls are territorial when it comes to their dad, at least I know that I am. If my mom and dad had gotten divorced, I don't believe I would have accepted another woman. If the girls do not immediately accept me, I will certainly understand. I would never try to take the place of Shelia. Hell, I honestly don't think that I am mother material. But, I am willing to try this instant family thing for the sake of love.

Mike and I are back to spending our nights together. We are limited to two nights a week, and we stay one night at his house and the other one at my house. He wants more, but that is all that I am willing to give right now. I am still slick punishing him for his little deception. There are still some things that he has not shared with me. If I had not hired an investigator, I would still be in the dark about his past. I am not sure why he chooses not to disclose this information. Maybe as time passes, he will. It has been hard to keep a tight lip about what I know. Besides, it is not that bad. I just wish that he trusted me enough to tell me.

Tish has been calling me leaving really strange messages. She has been heavily on my mind, and I have considered checking on her. Lord knows the girl is dealing with major issues. I think I will call her just to make sure that she is okay. However, I am not allowing her back into my life as she was before. I don't think there is anything wrong with checking on her. Besides, we were friends for over thirty years. I can love her from a distance. I am

going to call her now because if I wait until later, it won't happen. Mike will be over soon and he demands my full attention; no phones or social media.

"Hi Tish! It's Lisa. How are you?"

"I'm okay, I guess."

"How is your health and how is the pregnancy going?"

"My doctor has declared me as high risk, so I have to take a leave of absence from my second job. Other than that, I can't complain."

"Well, take care of yourself and avoid stress as much as possible."

"With Sam as my baby daddy and my man, that is impossible!"

"No comment! You were on my mind, so I decided to check on you."

"I'm glad you did! I really miss you and Carol. I know I messed up."

"Yeah! You fucked up royally!"

"Is Carol and Carl okay?"

"Their relationship has never been more solid."

"Whew! Thank God! I am glad to hear that. Do you think that she will ever speak to me again?"

"Honestly? Probably not."

"I will keep trying. Life without you two is cold and lonely."

"Tish, I do not want you to misunderstand this phone call. I am not allowing you back in my personal space because you caused friction between me and Mike, too."

"He ain't shit anyway! I was trying to do you a favor before you got in too deep."

"Really Tish! I see you are still on that shit!"

"Lisa! Why is it that every time I say anything to try and help you and Carol, both of you take it the wrong way?"

"Girl, you just don't know! You need to worry about Sam and his whole other family! You see Mike and I are solid. He is good to me and he spends his money on me. It's not the other way around. I'm done! Good riddance!" I quickly hang up the phone because I am officially over that bitch!

TISH

Lisa had some damn nerve. If she did not call to mend our broken friendship, then why in the hell did she call? I am so tired of everyone thinking that they can talk to me any way they choose. If Carol and Carl are so solid, then she should get over it. She could have included me in her birthday plans. I would never do that to her.

After work, I will swing by the laundromat to see how things are going. Sam assures me that everything is fine. I need to see it with my own eyes. Besides, I need to show my face so that the staff will know who I am. I allowed Sam to handle all of the hiring, except for Fred. I had to flex my muscle to make that happen. We have two weeks until the second grand opening. I pray that it is a success because I will no longer work my second job after next week. We've exceeded our forecasted financial goal for the first laundromat, which is grand.

"Hi Sam! How are things going? It appears to be very busy."

"Yes, it is! What are you doing here? I told you that it was not necessary for you to bother with coming by here."

"Oh, I just wanted to meet the staff and see operations for myself. I only know Fred."

"You do not need to meet any of my staff. You will not be working with any of them."

"Oh, I plan to show my face a lot more."

"Not!"

"Hi Tish!"

"Hi Fred! How is Sam treating you? Do you like it so far?"

"He treats me like a king! I love it, and I plan to be here for a while."

"Well that sounds great. Sam, where is your car?"

"It's at the dealership for maintenance."

"Glad to know that you are taking good care of it."

"Well, it is time for you to go! I will see you at home."

"No need to rush her, Sam. I am on break. Come with me to the break room and sit with me. We can grab a couple of drinks."

"Oh hell no!"

"Sam! What is the damn problem?"

"Yeah Mr. Bossman! What is the problem? I can show a little chivalry to the one person that is responsible for my gainful employment."

"Mother…!"

"Sam! Enough!"

"Yeah man, enough! Come on, Tish."

"You better return from break on time!"

"How are you and the baby fairing?"

"Okay, I guess."

"Well, you know that if you need anything, I am a phone call away. I am open to attend appointments with you, do shopping, decorate the nursery, whatever you need."

"Fred, that is so kind of you! I could really use all of the above since I am not talking to my besties. Sam surely has not come around."

"Well, that is sad. You are too damn good for him to be acting that way. But you must remember he is not the same man that went away eighteen years ago, no matter how much he tries to portray that he is. He has not been back in the real world that long, so he is still institutionalized."

"Interesting observation!"

"If he cannot be the man that you need, one that supports you and has your back like you have his; just know that I can be that guy if you want me to."

"Fred! Are you trying to make a move on me?"

"Hey! I am just saying it and putting it in the air."

"You are something else! I will keep that in mind."

"Remember, now."

I cannot believe that Fred just made a play for me under Sam's nose. I

must admit he boosted my self-esteem a few notches. It felt good to be pursued for a change.”

“Are you leaving?”

“Yes, but who is that driving up in your car?”

“Oh, that is my cousin Bianca. Remember the ultrasound you found? That’s her.”

“Why is she driving your car? “You said...”

“She took it to the dealership for me.”

“Oh okay. Well I’ll introduce myself on the way out.”.

“Oh, no! You are going to be late! She will be working here, so you will have plenty of time to meet her.”

“Okay. Then I will see you at home.”

“Yes you will. I’ll walk you to the car.”

“Sam!” His cousin calls as she exits the car.

“Hold on a second! Go on in and start counting the inventory.” Sam says to her.

“Okay! I’ll see you inside, dear.”

“Sam, I’ll see you later, baby.”

“Yes!” Then he slammed my car door like a crazy person. He could have shattered the window; then that would have been something else for me to pay for.

SAM

“That was a close call playa.”

“Shut the hell up, Fred before I...”

“Before you what? Before you give me some more of that dick? Trust me when I say that you will.”

“Never! You may work here, but that is it!”

“You got a real life soap opera going on here.”

“Worry about you and not my life. Worry about saving your money

because you will not be here for very long."

"Ha! We will see about that! Does Tish know about you and me? Does she know about Bianca and the baby? Does Bianca know about Tish?"

"Don't come up missing, Fred! You hear me?"

I am so tired of this punk. He has to come up missing for real. Maybe he and I can go fishing on the Wolfe River and he accidentally falls in. Or maybe I can take him for a long country ride on a cold bitter night and leave his ass out there.

TISH

Sam was acting very weird today. He was as acting as if he did not want me around. He refused to introduce me to his cousin and he has total resentment for Fred. Something seems off. Maybe it is the stress of making sure the business is successful. Whatever it is, it made him seem jittery. Maybe I can help out at the laundromat after my second job ends.

FRED

Sam actually believes that he is going to fire me. He has another thing coming. If he tries to fire me, I will move in on Tish. He will be my little secret and Tish will be my main chick. He has a good thing going and doesn't know what to do with it. However if he wants to play, I am game. Either way, I will make sure that he plays a part in getting my physical and financial needs met. Hell, he, Tish, the baby and I can all live together as one big happy family.

LISA

Carol and I are meeting for brunch today so that we can catch up. We really have not talked much since our New York trip. The poor girl has so much going on with her love triangle. I pray that it all ends well. I have her back no matter what. All of our lives, we have been each other's ride or die!

Tish has been our tag alone. Now we have tagged her out of the equation. She is really a piece of work. But, the more I think back, she has always been a fickle individual.

"Lisa! What's up chick?"

"Carol, we have a lot to talk about."

"Yes indeed. Let's order the mimosas and the food first. I am starving and thirsty."

"So am I."

"So, I will share last because I have so much to tell you! Hell, we may not even have enough time."

"Honey, I broke down and called Tish."

"That is not unusual for you. You always make the first move."

"True. But this time I made a big mistake. She had been heavily on my mind; plus I received some alarming voice mails from her."

"I received some too. She is just seeking attention and being a damn drama queen as usual."

"Yeah! It was bait; and like a fool, I bit!"

"What happened?"

"The conversation was brief. I explained to her that I was checking on her and the baby out of concern, but in no way was allowing her back in. Then she went off saying Mike ain't shit and that she was doing me a favor. She had no remorse. Nor did she take any responsibility for her actions."

"As usual."

"She went on to say that each time she tries to look out for us or give us advice, we take offense to it."

"I am convinced that she was dropped on her head when she was a born. Her energy is so negative and we have put up with it for years. She is very envious and jealous and she does not want anyone else to be happy because she is miserable."

"Oh wait! She asked about you and Carl. I told her that you guys were

solid. Then she asked if you would ever speak to her again, and I said "probably not."

"You are absolutely correct. She has come to the end of the road with me. Betrayal is one thing that I will not tolerate. I am loyal and I expect loyalty in return. She could rob a bank and never worry about me saying a word."

"I was so mad at her. I hung the phone up. I am officially over her."

"Well, it is about damn time! We can still love her from a far."

"I will drink to that!"

"How are things with you and Mike?"

"We are really good! We are back to spending nights together, but only two nights a week. He is still on punishment. As for New York, he really enjoyed himself and has suggested that we take another couple's trip."

"Oh! That would be cool."

"So, spill it! How was the Bahamas and how did the break up go?"

"Interesting! It was lovely, beautiful and romantic. You know Donovan is such a romantic guy. We had a penthouse suite at Atlantis. He gave me a Pandora bracelet that chronicled our relationship. It is so beautiful."

"Okay! So how did the break up happen?"

"Ha! Hold on! We had a private candlelight dinner on a yacht. He knows how to make a woman feel like a queen. I kept trying to tell him that Carl came through with a proposal. He would interrupt each time. It was like he knew, but did not want to hear it."

"Did you tell him?"

"Yes, finally! I told him on the day that we went to the aquarium. But here's the thing. He said that he did not care and that I was in Paradise Island with him in his arms; not Carl's, but his."

"Oh hell!"

"Oh hell is correct! He also said that I am only staying with Carl out of obligation, and that he is not going anywhere. He went on to say that he will

show up at the wedding and object if I proceed with marrying Carl."

"He does not mean that!"

"Lisa! I think he does. He said that I can make it easy on Carl and myself or hard. I tried to explain how much I loved him, but that I had to let him go. He was not trying to hear me. He ended the conversation by saying that he did not want to talk or hear anything else about Carl. I had no choice but to honor his wishes.

"Carol! You cannot marry Carl and continue to sleep with Donovan. Sleeping with him will give him false hope. Your commitment is to Carl!"

"Hell, I know that! But I cannot allow him to do something bad to Carl. I don't want anything to happen to Donovan either."

"Then you really need to go to the police!"

"If I do that, he may lose his job. Technically, he has not done anything. However, I do know that he is not going away without a fight. I tried to give him the ring and the bracelet back, but he refused them both. He has been calling and texting me ever since we got back, but I won't answer or respond. He wants to see me tonight."

"Hell no! You are not going! You can just hang with me and I will be your alibi. We will figure this thing out."

"Lisa, I have never been so confused and frustrated in my life."

"Have you thought about plans for the wedding? I sure have been thinking about your bachelorette party."

"A little bit. I've chosen the third weekend in June in Niagara Falls."

"I love that idea! Which side, Canadian or American?"

"Canadian! It's more picturesque. However, I have to start planning now in order to pull it off."

"Are you going to do the planning?"

"No! Your sister, Patricia. I will give her my ideas and allow her to do what she does."

"She is going to be thrilled to get the job! I am so happy for you guys. I

will not allow Donovan to ruin this."

"Thank you, bestie!"

"That is what friends do! We look out for one another. Have you decided on the color scheme?"

"You know my colors are going to be royal blue, white, and silver."

"Oh, I should have known. "Z Phi B!"

"You know it!"

"Carol!"

"Yes.“

"Who is that guy near the door staring at us?"

"Where? How should I know?"

"Over there by the door wearing black. He's walking this way!"

"Oh damn! It's Donovan!"

"Hi Beautiful! What's up with you? You are not answering calls, but you can text. Is everything okay with you?"

"What are you doing here? You cannot be here!"

"This is a public restaurant. Besides, I have been worried about you! We have not spent any time together or spoken to each other since the Bahamas."

"Excuse me, but she is with me! This is our time!"

"Who are you?"

"Lisa, this is Donovan. Donovan, this is Lisa."

"Pleasure to meet you, Lisa. I have heard a lot about you."

"It would be a pleasure under different circumstances. I have heard a lot about you, also."

"Good things, I hope."

"Until now!"

"Lisa, I don't want any hostility. I just want to see my beautiful queen. If she would respond to my calls, I would not have to intrude."

"How did you know that I was here?"

"Baby, I am the police. I know everything; and what I don't know, I can find out."

"I need space! It is too much going on with us."

"Donovan, you are being unreasonable."

"Who are you? Are you Carol's attorney?"

"I'm her best friend that is looking out for her best interest."

"Okay, best friend who is looking out for her best interest. It is in her best interest that she answers my calls and spends time with me whenever I ask her to."

"Donovan, I can't! We talked about this."

"Yes, and I. . . we decided that I was not going anywhere."

"No, you decided!"

"I have given you the consequences!"

"Your consequences will result in an ass kicking if you don't leave my friend alone."

"Lisa, Carol loves me and I love her. I am not going to give that up. She can stay with Carl. I have no problem with that. However, she is going to be with me, too."

"You are stalker crazy!"

"No! I am a man in love with a good, beautiful woman that I refuse to give up. So Carol, will I see you tonight?"

"No!"

"I'll ask again. Will I see you tonight?"

"She said no!"

"Can I please have some time to think, Donovan? Please! If you love me like you claim, you will give me some time and space."

"Carol, you are giving him false hope!"

"One week! However, I suggest that you answer your phone when I call to hear your voice!"

"I will. I promise!"

"I would hate for Carl to get run off the road during a police chase!"

"Donovan! That is not necessary!"

"Talk to you later, beautiful! I love you!"

"Ditto!"

"Say the words!"

I let out a sigh and say "I love you." Then this fool has the nerve to blow kisses after blackmailing me.

"Girl, he is crazy as hell! You have a big problem."

"I told you! He is not going away. He is serious."

8

LISA

I am so worried about my friend. I know she is strong and can usually handle any situation; but this Donovan issue is scary and sticky. I think she is way in over her head. She is planning a wedding and dealing with side piece who has turned out to be a damn fool that cannot handle separation. She and I are going to devise a plan. However, I have no clue as to what kind of plan!

It is movie and dinner night with Mike at my place, and I am choosing the movie. The one quality that I really love about my man is that he doesn't mind watching chick flicks and lifetime movies with me, which I love. If he does not like them, he has never indicated that he doesn't. For movie night we will watch Pretty Woman and Serendipity, my two all-time favorites. For dinner, Mike requested soul food like his grandma once cooked! Southern down home cooking it will be! The menu consists of Cornish hen, cornbread dressing, cabbage, hot water cornbread, black-eyed peas, homemade caramel cake, sweet potato pie, and freshly brewed iced tea. After eating all of this food, we may be too sleepy to watch two movies. However, I enjoy the time that we spend together. I think that the two nights a week gives us the space that we need. We don't get tired of each other and it makes our time together more special.

"Baby, dinner was delicious. I am stuffed! I think we should skip the movie."

"No! We can't skip the movie!"

"I am talking about going straight to the bed so that we can work off this food. Cooking like that turns me on."

"Everything turns you on! We don't have to go to the bed. We can do it

right here on this table.”

“I accept your invitation.”

“Freak!”

“That’s right! And you love it!”

“I sure do!”

Mike pulls my dress over my head, then picks me up and places me on the table. He sucks on my breasts as he spreads my legs with his knees. I am so wet that my panties are now soaked. He removes my panties with his mouth. He then takes cranberry sauce and spreads it on my body from my navel down to my vijay-jay. He licks it off slowly. I am so turned on that I cannot wait any longer. I grab his penis and insert it into my vijay-jay. For the next fifty minutes, we christen the entire kitchen area. We moved from the table, to the chair, to the counter, and finally the floor. We are sticky and dripping wet with sweat.

“Girl, you are wild! I did not know that you could ride like that! You could have allowed me to finish eating my dessert.”

“I couldn’t wait any longer. I was on fire like an incinerator.” We both laugh.

“For future reference, don’t ever cut me off and take control like that again. That is a turn off for me.”

“Why not? You don’t like it when I take charge?”

“Actually, no, I don’t!”

“Wow! Is there an explanation?”

“Yes! Don’t do it!”

“Well on that note, I am getting in the shower . . . alone!”

“No! I have not finished talking to you.”

“Mike, let me go!”

“I am the man in this relationship! I take charge, not you! Do we understand each other?”

“Mike! I really don’t understand what the problem is. I got caught up

in the moment and I wanted the dick; so I took it!"

"For me, it is an ego thing! Stroke it!"

"Sure!"

I saw something in his eyes that I did not like. If he wants to do all the work, then so be it. I will just lay there. In the meantime, I will just go with his flow. But me not being able to touch the dick is a serious problem.

Valentine's Day is approaching and I want to do something spectacular for Mike. He spends thousands of dollars on me and is always going above and beyond. I think that he has earned something very special from me. I may surprise him with a romantic trip somewhere. He has been talking about how much he misses skiing, so I think that I will call a travel agent on Monday. Maybe we can travel to Lake Tahoe since I have dreamed of learning to ski. That would be a golden opportunity and a win for the two of us. I have been so caught up in my thoughts that I did not realize I have missed several calls. Dang! My phone is vibrating again. I wonder who is calling because I don't recognize the number.

"Hello."

"Hi. Is this Lisa?"

"Yes it is. Who is asking?"

"My name is Shelia. I am Mike's ex-wife."

Oh Hi! How are you? What have I done to earn this call?"

"I am well. I probably should not be calling you. But as a woman looking out for my sister in Christ, I decided to call."

"What can I do for you?"

"Let me begin by saying congratulations on your new relationship with Mike. I wish nothing but happiness for you both. However, you need to know that Mike has abusive and violent tendencies at times; and he has been getting help by attending therapy. He mentioned to me when he was here that he felt as if his sessions were no longer needed. Also he feels as though he is wasting his time. The truth is that he needs those sessions like a heart

patient needs medicine. He is supposed to attend those sessions for the rest of his life, so that he can cope and control his behavior."

"I appreciate you for letting me know. Does he have a doctor here?"

"Yes. You can let him know that I contacted you and what we talked about. He is a good guy; but when he goes into that mode, he becomes a different person. It is up to you to help him and to make sure that he continues his therapy. It is imperative for your relationship with him! I do not want you to experience what I went through."

"May I ask what all did you go through?"

"I prefer not to say. It is the past. You will have your own experiences with him, be it good or bad."

"That's fair. I can appreciate your honesty and discretion. Thanks so much for calling."

"No problem. I look forward to meeting you soon."

Wow! That was interesting! Mike displays a few signs, but I think he's okay. I already knew about it; but if he stops therapy, then what? The other night was scary. I wonder if he has stopped his sessions already. I am definitely going to have a conversation with Mr. Mike about this matter. Now, I can use Shelia and he will never know that I had him investigated. Perfect timing!

CAROL

Donovan has lost his damn mind! I love him and the sex is mind blowing, but there is no way that I can continue a relationship with him. I am going to see him one last time; then it will be over for good. That is it! I have to begin planning my wedding and my life with Carl. Donovan will not be a part of my future. Who am I fooling? A part of me wants to continue seeing Donovan. If I could be assured that he would not interfere with my relationship with Carl, I would continue the relationship with him. Maybe I can continue the relationship with Donovan until my wedding, and then call

it quits. He just may agree to that scenario. That will give him time to find someone and get himself mentally prepared to accept that I will no longer be a part of his life.

I am meeting with my wedding planner today. Also, I have a date with my lover tonight. It sounds twisted and complicated, but I got this. Just the thought of Donovan makes my panties wet. Damn it! The truth is that I still desire him just as much as he desires me. I am playing a dangerous game that could end in a head on collision. Donovan knows that he has me in the palm of his hands, just as I know that I have him on a leash.

I have settled on the third Saturday in June at 3:00p.m. for our wedding date. The ceremony and the reception will both be held in Niagara Falls, Canada. The ceremony will be held on a yacht with the fall scenery in the background. I want the scene to be serene and breathtakingly beautiful. The reception will immediately follow the wedding. My colors are royal blue, white, and silver. My wedding party will include a matron of honor, maid of honor, seven bridesmaids, a flower girl, a ring bearer, a best man, and seven groomsmen. Save the date postcards will go out on the fifteenth of March. I have selected my wedding dress which is a Vera Wang design. Soon, I will round up the ladies in the wedding party so that they can take a vote on the four dresses that I have chosen for them to wear. Planning a wedding is hard work, and I still have a lot to get done. Patricia and I will meet again in two weeks to discuss the flowers, menu for the reception, decorations, and more. I want my wedding to be classy and elegant, but simple. Carl has left everything up to me, and I am sending him the bill.

I just left the wedding planner. Now I am in route to face this crazy ass man that I love and hate at the same time. I miss him and the way he touches me. I plan to introduce my plan of action to him. Hopefully, it will pacify and keep him calm for a while. In the meantime, I get the best of both worlds without drama.

"You made it! Hi beautiful! I knew you wouldn't disappoint me."

"Don't you dare hi beautiful me! What is wrong with you? You cannot go around stalking and making threats."

"Come here! You make me crazy."

He had the audacity to grab and kiss me. My body is melting like butter, but my mind says resist. Damn! I love the way he makes me feel.

"Back up! You are not off the hook! You know that this, us, is wrong on so many levels."

"I think that you and I are right. I feel it in my heart. You are all that I think about every day, all day."

"I think I have a solution that is a win for everyone."

"Let me hear it! I will be the judge of this win."

"We can continue to see each other up until my wedding date, which is the third weekend of June. That will give you and me time to wean ourselves from each other. Also, it will give you time to find someone else, and accept the fact that I am marrying Carl. I think that will work for us all. What do you think?"

"What do I think? I think that you are trying to over analyze and buy yourself some time because deep in your heart, I am engraved in it. You need time to let me go. Just as I am not willing to let you go, you don't want to let me go either. I do not like the fact that you are still trying to deny that it is me who you really want to be with. I think your idea is bullshit and you are out of your damn mind!"

"Is this something that we can agree on and carry out, though?"

"Possibly. How are you going to suggest that I find another woman? You know that you would not be able to handle that. You wanted to stomp a hole in Regina in Montego Bay. Besides, I may not want to be with another woman."

"I am good. I think you should get another woman to occupy your time because it is obvious that you have to much damn time on your hands when we are not together."

"Hey, I will agree to this little plan of yours if it means that we can now stop talking and start stripping!"

Laughing at him, I say "Cool. I need for you to sign this paper. All it says is that after the wedding date, you will no longer contact me for any reason."

"Are you really serious right now?"

"Yes. I am so serious. It is for both of our good."

"What happens if I sign and then change my mind later?"

"You will find out when that time comes."

"If I sign it, will this conversation be over?"

"Most definitely! Over and done with."

"There, I signed it. Now come on and get what you really came for."

"Your wish is my command."

"I love you, girl!"

"I love you, too!"

I knew that he would agree. He will do whatever makes me happy, especially if it will keep me in his presence. It is a win! Damn, I am good!

"You know I am going to want some time on Valentine's Day, right?"

"You are the side piece. You will get the fifteenth. Nothing has changed in that regard."

"I think that since I agreed to your terms, I should get something that I want. Just think about it and give me an answer later."

"No! If I give you an inch, you will take fifteen miles. Gosh! You have been bad and out of control."

"Oh so are we punishing now?"

"Yes!"

"I got your punishment here on the tip of my tongue!"

"Oh damn! Yes! Yes! "Yes you do!"

"I knew that I could get you to agree."

"Sucker!"

"You love this sucker! And you know that I am a good sucker!"

Well, I no longer have to worry about him attacking Carl or stalking me for a while. I am going to do my best to keep him happy. June is not that far away. I know that Lisa is going to think that I am insane when she finds out.

TISH

Today I feel awful. I have been cramping since late last night and I know that cannot be good. I did not get any sleep. Sam was complaining about me moving, so I moved to the couch. He did not show one ounce of concern for me. I am taking the day off. Hopefully I can get an appointment with my doctor to get a checkup. I hope nothing serious is going on with my little bundle of joy.

"Why aren't you dressed for work?"

"Because I was up all night cramping. And I still am."

"Yeah, you got on my nerves with all of that moving. I am glad that you finally moved to the living room."

"Would it hurt for you to show just a drop of concern for me?"

"Oh, I am sorry. I am not a doctor. What do you want me to do? I guess I was not clear when I said this pregnancy is of no concern to me."

"If the financial reports are profitable after you open the other laundromat, I want you gone!"

"Where will I go? Nowhere! But right here!"

"I can't do this relationship anymore. It no longer works for me."

"Who is going to want you besides me?"

"You will be surprised!"

I am beginning to hate him more each day. I was able to get an appointment scheduled with the doctor for later this afternoon because I am hurting badly. I will also need someone to drive me because I am unable to drive. Mom is at work. Lisa and Carol are out of the equation. Asking Sam is like asking a dog. The only one that I can think of is Fred. He told me that

if I ever needed his help, that he was only a phone call away. It is a damn shame that I have a man, and I have to call someone else to drive me to my appointment. Someone who is practically a stranger treats me better than the man I have loved and cared about for over twenty years.

"Hello Fred. This is Tish."

"Oh! Hi Tish. How are you?"

"Not good. I have been hurting since last night. I have a doctor's appointment for this afternoon and I am unable to drive. Can you please drive me?"

"Sure. Why though? Is Sam unable to?"

"No, he just refuses to show any concern at all for me or this baby."

"What time is your appointment?"

"Two thirty."

"No problem. I will be there at one thirty."

"Thank you so much."

FRED

I will tell Sam that I have a family emergency so that I can drive Tish to her appointment. If he does not want to support her, I sure in the hell will. He is stupid. I am going to move in on his territory before he blinks. He has the entitlement mentality, and thinks and feels that everyone owes him. Well brother boss man, keep on thinking with that mind set. If he cannot appreciate a good thing, I can show him how!

"Boss man, I have a family emergency and need the afternoon off?"

"What kind of emergency?"

"My sister is pregnant and may need to be admitted to the hospital."

"It must be something in the water. Yeah! Don't expect to get paid for that time off."

"In a few months, I won't need to get paid for time off."

"What does that supposed to mean?"

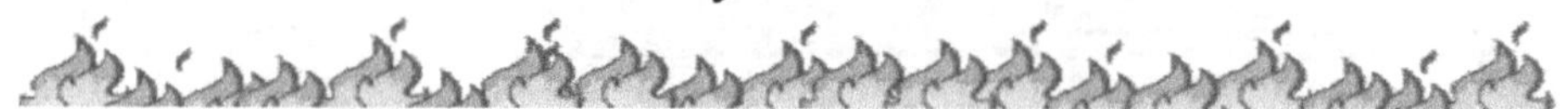

"Just watch me climb the social ladder. You may learn a few things, so take notes!"

"Get the hell out of my face."

"Gladly!"

TISH

I appreciate Fred. Sam may not like him, but he seems like a cool guy. For him to be a childhood friend of Sam, he treats him like crap. Now that I think back, Sam treats everyone like crap. I guess that we all tolerate him because we love him. I need space from him and I know that he needs space from me. These past few months have been pure hell. My home should be my place of peace; but as of now, it does not feel peaceful. Ouch! This cramp in my stomach is getting worse. Come on two thirty.

Oh thank God! Fred is here. It seems like these cramps are getting stronger by the minute. Lord, please let my baby be okay. It is too early to experience this type of discomfort without something being wrong.

"Hi lady! Are you ready?"

"Yes! My keys are on the table."

"Oh no! We can take my car."

"That is so kind of you. I am moving slow because I hurt badly."

"Do you think that I should call 9-1-1?"

"No! I will be fine. I just need help getting to the car."

"I got you! Here, lock arms with me."

Sam knew that I was not feeling well when he left for work this morning. He has not called nor texted to check on me. Although he is not concerned about the baby, he could at least show some concern for me. The doctor said that I am threatening a miscarriage. He is admitting me to the hospital to try and prevent it. "Little bundle of joy, I need you to stay in there. You best believe that your mommy is going to fight with every ounce of strength for you."

"Do you want me to call Sam?"

"No! He will just gloat. You can call my mom for me."

"Okay, will do. I am going to stay here with you. I am here for you all day if you need me to be."

Wow! He just made me cry. "Thank you, Fred!"

"Oh Tish! Don't cry! Just pray to God. Everything is going to be fine. Hang in there!"

"Just send Sam a text from my phone that says "in hospital."

"Will do!"

It seems like every little joy or happiness that I experience gets taken away from me. I have lost my two best friends. Now I am about to lose my baby. I cannot take too much more. "God, please show me what I am doing wrong in my life. If you spare my baby, I promise to change my ways and do your will."

"Your mom said that she is on her way. Sam said to keep him posted and that he cannot get away."

"Typical Sam."

"I am here. You don't need him!"

"Thanks for all that you have done for me."

"I am honored to be at your service, Ma'am."

"You are so sweet."

"Sam is such an ass! I will tell him to his face."

"When my mom arrives, please feel free to go if you need to leave."

"I am not going anywhere. I am here to the end. If you need me to move in and help out, I am available."

"You know that is a great idea! I do not know how this is going to turn out. But I know that I will need help for a little while. I sure as hell can't count on Sam!"

"Then it is settled! I am moving into your guest bedroom. How much will you need for expenses?"

"We will discuss that later. Welcome new roommate/assistant."

"Ha! I am in there! That was so easy! Sam is not going to know what hit him. I am bringing his high and mighty ass down slowly but surely. I will get revenge for Tish and it will be sweet!"

LISA

I am still a little bothered by Shelia's phone call. I don't know whether or not she was really being concerned, or trying to start confusion in our relationship. However, I have to inform Mike that she called to express her concerns. I, too, have some concerns of my own regarding Mike's behavior.

I have decided what I will do for Mike for Valentine's Day. I am taking him on a ski trip to Lake Tahoe. Carol and Carl will be joining us as well. We all need to experience a place of serenity in order to get a break from all of the drama. It will be a scratch off the bucket list for me and Carol. We both want to learn how to ski, so this will be a great opportunity to learn. Mike has been itching to go skiing, and I am sure that Carl will just sit by the fireplace in the lobby of the resort and drink crown. He will most likely leave the skiing to us; although he may try sledding . . . who knows?! I am just looking forward to our couple's retreat.

It is dinner and movie time again. This one is on Mike. He is cooking and selecting the movies. I am sure that the movies will be either action or drama. He has already given me a heads up on the dinner menu, and it will have an Italian theme. He loves Italian food! His biological make-up is partially Italian, so he really cherishes his heritage. I am not quite sure how I will approach him with my concerns. However, I do know that I will need to be gentle and not rush the process. Approaching an individual in regards to their mental state can be tricky. I want him to know that I love him and that I am here for him. We can get through this together. There will be no judgment from me. I support him one hundred percent.

I am on my way over to Mike's and I am wearing his favorite dress and

shoes. I also stopped by Victoria Secrets to buy new lingerie just for my man. Blue is his favorite color, so I went with a blue lace satin teddy. I have to remember to be less aggressive with him when it comes to sex. Sometimes I crave him so much that I lose control. I have to allow him to lead, which is the motto of our relationship.

"Baby, you are a few minutes late."

"Yeah. There was a little traffic jam that slowed me down."

"You look beautiful and sexy. I see you are wearing my favorite dress and shoes."

"Thank you. And I have a surprise for you under the dress."

"Can I take a peak?"

"No! It will be the dessert after dessert."

"My naughty, little Lisa. Come give your man a big hug and a kiss."

"I thought you would never ask."

"When we finish with dinner, I am going to spread spaghetti all over you and eat it off."

"Mmmmm! Oh baby, can we start with that scene now?"

"Girl, go put on some music while I finish up."

"Sure! What about Joe's "Love Scene"?"

"That is perfect! Play the entire "My name is Joe" playlist."

"You got it."

"Come on. Dinner is ready."

"You have done a great job with dinner. I love the little Italian vibe we got going on here."

"I am the best Italian chef that I know."

"I totally agree. Mike, I have to tell you something."

"It sounds serious. Is it good or bad?"

"One is a concern. The other, well, I am really not sure what it is."

"Spill it."

"I received an interesting phone call from your ex-wife."

"Who? Shelia?"

"Yes."

"What did she say?'

"She said that she was concerned about you. She mentioned that you were in some type of therapy and that you do not feel the need to attend anymore."

"What else did she say?"

"She stated that you had violent tendencies and that you need to attend therapy the remainder of your life in order to cope with your issues. She did not say anything negative."

"So you don't think anything is negative or wrong about what she shared with you?"

"No. If what she said is true, I want to help and be there for you."

"I have missed a few therapy sessions lately. I am pissed that she called you with that, and the fact that you entertained her."

"Mike! I am just trying to be honest with you. I could have kept this information from you and never said a word."

"Say what now?"

"I am not trying to fight with you. I am merely informing my man about a phone call that I received and the conversation that took place."

"Let me tell you something, Lisa. You should have told me immediately, not days or weeks later! So now, I will have to teach you a lesson on how things work!"

"Dang! You slapped me Mike! Why would you do that?"

"So that you will know your role as a woman for your man!"

"I have never felt so disrespected and humiliated in my life! Ouch! Stop hitting me!"

"I am so sorry, baby! Please forgive me! I lost it! I guess I do need to continue with my therapy."

"Yes, you do! If this happens again, we are over!"

"I love you and I would never do anything intentionally to hurt you."

"My face is red and bruised" I say to Mike as I cry.

"Tomorrow, I am going to therapy and I will never hurt that beautiful face again. Come here!"

Mike tries to comfort me as he embraces me with a tight hug, strokes my hair, and kisses my forehead. I cannot believe that I allowed a man to hit me and then I immediately forgave him. He has issues, but I know that he loves me enough to never allow this to happen again. I guess for the first time in my adult life, I have experienced the power of love. Love has caused me to forget every standard that I have ever set regarding interacting with men. I am still stunned that Mike hit me. I can no longer ignore the early signs that he has shown me, which I chose to ignore. However, I love him and I am going to help him. I will take him to every session if I have to. "Lord, help me! I need your help!"

Last night got crazy. I forgot to present Mike with the Lake Tahoe trip. We are meeting for lunch, so I will give it to him then. We are meeting up to talk about the incident and his therapy session. Last night is in the past. He realized that he made a mistake and he is taking the necessary actions to correct it. I admire a man who takes responsibility for his actions.

"Hi Sweetie."

"Hi Baby."

"Let me begin by saying again, I am so sorry."

"I know baby. All is forgotten and forgiven, Did you go to therapy?"

"Yes. I promise never to miss again. I know now more than ever how important counseling is."

"Enough about that! I have a surprise for you. You are always doing nice, over the top things for me; so I now have something to show my appreciation."

"What is it? You did not have to do anything for me. I do things for you because I love you and you are special to me."

"Here is an all-expense paid ski trip to Lake Tahoe!"

"Lisa! You are the best! I've longed to go skiing for quite awhile."

"I know. I thought Valentine's Day would be a great time of the year for a trip of this nature."

"Beautiful, smart and thoughtful! What more could a man ask for?"

"Carol and Carl will be joining us."

"That is great! I love you."

"I love you more."

I love that man with all of my heart and soul. But if he lays hands on me again, I cannot be held responsible for my actions; and I will tell daddy!

CAROL

My drama-filled life is on cruise control for now. Donovan is tamed, and Carl is no longer suspicious. The wedding plans are coming along just fine, and next weekend is Valentine's Day! Love is in the air! For Valentine's Day, Lisa and I are treating the men to a ski trip to Lake Tahoe. I am telling Carl tonight. He has been working so hard lately. He is either at work for sixteen hours or asleep. He has been working day and night since we returned from New York, so I am going to do something nice for him. Besides, I owe him due to my infidelities. Neither he nor I know how to ski, so I am curious as to what his reaction will be. However, the Carl that I know and love is always ready to travel. He says that "travel" is his middle name.

I have not and will not say a word to Donovan about my plans with Carl. I have learned from my past experiences that sharing too much information with him is not always a good idea. He mentioned that he wants us to spend the day together, but I told him that was impossible. We will spend time together before or after Valentine's Day. He has been quiet, so I don't know whether to be relieved or worried. Maybe he has found someone else to occupy his time. Nevertheless, he still checks in daily with a phone call and

a text message. I am meeting him on Saturday to discuss his demands for the love day. Whatever he wants, he will get. I do not want to deal with the drama that comes with the rebellion.

This love triangle is approaching a showdown in June. I have been thinking very hard about Carl and me moving away. He mentioned some time ago that he wants to spend his remaining years with DuPont behind a desk. He is now fifty and plans on retiring at the age of fifty-eight. That will be thirty-eight years of service on the job. DuPont's corporate office has openings all the time. He may consider transferring to Delaware. I am going to work on putting this idea into his head; so that by the time our wedding day rolls around, we will either have already moved, or will be in the process of moving. I believe that the only way to break free of Donovan is to move as far away as possible. Sometimes one has to remove oneself from a situation or the temptation. Just as sure as I remain in Memphis, my marriage to Carl will end before it begins. I don't want to be an adulterer. I want to be a good, virtuous wife to my husband. We could use a fresh start in a new environment. As a matter of fact, I will begin researching the area to gather facts on the cost of living and housing; and will apply for jobs at the local colleges and universities. Then he will know just how serious I am about this move and fresh start. Tonight, I am cooking all of his favorite dishes and preparing a romantic night. It will be full of surprises.

"It smells good in here. Someone has been busy. I smell pot roast and lemon pie."

"Yes Babe. I felt really good today; so I decided to surprise you since I knew you were getting off work early."

"Surprised I am. The vibe is so romantic. What did I do to deserve this honor? No! What do you want me to buy you?"

"Why must I want something for cooking your favorite meal?"

"And you are being nice and romantic?!"

"Don't spoil the mood."

"Hey, I am all in. I am going to enjoy the moment."

"I have another surprise for you. Here!"

"What is this? A ski trip to Lake Tahoe?!"

"Yes! Happy Valentine's Day! Mike and Lisa are going, too."

"Thank you, dear! But you and I don't know how to ski."

"I know. I was thinking that it will be a good opportunity to learn. Then I can scratch that off of my bucket list. Besides, there are other things to do such as sledding."

"Oh, I know. As long as I am with you, I am good. You know all I need is my crown and a spot to relax." We both laugh.

"I know oh so well. You know, I have been thinking and doing a lot of soul searching."

"Un huh."

"You mentioned a while ago that you would like to walk down your time at DuPont in an office."

"Keep talking."

"So, we could use a fresh start. I was thinking that since we are getting married, moving to Delaware may be great for us. The kids are all grown and gone. They can come and visit wherever we go."

"You are willing to move and leave Lisa? What brought this on?"

"Yes, I am! Lisa will have someplace to visit. I have been researching the area, and it seems to be very prominent and promising. I am going to apply for full administration and full professorship positions at local colleges and universities."

"Wow! You have been busy The company does have about six positions about to open up there due to guys retiring. I am sure more will be available soon."

"So, are you open to the idea?"

"Yes! If this is what you really want, let's go for it! What kind of time frame are we working with?"

"I am thinking by our wedding date. We can leave Niagara Falls and go to our new home."

"Okay! That plan sounds doable."

"We can begin looking for homes and go ahead and put this house on the market. By the end of May, hopefully we can begin to move out of here and close on our new home."

"It sounds like you have it all figured out."

"Yep, I am on it! We need this."

"I will put in a transfer request effective for the thirtieth of June. I can take some vacation time during the transition, and then be prepared to start working when we return from the honeymoon."

"A toast to a new beginning!"

"I will toast and drink to that! I love you, woman."

"I love you more, ole man."

Yes! I can get a fresh start with Carl and leave the temptations of Donovan behind. Speaking of Donovan, he and I need to make plans for Valentines. He sent me a text that read "Hot Springs", and I replied with "cool". We had a brief conversation about it, but I am not sure if those plans are set in stone. As long as he understands that Valentine's Day is off limits.

"What's up?"

"You, beautiful."

"So what did you come up with for us to celebrate Valentine's Day?"

"I have made reservations for us to be in Hot Springs on February eleventh through the thirteenth."

"Cool. That will work."

"I rented a house. Leave everything to me."

"What time do I need to be ready to leave?"

"Early! Around 6:00a.m. What is the rush?"

"No rush."

"I know you don't think that you are going to just leave my house

without giving me my time.”

"No honey. I am here at your leisure. We have about six hours.”

"I want the entire twenty-four hours.”

"You do? What if I say that you can't have twenty-four hours?”

"You won't!”

"You are so darn sure of yourself, aren't you?”

"Yes, I am! You can't resist this.” He then grabs me and kisses me on my ear and my neck.

Damn! You are right!” I love spending time with this man. He knows all of my weaknesses. That is why Carl and I have to leave this city.

TISH

I had a scare with my pregnancy. I am only a few months along. The doctor says that I must remain on permanent bed rest if I want to deliver this baby. I spent two weeks in the hospital, and my mom and Fred were by my side every day. However, Sam is another story. He came to see me twice during my entire hospital stay. Each time, he upset me by either talking about an abortion or a miscarriage, which he believes may be for the best. No mother wants to hear that, and no father should be thinking such thoughts. Sometimes I wonder if the prison system cut out his feelings and emotions.

I have to inform him that Fred will be moving into our spare room. I know that he will be upset; but I need his help and he is more than willing to help me. If Sam had been helping out, such drastic measures would not be necessary. I am so tired of him and I want him gone! If Fred's living arrangement works out, meaning if he pays on time and keeps up his end, Sam will be out. All Sam is good for is sex and stressing me out, and I don't need the stress anymore. Both of the laundromats are up and running; and they both are doing well financially. Soon I will see a return on my investment. Sam can finally stand on his own when I put his ass out. I will

not feel any remorse because he will be able to support himself.

"Sam! Before you leave for work, I need to have a word with you."

"About what?"

"I hired an assistant. Since I am on bed rest, I need help twenty-four seven. My assistant will be moving into one of the spare rooms this weekend."

"You hired an assistant to move in without consulting me first?"

"You are not involved in this pregnancy, remember? Not only are you not involved, but you make me understand each day that you have no plans to be involved. I need support and help around here. Besides, I am the bread winner and my name is on the lease. Enough said!"

"Why don't you ask your mother? And what does that last statement supposed to men?"

"My mom works and she is older. My last statement meant that I am the financial support of this house, you, the businesses, etc. I can hire anyone if that is what I choose to do."

"Your attitude towards me has been foul lately. I am going to blame it on your hormones and excuse it for now. That is the only way that I will not slap the taste out of your mouth."

"It is a combination of my hormones and being sick and tired of being used and pushed over."

"I love you. I have never used you."

"Ha! That is so hilarious. Every day you wake up, you talk down to me, eat my food, drive my car, and then go to work. Those are all examples of you using me. How many times did you show concern or visit me while I was in the hospital?"

"I came to see you! I had to keep the day-to-day operations going. I called you every day."

"Yeah! You did your little part as usual."

"I am tired of this conversation. Who is this assistant? When will she

move in? I can't believe you are moving a stranger into our home."

"I live with a stranger every day. You are not the Sam that I used to know. And to answer your question; it is a he, not a she. He is not a stranger. He will move in on Saturday. It's Fred."

"Fred Who?"

"Fred Smith, your friend. He has really been there for me. He took me to the hospital, stayed with me some nights, and he has offered to help with anything that I need. He said that he needs a roof and some extra income, and I need the help. So it's a win-win!"

"You have officially flew over the coo-coo's nest! Are you fucking him? When did the two of you become so chummy? That mofo will not be coming up in here. You have no idea who he is and what he is capable of! How did all of this take place?"

"It is settled and the plan is in motion, Sam!"

"Oh, we will see about that! That plan will not be happening! That mofo got me so messed up! I am out of here! You better not have any more contact with Fred!"

"Calm down! I do not see a problem. If you did the things that you needed to do, such drastic measures would not be necessary."

"If I find out that you two are fucking, the two of you will die! Believe that! That is a promise!"

"How dare you accuse me of infidelity?!

" You make me sick!"

SAM

Fred is a dead man. He showed up at my door and moved in on my lady! He forced his way into working at my business. Now he is moving into my home! He has for sure crossed the line with me for the last time.

"Fred! Fred! Where in the hell is he? Bianca! Where is that punk?"

"He is outside in the back emptying the trash and breaking down boxes!

What in the hell is wrong?"

"I am going to kill that mofo! That is what the hell is wrong! Fred!"

"What man? Let my collar go!"

"I am going to kill your ass! You think I am a punk? I am going to fuck you up!"

"Damn! You punched me in my eye and in my jaw! It's on!"

We start to go at it! I punched him; then he punched me. I see blood gushing from that punk's nose and I feel nothing but satisfaction.

"Is that all you got? Learn how to treat your woman right!"

I punch his ass in the mouth again! "You want to be me? You will never be me! You are fired! You are not moving into my home and stay the fuck away from Tish!" My hands are wrapped around his neck and I want to choke all of the life out of him.

"We will see what Tish has to say about all of this!"

"Sam! Stop! Let him go! What did he do?"

"Go ahead Sam and tell her! I'm sure she will find the facts interesting!"

"Shut the hell up! Get your shit and get off my property!"

"Gladly…for now! I am going to let you calm down and I will see you on tomorrow. Hell, I just may see you at home tonight! Ouch! You punched me in my stomach!"

"Sam! What is all of this about?"

"Mind your business, Bianca! Do not ask me any questions! Do I make myself clear?"

"I just want to understand what has you so angry. I have never seen you like this!"

"Go ahead and tell her, Sam!"

"Fred! You were asked to leave! I will call the police!"

"Bitch, you are just another hood rat with no clue! Your man likes to fuck men in the ass! I bet you didn't know that while you're walking around here like you're the Queen Bee!"

I then punch his ass in the mouth again and throw him out the door.

"Sam! What is he talking about?" Bianca asks as she cries.

"If you want to keep me and your job, stop asking questions and keep your mouth shut! You speak when I speak to you!"

"But Sam!"

I act like I don't hear her, then go into the office and slam the door shut. Fred's ass is going to go missing tonight!

FRED

I guess it's safe to say that Tish told Sam that I will be moving in on Saturday. I think that mofo broke my nose. When Tish sees the bruises on me, she will feel more contempt for Sam. That is why I only gave him a few punches to the stomach. He is the aggressor not me. He is digging his own little shallow grave. Now that hood bitch, Bianca, knows that he is not the hard thug that he is pretending to be. I have to call and check on my baby, Tish.

"Hi Tish."

"Hi Fred. How are you?"

"Actually, I'm a little banged up."

"What happened? Were you in an accident?"

"No! Sam attacked me at work."

"I am so sorry for that. I told him about our arrangement and he became very angry. He went as far as to accuse me of sleeping with you."

"Are you serious?"

"I am very serious."

"Look, I do not want to cause any problems for you guys. I don't want to lose my friend. Maybe we should reconsider this arrangement."

"No way! He is a grown ass man that needs to learn how to deal with adversity and consequences for his actions!"

"Are you sure?"

"I have never been so sure about anything! He will be fine. I am so sorry for what he did to you."

"No need for you to apologize, Tish. It's more important to know that you are okay because you do not need to be stressed. I can handle Sam."

"I am fine. You keep me calm. I cannot wait until move in day."

"Same here. I will see you later then."

Ha! Once I move in and get settled, I am going to deal with Sam. Tish and I will never have to worry about him ever again, at least not in this lifetime.

9

LISA

It is time for us to hit the slopes and Valentine's Day is only a day away. Lake Tahoe is gorgeous. The snow settled atop the mountains is beautiful. We are lodging at the Heavenly Mountain Resort which has a picturesque view of the lake, as well as great slopes and lifts. Mike and I arrived a day earlier than Carol and Carl because Carol had to take care of her stalker lover, which is just insane. Enough is never going to be enough with those two. In the meantime, I am going to enjoy quality time with Mike and get a head start on learning how to ski. My first lesson is in a few hours and I am so excited. Mike is already an expert skier; but as for Carl, well who knows. I am thoroughly loving this snow and cold weather. This is what I call Boo weather, and I have a Boo! The air here is fresh and crisp. I could get used to this.

After my ski lesson, I want to sit in the lobby by the cozy fireplace and drink coffee while cuddling with Mike on the sofa. When I mentioned the idea to him, he was all for it. So far our relationship is back to normal. He is in therapy and I have been attending Tae Kwon Do to brush up on my skills. If he tries me again, he will quickly learn who I really am. However, I feel confident that it will never happen again. Well, it is time to put on my new ski gear. I am too excited!

"Are you ready to try the slopes?" Mike asks.

"Ready? I was born ready!"

"Sure you were. It is fairly easy. If you follow the instructor's lead, you will be fine."

"Let's go!"

"Thank you so much for this trip baby. I love you to the moon and

back. It is so good to have a woman who listens.”

“Aww. I love you too, hon.”

Damn the ski instructor is fine! He has an Australian accent. I am such a flirt, so I need to contain myself. Now I wish that Mike had stayed back at the resort. This dude is model gorgeous. He is so fine and I can see his muscles through his coat. Ok, I'm done! No disrespecting my man to flirt with another man.

“Ms. Lisa, you have done well on flat land. Are you ready to try a small hill?”

“I don't know. What do you think Mike?”

“It's your lesson. The hills are the best thrills.”

“Okay.”

“I will be with you every step of the way.”

“I'm ready.” I take the lift up the bunny slope for my first downhill ski. I begin screaming as I glide down the slope with my eyes closed.

“Ms. Lisa! You need to see where you are going so that you will not run into a tree. You have to keep yourself safe! Let's try it again.”

I try it again with my eyes open and I succeed at my first lesson. Mike is hurting himself laughing at me, but that's okay. Before he knows it, I will be passing him on the slopes.

Here baby, drink this so you can warm up. You did very good on your first try.”

“Thank you dear.”

“Just one question . . . why did you close your eyes?”

“So I would not see over the hill. I just wanted to feel it.”

“You conquered two hills in one day. You are well on your way to becoming a champ at this.”

“I will try to be.” Mike and I sit on the sofa by the fireplace, drink coffee and cuddle for hours. It is calm and peaceful. I cannot wait for Carol and Carl to arrive.

Well, we survived the first day, now for day two. Today is Valentine's Day and it is going to be busy. I have another ski lesson, and we are going sledding with Carol and Carl. We will also be attending a dinner for couple's on tonight at the resort. I am about to explode with anticipation because I know that my gift from Mike is going to be spectacular. But now I am meeting up with Carol.

"Carol, I have a confession to make. I took a ski lesson already, so I am one up on you."

"Heifer! Trust and believe that I will catch up and pass you."

"So how was Hot Springs with Donovan ?"

"Nice, cozy, and freaky! OMG! We had a lot of freaky sex!"

"See, that's the reason you two cannot stay away from each other."

"I know! I need help. I am working on a solid plan to leave him."

"Do you mind sharing?"

"Not just yet. It is in motion. I will fill you in on the details later."

"I hope that it is nothing crazy."

"It's not. I promise! Well, I am going to see you later at the sledding post. I have to be at my ski lesson in ten minutes. Carl is joining me. Can you believe he is going to try it?"

"That will be interesting. I must warn you that the instructor is fine with an Australian accent."

"Oh really? Well, thanks for the heads up."

"See ya later!"

Carol is my best friend. The older we get, the stronger our bond becomes. She is finally marrying Carl. I pray that she gets from under Donovan's spell. I don't know what he has, but it is powerful. She knows that Carl is good for her and I know that she will fight to keep their relationship. It's my second lesson and I have already conquered two additional hills without much help from the instructor. By tomorrow, I don't think I will need him at all. Mike is a great skier and he looks sexy doing it.

I am glad to share this experience with him. One of the traits that I love about him is that he allows me to stretch out beyond my horizons. I can experience new things and feel comfortable in doing so. He will be right there cheering me on.

Sledding was fun! I think Carl had more fun than any of us. He wanted to stay out there all afternoon while we were ready to leave hours ago. I'm glad to see him enjoying the trip. He and my friend seem to be really happy for a change. Tonight is the couple's dinner and Carol and I have gotten dressed up for our men. Carol is wearing a beautiful, red and silver strapless chiffon dress with crystals accenting the neckline, and a long split displaying a teaseful view of her leg. My dress is red and white with crystals accenting the waist line. Our men are dressed to impress as well, sporting black tuxedos and bow ties that match our dresses. Everyone will pause when we enter the room!

"Bestie, you look gorgeous!"

"Thanks Lisa. So do you!"

"I think we are going to make all of the men jealous with these beautiful women on our arms. What do you think Carl?"

"Yes, I agree!"

"I think I can speak for Mike when I say you ladies did an awesome job with this vacation. A toast to beautiful, strong and intelligent black women!"

"I'll drink to that!" Carl says as we all clink our glasses.

"If it's okay with you guys, I would like to give Carol her gift now."

"Carl, I really was not expecting anything, especially after that big engagement ring and all of the wedding planning."

"You know that I was going to give you something on this day. In fifteen years, I have never missed a Valentine's Day gift."

"Aww, I hope that's us in fifteen years" I cheerfully say.

"Oh, hell! You didn't! The key to a Benz?!"

"Yes! It's that E-class that you have been drooling over."

"Damn baby! Thank you"! I love you! Love you! Love you!" Carol exclaims as she drowns him with kisses and smothers him with hugs.

"Oh gosh, save it for the bedroom " I playfully say as we all laugh.

"Lisa girl, all I can say is road trip!"

"Well Carl, you have certainly set the bar high. You are a hard act to follow! Happy Valentine's Day, Lisa! Now I have a surprise for my baby."

"Oh my God! Real pearls! I have always wanted my own pearls."

"I remembered you mentioning your mom's pearls and how you borrow hers on special occasions. You also said that pearls were on your wish list and that one day you were going to purchase some."

"Oh Mike, you remembered that? How sweet. Thank you, baby!"

"I have another surprise for you later."

So far, this trip has been perfect! This is me and Mike's first Valentine's Day together, and I hope there are many more to come. The night ended with all of us dancing, drinking, eating, and having a great time. As Mike and I enter our room at the resort, the ski instructor is lying in our bed naked with rose petals everywhere, and there are three glasses of wine.

"What the hell?" I immediately say.

"This is my second surprise. I saw the way that you were looking at him. So I invited him here to give you a threesome for Valentine's Day."

"Mike! This is a joke, right? You cannot be serious!"

"I am!"

"That would be considered cheating and I am no cheater! Thank you, but no thank you!"

"Okay man, you can leave."

Wow! I was not ready for that, and I really don't know how to feel about it. Mike has lost his damn mind!

CAROL

I am exhausted from those two back to back trips, but I must keep

pushing! There is so much to do in such a small window of time. Lisa and I have a lot of catching up to do. We did not have any opportunities for girl time while we were on our Lake Tahoe trip; so we are meeting for drinks at the Happy Mexican, our favorite spot. She told me that she is in shock, but did not provide any details. I am anxious to know what's going on. On another note, I have many things to discuss with her, especially pertaining to the wedding.

The surprise that Mike gave me on Valentine's Day is weighing heavily on my heart. I need her advice as to how to move forward. Hell, I need to know how I should feel considering our history. I am so confused. The funny thing is that neither he nor I have mentioned a word about it. Maybe with Carol's rational thinking, we can shed some light on Mike's intentions.

"Hi Lisa! Girl, I am tired and ready for some margaritas."

"So am I! I need about seven shots of tequila on the side."

"Damn! I was thinking four."

"You can have four, but I will have seven. Waiter! Can you bring us two large pitchers of frozen strawberry margaritas and eleven tequila shots?"

"So what has you drinking like a sailor?"

"Mike's ass!"

"Huh?"

"Okay. Remember when the men presented us with our gifts and Mike said that he had another surprise for me?"

"Un huh."

"Well honey, he had a surprise that I was not ready for."

"What was it?"

"Brace yourself!"

"Come on! Out with it!"

"A threesome with that fine ass ski instructor!"

"Shut the hell up! Are you serious?"

"I said the same thing to him."

"Ummm, so, what made him think it was okay to do that?"

"He said he saw the way I was looking at the instructor, so he knew that I was attracted to him."

"Girl! Well did you go through with it?"

"Hell to the no! I told him that would be considered cheating and I am no cheater! Thank you, but no thanks!"

"I have no words. Just give me a minute, or five."

"I don't know how I should feel."

"Have you two ever discussed a threesome?"

"No! We have not talked about the situation either."

"Maybe he was testing you."

"Testing me? How so?"

"To see how you would handle the situation. Maybe he wanted to know if he could trust you to not cheat if the opportunity presented itself. However, I personally can't say that I would not have taken full advantage of the offer."

"Your freaky ass!" I say to Carol as we laugh and take two shots.

"Real talk, I wish that Carl, Donovan, and I could all live together in holy matrimony. I know that shit sounds crazy as hell, but that's how I feel."

"You are crazy! But seriously, does he really love me? I feel dirty! Should I feel offended that he offered me to another man?"

"I don't think there should be any doubt about his love for you." It is very obvious by the way he looks at you and by the things he does for you. However, you two need to have an honest discussion about it. You have questions and he needs to give you answers."

"He definitely has some explaining to do."

"After you said no, did the guy leave?"

"Yes. Immediately! Mike told him to go."

"Did you two get busy?"

"Yes! All night! Hell, it was better than it has ever been!"

"Maybe you passed the test and it proved to him how much you really love him."

"Maybe, I don't know. He could not keep his hands off of me and his penis down."

"So, what's the problem, again?" Carol asks as she laughs at me.

"Hush girl! How are wedding plans coming along?"

"Patricia and I are working well together. I say what I want to happen and she makes it happen. Destination weddings can be hectic."

"Who have you selected for the wedding party?"

"Carl's sister, Sherry, will be the matron of honor; and you, of course, will be the maid of honor. My daughter, Carl's daughter, Patrice, Kesha, Cindy, and my cousins, Toni and Amber, will be the bridesmaids. My little cousin, Hope, will be the flower girl and my little cousin, Stephen, will be the ring bearer. Last but not least, my son will give me away."

"You have it all figured out, I see."

"I am trying. I have so much going on. Make sure that you are available for lunch on Saturday. I have scheduled a meeting with all of the ladies so that they can vote on the dresses that I have selected. I am kind of hurt that Tish will not be there. We all swore that we would be a part of each other's weddings, no matter what."

"Well, she messed that up. Have you received any more communication from her?"

"No! You will hear from her before I will."

"So, how is the Donovan situation coming?"

"Exhausting, but I am managing it. Hot Springs was cool. He had me hanging from the ceiling fans. I am lucky that Carl does not require much."

"Stop it! You are crazy! What is your plan to get away from him?"

"I am working on it. I will tell you all about it in a month."

"That sounds calculating. I hope it's a solid resolution."

"Oh trust me, it is! How would you feel if I moved out of state?"

"I'd be devastated! Why would you ask me something like that?"

"Carl has been talking about working a desk job for his final years with the company. He would have to transfer to headquarters in Delaware."

"You tell Carl that he cannot take my friend away."

"Okay, I will tell him. Well, I have to get going. Take care!"

"I will call you after I talk with Mike."

"Cool. I will anticipate that conversation."

"See you later!"

CAROL

I am enjoying my new Benz that Carl so generously gave me for Valentine's Day, although I am still trying to figure out all of the technology. He is so damn good to me. That is the main reason why I will not leave him. I get whatever my heart desires. Technically, I do whatever the hell I want. The heat is on, but I am cooling it down slowly.

I have made contact with a real estate agent in Delaware. Our house will go on the market for sale on Monday. Carl has put in for his transfer. Things are moving along. Next month, we are traveling to Delaware to look at homes. The agent sent us some pictures, but I need to physically see the house. I have not been able to break the news to Lisa regarding our plans to relocate. I believe she will give us her blessing after I tell her and give her my reasons for doing so. I got myself into this triangle with Donovan; and it is a damn shame that I have to move to the east coast to break that chain. Why did he have to catch feelings? Things were good. Why did I have to catch feelings? Why do I love the way he makes me feel? It's the Devil! Light complexion men are the pure devil! He has put voodoo on me. I can't seem to say no to him. The sad part is that I don't want to say no. I feel damn guilty, but I cannot control my desires for him. Unfortunately, he is like a walking time bomb. I never know what type of stunt that he will pull next. That is why I have been playing by his tune. I must handle him with

tender, loving care. He sent me a text this morning wanting us to meet at an address in Arlington at noon. I am very curious as to what he is up to now! My curiosity is a huge part of my issues with him.

"Hi beautiful! When did you get these new wheels?"

"Oh, it's a Valentine's Day gift from Carl."

"He is really trying to buy your love."

"He does not have to. You cannot be with someone for fifteen years and not have love for them."

"You two are just comfortable with each other. It is me whom you really love!"

"Honestly, I love both of you. I love different things about you both. Anyway, why did you request that I meet you here?"

"Oh yeah! I got mesmerized by the sight of you. I want you to come in and take a look."

"Okay. Are you planning on purchasing a new home out here? This neighborhood is gorgeous."

"I am thinking about it. I really want your input on this."

"Sure! I really love this kitchen! A lot of women dream about having this much space and all of the latest cooking technology. The spiral staircase is a major attraction feature. What is the square footage?"

"Sixty-five hundred. So, do you like what you see so far?"

"I do! I am sold on the kitchen alone."

"Wait until you see the master bedroom!"

"Oh my God! There's a fireplace in the bathroom with his and her everything, and a jacuzzi. This house is spacious and fabulous!"

"We could have some serious romantic nights in here."

"I probably would never leave the bedroom area."

"That is what I like to hear. The patio and the man cave are every man's dream. I already have ideas as to what I am going to do with both. I am so glad that you like it! I put a bid on it for us on yesterday."

"Us as in you and I?"

"The one and only us! Come on baby! Take a chance with me. Say that you will marry me, live in this house with me, and have a baby with me."

"Donovan! You said you would not pressure me about the proposal and you would accept the fact that I said yes to Carl."

"I know. I do not mean to pressure you. I just want to keep my bid in. Hell, I will buy you a seven forty-five BMW! Give Carl that Benz back!"

"Oh Donovan! You really know how to stress me out! You know that nothing about our circumstance is that simple."

"Yes it is. The two of you are not married. That is why you're with me every opportunity you get. It took him fifteen years and a threat to propose to you! Yes, I am turning up the heat! Again, I say, you are with him out of obligation."

"Donovan! Donovan! Donovan! No, that is so far from the truth! Deeply, I truly love Carl." "Hell, I love you, too!"

"I know you do. That is why you need to switch lanes. You do not have to give me an answer today or tomorrow. Just think about it long and hard. Will you promise me that?"

"Oh man! I guess!"

"At least it's not a no. Come here girl!" he says as he embraces me with a kiss and hugs. These hugs and kisses get me every time. "I love you so much! You really have no idea how much."

"I am beginning to see."

"Are you spending the afternoon with me?"

"You know I am! However, I can't spend the night. Am I clear?"

"I see your mouth moving but I can't hear anything coming out."
I lightly hit him on the arm with my fist. "You heard me loud and clear."

"Can we go down to the river? Will that be too open for you?"

"No, that's cool. Carl is tied up at work for the next twelve hours."

"Good! Let's go!"

We spend hours on the river; sitting, talking, and walking. He is doing most of the talking about our future. The cold hard truth is that he and I do not have a future. My future is with Carl. I am making wedding plans for me and Carl. I keep telling him my future is with Carl, but he refuses to hear me. Today confirms that moving away is my only option if I want a happy life with Carl. My phone then rings and breaks my concentration.

"Who is calling you during my time? I already share you with Carl."

"Actually, it's Carl. Please be quiet! I have to answer."

"No you don't! You better not answer!"

"Do not act like that, baby. I am here with you and I am not leaving. I'm simply answering the phone. If I do not answer, he will get suspicious."

"I shouldn't have to be quiet. We are in the park, a public place!"

"Please baby! Do it for me." I then answer my phone.

"Hello."

"Hey Sweetie! Where are you? What are you doing?

"I am out and about enjoying the sunshine and the Benz."

"Well, I am working hard. I just wanted to check in on you. Do you think you can bring me some lunch about seven?"

"Umm, sure! What would you like to eat?"

"You! But I will settle for some barbeque from A and R."

"Okay Babe. That's not a problem. I will see you in an hour."

"See you then."

"Bye!"

"What the hell? Where do you think you are going in an hour?"

"Carl wants me to bring him some lunch from A and R."

"Not going to happen!"

"Baby! Snap out of it! You are losing it! The man just bought me a Benz! Taking him lunch is the least that I can do!"

"This is my time! You are not leaving me to take him some food."

"You know what? You are tripping! I'm out!" I start to walk away from

him and he pursues me.

"Bring your ass back here!"

I pick up the pace and then begin to run. "No! I will meet you back at your house; but I am leaving." I make it to my car and close the door before he gets there. He beckons for me to roll down the window or open the door. When I refuse, he kicks my car door.

"You have truly lost it! I will not be seeing you later!"

"If you don't, believe me when I say you will regret that decision!"

"I am sick of your threats and I don't take kindly to idle threats."

"Oh, it's a promise! Try me if you want!"

I put my car in reverse and drive away as fast as I can. I am driving so fast that my car tires are screeching. This mofo has really done a three sixty. I am a little afraid to see him later and afraid of what the fool will do if I refuse. This has gotten too far out of hand. He is acting possessive and I don't like it at all. This incident strongly confirms that I have to play him gently until June.

DONOVAN

I love Carol with all of my heart. I think that I may have scared her a little. I just get so damn upset when she caters to Carl's punk ass! I cannot stand him! She is loyal to the wrong man! I proposed to her within two years, not fifteen. I can offer her everything that Carl does and more. I just have to make her see it. I am going to send her flowers and an edible arrangement to show her how sorry I am for my actions earlier this afternoon. The next time that she graces me with her presence, I will never let her leave again. Love will make a man take drastic measures.

TISH

Sam attacked Fred because I hired him as my assistant. I think he feels threatened by Fred. He is lucky that Fred decided against pressing charges

for assault. His attacking Fred will not change my decision. He isolated me from my friends and now he is trying to do the same with Fred. It seems like he has a problem with anyone who shows me support or cares for me. Fred said that he made all types of idle threats against his life. He told me that if Fred moves in, then he is out. I told him "goodbye" because all he does is stress me out. He is the main reason for my pregnancy being high risk. Fred moves in on Saturday and he will continue to work part time at the laundromat. Sam needs to put on his big drawers and deal with it!

SAM

When Fred comes to work on tomorrow, I have a big surprise for him. He will not be part of my life, nor Tish's life. He thinks he has one up on me, but he has another thing coming. Tish is so damn gullible that it hurts. I know I am not the best when it comes to providing emotional support, but turning to Fred is unforgivable. The fact that he is trying to move in on my territory infuriates me!

FRED

In two days, I move into my new home. My plan to make Tish my girl is on track. I am going to be the best damn man possible for her. She deserves better than Sam. I am going to be her knight in shining armor. I am going to be a father to that baby and "Mr. Too Damn Good" to Tish. Sam is going away for a while, far away! My people are going to grab him on Saturday night when he closes shop. He will no longer be a womanizing, manipulating, wanna be man. By the time he is found, Tish will have forgotten all about him or his existence. Hopefully, he will have lost his mind and his will to return home. I am taking the remainder of the week off so that I can finish packing and get moved in. As of Monday, I will be the man in charge of those laundromats. The first person that I am going to fire is that hood rat Bianca. I am sure she will be the first one to notice that Sam

is missing. I will call in to work now while I am thinking about it to inform Sam that I won't be in for a few days.

"S and T Laundry."

"Hi man! This is Fred. I was just calling to inform you that I will not be returning to work until Monday."

"No! You will return tomorrow if you want to keep your job!"

"You know I actually work for Tish. My main job is being her assistant. The laundromat is only part-time. Oh yeah, she owns that too." "I cannot afford for you to miss tomorrow. I am already short of employees and I need you here. Everyone is worn out from covering time that you have already taken."

"Well, you would not be short staffed if your ego had not gotten the best of you. I should sue you for the time off since you caused my injuries."

"Mofo! This job doesn't have benefits."

"Being best friends with the owner and living with her sure has benefits. Are you threatened by me, Sam?"

"Why in the hell would I be threatened by a gay faggot?"

"Really, Sam?! Are you going there? Since you are, for the record, Tish is going to be the woman who keeps me straight! By the way, how are things with you and the hood rat? I know she has questions; but maybe not. She looks slow to me."

"I hate your no good for nothing ass!"

"See you at home on Saturday, boo! Oh, and don't worry, I don't want those ten inches anymore. That is just disgusting!"

"You better not try anything with Tish!"

"Bye boo!"

SAM

I have to come up with another plan. Fred will not be coming in to work on tomorrow. Not if I can help it! So now I have to tell Tish about his sexual

preferences. That will change her mind about hiring him or allowing him to move in. She would never have approved of that if she knew. There is no way that Fred and I will live under the same roof and share anything. It will be a cold day in hell before that happens.

TISH

Sam called to say that he is taking me to dinner. Why is he being so nice all of a sudden? He is up to something. Whatever it is, I am going to enjoy this free meal and hopefully some positive conversation for a change.

"Why are you being nice to me all of a sudden?"

"What do you mean?"

"By inviting me to dinner and opening doors. Chivalry is not you!"

"Damn! Your opinion of me is now gutter low. I do the best I can!"

"Cut the red tape. What do you really want?"

"I am trying to work on changing. I want to be here for you and the little one a lot more."

"That is hilarious. Is Fred the cause of this sudden change of heart?"

"That mofo does not contribute to my existence or well-being in no shape, form or fashion."

"You could have fooled me. All of a sudden, you have become nice and supportive since he agreed to be my assistant."

"Tish! There are things that you do not know about him."

"Like what? Hell, some days I don't know you!"

"I don't know how to say this any other way but to just say it. That mofo is gay! He tried to make a move on me!"

I laugh at Sam until I almost pee in my pants. My stomach is now cramping and I can hardly breathe!

"Sam, is that the best you can do? Do you expect for me to believe that a childhood friend of yours is gay?"

"He is not a childhood friend. I knew him from Fed lock up. He is using

you to get to me. And now he wants what I have, including you! Whatever it takes, he is willing to do it!”

“Sam! Stop it! You are such a liar! You have lied so much until I no longer know when you are telling the truth!”

“Tish! This is real talk. No bullshit.”

“You are wasting your time. I am following through with my plans, so keep doing you.”

“Tish! He will not be moving in. End of discussion!”

“Whatever you say, dude.”

Sam has reached an all-time low. He must think I fell off a wagon or something. He is just jealous that someone is showing me some affection. Fred is a gentleman. He is a really nice guy that needs a hand up to help him get back on his feet; and I need a friend and some emotional support. Sam is jealous! Ha! I love it! I will call Fred now to make sure he is still moving in on Saturday.

“Hi Fred.”

“Hi love.”

“How is the packing going?”

“Hectic, but I am almost done.”

“Great! You know Sam is still trying to rain on your parade.”

“Please say it is not so.”

“Oh yes it is so! But I’m not backing down. We have an agreement and that’s all to it.”

“Thanks for letting me know. See you on Saturday, boss lady.”

“You’re welcome. See you soon!”

FRED

Sam is constantly trying to drop salt. Before he goes missing, I think it is my Christian duty to inform Bianca about Tish and the baby. I will also tell her where he lives, who really owns the laundromats, and who is paying

for his car. His world is going to turn into a whirlwind! I am going to drop my original plan. Seeing him crumble and lose all that he has achieved will be satisfactory for me.

It is move in day. I am up making sure that I have all my things packed and sorted. Today is the beginning of a new era in my life. I am going to roll up my sleeves and immediately jump in to help Tish. If I have my way, Sam will not last a week with me around. I keep him rattled and he cannot control himself. I will not allow him to upset Tish, or cause chaos in my new home. Tish has basically developed hate for him due to his wicked ways. The only thing that I have to do is continue to exploit the situation. The doctor's order requires that she remains calm. With Sam around, remaining calm is almost impossible for anyone.

TISH

My new assistant has arrived and his room is ready. He just needs to move in and get settled. Sam left super early this morning, and that's a good thing. At least Fred's move in will be peaceful. Sam purposefully made so much noise as he prepared for work this morning. However, I know he is just acting out. He used profanity all morning and kept saying "two grown ass men in one house is not going to work." I feel that sensible adults can make any situation work. I am just happy to have some company around in this condo. Sam is barely home, so it gets very lonely sometimes. When he is around, it still feels almost like he is absent. Fred's presence is going to breathe life into this place.

"Tish darling, good morning!"

"Good morning! I made a pot of coffee for you and the movers."

"That was not necessary. You are supposed to be on bed rest. That means you stay in bed."

"Making coffee is not work. I just wanted to welcome you with some southern hospitality. I also have some Krispy Kreme donuts."

"Well, your new assistant is here at your call twenty-four seven. I will make the coffee from now on. I really appreciate all that you have done and are doing for me. I need for you to sit here with the remote and look beautiful."

"Why thank you Fred; but I am not helpless. I can do a few things".

"I know. But I want your main focus to be on holding that baby for the next seven months. Once I bring all of my things in, I am going to make a store run. You make a list of all that you need; food, supplies, etc."

"You do not have to do that today. You are not officially on the clock until Monday."

"I am starting the clock on today because today is your day! I will make dinner and later we can watch movies. "Include some movies that you would like to watch on your list. We are going to relax and have fun!"

"I knew this arrangement was going to be perfect. I like having you around already!"

"I like being around. I am going to treat you so good until you will never want me to leave."

"For some unknown reason, I believe that whole heartedly."

Sam has been calling me for the past two hours. I refuse to answer. He only wants to argue and try to convince me that Fred is not right for the job. I am not in the mood to argue with him and the deal is done. Fred is here and at my service.

"Wow! You tried to buy the entire store didn't you?!"

"Nah, but food and supplies will not be an issue for awhile."

"I like how you think. I knew you were the right man for the job."

"Indeed, I am. I got Popeye's for dinner. I was going to cook, but the move has worn me down a little."

"That's fine."

Fred and I are enjoying each other's company. Dinner was enjoyable and we are now relaxing and watching movies. Not long after, Sam finally

arrives home.

"You two are a little too damn cozy! What the hell is going on here?"

"Look man, I am not going to argue and fight with you" Fred says.

"Please do not disturb the only peace I have! I have not felt this peaceful in months."

"So Tish, what exactly are you saying?"

"I am saying if you do not like Fred's presence, there's the door. I will be in my room."

"Dude, she cannot get upset. I really just want to co-exist with you and get along, and do my job by looking out for Tish. If you cannot keep the peace, you need to pack and leave."

"You think I'm going to allow another man to live with my woman of eighteen years and I just leave? That's not happening!"

"Well, that means you will accept the terms and not argue and upset her. Also, I need you to understand this; the next time Tish seems be upset because of you, the police will be called and you will be escorted out!"

"You will go down, bro! Trust me, you are going down soon."

"It looks like your boat is already capsizing."

"I am going to cut your balls off and shove them down your throat!"

"No need to lash out with harsh threats. May the best man win! Besides, you got your little family with Bianca. Oh, that reminds me, she doesn't have anything. I wonder what her thoughts will be if she knew that everything you have belongs to Tish."

"I am my own man and I make my own way!"

"Yeah, right! Let me get back to Tish before she starts to worry."

10

LISA

Mike and I have not talked about what happened in Lake Tahoe! I have plenty of questions but I am just not sure how to approach him. Carol said the only way to get answers is to ask questions. It is eating me up inside. Nothing else in our relationship has changed. Everything is still good! However, he knows that I have something on my mind. Lately he has started every conversation with me by asking is everything okay, and I always tell him yes.

Today, I am going to get this heavy load off my chest. I need honest answers from Mike. Next month, our relationship will move up the ladder another notch because I am meeting Shelia and the girls. I already have to deal with enough pressure from that situation, so I don't need what happened in Lake Tahoe to add to it. I now realize why I have often chosen to be alone. Relationships are hard work and can be complicated. Love will make you do stupid things. Sometimes love will make you forget who you are as a person. Love will make you overlook obvious signs, and will make some lose their minds. Love generates powerful emotions. However, love can be a good thing, too; because God is love! I love Mike and at this point in the game, I have come too far to turn around. We are going to dinner and out dancing tonight. I hope that my bringing up Lake Tahoe does not ruin date night.

Mike is always the perfect gentleman. He opens doors and greets me with flowers and gifts. He drowns me in kisses and smothers me with hugs. Yet, I still find things about him that I question. My mom says that most women do not recognize a good man. If this relationship does not work out, I will officially be done with dating. I will just be an old, single, cougar for

the remainder of this good life that I have.

"How is my queen feeling?" he asks as he kisses me on the cheek.

"I am great now that you are here."

"I love you!"

"I love you, too."

"Lisa, what's on your mind? And please don't say nothing because I know better. You have been very distant."

"I have some questions and I need honest answers."

"I am always honest with you to the best of my knowledge."

"Lake Tahoe. Why did you invite another man into our bed?"

"Honestly! It was a test of trust. I knew you were attracted to him and so was he to you."

"How did you know he was attracted to me?"

"He asked if we were an item because he was interested."

"I felt dirty. I felt as if you did not love me."

"I'm sorry for making you feel that way. But, I had to know if you would act on impulse or not."

"Oh, so that meant you did not trust me. I am hurt!"

"Lisa! Baby! You have to understand and know that I feel awful. I had no idea that you were harboring these feelings."

"So what would you have done if I had given in?"

"I would have left! I cannot tolerate seeing another man touch you!"

"Why put me in such a compromising position? If I play the devil's advocate, I might have given in just to please you, thinking that you were into that kind of thing."

"You know me well enough to know that I am selfish and territorial when it comes to my woman. I tried to test you, but my gut told me that you would not do it."

"I do not like damn games! The next time just ask me and not test me. You are on strike two!"

"What was strike one?"

"You have one more strike and we are done. Strike one was when you hit me and strike two is this fucking test as you call it. I am a grown ass woman and I do not have time for games! If you hit me again, I am going to Tae Kwon Do your ass."

"Damn girl! Calm the hell down!"

"You know what, this date is over. Take me home!"

"No! You are not running anything but your mouth. You can't keep running every time we have a disagreement."

"Do you want to try me, today? Huh Mike? Is that it? Pull the damn car over!" He pulls over to the side of the road. I chop his ass in the throat and he gasps!

"What is wrong with you woman?"

"I have a lot of built up frustrations and you are playing games!" I chop him in the stomach and he gasps again.

"Ouch! I can't breathe!"

"Good. That's what your ass gets!" I jump out of the car and begin walking as fast as I can.

"Get back here! I am not going to let you walk out here alone!"

"Leave me alone before I give you some more of this ass kicking that you got brewing!"

"Get back here, now!" He catches up with me and grabs my arm.

"Mike, let me go!" I then kick him in his knee.

"Oh shit! Girl, you are crazy!"

"You damn right!"

"Let me take you home, please. Will you help me back to the car?"

"Hell no! I'll wait for you to get back to the car. I'm driving!" I walk swiftly back to the car.

"Oh! Oh my knee!"

Mike limps back to the car and gets in. I take off as fast as I can with the

tires screeching. I am so damn angry. I want to drive him off in the woods and leave him there. It's a long drive back to my house and we both remain quiet. As I pull up to my house, Mike finally decides to speak.

"Lisa, can we talk please? Are you calm?"

"Ask me that in three weeks. Don't call me, I will call you!"

"I know that you are not serious!"

I get out of the car and slam the door as hard as I can. I have never allowed a man to disrespect me and I am not about to start.

"Lisa! Baby! Lisa! I said I was sorry!"

I keep walking and do not look back. I refuse to acknowledge him.

CAROL

I need to meet with Lisa so that we can finalize some wedding plans and details for the bachelorette party. It has been an entire week since my last encounter with Donovan. I am afraid of someone for the first time in my life. The furious look in his eyes was disturbing. I see now that there is truth to the saying that you cannot end a relationship with someone and continue to sleep with them. I need to make a clean break. I guess I was so self-absorbed that I took his proposal for granted. Now, he is buying houses and trying to compete with Carl. The web that I have weaved is crazy! Maybe conversation and drinks with Lisa will give me some insight for handling my situation. Sometimes talking things out can help shine some light on problems and provide possible solutions.

LISA

It has been three days since I kicked Mike's ass. I don't know what came over me, but I needed that release. Now I feel better, but I am still not thinking straight. He calls and texts me at least fifty times a day. I know I was clear when I told him not to call me. I will call him when I get good and damn ready. I still feel some type of way about his damn test. Every time I

think about him saying the word "test", I become infuriated. I thought we were adults. However, after I calmed down, I realized that I may have overreacted. I'm about to meet with Carol, so I will get her opinion on how I handled things.

"Hi Lisa. What's going on?"

"Too damn much! What's up with you?"

"I am watching my back these days. That's all I can say."

"Oh my! This is going to be good. What happened?"

"Honey, Donovan has flown over the coo-coo's nest!"

"What's new? He did that when he followed you to Montego Bay".

"I don't know where to begin. About a week ago, he texted and asked me to meet him at an unfamiliar address. When I got there, I was in awe. The house is in a new subdivision in Arlington and it's extremely gorgeous. He then informs me that he has put in a bid on it and wants me to come live in it with him. He wants me to give Carl back his Benz and take a chance with him. He even offered to buy me a 745 BMW!"

"Lord! I told you to stop sleeping with him a long time ago. Now he is whipped and you cannot get rid of him."

"There's more. I spent the entire afternoon with him on the river. While there, Carl called my phone and Donovan became livid. He told me not to answer; but when I did, he made a point of talking in the background."

"Why did you answer?"

"Because Carl kept calling. He wanted me to bring him some food to the job. Anyway, Donovan went on to say that I was not going anywhere and even got a little physical. But the nail in the coffin came when he kicked the Benz. I was scared as hell, and still am. I have not had any communication with him since."

"He has gone mad. Has he tried to contact you?"

"Yes girl! He has sent roses and edible arrangements with notes of apology almost every day."

"Where is he sending them to?"

"My job. I want to respond, but I am going to use this time to reflect and make a break for it."

"Be reasonable. He is not going to give up! Prepare for battle."

"Staying away is so hard. Today makes one week; but shit, I am watching my back every day."

"You should. He may be in here somewhere or outside waiting."

"I pray not. Enough about me. Did you have your talk with Mike?"

"Yes. The bastard said that he was testing me! So I asked if I had given in then what? He said that he would have walked away. He went on to say that he is territorial and he could not stand to see his woman with another man. Baby, I snapped and beat his ass!"

"You did what?" Carol asks as we laugh.

"I put some Tae Kwon Do moves on his ass. That incident made me feel dirty and not loved by him. He offered me an apology and said that he was only testing me."

"After you kicked his ass, what happened?"

"I drove home and then told him not to call me; but the fool has still been calling and texting all day, every day; not to mention the emails and deliveries. Did I overreact? I just felt so disrespected."

"I cannot say whether or not you overreacted. But, I would have loved to witness it all. I guess it is safe to say that it is a full moon and the men in our lives have gone mad. Are you going to forgive him?"

"You see, that is what has me worried. I get so angry when the thought of it creeps into my mind. For some reason, I cannot let it go."

"Let's keep drinking; and just maybe we will figure it all out."

"Let's talk about the bachelorette party. I have three suggestions; Atlanta, Las Vegas, or San Francisco."

"Those sound great, but I don't want to burden anyone financially. The wedding is already a destination wedding; so combining a destination

bachelorette party with that may be too much."

"All of the places on the list advertise reasonable packages daily."

"I don't know. Come up with some numbers and we can go from there. However, I strongly suggest doing something locally, like maybe taking a boat ride on the Memphis Queen or something."

"Okay. I will consider that. But I prefer to travel some place."

"So do I. But everyone may not be able to just plan and go at the last minute like us."

"Alright! Alright! No matter what, there better be strippers."

"Agreed!"

"I will drink to that."

"Well I have to get home to Carl. I promised him a date tonight."

"Now you are doing the right thing with the right man! Tell Carl that I said hello."

"Will do. Stay out of trouble."

"I will try!"

CAROL

Who is that sitting on my car? I know that is not who I'm thinking it is. Damn, it's Donovan!

"What are you doing here? Why are you here?"

"I wanted and needed to see you. You are not responding to my calls or my texts. I just want to make sure that we are good. Have you been getting my daily gifts? Why are you standing over there?"

"You scared me! Now I don't trust you!"

"Baby! I would never hurt you! Come here and let me touch you."

"No! We need a break from each other."

"You've had a week. That is long enough."

"No it's not, because you have been sending me gifts and trying to contact me. I need time to evaluate us, you, hell, everything!"

"Are you taking a break from Carl? You better not be giving him any of my loving!"

"Man, do you hear yourself?! It's talk like that which has me afraid to be with you now."

"Carol! You know that I would never do anything to hurt you. I don't know what came over me. I did kick your car door, but I did not lay a hand on you. I have never hit a woman. I am a lover! You know that. Now come here and stop acting silly. Come on girl" he says as he grabs my hand. "See, I am not going to harm you."

"We have lost sight of our relationship. I think a break from sex will be good for us. I need to know whether or not our relationship is based on sex or not." He then kisses me on my cheek.

"For me, it is not. I really genuinely love you. I know what I want, and that is to spend the rest of my life with you. I don't buy rings and houses for just anyone" he says as he kisses me on my ear and holds me in his arms.

"Stop that! You know I cannot stand that! Look, the break is happening whether you like it or not. I have made up my mind about that!"

"Okay. No sex will be hard; but if that makes you comfortable, then hey, it is what it is."

"We cannot spend any nights together nor take any out of town trips together."

"Well, can I at least see you to get a hug and smell you? How long will this last?"

"I will agree to seeing you, but only in public places. That way we will not be tempted to have sex."

"There's that beautiful smile! Hmmm. What kind of public places?"

"I don't know yet. I will let you know. I am thinking sixty days."

"Sixty days! Oh hell no! I will agree to a compromise."

 "How about forty-five days?"

"Damn! You are a hard negotiator. I brought this on myself, so I guess I

will have to live with it for now."

"No more gifts and showing up unannounced either!"

"What about if I just drive by to look at you and don't say a word?"

"I will let you know."

"Damn! Can you at least respond to me when I call or text?"

"Yes. I have to go!"

"See you later."

He opens the door for me and kisses me! I am so turned on, but I will not give in. I have a date with Carl. Building my life with Carl is my main focus right now, so Donovan has to go! I am proud of myself. I just need to pray for God to grant me the will power that I need to stay away from Donovan.

Carl and I are going to see Anthony Hamilton in concert. Thanks to Donovan, I am running late. The good thing is that Carl knows that I don't have any sense of time. Being on time is not one of my strong attributes, so he expects me to be late. If I am on time, he thinks that something is wrong with me. I have already laid out my outfit, I just need to shower and get dressed. He is doing what he does best, and that is to wait on me. Hmm, I don't see his truck. For the first time, I guess he will be late as well. As I walk into the house, I see that Carl is actually home.

"Sorry honey! I will be ready in thirty minutes."

"Sure! No need to explain. This has been going on for fifteen years."

"Where is your truck? How did you get home?"

"My brakes went out because the brake line was leaking fluid. I had it towed to the dealership and Ty dropped me off."

"How did that happen? Did you have an accident?"

"No. When I left for lunch today, I pressed the brake to stop at a light, and it would not stop. I thank God that I had just left the parking lot and was not driving fast. No one was in front of me, so I was able to throw it into park quickly."

"I am glad that you are okay! Why didn't you call me?"

"It was no big deal! I knew that you and Lisa were working on the wedding plans, so I didn't bother you. The mechanic said it looks like the brake line has been cut."

"Huh! Are you serious?"

"Yes!"

"Are you going to get a rental?"

"No. It will be ready on tomorrow. I will just have you drop me off at work and pick me up." Then, we can pick it up when I get off. Besides, it will be good for us to spend that little extra time together since we rarely have a chance to do."

"Okay. Well I'm ready."

"Wow! That's record time for you! Time does change some things."

"Ha! Let's go see my next husband when I divorce you."

"You ain't going anywhere and I am not worried about Anthony."

"You should be."

"I like this new us. I am looking forward to our new beginning."

"Carl, so am I honey."

As we are driving along I-40 in route to the concert, Donovan passes us in the next lane over. This had better be a coincidence and not his stalking tendencies! I am not going to allow him into my thoughts and ruin this night. This night belongs to Carl. I will deal with Mr. Donavan on tomorrow. He has the Audacity to send a text "If you take a break from me, you need to break from Carl." I refuse to entertain him!

TISH

Sam seems to be accepting Fred's presence as he's finally starting to act sensible. Maybe the threat of me putting him out has made him think twice before he speaks. Since Fred came to live with us, Sam has been spending more time at the house. He made it home in time for dinner three nights in a row. It has even been peaceful and no arguments. Sam has been a little nicer towards me and he is sleeping in the bed with me. The shocker is that he tried to make love to me, but I told him no. I do not feel turned on by him anymore. I still love him, but I am no longer in love with him. I never thought this day would come. However, things change and people change. Carol and Lisa would be proud of me. Oh how I miss by besties! Maybe one day we will mend our friendship and let go of the hurt and pain.

My little bundle of joy is growing. So far, there have been no more threats of a premature birth. Fred has been very attentive and awesome. I literally do not lift a finger. He cooks, cleans, does the laundry, chauffeur and whatever else I need. Most things are done without me having to ask or worry. My mom is at peace now that I have hired Fred to assist me. She wants this grandchild to arrive healthy. I have a doctor's appointment later this afternoon, and I hope and pray that all is well. I try not to worry, but being on bed rest the entire pregnancy is going to be challenging.

SAM

Fred has inserted his way into my life. I am trying to come to terms with it. Aggressive measures are not working, and neither are threats. I am going to find a way to beat him at his own game. He is conniving and manipulative; but I have to be become better at it than him. He has Tish eating out of the palm of his hands. She now looks at him the way she used to look at me. Nevertheless, she is loyal to me and I know that she would never cheat on me, at least not physically; but emotionally is a different story. I trust her, but Fred cannot be trusted.

I knew I had messed up when she turned me down for sex; so I need to turn this thing around fast. I have to change my way of thinking and change how I treat Tish. That means I have to support her and accept this baby. There is no way that I am going to allow Fred to take the woman I have molded and shaped just for me for eighteen years. Hell, I am not going to

allow him to take any woman from me. I am going to change; and eventually Tish will view me as her king and not the thug she fell in love with years ago. She has matured and I was not ready for that. The game has changed and so will I, starting today! I am going to surprise Tish with baby furniture for the nursery.

BIANCA

Fred mentioned something that has been on my mind a lot lately. When he comes in for work, I am going to interrogate him. I really don't know much about Sam or his family. Our relationship moved so quickly, and I ended up pregnant two months after I met him. I have only met his mother, and I saw his sister in passing. I don't know where he lives, eats, or sleeps. We never really go on dates because we are always at my crib eating fast food. Whenever I ask him questions, his answers are very vague and he becomes agitated.

I am appreciative of how he has stepped in as a father figure for my son. Although he is good to me, I still need some answers. Love will make you overlook things that may be harsh and hurtful in reality. To be honest, I do not know Sam's birthday or where he was born. He has been very supportive during this entire pregnancy, and he is responsible for me having this job. However, I am not sure what type of work he did or how he made his money prior to the opening of the laundromat. He told me that he was a business man and I did not question him. He encouraged me to go back to school because he said that no man wants to be with an uneducated woman. Thanks to him, I will get my G.E.D. next month; and I plan to enroll in classes at the University of Memphis after the birth of my child. Overall, he has been good for me and to me.

FRED

Today will be my first day back at the laundromat since Sam beat my ass. My new job as an assistant to Tish is demanding, but cool. I love taking

care of her because she is such a sweet soul. How she ended up with a man like Sam is beyond me. Now that I am there, he is spending more time at the house, and that is not going to work for me. He is too late and Tish can see through him. If she can't, I will make sure she does. The sight of me makes his blood boil and I am going to feed into it every chance I get. His days with Tish are numbered.

Today I am only working the morning shift because I have to drive Tish to her doctor's appointment. Besides, she needs me more in the afternoons and evenings. Truth be told, I don't trust Sam and I will not be closing the business on nights. All of a sudden, he wants to be home nights; but I know that's only because I am there and he feels threatened by me. Tish and I are developing a great relationship and he is jealous; but that's okay. He is getting ready to catch hell from Bianca because today, she is going to learn the truth about her thug love, Sam. I am going to sing like a canary.

"Good morning, Bianca! Did you miss me?"

"You as a person? No. But you as a co-worker, yes! I need your help around here!"

"Where is Boss man? Did he not step up to the plate?"

"Yes. He was running back and forth between both places."

"Are you sure that was the case? He may have been occupied by something else."

"What are you implying? You know what? Forget it! I need to ask you something."

"How may I assist you?"

"How do you and Sam know each other?"

"The answer to question number one is because God is good and he has really blessed me. The answer to question number two is we were locked up together in the Federal pen for about ten years. He had already been there eight years prior to my arrival."

"Federal Pen? He was locked up for eighteen years?! Where?"

"Leavenworth, Kansas."

"Wow!"

"How much do you really know about him?"

"I honestly don't know much at all. We met at a gas station, and within a couple of months, I was pregnant. He's been there for me and he has been good to my son, too."

"Have you met any of his family?"

"I met his mom and saw his sister in passing. He does not talk much about himself or his family. Maybe you can shine some light on some things. I have been really bothered by that statement you made about him sleeping with men. Were you saying that because you were angry? Why were you two fighting?"

"I will be glad to share as much as I do know. Sam lives with a woman who is an angel and takes good care of him. She held him down for the entire eighteen years he was in prison. She visited him regularly, brought his mom to visit, and kept plenty of money on his books. They live in a condo overlooking the river. That car that he drives, she makes the payments."

"He told me he paid cash for that car!"

"Negative! She fronted the money for both of the laundromats. He has nothing of his own. And yes, he will screw a man. He was locked up with men for eighteen years; and sometimes the fist is not enough, especially for men like Sam who live and breathe to have sex. He has never been penetrated, but he enjoys giving it."

"I feel so stupid!" Bianca says as she begins to cry. "I need to have a conversation with her. Does she know that he sleeps with men?"

"No! I am sure that she doesn't'! Did he tell you that she is pregnant also? Her pregnancy has been classified as extremely high-risk, so she is now on bed rest for the next seven months."

"What does she look like?"

"She is plus-size, very pretty and dresses well. Professionally, she is a college professor and social worker. She's been in here before. The first week we opened, she was leaving at the same time you arrived. Sam walked her to her car, and she was driving a white Lexus SUV."

"Yes! I remember! He rushed her to her car and demanded that I begin the inventory. I have been driving another woman's car! I feel sick. Oh my God! I need to go to the bathroom!"

As Bianca runs toward the bathroom about to throw up, I yell out "Hey! Are you okay?"

"Hell no! I am not okay. I just found out that my baby's daddy is a fake and our relationship is a complete lie! What is her name?"

"Tish."

"I have to meet her. I need to speak with her. I need to get checked out! Lord! I may have aids and my baby, too! " Bianca is now crying almost hysterically.

"You may not need all of that. He uses condoms and he is clean."

"How in the hell would you know? Have you ever...?"

"What? Slept with Sam? Yes! We were exclusive for ten years. But I am no longer that way."

"Ewe! Just disgusting!"

"When he got out, he always kept money on my books. But a few months before I got out, the money stopped coming. So when I got out, I hunted him down. The rest is history."

"He has played all of us like a trumpet!"

"Yeah! Sam is a user! All he does is take and take from people! Tish does not deserve to be treated like that."

"Hell! Neither do I! I am innocent in this mess too! If it was not too late, I would have an abortion tomorrow. I have to get out of here! I do not want to be here when he arrives. I need some time to think."

"I'm sorry you found out like this. I will let him know that you were not

feeling well. Go on home and get yourself together.”

“Thanks Fred. Thanks for everything!”

“It has been a weight-releasing pleasure.”

BIANCA

I am so disgusted! I feel dirty and sick! I have been sleeping with a complete stranger. I know nothing about the man that I love! I have major decisions to make. I refuse to raise another child alone. I need to meet this Tish chic and see Sam’s other life with her. Tonight when he leaves work, I am going to follow him.

FRED

Well, Bianca sure knows the truth now. What she chooses to do with it will be interesting. One thing for sure, she is a drama queen. She is going to go ham on Sam! Sam is about to catch hell on so many levels, and his world will no longer be as he knows it. I am positive that Bianca will have no problem telling him about all of the information I gave her, and I don’t care! I told him that his demise was on the horizon and to prepare himself. Oh, here he comes now.

“Where is Bianca?”

“She was feeling awful so she went home early.”

“She did not consult with me! I am going to call and tell her to get back here.”

“The girl is pregnant! Pregnant women have bad days. You are just ignorant when it comes to the needs of women. You may fool Tish, but you know that I know all of your secrets.”

“Shut up Fred! This heifer is not answering her phone. I know one thing, she better get her trifling ass back to work!”

“Oh! I will be leaving at one to take Tish to her appointment.”

“Oh no you’re not! I’ll take her. You need to stay here because Bianca

has already gone AWOL!"

"This is my part-time job and Tish is my full-time job. She is my first priority! Don't go acting like you care now."

"I do care! She is my woman and she is carrying my baby."

"For a second, I almost believed you. I just enjoy that sweet lady."

"Watch yourself, boy!"

"I got your boy; but I do not engage in such activities anymore."

"It is only a matter of time before you get that urge, and I am going to make sure that Tish finds out exactly who you are!"

"Compared to you, I am a gift from God to her! So, don't be jealous; it is not a good look on you."

"Go to hell, Fred! I will be in my office."

Sam is going to get the shock of his life when Bianca shows up at the house. I cannot wait to see the egg on his face and how he tries to weasel his way out of it. When Bianca shows up, that will definitely be the end of him and Tish. It will be my job to throw him out on his head, and I am going to take great pleasure in doing so. Then Tish will be all mines!

11

LISA

I finally picked up the phone to call Mike. I am still hot over his test, but I am slowly getting over it. He has been begging me for my forgiveness. My attitude towards him remains hostile; but if he is willing to tolerate it, then oh well. Next week, he and I are traveling to Charlotte for my formal introduction to his ex-wife and his girls. I will put on the perfect show in from of them, but he has a lot of ass kissing to do in order to make this right. He keeps begging to see me, but I think I will make him wait until we leave for Charlotte. Next time, he will think several times before he decides to play me.

As time draws near for Shelia and I to meet, I get butter flies in my stomach. I am curious to know if Mike confronted Shelia regarding the phone call to me. After I told him about Shelia's phone call, he turned into a man that I do not care to know! As a woman, I appreciate her looking out for me, whether her intentions were good or not. If my bond with the girls is not instant, I am going to reevaluate my entire relationship with Mike. I cannot handle any more surprises, drama, or mountains with him. It will be easier for my sanity to just end it.

It has been hard fighting with my sexual desires for Mike. I'm glad I held on to my bedroom Kandi collection. It has come in handy every night for the past three weeks. Perhaps I really don't need a man; besides, it lasts longer and I don't have to wait for it to recharge. It stays hard, firm, and ready! With Mike, I got caught up in the material things and the chivalry. I let my guard down too fast, but I am now back on high alert.

Mike still has a limp from that knee chop I gave him. I feel a little bad, but not enough to apologize. I decided to meet him at the airport instead of

us riding together. His feelings were hurt, but he knows how I feel. I don't know the game plan for this trip because when he tried to share the details, I showed little interest. The only detail I know is that our flight leaves Memphis International at 10:45a.m. I told him that we could discuss the other details while on the plane. He accused me of being a total bitch; and to some degree, he is correct! It is time he realized who I really can become if need be.

"Hi baby. Damn! I missed you."

"I missed you a little bit." He kisses me on my cheek and tries to sneak one to the mouth but I am not going.

"Just a little?"

"Yep! A little."

"Come on baby. Let's leave all of this here in Memphis and enjoy this trip. I have some special things planned for us . . . just you and me. I got us tickets to a Charlotte Bobcats game."

"Sounds nice. I've never visited Charlotte, although I have heard great things about the city."

"It's growing and has great economic potential. I just need you to loosen up and enjoy the trip. Our relationship has hit a wall; but if you are willing, we can climb over it together."

"We are good. Once I get past meeting your family, I will be able to relax a little."

"You will be fine! Meagan and Sydney will love you. Who cares what Shelia thinks as long as she respects you and our relationship, and allows you to bond with the girls."

"Did you confront her about the phone call that she made to me?"

"Yes, I did! It was for my good, though. I had fallen off the wagon. I did not appreciate you finding out something so personal from another woman. It was supposed to have come from me, not her. However, it is a part of me that I hate, but I've come to terms with it and I'm dealing with it.

It is just one of those things that's hard to share."

"Mike, I love you. I feel that I can share anything with you; good, bad, or ugly. It hurts me that I have to find out second hand information about you!"

"Baby, I know! I am a work in progress and will do better."

"I know. We all are."

"You are perfect."

"No, I am far from perfect. However, I try to be an open book for my lover, so I expect the same in return."

"That is fair."

We have arrived in Charlotte and it is a beautiful city. I'm hoping that I will accidentally run into Cam Newton because I am a big fan. If I do not see any other sites, I am only interested in Bank of America Stadium. I am on the hunt for Cam! Mike always chooses the best hotels. We are lodging in Uptown Charlotte, which means downtown in other cities. Shelia suggested that we stay with her, but I felt uncomfortable and so did Mike. That would be too much, too soon.

The first order of business is to meet the family. We just pulled up to the house; and I must say that Shelia is living well! She lives in the affluent area of South Park. Mike said as a couple, they lived in Ballentyne, which is also a very affluent area.

"Hello Shelia."

"Hi Mike! Good to see you. And you must be Lisa. It is great to finally meet you."

We all exchange friendly hugs and I say, "Hi! Same here."

"Well come on in. The girls will be here shortly. I thought we three should chat first, as Mike suggested."

"This is a little awkward. Shelia and Lisa, I want us all to get along and I want us all to be in agreement on matters regarding the girls. Shelia, please know that Lisa is a good person and she would never do anything to hurt my

kids. However, I want them to respect her. So that will require both of you communicating and backing each other up. The girls do not need to see any divisiveness.”

“That’s fair. The only thing that I ask is that when it comes to physical discipline, I prefer that you handle it. I am not saying that Lisa cannot correct them when they are wrong; but I want you to take care of the discipline.”

“How do you feel about that, Lisa?”

“I am okay with what you all decide. This is all new to me. I don’t have children, so this is going to be a learning experience. However, I love Mike so I am willing to try this.”

“Lisa, you must mean what you say and say what you mean. You cannot be their friend because children will try to play adults against one another. I trust you with them. I knew you were an okay chic when I called you. You remained a lady throughout the entire call.”

“Thank you.”

“Daddy! Daddy!”

Meagan and Sydney are excited to see their dad. You can feel the love and the bond that he and the girls share. It reminds me of my relationship with my dad. He is still my hero, and you can see that Mike is their hero, too.

“You girls are getting so big! I’ve missed you guys so much!”

“Yeah Dad. I missed you this much!” Sydney opens her arms wide to express how much she has missed Mike.

“I missed you this much daddy.” Meagan competes with Sydney by opening her arms wider to express how much she missed her dad.

“Come here! I want you two to meet someone. Sydney and Meagan, this is Lisa.”

“Hi Ms. Lisa.”

“Hi Ms. Lisa”

"Hi Sydney and Meagan. Your dad has told me a lot about you two." Sydney does the sweetest thing that brought tears of joy to my eyes.

"Can I have a hug?" Sydney asks.

"You sure can!" Sydney and I embrace in a big hug. She is so adorable. Meagan is slower to embrace me, but she eventually warms up.

"You want to see my new doll house, Ms. Lisa?"

"Oh, I would love to Meagan."

"Lisa, you are in there!" Mike says.

Meagan, Sydney, and I proceed to their rooms. Their rooms are like fairy tales. These young ladies are so precious and beautiful. They overwhelm me with all of their dolls and video games.

"Lisa! Girls! Come on so that we can go to dinner."

Wow, today has been great. We had a wonderful and exciting time with the girls. I did not want Mike to take them home. I wanted them to spend the night with us! But Mike said "no" and that we have an entire week to spend time with them. They did not want to leave us either. I think that the girls and I are going to be just fine.

"Mike, I love them already. They are so smart and adorable."

"I knew everything was going to be fine. You have my heart and the hearts of my girls as well."

"Aww, I feel so special. I am just so full of emotions right now. Shelia seems cool, too."

"Yeah, she's alright. She seems to be okay with you as well. That is a good thing because she looks down her nose on every one that she meets."

"Really?"

"Yes! The fact that you won the girls was enough confirmation for me. I love you, Lisa! I really want us to work hard on our relationship. I know I come with baggage, but I am worth the effort."

"I don't know about all of that! I'm just kidding. I am willing. I am a work in progress as well. I love you and want to spend more time with my

two new best friends."

"I just want and need all of the women in my life to all get along. I think you all are the perfect combination."

"I don't know about perfect, but we are going to be good together."

Seeing the love and bond that Mike shares with his babies is such a turn on for me. The way he took charge when he, Shelia, and I talked showed me that he is a man in charge of his life. He is a man on top of his game. This week is going to be an adventurous ride, but I am up for the challenge.

We are spending every day with the girls, except for Friday. Mike said that will be our time alone. He believes in adults having their own space. Time with the girls will include a NBA game, the zoo, shopping and more shopping. If he keeps this up, I may just reward him on Friday. Being around Sydney and Meagan has me thinking of having children of my own. Mike and I will make some beautiful babies. I am thinking two sons. Having a son is every man's dream legacy because they want someone to carry on their name. However, my biological clock is ticking which means we don't have much time.

Meagan and Sydney are some wonderful, loving girls. If this thing with Mike works out, I know that they will be the daughters that I never had. I will never try to take Shelia's place, but I know that my time with them is going to be priceless. We will have them for the entire summer. I am ready and so are they! The smile on Mike's face when we are all together is so precious. He is a real family man, just like my daddy. It has been said that women often marry men with similar characteristics as their fathers.

Our stay in Charlotte is coming to an end. I am so glad that I didn't allow the devil to cheat me out of this experience. I like this city. If Mike ever decides that he wants to return to be closer to those beautiful young ladies, I will definitely nurture and encourage the idea. Tonight is our adult time. I finally get to experience night life in Uptown Charlotte. I love the Southern, down home, friendly atmosphere. I can get used to this place.

"Baby, what are your thoughts on this whole experience?"

"I am so glad that you included me. I am in love with your babies and I am in total awe of this city! This experience, especially seeing you as a devoted father, has made me see you in a new light."

"Seeing you bond with my babies brought so much joy to my heart and tears to eyes. All a man wants is for the important women in his life to be bonded together. You stole their hearts just like you stole mines."

"The way you took charge and demanded that all of us respect each other was such a turn on! I could no longer hold on to the anger that I had towards you. You reminded me of the kind of man that my dad is. That speaks volumes because I love and respect my dad to the moon and back."

"I love you and I want to spend my life and eternity with you. Will you marry me, Lisa? You don't have to give me an answer now. But, please accept this ring as a token of my love for you."

I can't hold back the tears nor the look of surprise on my face. "Mike, when did you find time to purchase a ring without my knowledge?"

"After you got mad and left me, I told myself that if you ever came back, I would keep you in my life and spend the rest of my life making you happy. I just needed to see how you would interact with my babies."

"We still have issues to work through. I won't say yes right now. Will you accept a maybe?"

"Maybe is acceptable for now; but will you please take me off this punishment? I want to tear your clothes off and make love to you on this table right now!"

"I thought you would never ask!"

"Check please!"

CAROL

I have to do something about Donovan. He is stalking me every opportunity that he gets. I am not certain, but I think he is trying to harm

Carl. I can't prove it, but I am sure that he had something to do with Carl's brake line being cut. I don't want Carl getting hurt or losing his life due to my infidelities. I have to be a woman who is loyal and loves her man. So I must handle Donovan by any means necessary. On the flip side, I don't want Donovan to lose his job. If I go to Internal Affairs to file a report against him, there will be consequences that could cost him his livelihood. I love them both, but I have to betray one to save the other. Donovan has placed me in a horrible position and I don't like it!

An Internal Affairs report will air a lot of our dirty laundry. I will have to give details of our affair that I don't care to discuss with strangers; and Donovan won't take that lying down. There has to be a better solution. Internal Affairs must be my last resort. I convinced him to allow us space; but for some reason, he feels that I should also have space from the man to whom I am engaged and live with. I had convinced myself that a break would help him calm down and act rational. However, that is not the case. Usually cutting off the pocket book will put a man in check. I have tried giving him the ring and the other gifts back, but he refuses to accept them. He really thinks that we are engaged, not to mention that he initiated the process of buying a house for us. The loan officer emailed me papers on yesterday. My plan was to keep him close by continuing to get good sex until my wedding, and then disappear by moving away. We are still planning to move away, but sleeping with him again would be like me committing suicide and putting a hit on Carl. I am usually very clever. It is time to put my brilliant mind to work and deal with Donovan once and for all!

I have a plan that is going to make Donovan think that I am crazy. He will no longer want to be with me. Carl and I can live happily ever after. Unfortunately, the drawback to the plan involves me screwing him one more time. I don't want to, but I have to do whatever it takes to end this fiasco.

"Hi Donovan."

"Hello beautiful. You sound sweet and you just made my day!"

"I miss you. I try to deny it, but the love I have for you is real."

"I have been losing my mind. I just need to touch and smell you."

"I am so torn between you two. The things that you do to me make me feel like... I can't describe it. I need to be with you. I need your touch!"

"You know you can come and get it anytime you want. You don't have to ask. Remember, you are the one with the baggage."

"What does your schedule look like tonight?"

"I will make time for you. I get off work at ten. I will leave the key under the mat so that you can let yourself in."

"Great! I will arrive around nine. I will be ready for you."

"Are you spending the night?"

"Yes."

"See you soon, beautiful. Love you."

"See you. Love you more."

He just doesn't know what I have in store for him. I am going to rock his world one last time. Tonight is going to be a night that he will never forget. He is going to remember this night for the remainder of his life. I have to make sure that I have all I need on my list. Let's see: Handcuffs, gun, lingerie, pumps, floating candles, rose petals, three bottles of wine, chocolate strawberries, and a blindfold. Check to all! There can be no room for error.

The mood is so right up in here. Luther Vandross is playing softly in the background. There is a trail of rose petals leading from the front door to the bedroom. I am wearing a black, crouchless lace teddy with red pumps while lying on the bed, sipping wine, and waiting on Donovan's arrival. He should be walking through the door in about five minutes. His bath water is ready with floating candles and a glass of wine. Also, I have chocolate strawberries and two bottles of wine with two wine glasses on the night stand. I have already drunk one bottle by my damn self.

"Carol! Baby!"

"Yes honey! Follow the rose petals."

"Damn! It smells good in here. You are looking so sexy; like a box of caramel chocolates that I want to tear into. Come here, girl! I have been feigning for this."

He lies on top of me and we start to kiss. He then licks me from head to toe. "Wait a minute! I have bath water and a glass of wine waiting for you in the bathroom. Go relax and I will be here ready, waiting, and wet!"

"Damn! I am ready now, but I'll let you drive tonight."

"Good!"

"Are those chocolate strawberries?"

"Yes, your favorite."

"What are you planning to do with those?"

"You will find out in due time."

"I feel like a king tonight."

"This is your fantasy! You can be whomever you choose."

I am on the second bottle of wine and waiting on Donovan so that we can play house. He is finally done with his bath and his penis is standing at attention. I wave my finger for him to come closer to me.

"I have a surprise for you. Lay down! I need you to trust me and follow my lead."

"Your wish is my command. Oh shit, handcuffs! I like this already."

I handcuff both of his hands to the bed and ask, "Would you like me to feed you some strawberries?"

"Yes, please!"

I feed my man as he wishes. Eating strawberries is sexy foreplay! I take a slow bite out of the strawberry as he watches, and then lick his lips with my tongue. I place juice from the strawberries on his nipples and slowly lick it off. He wants to hold me, but he is handcuffed and can't. He begins to moan and tell me how good it feels. I feed him another strawberry and lick the juice from his lips. I take a slow bite from another strawberry and allow him to lick the juice from my lips. I bite into the strawberry again and allow

the juice to drip on the head of his penis; and then I slowly lick it off. I suck his penis until he screams for me to stop!

"Come on girl and ride it! The foreplay is killing me!"

"Are you sure that you are ready for the ride of your life?"

"I stay ready for you. Take that damn lingerie off. I wish I could rip it off. Put some of that strawberry juice on your nipples."

I slowly take off my lingerie as I stare into his eyes. I allow him to bite the strawberry so that I can place juice on my nipples just for him. I put my nipples in his mouth one a time and he licks and sucks on them like he is starving and deprived of food. I straddle him, grab his penis and put it inside of me. I begin to slowly ride him, sitting lower and lower with every thrust. We both are now screaming and I know that the neighbors can hear us. That was the best orgasm that I've ever experienced!

"Don't ever make me wait that long again. There are no words to describe that. You act like you missed me."

"I told you that I did. Maybe you will quit stalking me now."

"It is not stalking. It's protecting and keeping you safe."

"Safe from whom? You? You are the only threat!"

"I can't help it! I have to see you even if it is from a distance."

"Carl said that his brake line on his vehicle went out last week. The mechanic said that the brake line had been cut. Do you know anything about that?" I kiss him on his ear and on his neck.

"How would I know?"

"Maybe because that is the same day you showed up at the restaurant where I was; and you followed us. Your behavior has been erratic. You can trust me and tell me. I just need to know. Do you really love me that much that you would hurt someone else?"

"Can you let me out of these handcuffs? I am feeling sticky. Let's take a shower together and make love some more."

"Are you avoiding the question?"

"Carol! Quit playing, baby."

"I am not playing! I am not taking those handcuffs off until you answer my question?"

"Hell yeah! He does not deserve you! You act like you can't see that I am the man for you. So I had to take measures to secure our future together. You were acting crazy and talking foolish by saying we should no longer see each other. I lost it, okay! You happy now?"

"I find it disturbing that you would make an attempt on someone's life! I think you need to stay handcuffed to that bed and think about your actions for a few days."

"All I have been able to think about is you and how to get you away from Carl. Uncuff me dammit!"

"I don't think so!"

"Have you lost your mind woman?"

"Yeah. You make me crazy!" I then clean the sticky juice off of him and put his boxers on him.

"I have everything that you just said on record. I recorded it on my phone. If you try to hurt Carl again, I will take this to Internal Affairs."

"So that is how you do it now? Fuck my brains out and trick me!"

"You left me with no choice!"

"It still doesn't change how I feel about you. Tonight has made me want you more!"

"Well, I guess you are going to be in that bed until you change your way of thinking. I will be back on tomorrow to check on you."

"How am I supposed to eat, use the bathroom, etc."

"When I secure this recording, I will be back to let you go. By the way, I know that you are off work for the next two days. I may give you some more action tomorrow if you are talking right when I return."

"Carol! Carol! Dammit! That damn girl is crazy as hell!"

TISH

Being on bed rest sucks! I can barely do anything for myself. It is a beautiful day and I can only enjoy it by sitting on my balcony. I want to go down and walk on the river. I want to go shopping in the mall for my baby. I shouldn't complain because I have lots of help and support from Fred and my mom; but it is hard waiting for others to take care of me when I am used to handling things on my own. Believe it or not, Sam has also been nice to me. He asked if I needed anything. I wish I knew whether or not he was sincere or just competing with Fred. Fred is the best!

"Tish! It is such a lovely spring day! I am going to fire up the grill. Why don't you invite some friends and family over?"

"I like that idea. I will invite my mom and my cousins. My only two friends are no longer talking to me. I can thank Sam for that."

"That is a shame! Keep reaching out to them. Do not give up! Eventually, they will come around."

"I doubt it! I haven't heard from either of them in three months."

"Well, forget them for today. I know that it is hard being cooped up in here all day every day. The view is beautiful, but it's still hard. So I just want to bring a little joy and fun to you."

"I really appreciate you! What time should I tell them?"

"Tell them it will start around six. I have to work a few hours at the laundromat today."

"Okay! That's a plan. It will be nice to have some people around."

SAM

I have a surprise for Tish. Maybe this will make her see that I am really working hard to change. I want her to know that I do care and that I do have a heart. I can never really get any alone time with her because Fred is always around and in her face. Since Bianca has disappeared and gone AWOL, I have to spend more hours working. I have placed an ad for her position; but

so far, I have not interviewed anyone worth hiring. Fred is too busy trying to impress Tish. I can't stand him! My main priority is finding a way to get him out of our lives once and for all.

BIANCA

It has been three weeks and no contact with Sam. He has been calling me, my parents, and my siblings. He randomly comes by and knocks on my door, but I just look at him through the peep hole. He sends me all types of crazy, threatening text messages, but I still will not respond. I have been using this time to reflect on my life and make decisions regarding my relationship with him. I have decided that I will give this baby up for adoption. I just refuse to raise another child alone. I will be attending college this fall and a new baby does fit into the puzzle. Everything regarding our relationship was a lie and I don't want anything that reminds me of him. Before I am completely out of his life, I am going to give him a grand finale. Tonight, I am going to pay him a visit at the home that he has built with Tish. She is going to find out what her so called man has been up to. He is lucky that my HIV test came back negative. The doctor says that I will need to get tested again in six months. What kind of man lives off the hard earned money of a woman? The man is supposed to be the provider. I can see how she got sucked in by him all of these years. He is smooth and the sex is to die for.

SAM

"Look at what I bought, Tish!"

"You bought something for someone other than yourself?"

"Funny! I bought something for the baby. You are going to love it."

"Wow! I am impressed! What is it?"

"Close your eyes and give me your hand."

"I don't feel like all of that right now. Just show me!"

"Damn, Tish. I am trying here. Can you just humor me, please?"

"Okay, Sam. Damn!"

"Open your eyes. Surprise!"

"Oh wow! When did you have time to get this in here and put it together without me noticing?"

"You never come in this room. So while you were asleep at night, I brought it in piece by piece and worked on it. So how do you like it?"

"I love it! It is beautiful! I am just overwhelmed by your actions. You actually bought all of the furniture for the nursery!"

"I just want you to know that I am trying to change."

"Well, this is a good start. Thank you!"

"I am glad you like it. I have to get to work now. I'll see you later."

"Fred is having a little get together this evening. If you can get away, you should attend."

"Where? Who gave him permission to have a party at my house?"

"It is for me! Since I can't go out, he decided to fire up the grill. I am inviting a few people."

"Like who? You don't have any friends."

"Thanks for reminding me, Sam! But I do have family."

"You know, I live here too. I should have been consulted before you all decided this."

"I don't have to consult you. My name is on the lease! Now, go to work and have a good day."

"I am tired of being disrespected" he says as he slams the door shut on his way out. He is just upset that Fred thought of the idea and not him.

FRED

Tonight will bring a little joy to Tish. I know that I bring her joy; but being around others will be healthy for her. It's the little things that mean the most. After tonight is over, I am going to work on helping her mend her

relationship with her friends. It is obvious that she misses them. She seems to be a little miserable without them. During this time in her life, she needs her girlfriends. I can see the sadness in her eyes whenever she talks about them. I can't replace them because a bond between friends is irreplaceable.

As soon as Sam hits the door, I am out of here. I don't want to hear anything he has to say. My advice to him is to get on my level. Lately he has been trying, but it is almost a little too late. Here he comes now looking like he's mad at the world when I know that he is only furious with me.

"Who in the hell gave you permission to host a gathering without first consulting me? You may live there and have a spell on Tish, but I am the man of the house! Your disrespect will not continue."

"Ha! I almost believed you for a second. You are just upset because I came up with the idea and not you. This gathering is for Tish. She needs some joy in her life, especially since she has been cooped up in the house all day, every day. I thought she could use a little time socializing."

"Yeah. You are always thinking. Too damn thoughtful! Whatever you can do to undermine me is all you can think about."

"You do that all on your own. All I do is sit back and capitalize on it. Oh well, I am through losing brain cells talking to you. I am out! I have a social gathering to prepare for."

"Get the hell out of my business and my life!"

"You mean Tish's business, not yours!"

"Mofo!"

I can't help but laugh at Sam. He is such a joke.

TISH

It feels good having my family over. We are having a great time. Everyone is excited to see one another; and laughter and music is filling the room. The smell of barbeque and fresh air from the river is making a nice aroma. Life does not get any better than this. I get to socialize with

someone other than Fred and Sam for a change. Fred has done a great job pulling this together. My mom thinks that his feelings for me go beyond an employee. She says that she can see it in his eyes. She likes the way he takes care of me. Truthfully, he takes excellent care of me. His presence has forced Sam to do a little better. Suddenly, the doorbell rings!

"Who is that ringing the doorbell like a maniac?"

"I will get it Tish."

"No, you concentrate on the food. I can get it."

I open the door and there is a strange female standing there. She kind of looks familiar.

"May I help you?"

"Yes! Is this Sam and Tish's residence?"

"Yes it is. Who are you? Why are you looking for me and Sam?"

"Can you step outside? I mean you no harm. I just need to speak with you privately."

"I don't know you! What is your business with me? What is your business with my man?"

"Who is it Tish?" Fred asks.

"Someone who needs directions. I am listening, Ma'am."

"My name is Bianca Jones."

"Oh! You are Sam's cousin. Why didn't you just say that? Come on in and join us."

"No! I need to talk to you! Why do you think that I am his cousin?"

"I found your ultrasound picture in his pocket. I confronted him about it and he said that it belonged to his cousin. He explained that he had taken you to the doctor and that you left it in the car. So he, being such a great guy, put it in a safe place for you."

"That lying, no good, son of a bitch!"

"Why are you talking about him like that? He is your family!"

"I need you to listen real good to what I am about to say. Don't say a

word until you hear me out. I am not Sam's cousin! We have been dating eight months and I am pregnant with his baby! He has been a great fill in father to my son and he has been great for me. He's even convinced me to return to school to get my GED, and I start college in August. I have been working at the laundromat as the assistant manager."

"Wow! I am pregnant also; and high-risk at that! Sam has nothing! Everything he claims he has belongs to me. I held him down while he walked down an eighteen year prison sentence! That car that he drives, I make the payments. This condo is in my name. Those two laundromats are a result of bank loans that I signed for! He told me to get an abortion because we did not have time for a baby. I can't believe that after all I've done for him, he would betray me like this!"

"Before the laundromats, where did he work?"

"Why? Nowhere!"

"He had to work somewhere because he gave me four thousand dollars to get an apartment and some furniture."

"That bastard got that money from me! I took out a loan because he said he needed to pay a gambling debt! You know what? I am calling him, now! You stay right there."

"He has played us both! I didn't know you existed. I saw you at the laundromat one day, and he was walking you to the car so fast. He said you were his sister. I drive the car and everything."

"I am calling his ass right now!"

"Hello."

"Sam! I need you home now!"

"What is going on? I am working."

"The condo is on fire! Fred has set the condo on fire!"

"What? I am on my way!"

"He will be here shortly. Why don't you come in and have a seat? Everyone, I would like for you to meet Bianca. She is a friend of Sam."

"Bianca! What are you doing here?" Fred asks.

"I came to give Sam my two-week notice. Wait! Do you live here?"

"Yes! I am Tish's assistant."

"And you work at the laundromat? You are on a role."

"Watch yourself!"

"Oh my stomach is cramping! Sam is on his way home. Bianca has told me an interesting story about she and Sam's relationship."

"Stay calm, Tish! You don't need to stress over anything. Sit here. Why is he on his way?"

"I called his ass. He is going to face both of us tonight!"

"That is not a great idea. You are already cramping."

"It is what it is. He is getting the hell out of my life tonight because we are done for good!"

"Same here! It is too late for me to abort. However, I will be giving this baby up for adoption. Tish, did you know that he sleeps with men? I also found out that he had an exclusive boyfriend for ten years while he was away in prison."

"Ohhh, my stomach! Fred, I need to throw up."

"Ma'am! Don't tell her any more. You are upsetting her!" Fred says with a stern look.

Sam then walks in and sees Bianca. I can tell by the look on his face that he is furious.

"Oh hell! What is going on? Tish, I thought you said the condo was on fire. Bianca! Why haven't you been to work?"

"Really, Sam? I know all about your little escapades. Give me the keys to my car, the condo, and the laundromats; then get all of your shit and get out! We are done!"

"I now know everything too! You don't have anything nor own shit! Our entire relationship has been a lie and I am giving this baby up for adoption. Don't ever contact me again!" Sam then starts to beat on Bianca.

"Bitch, you think you can show up at my house, ruin my life, and walk out the door?!"

I try to stop Sam and accidently get hit in the stomach. I then start screaming, "Stop! Stop it Sam! Fred do something!" Fred then hits Sam a couple of times and he falls to the floor. He appears to be unconscious. I try to sit down and notice blood running down my leg. Fred then grabs me so I wouldn't fall and eases me into a chair. Sensing the severity of the situation, Fred calls 911 for help.

"911, what is your emergency?"

"Oh, Tish baby. Yes! A woman is losing her baby. She is a high-risk pregnancy! Please send an ambulance and hurry! Also, there is an unconscious male and another pregnant female with a bloody nose! We need help fast!"

12

LISA

Carol and I are meeting up to discuss our latest life experiences. She wants to pick me up which is odd. We normally meet at our regular spot, but she said she needs my help. It must be something related to the wedding. I am still on cloud nine from my trip to Charlotte. I accepted Mike's ring, but I am still on the fence about marrying him. I think we should have a two-year engagement. I have to make sure that his abusive nature is under control. If it all works out, I am going to give him some babies and love on his beautiful daughters. Seeing Mike as a father wipes out his abusive tendencies, but I can't forget about it. It is a reality that I have experienced. However, I don't think he will tread down that path with me again.

CAROL

Lisa is waiting for me to pick her up. I need her to stand guard on Donovan while I take those hand cuffs off of him. He has been handcuffed to the bed for about sixteen hours. I know he is furious. He probably wants to beat my ass and kill me. I'm taking Lisa because if he tries anything, she can put some of those Tae Kwon Do moves on his ass. And if that doesn't work, I have my gun. I will shoot him in the foot. I don't think it will come to that, but it is better to be safe than sorry. Now that I have some leverage on him, maybe, just maybe he will back off of trying to hurt Carl. It hurt me to do that to him because deep in my heart, I really love the man. I just cannot be with him. I know that he loves me because his crazy actions show that he does. I just needed to show him that I am just as crazy as he is when I feel backed into a corner.

"Hi Carol! I'm so excited. I get to ride in the Benz. However, I am curious as to what you have going on."

"Enjoy this ride because it is going to be interesting. We have to make a stop before we go to lunch."

"Okay. A stop where?"

"Last night after playing a kinky game of sex with Donovan, I handcuffed him to the bed and left him there all night to teach him a lesson." Lisa then starts laughing uncontrollably.

"Wait! What?! I am confused."

"You know that he has been stalking me and Carl. Before now, I couldn't prove it; but now I can. Girl, this fool cut the brake line on Carl's truck! Luckily, the brakes went out soon after he left the parking garage and not on the highway. He was approaching a stop light when he noticed it; so he was able to pull over to the side and stop."

"Oh hell no! Shut up!"

"Yeah! The mechanic said the brake line had been cut. So, I had to take drastic measures. I handcuffed him to the bed and got him to confess while I recorded it on my phone. What worries me is that he keeps saying that Carl does not deserve me and that I made him do it. So, I told him that I was going to leave him handcuffed to the bed until tomorrow so that he can think about his actions and the things he says. Girl, he was livid!"

"Carol! You are crazy as hell! Lisa says while still laughing. "So, what part do I play in this? The things that we do for each other seem to get crazier and crazier."

"You are going to stand guard while I take the cuffs off. If he makes one wrong move, you are to kick his ass using Tae Kwon Do. And if that doesn't work, I am going to shoot his ass in the foot!"

"You got it all thought out, huh?!"

"Yeah girl. My other option was to call the police and pretend to be a concerned family member. I was going to say that we are worried because

no one has heard from him, and then ask them to do a wellness check. But, I thought that would be embarrassing if his co-workers found him handcuffed to the bed. It would raise many questions."

"So, he is trying to hurt Carl and harass the hell out of you! What's a little embarrassment? You love him! That's the issue. Why don't you just file an internal affairs complaint against him?"

"I don't want him to lose his job. Besides, I will have to disclose a lot of dirty laundry about our affair to total strangers."

"You love him. Admit it! After all that he has done, you are still trying to have mercy on him. And once again, you're trying to handle something on your own!"

"No! I asked you for help this time. We're here. Come on!"

"Do you have a key?"

"Yes! He leaves the spare key under the mat for me." I open the door using the key and he immediately calls my name.

"Carol! That had better be you. My damn bladder hurts and I am hungry! I can't believe you left me incapacitated!" he says while trying to kick at me.

"Wait a minute partner!" says Lisa as she chops him on the knee.

"Ouch!"

"Be still and stay calm. Have you given any consideration to what we discussed?"

"The only thing that I have been focusing on is my bladder and how to keep from pissing on myself! My bladder hurts so damn bad! Please let me use the restroom."

I finally remove the handcuffs. He can barely move as he slowly gets up and makes his way to the bathroom.

"Ahhh, relief!"

"We're out! We have to go!" Lisa and I quickly head for the door.

"I am going to deal with you as soon as I recuperate from this. I still love

you and that will not change!"

"Come on girl!" We both get in the car and slam the doors. We laugh until our stomach hurts and we can barely breathe.

"That fool is not done! I hope you know that."

"I think that will slow him down and make him think twice before acting. I'm sure he now thinks that I am crazy."

"Well, he now knows what I have known for years. There is never a dull moment with you as my bestie!"

"I try! I need that drink now. Let's get wasted!"

"Due to all of the drama you have going on, I haven't had a chance to fill you in on Mike and our trip to Charlotte."

"What happened? Did you meet Shelia? What does she look like?"

"It was a great experience. Shelia is beautiful and really nice. She's is half black and half Puerto Rican. Mike laid down the rules of how he wanted this trio to work. It went rather smoothly."

"Did you all talk about her phone call to you?"

"Mike and I discussed it, and he said that he knows she is just genuinely concerned; but she nor I ever mentioned it. His daughters are so beautiful and adorable. They stole my heart. Meagan and Sydney were so warm and open to me. Sydney even asked me for a hug and I melted like butter. I now want some babies! Mike as a father reminds me so much of my dad."

"That is so beautiful, step mommy! You want babies? "I will finally get to the opportunity to be a Godmother!"

"Can you believe it? If I don't have any, I know those girls will be just like my own. We bonded instantly. We are keeping them the entire summer and I can hardly wait. I am going to take them to the wedding."

"You are in love with them!"

"Yes, I am! Oh, I almost forgot. Look!" Lisa waves her hand in my face and I scream.

"You got engaged?!"

"He proposed. I have not given him a definite answer. I gave him a maybe, and he said that was fine for now. I want a long engagement, like two years."

"Why? Is there something that you are not telling me?"

"Yes! I am not ready to talk about it. We are working through something. Mike is also working on something. I have to know for sure that the situation is controlled before I say yes and marry him."

"I hate it when you do that."

"Do what?"

"Keep information from me. I tell you everything!"

"I tell you everything, too. I have never kept anything from you."

"No. You just wait five years to tell me."

"I promise I will tell you in due time."

"Alright! Thanks for helping me with Donovan."

"No problem. Let me know if you need me to handle him again. He is a piece of work!"

"You know it. He kind of acted like he liked the handcuffs."

"The freak probably did."

"The good thing about today is we did not have to worry about him showing up!"

"You got that right. Let's get out of here. Care to go to the mall?"

"Sure! We have not shopped together in a while. Plus, I need to look for silver jewelry for the wedding party."

"Charming Charlie will probably be your best choice."

"Okay, we can start there." I can say will all honesty that Lisa is my ride or die friend.

LISA

The past few weeks have been quite interesting and adventurous. I became an instant stepmom, a partial fiancé, and acquired a desire to give

birth. Carol then took me on an escapade. It is amazing to see the effects that life experiences and aging can have on an individual. It can alter your entire way of thinking. I feel like I am going through some sort of mid-life crisis. My mind is never at peace, and I am always thinking and imagining things, like my future with Mike.

Well, it's date night again and tonight is Mike's turn to host the party. He said he has something different and special planned. I cannot wait to see what he has up his sleeve. Whatever it is, I know that it will be romantic because he is a very romantic guy. That is another quality I love about my man. He is not afraid to show emotions.

I have not mentioned the proposal to my parents yet. I don't want them getting all excited in the event things don't work out. As soon as my mom finds out, she is going to take over. This will be the wedding she has waited for, so I must mentally prepare myself for that. Dad is not going to spare any expenses. Anything that mom asks for will happen. My opinion will not matter. The smart thing for me to do would be to plan the wedding on my own, and then send them an invite. However, I know that would cause so much chaos, especially since my sister is a wedding planner. I wish I could tell her so that she and I could secretly plan; but Patricia cannot hold water! The only person that I can trust with a secret is Carol. That's why I chose to reveal the proposal to her first.

I am in route to date night. Mike has been very secretive about it, and I am about to explode from anticipation. As long as it includes good sex, I will be overjoyed. As I pull up, I see several cars. I wonder who they belong to. Date night is supposed to be between Mike and me, so what is really going on?

"Come on in baby. I have been waiting on you. You are a little late."

"I'm sorry. I stopped to get more wine so that we don't run out this time. Who does all of those cars belong to? I thought this was date night?"

"It is date night with a twist. Come sit here and relax."

"This better not be any swinger's foolishness!"

"No girl! Sit back and trust me. Those cars belong to models. I have brought New York's fashion week to you. I flew in a bridal boutique owner from New York! She has put together a wedding gown fashion show just for you."

"Oh, but I thought..."

"I know, just trust me."

I am now boiling with anger. I have not agreed to marry him. I said maybe! What makes him think that it is okay for him to have a say in my wedding gown selection? Now I am feeling pressured, and he promised me that he wouldn't. It is bad luck for the groom to know what the gown looks like before the day of the wedding. Besides, it is too soon to look at wedding gowns. I have to say yes to him before I can say yes to the dress. I did not plan on this happening for at least a year and a half. I am going to put on a happy face for now, but he is going to catch my wrath when this bootleg fashion show is over.

"What's wrong, honey? You haven't said much. I really like that one and I think it will look great on you!"

"I am just sitting back and taking it all in."

"Do you like any of the gowns? I know how you love Vera Wang's designs; so I asked the owner to bring as many of those as she could find."

"All of the dresses are beautiful. There are so many to choose from. I am just in awe right now." Honestly, I cannot wait for this torture to end. I probably should feel appreciative since he went through all of this; but I see it as trying to pressure and control me.

"Lisa, that one with the diamond neck line is the winner!"

"Umm, I don't know. Do you expect a decision today? I am not mentally ready to decide on a dress."

"Okay then. I will have her place the dresses on hold until you can decide."

"Thanks!"

"My smile has changed to a frown of frustration. I dare not be rude to the models or the store owner, for they are innocent in this little charade. I thank her for the hard work and inform her that I will follow-up as soon as possible. As an alternative, she kindly offers to leave the dresses. Once I make a decision, I can then ship the remaining gowns back to her. I agree to oblige against my better judgment. Now that the coast is clear, I can let Mr. Hampton know how I truly feel.

"Mike! You are breaking all of the traditions that I like and believe in. The groom is not allowed to see the dress until the wedding day!"

"I don't believe in all that superstitious stuff."

"Well, I do! Besides, I have not said yes to you; so what makes you think that I am ready to say yes to a dress?"

"Why are you so rattled? Many women would be excited that their man had the means to bring a top designer show to them, in addition to writing the check and sparing no expense!"

"Mike, you are missing the point! Shopping for a wedding gown is something that women do with their mothers or their girlfriends."

"Is that all? Well next time, I will invite them to help you make a decision. Excuse me for going all out to make my woman happy and be supportive through this process. I was trying to do what makes you happy!"

"How do you know what makes me happy? Did you ask me? Hell no! You did not! This is just you being controlling and using this as a tactic to pressure me into saying yes!"

"What did you just say?"

"You and your controlling ways have to stop!" That statement must have hit a nerve because he forcefully grabbed my arm and it hurts. I am trying not to kick his ass again.

"I am not trying to control you or pressure you! I am trying to be the man in this relationship!"

"I suggest you let me go before I put your other knee out of commission!" He clutches my wrists tightly as he lifts me off of the floor.

"Girl! You better learn how to talk to me without disrespecting me!"

"Mike! You are hurting me!"

"Good! Now you know that I mean business!" He lets me go and I feel my anger getting the best of me, and I can't control it. Without any further thought, I drop kick him.

"Now, you know that I mean business!"

"Ohhhhh! Are you crazy?"

"Hell yeah, I am crazy! Get up! Come on and get some more!"

"I don't want to fight with you! I am done with this. I am leaving so that I can cool off. I will be back later!"

"Yeah, you do that! That is the best idea you've had in a while." Date night turned out to be a total disaster and a waste of my time. Mike is going to get the picture one way or another.

CAROL

It has been two weeks and there has been no contact with Donovan, except for a text saying "I forgive you, I love you, I miss you, can I see you?" I responded with "I'm sorry, I love you too, Miss you, Not for a while." Maybe I put a little fear into him. That was my intention. I just wanted to get his attention. I want him to grasp his mind around the fact that we cannot be together. I love him, but I love Carl more. When Carl proposed, Carol and Donovan became null and void. I really regret that we crossed the lines. I always pictured Donovan as my go to guy for life.

Carl and I leave for Delaware in the morning. We are moving forward with our plans to move, as well as with the wedding. Time is winding down. We have a little over two and a half months left to complete everything. I hope that our trip to Delaware is successful. Finding housing can be a tedious process. I want to put a contract on a house so that I can feel like

something is being accomplished. It seems like I have many projects in the works, but nothing is being completed. I need this transition to be as smooth as possible. Carl seems to be just as excited as I am because he has told everyone. I have yet to reveal to Lisa that we will be moving. I guess I will break the news to her at the next girl's night.

Donovan has been texting and calling me all day. I spoke too soon! He wants to see me, but seeing him is not an agenda item, especially since I pulled that little stunt. He may try to beat my ass or handcuff me to keep me from Carl. I have to be smart from here on out when it comes to dealing with him. We are in route to Delaware. However, I may make plans to see him when I return. I really do miss the things that he does to me; but I need to be strong. If I can go two weeks with no Donovan, I can continue.

We have arrived in Dover. DuPont has laid out the red carpet for us. The real estate agent has four properties for us to view. Our dilemma will be whether or not to choose a huge house with a yard, or a condo that does not require yard maintenance. Carl believes in the big house so that our children will always have a comfortable home to return to. My motto is to have an extra room for them, but I don't want them to become too comfortable. I don't think we need a big house because it's just the two of us. I am going to try and follow his lead; or at least allow him to believe that he is leading.

All of the communities are fairly new, and all of the properties we saw are new. I like being the first to live in a home. That means that the house has no history. I think we will like it here. I know that Carl is going to love it. It is a very calm, settled, peaceful place. It is perfect for retirement.

"Carol, I want to put a contract on the house with the pool."

"I like that one, also. However I don't think we need that much house. I am thinking long term. The condo at the Paddock has just as much space and bedrooms as the house. It has a pool as well. And being that it is a community pool, there will be no pool maintenance or yard work. You are

not getting any younger and you know that I am not going to do it.”

“Your point is taken. However, I am thinking about holiday celebrations with our families and parking. Eventually, our family will extend with grandchildren and in-laws.”

“The paddock has a state of the art pool and club house that is available to us at our leisure.”

“I respect your opinion, but that house is my dream house. The house payment is my bill, therefore I am making an executive decision as CFO of this family.”

“Can we take a few days and think on it?”

“No! If we snooze, we will lose.”

“Make sure that you include a maid in the budget. I am a career woman not a housewife.”

“I will consider bringing in one a couple of days a week.”

“Well, I guess it is settled. We have found our new home.”

We accomplished our goal. Finding a new home was our main objective, now we are headed back home to work on completing all of the other unfinished business. We still have to sell our house and finish planning for the wedding.

“What in the hell?”

“Oh my God! “What in the world?”

We arrive home to find that someone has toilet papered Carl’s Tahoe, and vandalized it with spray paint leaving a message that says “Cheating bitch” on both sides.

“Who have you been screwing around with?” I ask.

“No one!” he says.

“Someone is pissed at you! Whomever it is knew that we were out of town! You are slipping! You allowed your bitch to find out where you live!”

“I am not cheating! This must be your crazy ass boy toy, Donovan!”

“Wrong answer. I have not communicated with him in ages, and he is

not my boy toy. We were only co-workers. It's probably the heifer who sent the letter to the house a few months ago!"

"Whoever it is apparently wants to divide and conquer us. We need to unite and find out who is trying to break up our happy home."

"I'm not stupid. This is the work of a female and you know it, Donovan!"

"Who did you just call me?"

"Carl!"

"No! You called me Donovan. Apparently, he is on your mind. He probably did this!"

"Don't you dare try to turn this around on me! This has female written all over it."

"I'm calling the police. We will deal with who did it later."

"Yeah do that! In the meantime, you will not be living here. I feel violated in my own home due to your infidelities."

"I am not going anywhere! I will sleep in another bedroom, but I am not leaving! That is exactly what the perpetrator wants! I just put a contract on a half a million dollar home, so we are glued together for life!"

"Well, I will leave!"

"Like hell you will! We are living together, mad as hell and all!"

"Ugh! Old ass!"

It seems like for every step we take forward, we end up moving five steps backwards. I know that Donovan is capable of doing this; however, he didn't know we were out of town. Besides, he knows that I mean business when it comes to Carl. I go through all of that to protect Carl, and now he's had some floozy vandalize his vehicle. I can't leave but I can get away for a few hours. Donovan has been begging to see me and I need the comfort of his arms right about now.

TISH

My life has been turned upside down. Reality has hit me in the face. A man that I loved, stood by, and held down does not give a damn about me.

He only cared about the material things that I was able to provide for him. I have loved this man my entire adult life. He is the only man that I had sex with. For eighteen year, I have saved myself only for him. Yet, he has betrayed me in so many ways. He has impregnated and been supporting another woman, all while treating me like dirt and demanding that I get an abortion. Our child is no longer an issue now. All of the stress from last night caused me to miscarry. I am devastated! My little bundle of joy is gone and so is Sam. Sam got arrested for assaulting his pregnant girlfriend, which led to a parole violation. He is out of my life for good! I will not be his support system this time around. All of this went down in the presence of my mom and my family, so I couldn't take him back even if I wanted to.

FRED

I have finally made it to the hospital and my worst fear is confirmed. Damn! Tish lost the baby. I feel so sorry for her. However, I am not sorry that she found out about Sam's little secrets. He is now out of our lives for good. I am going to testify to make sure that he never returns. I will be Tish's shoulder and support, and I will nurture her back and make her a happy woman for a change. I am going to be her king and she will be my queen. Maybe she and I will have a couple of babies. And if we don't have any together, maybe we will adopt. It is going to take some time before she trusts another man. Shoot! It may take a lot of time for her to reciprocate romantic feelings for me. One thing that is for certain, I have nothing but time. Time will be my best ally.

It felt really good to knock the hell out of Sam. He tried to press charges against me, but it did not stick. The police saw the incident as a man defending women against an abusive man. I warned him that his demise was near, but he refused to listen. With him gone, I can focus all of my attention on Tish, her health, and her well-being.

"Fred, I am really going to need your help now."

"I'm here! Just let me know whatever you need."

"I will need you to take over managing the laundromats. Be sure to hire adequate staff. The business is doing well, so I want that to continue."

"Sure, no problem. What about you? You are going to need help while you heal."

"My mom is going to stay with us for three weeks to help us transition into a normal routine. She will be with me during the day, and you will be here during the night. I just need all of the love and support that I can get right now."

"I promise that I will not disappoint you."

"I know you won't! You have proved to be a good, hard-working man; and I appreciate you!"

"I am so sorry about everything! I tried to keep you calm."

"I know, Fred. You did everything you were supposed to do. You did nothing wrong."

"I feel partially responsible. If I had not insisted on that cookout, then maybe none of this would have happened."

"No Fred! You have to know that you did nothing wrong! Unfortunately, this was inevitable. Sam created a web that entangled us all and caused us all to pay a high price, especially me!"

"Sam's existence is no longer a concern. It will take some time, but you will get over him."

"He is all I've ever known!"

"Well my friend, you have been missing out! There is a whole world out there that you have yet to experience. There are still some good men around that will love you unconditionally."

"Maybe. I just may become a nun." We both laugh.

"You are going to be just fine. No need to worry. Fred is here!"

"Thank you for all that you do."

We hear a knock on Tish's hospital room door. As we both turn to look,

Bianca peeks her head in and asks if she can come in.

"Tish, are you okay with her being here?"

"Yes. She is a victim as well."

"I just wanted to check on you. How are you in spite of everything?"

"I'm here. That's all I can say. How are you and the baby?"

"We are okay, as well as can be expected. Thank you, Fred, for defending me."

"No problem. That is what a real man does."

"Tish, I need to ask you something. I have decided to give this baby up for adoption. I am sorry for you loss. You lost a lot on last evening. I know that you don't really know me, and I know you loved Sam. Would you consider adopting this baby? It is the one good thing that Sam did. However, I just cannot raise another child alone. I feel like you would give this baby a good loving home."

"Oh my! I don't know, Bianca. Too much is going on right now."

"I know this is a lot to throw at you. You don't have to give me an answer right away. Just give the idea some consideration if you don't mind. I will leave my information with Fred so that you can contact me when you make a decision. Take care and I hope to see you later."

"Fred, I am speechless! I was not expecting that. I have so much going on in my head. My life as I knew it is no longer, and it is depressing. I lost my baby, but God has presented me with the opportunity to be a blessing to another. I don't know what to do. Sam has been a part of my life for half of my life. I can't just shut my feelings off like water. If I decide to become the mother of that baby, I will always have a piece of him. I will consider it. But before I make any decisions, I have to get myself together."

"Fred, will you make sure that the baby furniture Sam bought is gone by the time my hospital stay is over?"

"Sure. I will return the room to its original state."

"Thank you."

"Keep your head up. Everything is going to be fine."

I will be damned if I allow Tish to raise that bastard child that Sam created with that hood rat. Tish is emotionally unstable and is not thinking clearly. The fact that she is considering it shows that she is not well. Bianca is running a game and I will not allow it! I think I will call Tish's besties. She really needs them. I will be there no matter what, but I think she will need more than I can give. Maybe now that Sam is out of the picture, they will be willing to give here another chance. I recall Tish saying that Lisa was more forgiving than Carol. I will contact Lisa first and see how it goes.

TISH

Sam has been trying to call me, but I will not accept his calls. He even tried getting his mother to call me with a sad story about needing to hire an attorney. I am still in the hospital grieving the loss of a child, and the only thing Sam can think about is his self. I responded to her nicely by saying that "Sam and I are no longer together, and I am no longer his financial or emotional support. Please do not contact me again on his behalf". It felt good to say that to her. The nurse said that I should get out of bed and take a walk. A walk may make me feel better. The truth is I do not want to get out of bed. All I want to do is sleep. Nothing will make me feel better. I do not want to feel better. I just want to be left the hell alone. Is that too much to ask?

13

LISA

I received the most disturbing call regarding Tish from some gentleman by the name of Fred. The poor girl has been going through and she has slipped into depression. She was admitted to Lakeside which is a mental hospital. I am going to meet Carol shortly to discuss us possibly putting our differences aside to show our support for her. I cannot imagine the pain that she is feeling. We all are going through something with these men in our lives. I just don't know what will become of my relationship with Mike. It gets rocky, and then it smoothes out again. No relationship is perfect and I know that a healthy relationship requires work. I am willing to put in the work. I honestly think Mike and I need professional help. We talked about it earlier in our relationship, but never followed through. I am going to suggest, and demand if I have to, that we seek counseling. If counseling does not help us, then I will know that we are not meant to be.

CAROL

I have managed to stay away from Donovan. I was so tempted to reach out to him after we returned from Delaware. He has been turning up the pressure to see me, but I have been resisting. I have not physically been with him since the handcuff situation. We have only communicated via phone. I am still pissed at Carl about the floozy that vandalized his car. He swears that he is not cheating and has no idea who may have done it, other than Donovan. But I don't think he's responsible. Vandalism is the work of a female. I know from self-experience. I vandalized a few vehicles when I was younger. Whoever she is, she must be young. Maybe some little young thing paid him some attention during his mid-life crisis. He probably

refused to give her something that she asked for. He does not have money for anyone because I account for every penny. If he's cheating, he's damn sure not neglecting home!

"Smooches. How are you?"

"Mad as hell! But we will talk about that later. What about you?"

"I am an emotional wreck, and I really don't know where to start."

"Maybe by the time we get wasted, nothing else will matter."

"If only life and relationships were that simple. I need to tell you something. Please hear me out before you respond!"

"Okay. It sounds serious."

"I received a disturbing call from a gentleman by the name of Fred regarding Tish."

"Who is Fred?"

"He said that he was her assistant."

"Assistant? What is going on?"

"He said that Tish tried to commit suicide by cutting her wrists."

"Oh my God! Why would she do that? I am willing to bet that damn Sam is behind it!"

"Yep! He has a lot to do with it. Apparently, Tish found out about the other woman and the baby. Also, Tish's pregnancy was high-risk."

"What do you mean was? Did she lose her baby?"

"Yes! The stress of Sam and his antics were too much. Also, she found out that Sam has been sleeping with men."

"That's why I never liked him! He brought too much baggage and unnecessary drama."

"Well, Tish and Bianca confronted Sam; and he in turn attacked Bianca. Now he has gone back to lock up for violating his parole."

"Poor girl! After all she's done for him over the years. He is trifling for coming home and treating her like that."

"Lisa, I know you can't stand her now. Hell, neither can I! But I was

wondering whether or not we can put our differences aside to support her. She is going through pure hell."

"Yes! I can do that. I don't have to trust her to be there for her."

"Oh good! Let's go see her when we leave here."

"Okay! We can do that. Now, I have to tell you something important and my reason for being upset with Carl."

"I am listening."

"Carl and I are moving out of state immediately after the wedding."

"Noooo! Carol you can't leave me! What will I do? When did you two decide this?"

"I have to do something to get away from Donovan. Carl had been talking about working in the corporate office for the next few years until retirement. I am desperate and it seemed like the golden opportunity."

"That is a stupid plan! That fool is going to find you! The only way to deal with him is head on; face to face." Running away is no solid solution. What about the other tactic?"

"So far it has worked. Carl and I need this new beginning. I have to free myself from Donovan. He is like an addictive drug. I have to remove myself from him permanently."

"Do you hear yourself? You are willing to allow him to push you away from your life, your family, and your friends?"

"Calm down! Look at it this way; you will have somewhere to visit."

"I do not want to visit! I want you here for margarita nights!"

"I will be a text, phone call, Google talk, Facebook message, and a tweet away. Nothing will change. We can make margaritas in the kitchen and skype while we sip."

"So you just got it all figured out." Lisa says as she breaks into tears.

"Yes. It will work out. Oh, I forgot! I will also be a plane ride, train ride, and a drive away if you need me." That makes Lisa laugh.

"So where are you moving to?"

"Dover, Delaware. We put a contract on a home a couple of weeks ago. I wanted to tell you sooner, but I just couldn't bring myself to it."

"I hate Donovan's ass! I may kick his ass my damn self if we ever cross paths again. I still do not think that moving away is the answer. A damn fool will find a way!"

"This feels right! Now, let me tell you about Carl. When we returned from Delaware, someone had toilet papered his Tahoe and spray painted "cheating bitch" on it."

"Are you serious?"

"Very! I told him that I felt violated and that he was slipping. He tried to flip the situation on me by saying that Donovan did it, but that is the work of a female."

"Carol! He may have a point. Donovan is a piece of work."

"I had no contact with Donovan prior to us leaving for Delaware. He didn't know that we were gone."

"Donovan is the police!" He knows your every move, even when you think he doesn't. He manages to show up every time you and I have drinks. He is probably outside lurking as we speak."

"No way! That work has female stamped on it! I will never believe that it was Donovan."

"I bet if you handcuff him again, you will find out it was him."

"Nope! Carl's floozy."

"Okay! It will come out; and when it does, I am going to say we, as in Carl and I, told you so!"

"Whatever!" What is going on with you and Mike?"

"Don't try and change the subject. You are avoiding the issue."

"If he comes to Delaware, I will know just how crazy he is, and I will be the left with no choice but to go to Internal Affairs. I am really trying not to jeopardize his job."

"He is trying to jeopardize your relationship!"

"Enough about me. How are things with Mike?"

"Crazy as hell! You know that he proposed and I said maybe, right?"

"Yes."

"Well on date night, he brought in a boutique owner and some models from New York for a private wedding gown fashion show just for me. He said he wanted to bring New York Fashion Week to me."

"Ma'am! What is the problem?"

"That stunt was about his controlling ways and him putting pressure on me to say yes."

"Do you think that you may be overreacting?"

"No!" The dresses were all by Vera Wang. This is just one of many controlling things that he has done. I will not be pressured by a man. Before, I say yes, we are going to counseling."

"Wow! That bad, huh?!"

"It has potential to be."

"Before you say yes or invest a lot of time in the relationship, make sure that he is worth it."

"I am! I am going to demand that we seek counseling."

"That is a great idea."

"Come on so that we can drop in on Tish and pray for her. Be nice!"

"I will try my best to be good. I will do the best that I can."

I don't care for Tish's ways, but I have known her since the age of five. I would not wish what has happened to her on my worst enemy. I am going to support her through her trials, but I will never trust her or hang out with her again.

LISA

It was really hard for me to see Tish in such a sad place. I am going to continue to pray that she pulls through. Her relationship with Sam has almost ruined her. That is why I am going to move slowly with Mike. My

life and the things in it are changing. One of my besties is moving away to get away from a man. The other has allowed a man to cause her to lose control of her mind. I have a man who loves me, but he wants to control every aspect of my existence. Carol is in a bad situation with one man, but she is in the best situation with the other. Carl loves her no matter what she does. He loves her unconditionally and gives her whatever her heart desires, with no strings attached.

I have not spoken to Mike much since the fashion show. Every time we attempt to talk about it, the conversation leads to an argument. He does not get my point. In my opinion, he does not have a point. The only thing that we can both agree on is talking to a professional. We are scheduled to see a therapist today. He wants to ignore the situation and pretend like everything is fine. He wants to paint a pretty picture for his parents and the girls, and expects me to go along with it. That is not happening. He told his parents that we are engaged, when the truth is that I have not said yes. I said maybe. The girls will be coming to stay for the summer, and that is going to complicate things more. Before they arrive, we need to have ourselves together. I hope this therapist is worth the money.

"Hi love."

"Hello dear."

"I've missed you. I am so glad to see you!"

"I kind of missed you, too."

"Lisa and Mike! I am Dr. Anderson. You both can step into my office now, I am ready for you. How are you both doing, today?"

"As individuals, we are fine. As a couple, were are not."

"I don't think anything is wrong. Lisa has a tendency to overreact."

"Well, maybe we will get to the bottom of your issues. I always inform my clients up front that issues will not be fixed in one session. Both parties must be willing to be honest and do the work. The most important and most essential part of therapy is being able to look at the man in the mirror and

take responsibility for the man in the mirror. If you both take that piece of advice, your relationship will mend together and be healthy. Lisa, let's begin with you. What are your concerns?"

"Mike has a controlling nature. He wants to control every aspect of my life and this relationship, from the clothes that I wear to how I have sex."

"Can you elaborate?"

"Yes! Once when we were having sex, I grabbed his penis. When we were done, he told me to never do that again. If I cannot touch the penis when I am in the mood, then that is a major problem. The latest thing is he proposed to me. I said maybe, not yes. He takes it upon himself to bring models in for a fashion show of wedding gowns. Wedding gown shopping is something that women do with their mothers and girlfriends. It was a nice gesture; however, it was one of many things he does that I consider to be controlling."

"Mike! I want you to respond before I interject."

"I will admit that I do have a controlling nature. I am in therapy for it. I am a work in progress. However, I don't see anything wrong with doing something nice and going all out for the woman that I love. As for the sex thing, I like to take my time and please my woman from head to toe. I do not like to be rushed. The incident that she is referring to, she rushed me."

"You two are having what we call a power struggle. Mike you have the cave man syndrome; and Lisa, you have the strong woman attitude. Lisa, in later sessions, my goal for you is for you to learn how to allow a man to lead, but at the same time be a strong woman that is not defined by a man. Mike, my goal for you is to get rid of those cave man ideas, such as I am the man and what I say is the law. There is hope for the two of you. Like I said in the beginning, you both must be willing to do the work. Are you guys willing to do the work?"

"Yes! I love her with all of my heart. I want her to be my wife and I want to spend the rest of my life with her."

"That is why I am here. I love him and I really want this relationship to work. He has some great qualities, but the cave man in him always seem to take over."

"I have homework for the two of you. Your assignment is for the two of you to give each other an awareness check. Lisa, whenever Mike does something that you think is controlling, you need to let him know at that moment. Mike, you must be willing to accept the awareness check and work on correcting the behavior. Mike, when Lisa does something that makes you feel like she is not allowing you to be a man, let her know at that moment. Lisa, you must be willing to accept your awareness check and work on correcting the behavior. Here is a journal for the two of you. You are to write down the behavior that you want the other to change. This will give you an idea of how many times you gave an awareness check. Bring your journals to the next session and we will discuss it. Do either of you have any questions?"

"No!"

"None!"

"Well, we will close this session. I will see you in a couple of weeks."

"Mike, how do you feel about our sessions with the therapist?"

"Inspired! I think this will really help us take a look at ourselves."

"So do I. I will just have to keep calm when you call me out."

"Same here; and no karate shit from you."

"What does that supposed to mean?"

"If you do not like what I say, you may put some of those karate moves on me. Those moves encourage me to attend my sessions every week. Hell, I am afraid not to attend."

"You play too much!"

"Hell! I am not playing. I still have a limp and knee pain. I love you but you are something serious. Come on let's go have a romantic dinner and some mind blowing sex."

"I like the sound of that!"

"Oh yeah, the first step to correcting my behavior is to let you grab the dick and do whatever your heart, mind, hand and mouth desire."

"You will not be sorry!"

CAROL

Carl has been walking around here like he is so innocent. I know his floozy is the one who trashed his truck. Being the woman of grace that I am, I am going to leave the issue alone. If she wants to continue to play second fiddle, then she can be my guest. He just bought me a Benz a few months ago and signed for a half a million dollar house, in addition to moving and wedding costs. I don't know what she is getting out of the deal; but for her sake, I hope it's worth it. Speaking of the wedding, Carl and I have an appointment with a baker regarding our cakes. He does not want to be a part of any of the other planning. However, I demanded that he at least choose the groom's cake. I already know that he wants a Dallas Cowboys cake, but he needs to be responsible for his own details such as the design and the flavor.

Tish has allowed Sam to send her over the coo-coo's nest. I knew that would eventually happen. I cannot stand her, but I hate to see a strong, educated sister allowing a man to drive her insane. I hope and pray that this Fred character truly has her best interest at heart. He seems genuine and concerned about her and her well-being. My only question is where in the hell did he come from? Lisa and I have made a pact to visit her at least once a week until she is better.

A couple has placed a contract on our home. I am in the process of trying to decipher between what I will keep and what I will throw away. There are a lot of memories in this house and fifteen years of everything. This is going to be a task for me because I have a hard time letting go of stuff. Everything in this house is precious, important, and valuable to me.

Soon, one of my children will be returning from college and one will be graduating. Maybe they will help me with all of this. My daughter suggested a yard sale, but I'm not sold on the idea. Carl has made it clear that he wants all new furniture for the new house, and I totally agree. I hate packing!

It has been two months and I have avoided physical contact with Donovan. I know he is growing impatient because I saw him ride by my house on yesterday. He has given me until the end of the week to set up a date with him or else. I am not sure what the "or else" means, and I don't want to find out. I have been praying and believing that God will remove Donovan out of my system and remove me out of his. My feelings for him are not as strong as before; although I would be lying if I said that I still do not desire him. I am trying to stay focused on my future with Carl, which is where I belong. My thoughts are interrupted by knocking and ringing of the doorbell. I answer the door and I see a face that should not be here under any circumstances.

"Hello beautiful!"

"What in the hell do you think you are doing? "How dare you show up at my door!"

"How dare you avoid seeing me! I have been watching you. I see you have been busy choosing wedding cakes and shit!"

"You have to go, now! You cannot be here. I just got home from work and Carl will be here shortly."

"Well, you may have a problem. Are you going to invite me in?"

"Like hell! Are you stoned out of your mind?"

"Hell yes! Nobody will know I am here. I parked around the corner and down the street. I am that in love with you, but you have been taking my love for granted. I will no longer be your secret. So, can I come in?"

"Only for a second, and then you have to go. What do you want from me?"

"That is interesting. Now that I am here in your house, you suddenly

care about what I want!"

"I have always cared about what you want, but you got to go! I will do whatever you want. I will meet you at your house later. I can be there around eight."

"That's fine; but you owe me, and you are going to pay up now!"

He grabs me and holds me tight, then kisses me. I try to pull away, but he pulls harder and begins to kiss me on my neck. "Donovan! No! No! Oh! Ohhhh."

"I know you want it!"

"I do, but not here. That's not a good idea."

"It's a shame that you have driven me to this." He picks me up and carries me to my bedroom.

"No! Put me down! You have to go! We cannot do this here. I swear, I will yell rape. I will go to IAB before you can say I!"

"I want you and I am going to have you, here and now!"

"Let me up, Donovan! I mean it! Let me go right now!" Suddenly I hear the garage door opening.

"Your honey is home! You got lucky! I am leaving, but you better be at my house at eight!"

"Go! Here go out this door! I will be there."

"You better not be a minute late."

I rush to fix my clothes and the bed.

"Carol! Carol! Where are you?"

"In the bedroom, honey. I'm lying down."

"Did I hear a male voice?"

"What? A male voice? No! That is the TV."

"Why is the patio door unlocked? I have told you about leaving that door unlocked over and over. What were you doing? I thought you were lying down?"

"I opened it to get some fresh air on this beautiful spring day while I was

lying down. After I got sleepy, I closed the door and just forgot to lock it."

"That is dangerous! Please stop doing that! This neighborhood is not what it once was."

"I know. You are right. It will not happen again."

"Give your man some cuddle time."

"Sure! Come on."

"Let's grab a dinner and a movie later."

"That would be lovely, but I have a committee meeting at eight."

"Oh. Can you skip it this time?"

"I wish I could, but we are planning our final event for the year, and you know that I am the chairperson."

"Well, let me give you something to think about at your meeting."

"Come on daddy."

Whew! That was close! I am going to do something bad to Donovan if he keeps playing with me. Carl was very frisky, and now I have to please Donovan. After tonight, Donovan and I will be done. I am going to get this last piece, and then on tomorrow, I am going to visit IAB. That is the only way that I can stop him from his antics.

As I arrive at Donovan's house, I begin to feel nervous, angry, disrespected, and a little love for him all at the same damn time. I am nervous because I don't know what to expect. I feel like he ultimately disrespected me by showing up at my house. I am angry because he continuously tries to jeopardize my relationship with Carl for his own gain. In spite of all of that, the love I have for him is what allows me to always forgive him.

"Why are you sitting here in the car?"

"I still have ten minutes before I am considered late."

"Ha! That's sarcastic. Come on in."

"I'll be there in a minute."

"Wow! You are acting funny. Are you angry with me?"

"You show up at my house and try to force me to have sex with you in the bed that I share with another man; not to mention that you almost got us caught. How in the hell do I supposed to feel?"

"If you would have made time for me, I would not have stooped to such measures."

"So you are going to rationalize it and not take responsibility for your actions? I am beginning to think that you are not the man I thought you were!"

"What kind of a man is that?"

"A man who knows his role as the other man. "You are acting like a little bitch!"

"I'm sorry that you feel that way, but I am not going to apologize for loving you!

"You really do not get it! Just move so I can get this over with." I exit the car and slam the door. I walk as fast as I can toward the house. Donovan runs behind me and grabs my hand.

"Hey!" I pull away and he grabs me again.

"Hey! Come on baby, calm down! Don't be angry with me." He tries to kiss me on the mouth, but I give him my cheek.

"I am not in the mood."

"I'll take care of that! I don't like it when you act this way."

"I am confused as to how you expect me to act!"

"Just come on in, relax and allow me to take care of you like I always do."

"It seems like you are trying to hurt me these days."

"I am insulted! I would never try to hurt you! I love you! I just cannot stand you being with him. I can give you everything that he can and more. I have been trying to show you, but you keep ignoring the facts."

"Donovan! All of that may be true; but here are the cold hard facts. I was with Carl when we got started with this fling. It is a fling that led to us

having feelings, then to falling in love. I never lied to you. I have always been honest with you about everything. I share everything with you regarding my relationship with him. We started this relationship because we were attracted to each other, and because I was ready to get married, but Carl wasn't. Now all of that has changed. You knew that there was always that possibility!"

"True. However, I do not have to accept it!"

"You know what? I am done talking. Let's get this over with!"

"Now you are talking. "Let's get busy!"

What can I say? Obviously, nothing! I guess I am going to continue screwing him until my wedding day.   What the hell? It is mind blowing and He knows how to touch all of the right places. Who am I fooling? I like what he does to me and how he makes me feel. I have two months and counting.

14

TISH

This therapy thing has been good for me. For the first time in my life, I am figuring out my worth and who I really am. I am focusing solely on me and my well-being, and taking charge of my life. I had no idea how lost I was. I was so lost in Sam. I made him my world without any regard for myself. I no longer like the old Tish who defined herself by a man. I have a new attitude; but I still have a lot of work to do. The therapist said that I am progressing well and that I may soon be released; but not until he feels that I am ready.

My mom said everything at home is fine. She is handling my finances and personal business. Fred is managing the businesses, which is still going well according to him. The financial reports sent over by the accountant shows that business is booming. I must admit that Sam's idea for the laundromats was brilliant. Too bad he will not experience the fruits of his labor. During my meltdown, I realized that Sam really did not know any better, so I forgive him. Forgiveness is the beginning of the healing process. If I hold on to all of the hatred I felt when my world began to crumble, then all of this therapy will be a waste of time.

I now realize that Carol and Lisa are the best friends in the world. I could not ask for any better, more supportive friends. After all of the malicious stunts and verbal abuse that I subjected them to, they are still there for me. They take time out of their busy schedules to visit me every Saturday. Also, they help my mom out whenever she needs it. I have a great support system from two bold, gracious ladies.

One of my assignments is to write Sam a letter. Funny! I have a lot

to say! There is not enough paper to hold all of the words that I have for him. However, my letter is going to be short and sweet. I will not allow him the satisfaction of believing that he still has power and control over my thoughts. I just want him to know that I do forgive him. I have to write Bianca a letter as well. I actually feel sorry for her, but not enough to adopt Sam's bastard child. How dare she ask me to make such a sacrifice? Fool is not stamped on my forehead. God is going to bless me with an awesome gentleman who will love me and treat me like the queen that I am. God is also going to give me another chance at motherhood; and this time, I will be in the right situation with a good man. God is turning things around just for me. Part of my getting better includes believing in God and knowing that He is the center of my life and my joy. Without God, there is no joy or happiness. Another thing I realized is that if God does not want you to have something, then you will not receive it, no matter how hard you pray about it. God has a plan for everyone's life and his plan surpasses any plans that we may have or want.

Fred has been the best thing that has happened to me in a long time. He has been absolutely awesome! He visits me every day and he sends me little gifts along with daily inspirational quotes. He stepped in just when I needed him. I look forward to his daily visits. My therapy sessions made me realize that my relationship with Fred began due to my dysfunctional relationship with Sam. I was so desperate for attention from a man that I moved a stranger into my home. God had to be looking out for me; and so far, he has been great. He is a very good friend, but I will never have any romantic feelings for him. I am not going to make the mistake of jumping into a relationship with anyone else until I am ready to handle it, and until I have a sign from God. My mother said to pray and ask God for the kind of man that I want, and then wait patiently for him. I am going to do just that!

"Oh! Hi, Fred. I didn't hear you come in."

"You look like you were in deep thought."

"I was. I was reflecting back over my life and evaluating the changes I need to make."

"I hope those changes will still include me and allow me to remain a part of your life."

"I don't know what part you will play yet, but I know you will play an intricate role."

"I'm glad to hear that! I am going to take good care of you."

"I know you will. You are a good person."

"I took it upon myself to change your phone number so that Sam cannot contact you. I hope that was okay. I also texted everyone in your phone list to inform them of the change."

"Thank you for that! But wait, Sam's mom and sister were in my contacts. If you texted them, he will still get the number."

"I actually deleted them."

"Mr. Thoughtful. I should have known you were on top of things."

"I try! That's who I am!"

"You know I have done a lot of soul searching, and I realized that I have not been a very pleasant person. Sam was the cause of all of that."

"He is no longer a factor! Try not to allow him to enter your thoughts. Twenty years is a long time, but you are strong. You can do it."

"Pieces of him disappear from my mind and heart daily."

"Good! That is proof that you are healing; and you will soon be able to start living your new life."

"It will be a new life, indeed! I know it is going to be challenging trying to reinvent myself, but I accept the challenge. I want to thank you for reaching out to Carol and Lisa. They have been great to me, and they visit me every Saturday."

"I knew you needed them in your life now more than ever."

"Indeed I do! Mr. Thoughtful strikes again! So, how is the new staff working out?"

"Everything is going smoothly. I used a personnel firm which was the best decision."

"Great! Looks like you have it all under control."

"So far, everything is good. Occasionally, your mom drops in to check up on me."

"That is my mom. She means no harm."

"No harm taken dear. I know she means well, and I actually like having her around."

"If she gets on your nerves, just let me know and I will talk to her."

"No problem. I have to get back to work. I just needed to see that beautiful face of yours."

"Thank you. I love your visits. See you on tomorrow!"

"Okay, see ya!"

He sure knows how to make a girl feel special. I think I am beginning to develop a strong like for him.

LISA

Mike and I have been making great strides in our relationship. We owe it all to therapy. Mike is slowly getting a grip on his controlling ways, and I am learning to own my faults as well. We are happy! I no longer feel as though I have to walk on egg shells. I think that by the time that we complete therapy, I will be able to give him a definite answer to his proposal. Next month, Meagan and Sydney will be here for their summer vacation, and I am looking forward to spending time with them.

Carol and I will be meeting to make some final plans for the wedding, as well as for the bridal shower and bachelorette party. I am going to miss my friend when she moves away. I know she is doing what she feels is best for her family, although I totally disagree with her approach. But who am I to question her decisions. I cry at the thought of her moving so far away. Maybe if this thing with Mike works out, I can convince him to move

back to Charlotte. That will put me a little closer to Carol.

"Smooches, my friend. I'm here! How are you?"

"I'm excited for you and mad at you at the same time. I'm excited to be a part of this important event in your life. However, I am mad that you are allowing Donovan to run you out of town."

"Oh honey! You are going to make me cry. Speaking of Donovan, I have to tell you about his latest stunt. I am sick and tired of his antics!"

"What now?"

"I will tell you when Patricia leaves. She will be joining us as well."

"Oh, okay. So, how are you feeling? Are you the least bit nervous as the date gets closer?"

"Yes, I am! The truth is I am nervous about everything; the wedding, the move, and becoming a new wife. I know it sounds crazy. Shoot! I have been acting as his wife for fifteen years. I have only waited my entire life for this! I am sad that my mother did not live to see this day; but I know she is watching and will have a front row seat from heaven."

"Aww! I'm sure she would be proud that you and Carl are finally going to be official. But I also know that she would want to beat you about Donovan."

"I am going to drink and totally agree with you on that. However, momma was no angel herself before she transitioned."

"There's Patricia. Hey, over here!"

"Hi ladies!"

"Big sis, you are losing weight and looking good!"

"Thank you, hon. I'm trying."

"Well, your hard work is paying off. You look fabulous!"

"Let's get busy. I have another meeting after this. Carol, you and I will need to arrive in Niagara Falls seven days prior to the wedding date."

"Why so early?"

"So that we both can be assured that everything is in order and arriving

on time. I'm not trying to scare you, but destination weddings can be hectic. You are a perfectionist, so I don't want any last minute problems or headaches."

"I see."

"I can change my travel plans to go early and help out as well, especially if that will help relieve some of the stress. Mike and the girls can do without me for a few days."

"Thank you, Lisa."

"That's what maids of honor are for."

"I am going to go over this list, and I need you to tell me whether or not everything is okay." Patricia says.

"Damn! I had not realized the price tag for this wedding. I am worth it though."

"Oh, you can be assured that amount will increase before it's over."

"Make sure that Carl gets the bill! How much do I need to write a check for today?"

"Fifteen thousand. That will complete the final payments for the venue, photographer, DJ, caterer and the cake."

"Damn girl! Just how much is this wedding costing?" Lisa asks.

"I will let you know when I am done. So far, I have spent twenty-five thousand, and that does not include this check. I never meant to spend that much. Fortunately, Carl is loaded; and I have a stash that I have been building for twenty years. I have saved for this day because I want the fairy tale wedding. My dress and shoes used a large chunk of that twenty-five thousand. You know I have to have some bling! By the way Patricia, do you think we can add on a live band as well?"

"Yes! I will look into it."

"Make it happen."

"You and your expensive taste! When I get married, I am borrowing your dress. I'm sure it can support two brides for that dollar amount."

"When your day comes, I know you are going to be different!"

"So true. Nothing compares to the feeling of seeing yourself in your own wedding dress."

"Well, I think I'm done here. I will call you if I need anything else."

"Okay. Oh, how many people have already returned their RSVP?"

"Of the two hundred twenty-five people invited, one hundred eighty have confirmed. The rest have until next Friday. I will not be able to accept any more beyond that date because I have to give the caterer and the venue a final count. I may send out another reminder on Monday."

"Okay, cool. See ya!"

"Bye now."

"Now, let's plan the fun. What are you going to do about Tish?"

"What about her?"

"Carol! You know you have to let her be a bridesmaid, now."

"Says who? I will invite her to be a guest, maybe; but having her as part of the wedding party is a big fat negative! Next topic!"

"Carol, you are crazy!"

"No, I am keeping it real. I told you that I am going support her until she flies back from over the coo-coo's nest. As for besties, we will never have that type of relationship ever again."

"I thought you would have changed your mind by now. But you are not as forgiving as I am."

"And you shouldn't be either! Now, about the bachelorette party; I want chocolate and caramel penises swinging from the ceiling."

"That means strippers. I'll find the finest one to jump out of the cake."

"Yes! Yes! Yessss!"

"For the location, we need to choose between the Marriott downtown or Embassy Suites. I think the Marriott will be the better location. Also, we can hit up Beale Street and some clubs after the party."

"I like that! Marriott it is. I will confirm with the hotel today and send

out invites on tomorrow."

"I want the bridal shower to be an elegant affair. My future sister-in-law has taken the lead; but I am going to give you her information so that you can touch base with her. You know what I like and what I don't like."

"Gotcha!"

"I want us to have fun. Just make sure that she does not turn it into a church service. I am so serious. She will probably pull out holy oil at the bachelorette party. Here are both guest lists. I think that covers everything."

"Okay. I am all over this. I will update you on Tuesday."

"Sounds great!"

"I will see you later."

"Later!"

Shoot! I lost track of time. We had so many details to cover. I was supposed to be at Mike's two hours ago. This will test whether or not the therapy is truly working. I would call, but I need to see what his reaction to my being late is going to be. Let's see how this will play out. I may or may not have to kick his ass.

"Hi baby!"

"Hi dear! I am sorry that I am so late."

"I know you all were planning, so I am okay with that."

"We had a lot of unfinished details."

"That is to be expected. The wedding is less than two months away."

"Look at us!"

"What?"

"Nothing. We are getting along without any friction."

"Yes! I told you! I am in this for the long haul."

"Well I'm glad!"

"I love you, Li-Li"

"I love you too, Mike-Mike."

CAROL

My wedding day is quickly approaching. I have a little over a month and a half left. My "to-do" list does not seem to be shrinking any. The majority of the wedding plans are complete. I just pray that it all gels together smoothly. I hope my day is perfect! Unfortunately, the discarding and packing of things in preparation for our move is not going well as I would like. However, I am moving along. Carl acts like he is unbothered by it all; but I seem to be stressing. It seems as though my day never ends. When I go to bed at night, there are still plenty of things left to do. I thank God for my wedding planner and Lisa. Without the two of them, I would probably be in a room housed next to Tish.

I now know that I will only get married once because planning a wedding is too much damn work, especially when you want it done correctly. I have also realized that after all Donovan has put me through, I will never cheat again; no matter how unhappy I am! It is not worth the headache. I will keep my good stuff to myself. To appease him, I have to dance to his beat until we move away. In a month, he is going to look for me and I will be long gone without a trace. Sadly, I am going to miss him, but he is a ticking time bomb just waiting to blow my world up for his gain.

According to Donovan, he will be closing today on what he refers to as "our house"; and he wants to go furniture shopping this evening. If that will keep him happy and calm for the time being, of course I will oblige. Besides, it will give me an opportunity to gather some decorating ideas for me and Carl's new home in Delaware. Too bad this area does not have an IKEA store. I have been browsing their website, but I like to lay and sit on furniture before I spend my money. Hopefully we will be too tired from shopping to think about sex afterwards. I'm sure that is just idle thinking because we cannot keep our hands off of each other. Our chemistry is explosive! What can I say? If he wasn't so crazy, it would be nice to keep him so that I could get away from Carl when needed. That's out of the

question though. There is no chance of that ever happening. When I move, I am changing my phone number, my last name, and any other traces that may lead to my whereabouts.

Dang! I am a little behind schedule. I guess I will give him a courtesy call to let him know that I am on the way. Who is calling me now? Oh, it's him! I just cannot catch a break!

"Hi beautiful. Where are you?"

"I am a couple of exits away. I will be there shortly."

"I was just making sure that you did not bail out on me."

"No sir. Whatever Donovan wants, I try to appease."

"Oh snap! It's like that now? Actually, it should be because you love me and want to spend quality time with me."

"I do. But lately, it seems as though you force me to spend time with you. If I don't, you pull your little unnecessary antics. It's like I have no say; and that takes away some of the enjoyment from me. But all is well."

"What does that supposed to mean?"

"Nothing. Just all is well."

"I am excited to allow you to decorate our new home. How long before your house will be sold?"

"Maybe in about a month and a half."

"Good! We can finally be together with no Carl."

"I'm here."

"Where?"

"I'm parked in front of the store. Where are you?"

"I am parked on the side. Stay there, I will drive around."

"Welcome to Great American Home Store! How can I assist you today?"

"We just closed on our new home and we need to buy new furniture for every room. We have over five thousand square feet."

"Congratulations! We have a great selection to choose from. Where would you like to begin?"

"Let's start with the living room and then go from there."

"Sounds like a great plan."

"Whatever she wants! I am just supplying the payment."

"I will definitely spend all of your money."

"I know, but anything for you."

We have been in this store for four hours and I am exhausted. Shopping for his home did give me a lot of great ideas as to how I want my new home to look. I have to admit that I enjoyed this shopping experience with him; even though this entire experience is a lie.

"Come on over to my place so that I can rub your feet and give you a good massage as a reward for all of your hard work."

"No, I am exhausted! Can I have a rain check? I think I will just head home since I have to work tomorrow."

"Oh, come on. Just for a couple of hours."

"Our couple of hours usually ends up being all night. I have a lot going on at work. So, I need to just go home and go to bed."

"Is Carl home?"

"No, he's at work. I will have some alone time which is what I really need. I'll make it up to you this weekend. I promise!"

"Okay. Go get you some rest and I will check on you later. Hey! I have been meaning to ask you whether or not you have told Carl that you will be leaving once your house is sold? Does he know that there will be no wedding?"

"I have Carl under control. Those are questions that you do not need to concern yourself with. Besides, I am too tired to discuss anything at the moment."

"Okay. But know that we will have this discussion."

"Sure. I will see you later."

"Love you!"

"Love you as well."

My business with Carl is none of his business. There will be no discussion and I will be Mrs. Sullivan in a month and a half. He thinks that he is running something, but he is in for a rude awakening. The day before I leave for Niagara Falls, I will be filing that Internal Affairs complaint.

I am going home to my future husband which is where I belong. Carl loves me! This I know. He has to because being with me is not easy. He does not deserve the things that I have done, and it will all stop when I become Mrs. Sullivan.

"Carl! "What are you doing here? I thought you were working."

"I was. My time is winding down and things are slow. So I decided to come home and do some packing, especially since you have been working so hard at it. Where have you been?"

"Furniture shopping. I got some great ideas for our new home."

"Okay good. But I have the say when it comes to the man cave."

"I will think about it."

"When is your last day of work?"

"I have two weeks left. Semester exams begin next Monday. As time draws near, my heart races and my stomach flutters. We have a lot of changes happening at the same time."

"True, but we got this! We have always been successful at handling all of our challenges."

"I know. Sometimes I act like a brat and unappreciative; but I love you, and I appreciate you from the bottom of my heart."

"That would be all of the time, missy."

We share a laugh and a hug. "Have you and all of the guys gotten fitted for your tuxedos?"

"Yes! The only thing the store has to do is ship them out on time. You know men typically handle their business."

"Okay. I am both mentally and physically exhausted."

"Come here and let me give you one of my massages. They always seem

to put you to sleep.”

“I thought you would never ask.”

“Just relax. Everything is going to fall into place.”

“I can’t help it. You know it’s my nature to worry.”

“Well, I’m not worried. You know why?”

“No. Why?”

“Because I am marrying the strongest, boldest, most authentic, beautiful woman in the world!”

“Awww, thank you, honey.” This is a real genuine moment with Carl. I know that in our new home with our new beginning, we will have another sixty years of moments like this.

CAROL

Lisa and I are going to visit with Tish. During our visit, I will fill her in on the wedding plans and give her an invite. That is all that I am willing to give. She will never get the opportunity to bite me again. She is now in the category I call distant associate. I cannot be a friend to someone that I can’t trust. I have the belief that friendships are based on loyalty and trust. If loyalty and trust do not exist, the friendship is doomed. A true friend is neither envious nor jealous. A true friend only wants the best for you and wants you to be happy. Lisa and I have that in each other. Lisa wants me to give Tish more, but my heart will not allow it. I cannot trust her with the information about my move. Lisa can use her as a substitute since I will be leaving. Honestly, I am the one and only. There is no substitute for a friend like me.

LISA

I am proud of Carol. She is making progress when it comes to Tish. She invited her to the wedding; however, I feel that she should at least make her a bridesmaid. We made a pact at the age of ten that we would be maids of honor in each other’s weddings. The pact was two maids of honor no matter

what. But I know that things can change in the blink of an eye with Carol. Never in my wildest imagination would I have thought that our friendship would encounter such a rift. Life is full of lessons, twists, and turns. I think Tish has learned her lesson. Lord knows the poor thing has been through the fire and the flood. From the expressions on her face, she really enjoys our visits; and she is glad that we are a part of her life again.

TISH

Lisa and Carol should be arriving for their weekly visit shortly. I am looking forward to my opportunity for girl talk and healthy conversations. I cannot wait to share the good news of my release with them. I want our girls' night back again. Maybe that can be a goal we can work towards as we rebuild our friendship and sisterhood. Life is short, so I am not going to rush it; even though I feel like my being in this facility is preventing me from enjoying life. Regardless, I now know that the bondage Sam had me under prevented me from enjoying the simple things in life.

"Hi ladies!"

"Hello ma'am."

"What's up girlie?"

"I was just thinking of the two of you. I am ready for some girl talk. Oh! I have great news." "Let's hear it. Spill it!"

"I am going home on Wednesday."

"That is great news! Congratulations!"

"Yeah. I am happy, but a little afraid."

"Take it a day at a time. That's all you can do. What about work?" "I probably won't return to work for a couple of months. Besides, the doctor has to clear me to return to work; and he will probably say that I am not ready, which is okay with me. I need a little me time out in the world."

"Well, I have something to give you." Carol says.

"Oh! You and Carl are finally tying the knot. Niagara Falls! You always

said that would be your place of choice for your wedding. Congratulations! I will be there!"

"Book your flight and hotel as soon as possible. I will RSVP to Patricia for you. She is going to get me for messing with her final count."

"She will be just fine. Plus, she is getting paid very well!" says Lisa.

"If you need me to do anything, please let me know. I will have plenty of time on my hands. May I bring Fred with me?"

"Sure! What's with you two anyway?"

"Where in the hell did he come from?" Lisa asks.

"You are not going to believe this. He is a childhood friend of Sam's. He has been great ever since the day that he showed up at my door. He is just a really good friend and a good guy that needed a second chance."

"So, he just showed up after all this time looking for Sam, and you welcomed him with open arms?" Carol curiously asks.

"Yep! He is nothing like Sam. They are from two different worlds. He has been instrumental in helping me get Sam out of my life."

"Well, he's alright with me then! I like him for that reason alone."

"It is no secret that the two of you are no fans of Sam, and I finally realize why, after all of these years. My light bulb finally came on."

"We all have dark moments."

"Not for twenty years! Speak for yourselves."

"Carol! "Stop it!"

"Okay, but I am just saying. I can admit that I won the award for the longest dark moment! Better late than never!"

"That is a true statement."

"Ladies, can we please change the subject? I don't want to relapse."

"Definitely! The bachelorette party is going to be off the chain!"

"Chocolate and caramel strippers! Strippers and more strippers!"

"Male, I hope!" I say curiously.

"Hell yeah! Why in the hell would I want to look at female parts? Hell, I

have my own. You might need to stay here a few more weeks!"

We all laugh. "Carol you have not changed one bit!"

"Why would I? I am who I am."

"Yeah, crazy with no filter!" Lisa says.

"Yep! I own it! So, how is the bridal shower coming?"

"Great! I think I have almost taken over. You were right when you mentioned church service."

"I told you!"

"The theme is "Sex in the City", and she almost stroked out over it."

"Who?" I ask.

"Carl's sister. She was relentless in insisting that she host the bridal shower. I didn't have the heart to tell her no; so I asked Lisa to connect with her to ensure it does not become a church service. We want it elegant, but fun and enjoyable."

"Sherry is known for turning something fun into Bible study."

"Yes, she is."

"So I see I have a lot of fun and entertainment, as well as travel to look forward to. I am going shopping the minute I get out of here because I have lost a few pounds."

"It is good to see you smiling and excited again."

"It feels good!"

"I must get going. I have a lot to do within a small window of time."

"I wish you guys did not have to leave."

"So do I. However, as the maid of honor, my job is never done."

"Take care, Tish. We will see you on the outside!"

"Bye ladies!"

"See Ya!"

15

TISH

Today is a fresh new beginning for me. I am finally leaving Lakeside and prepared to face the world as a new woman with a new attitude. The first thing that I want to do is shop for new outfits for Carol's wedding festivities. I am so happy that she invited me to her wedding. On the other hand, I am sad and disappointed that I am not a part of the wedding party. However, I understand her reasoning and have no choice but to accept it. I betrayed her, and betrayal for Carol is a no-no! I'm sure that her decision to invite me to her wedding was a big step for her. Had I not gotten ill, I most likely would not have been invited. I can only blame myself for that. I was unhappy and miserable; and I wanted company. Unfortunately, I chose the wrong individuals to take my frustrations out on.

I hope Fred cleared his schedule today because I plan to shop the entire afternoon. Also, I am going to ask if him to attend the wedding with me. I hope he accepts. I don't want to be the only female attending the wedding without a date.

"Hello dear. You look great!"

"I feel great! I feel like a new woman with a new lease on life."

"You sure do look like it. What's the first thing you want to do? I am taking the afternoon off to cater to you."

"Great minds think alike. I was hoping you did because I want to go shopping. Carol is getting married next month and I need new clothes for the wedding and festivities."

"Sounds like a plan. Let's go!"

"The wedding is in Niagara Falls. Would you like to go with me?"

"Yes! I would be honored. I have always wanted to visit that place.

I used to watch the travel channel and dream of traveling to places like that. How long will we be away?"

"I believe we will be gone four days and three nights."

"How much do I need to give you for travel expenses?"

"Nothing! I invited you."

"No! I am a man and I pay my own way. Remember, you are starting fresh. At least allow me to pay for the airline tickets."

"Oh wow! That is so kind of you."

"I make a good salary. There is no way that I am going to allow you to pay my way. If we were or ever became a couple, I as the man would pay for it all. That's how my dad told me it works."

"Well I don't know anything about that. I have been paying for almost everything my entire dating career."

"That just confirms that you have never dated a man."

"How is it that you and Sam are from the same backgrounds, but are totally opposite?"

"I chose to take a different path. I treat women the way I want my mom and sisters to be treated."

"So, you do have family?!"

"Yes! I recently reconnected with them. I felt that I needed to make something of myself before showing my face to them again. I thank you so much for taking a chance on me and believing in me."

"Thank you for appearing in my life at the right time. We were good for each other."

"Yeah, I guess that is a good way of looking at it. What is your first store of choice?"

"Macy's."

"Macy's it will be. So to be clear, I will pay for the airline tickets and half of the hotel. Are we getting separate rooms?"

"No, I was thinking double beds. That is all the hotel had available since

I received my invitation late, and she has invited over two hundred guests."

"That will be cool. I plan to photo bomb all of the pictures."

"Just be sure you stay out of Carol's pictures. She is vain and she loves for her pictures to be perfect. She just may come out of her wedding dress on you."

"Nah, I am just kidding. I would never do anything to embarrass the sweetest, most gentle woman that I know."

"Stop. You are going to make me blush and cry."

"Well, it's the truth! Come on, you and I both have shopping to do."

I learn something new about Fred each day. Today, I learned just how much of a man he really is. Also, he has a family that loves and cares for him. I wonder how much more is there to know about him. I am now intrigued to find out. I plan to keep him around for a long time. Who knows, maybe he and I will become closer than close. I know it's too soon to be thinking about a relationship. However, it is not too soon to think about having hot sex. Damn, he is looking mighty sexy in that muscle t-shirt and those jeans. I need a shower.

CAROL

Yippee! I just received a job offer from the University of Delaware as Dean of the Computer Science and Mathematics Department. This move is definitely a winner for us in so many ways. It all began as a plot to get away from Donovan, but it is turning into mega blessings. I am taking Carl out for dinner tonight, or maybe I will cook and we stay in. Everything is falling into place. We close on our new home next Friday, and the buyers for this house are scheduled to close in two weeks. My wedding plans are complete. The only baggage I have left to deal with is crazy ass Donovan.

Yes! He is crazy! He has it in his mind that I am going to leave Carl. I never told him such foolishness. I have been playing our entire relationship over and over in my mind, and I can't recall at what point he turned into a

crazy man. I have been completely honest with him, but he hears what he wants to hear. I am so exhausted from playing this twisted game with him. I will not lie and say that I do not love him, but I need him to accept that I love and chose Carl. I feel really bad about what I am about to do to him, but he has left me with no choice. He pushed me into a corner, and now I am scratching my way out! I would love to share my plans with him, but I can't. I miss sharing things with him. He and I both lost sight of our relationship. I feel like a professional liar and manipulator, but I have to beat him at his own game. There is no room for error!

"Guess what, Carl?"

"What?"

"I have a new job in Delaware"!

"Congrats baby! Where?"

"The University of Delaware. The position they offered me is Dean of the Computer Science and Mathematics Department."

"We have to go celebrate tonight."

"I was thinking the same thing, but then I thought about cooking."

"No way! This is your moment. I am taking my sweetie out."

"You will not get an argument from me."

"I am going to shower and we can leave around seven."

"That sounds like a plan."

"Be thinking about where you want to go."

"I already know!"

"Where?"

"Benihana."

"Benihana it is."

Shit! Donovan is texting me trying to make plans for us to meet at the house tomorrow. It's moving day for him, so I will appease him. I will be there to meet the movers and receive the furniture delivery because he has to work in the morning. Who works a double on their moving day? I have

assured him that I have it under control. I can even spend the night with him in the new bed because Carl is working a double on tomorrow as well. I have gone as far as telling him that I will be moving in with him in six weeks. The truth is that I will be in Niagara Falls awaiting my wedding day. In three weeks, Carl and I will be settling into our new home in Delaware. I am going to disappear from Donovan without a trace.

Life is so crazy. At the end of last year, I was actually contemplating leaving Carl for Donovan. I had no proposals, and then I got two. Now, I am in the midst of a maze that I created. I'm not too worried though. I am a paratrooper and I always win. On another note, my celebration dinner with Carl was spectacular. Our relationship is back to how it once was, and I love the new us!

It is moving day for Donovan. I'm at his house waiting on the movers and the new furniture. The house is immaculate. Hopefully he will find someone else to share it with; that's if he ever gets over me and the severing of our relationship. I am going to be responsible for messing up a good man. However, he brought this upon himself because he refused to listen. I cannot worry about that now. My focus for today is to organize his house and get things in order. Tonight, we are going to christen at least two rooms in this house, one being the master suite. I am going to go all out for him. After this, he has one more love making session with me and then we are history!

LISA

Summer break is finally here and I get a break from my name being called a thousand times a day. I love my job, but summer breaks are essential to my mental stability. My summer is already filled with activities, to include Carol's wedding functions and the arrival of Megan and Sydney. I am going to become an "instant mom" and I hope everything goes well.

Mike has insisted that I move in with him for the summer to prevent

bouncing the girls back and forth from my house to his. He said that stability is important while we are making the transition to become an extended family. From my experience with children, he is accurate; so I am going to move in. However, I feel a little immoral living with him without being his wife. I guess it is a little late to think about my religious morals with all of the pre-marital sex that we have. We have great pre-marital sex!

I have been working on daily schedules and activities for Meagan and Sydney. I want to keep them active and busy so that they do not get bored. It's important to me for them to have a good time with us, and have lots to share with Shelia about their experience. My responsibilities are a little over whelming. Acting as "instant mom" along with the responsibilities of being the maid of honor will keep me busy every day. However, I would not have it any other way. I love Mike and there is nothing in this world that I would not do for my bestie, Carol.

Tonight is date night for me and Mike. It is the last hoorah for us for a while. I am going to do something very special for Mike tonight, and I think he is going to love it. I have been secretly taking pole dancing lessons. Tonight, I am going to display my skills with Mike. When he arrives, I will be sitting on the pole naked. I think I will dance to R. Kelly's "12 play". That should give him a hint of the kind of night I want to have. The original theme for tonight was sexy lingerie and pajamas, but I think I am going to change it to naked and anything goes! It is summer and I am ready to let my hair down.

"Lisa! Lisa! Honey, where are you?"

"Follow the signs dear! You are on a scavenger hunt for me."

He laughs loudly. "Oh my! What are you up to?"

"You'll see when you find me! There is a surprise waiting for you."

"Okay! A good one, I hope."

"It is a surprise that you will never forget!"

"It's hard to follow your voice on the intercom system."

"That's why you should follow the signs for clues. I am waiting!"

"You are something else."

"I know!"

He finally found me. "Oh shit! What is this? Girl!"

I come down from the pole and give him a slight push. He sits on the bed. The music pops on and Mike is smiling from ear to ear. "Sit back, relax, and enjoy the show." I began to dance for Mike. I start with a lap dance, and he is standing at attention before I can finish. Now to the pole. I am going to show him skills that he never knew I had.

"Damn Girl!"

His mouth is wide open as I swing upside down with my legs wrapped around the pole. I slide upside down from the top of the pole to the bottom. Mike leaves his seat and comes over to me. While I am upset down on the pole, he takes one of my legs to gain access to my vijay-jay. He begins to eat me like I am a full course meal and it feels so damn good! Somehow, I move my legs from the pole and wrap them around his neck. Damn! I got skills and so does he to make me move like that. Finally, he lifts me up and carries me to the bed. There is no interruption with me as his main course meal. He finally comes up for air and we make love for well over an hour.

"When did you learn how to pole dance?"

"I have been taking lessons for about two months now."

"I cannot describe what I am feeling ring now. But, I never want it to stop! Making love to me like that, you will never get rid of me."

"Who says that I want to? I took those lessons for you!

"Thank you! Did I say thank you?" We both laugh and cuddle.

"I wanted to do something kinky and special before the girls arrive, and leave you with something to reminisce about when things get tough this summer."

"You think it will be tough?"

"I don't know. I am nervous. I just hope I do a good job keeping those

little ladies entertained."

"Don't worry, baby. You will be fine."

"I have been working on a schedule of activities."

"The teacher in you never shuts down."

"No. It doesn't."

"I am starved, but I am too weak to get up."

"So am I. Dinner is ready, though."

"I just want to lay here and hold you."

"Oh! We never got to the chocolate strawberries and wine."

"In the heat of the moment, I ate exactly what I wanted!"

"Ewe! Michael Hampton! You are nasty!"

"That's why you love me."

"Indeed it is. Shut up and eat some of these strawberries. We need to regain our strength."

"After all of that we just experienced, it may be a while."

"That confirms I did an excellent job."

"Hell yeah! I'm tapped out! I don't ever recall that happening."

"Whoever said plus-size women can't pole dance has never met me."

"In this lifetime, they never will! This is all mines."

"Come on, let's try to shower and make it down stairs."

"No! Let's relax in the Jacuzzi."

"That is a better idea! I love me some Li-Li!"

"I love me some Mike-Mike. Grab the wine and strawberries."

Mike and I soak, relax, and eat chocolate strawberries in the Jacuzzi for hours until we become wrinkled.

CAROL

I have been sitting in this parking garage for two hours. I am in such shock that my legs are trembling. How in the hell did I test positive to a pregnancy test? Who gets pregnant at forty? Why is this happening to me a

month before my wedding and two weeks before I move? The real twist to this saga is I am unsure of who the father is. According to the due date, it happened the day that I slept with both Donovan and Carl within a four hour time frame. Who am I fooling? It has to be Donovan's because Carl has been shooting blanks for years. The one time that the condom breaks with Donovan, I become pregnant. However, it's still possible that Carl took some geritol, ginseng, or something. It does not matter because if I decide to have this baby, Donovan will never know; and Carl will be the father by default. I am keeping this to myself until after the wedding and after Carl and I settle into our new home. I have a major decision to make.

What will I do with a new baby this late in life? I don't have time to raise another child. We have too much going on. Carl and I both are beginning new positions in our careers; and hell, we are both to damn old to be running after a two year old. I can see it now. The child will be out of control because we are tired and old. What will our adult children say? The more I think about it, this baby cannot and will not happen. My, how quickly does things change? Once upon a time, I would be the first to condemn someone for having an abortion; but here I am now, thinking about it with very serious consideration. A baby is not in my plans because my life is way too complicated to bring another life into it. I do not want to be responsible for anyone but me, and I have earned the right to be selfish. I have my children already and I am happy. They are self-sufficient adults that rarely need me. A baby needs a parent who is nurturing, and I don't have any nurturing left in me. Yep, this is one of those secrets that no one will ever know about. I am taking this one to the grave. God, I am asking you for your forgiveness in advance. I am making this phone call to set up an appointment for next week if possible.

I am meeting Donovan later for dinner. I have to put my big girl face and panties on for the last song and dance of this relationship. He insists on having dinner in "our new home". There will be no hot sex tonight because I

am not in the mood. I am putting on this pad so that he will immediately know that it's not happening. I am way too stressed for that. My main focus right now is on getting rid of this baby next week before anyone finds out about it.

Donovan has a special request for dinner tonight. He wants me to prepare lemon pepper fish, spaghetti, coleslaw, garlic bread and homemade caramel cake. I put a lot of time and effort into this meal because it will be the last time I see him or spend time with him. I know I've said that before; but this time, I am telling the truth. We, as in Carl and I, are permanently leaving for Delaware in a week. Our house has been sold and we are almost finished packing. The movers will arrive on Saturday morning, and I have a garage sale lined up to try and sale everything that we have decided to leave behind. My plan is coming full circle. Finally, I will no longer have to lie and sneak around. I can be the devoted woman to Carl that I was meant to be. I will no longer crave life on the wild side. In other words, I am going to be still, act my age, and be happy with what I already have. I now know that the grass is not always greener on the other side.

"Baby! Dinner smells good."

"Thanks! It is what you requested."

"I cannot wait to taste it and you."

"Unfortunately, there will be no eating me tonight. Mother nature has made her arrival."

"It's not her time. She is not due to arrive for another week."

"She decided to arrive early."

"Oh well! We can cuddle in bed and love on each other while we enjoy the sky view from the bedroom."

"I like the sound of that."

"Carol, you make me so happy. I know I act crazy sometimes, but I mean no harm by it. I just want you all to myself. When I think about you being with Carl, I lose control. It's like I temporarily lose sight of reality. I

feel so much contempt for him."

"Why? He has not harmed you in anyway. He doesn't even know you that well."

"He is the only thing that keeps you from me, and prevents you from completely loving only me. I know that you love me, but you also love him. You feel a sense of loyalty to him that I cannot unlock."

"Why are we talking about this?"

"Because I need you to really understand me and why I do the things that I do."

"It is hard to walk away from fifteen years. Overall, the relationship has never been bad."

"I know! I feel like he has taken you for granted all of these years. It took him fifteen years to propose, which is ridiculous. I knew within a year that I wanted you to be my wife. But, I knew you belonged to someone else. When you opened up and confided in me about your relationship with him, I knew I would be a better man for you. I promise you that I have been trying ever since."

"I know you have. Can you truly with all honestly accept any outcome that may happen?"

"Honestly, No. I feel that I have done a lot to prove myself to you. I deserve the prize."

"Interesting answer my dear. I don't know what to think or how to feel about your answer."

"You asked for honesty."

"I did. I no longer want to talk about this. Let's enjoy our night. When we finish dinner, I want to enjoy a night cap on the balcony."

"Agreed. This meal looks delicious! I finally got you to cook for me. I've always heard about it, but never experienced it."

"I am a country girl, so you should know that I have cooking skills."

"You got skills in every area."

Donovan winks his eye at me and we share a moment of laughter as I set the table. He pulls out my chair and we enjoy the meal I have prepared. After we finish dinner, we both clear the table and clean the kitchen.

"Let's have that night cap you suggested."

"Sure!"

Donovan grabs two wine glasses along with a bottle of wine. We sit on the balcony, sip our wine, and enjoy the stillness of the night. We hold hands, laugh and talk for a couple of hours. It is as if nothing or no one else matters. We move to the bed and we cuddle, kiss and talk some more.

"Let's get some sleep. I have to work tomorrow; but you, Ms. Off for the Summer, get to sleep in."

"Don't be a hater! It does not become you."

"I love you! I can't wait to have more nights like this with you."

"Same here, honey."

My last night with Donovan was perfect! I will never forget him. He came into my life during a much needed time, and I will always be grateful to him for that. It is said that time heals all wounds. I hope someday he will forgive me for the way I plan to leave him . . . without a trace!

CAROL

Guess what day it is? It is the day of my bridal shower! I can't believe it is really happening! My wedding is around the corner. I am ready to hang with the girls and open presents. Lisa said the theme is "Sex in the City." I wonder what all that consists of. She has been very secretive. I am just glad that she took the reins from Sherry. I am so happy today. If I feel this happy on today, I might explode on my wedding day. For the next three weeks, I am the "Queen Bee" and everyone will cater to me! Today, which is more of a sophisticated affair, is only the beginning. Next week will be wild because the bachelorette party will be in full effect. We are going to be buck wild and uncensored; and whatever happens at that party must stay at that party!

LISA

I am wrapping up last minute details for my girl's bridal shower. She is going to love what I have planned for her. It will suit her taste just fine. It is going to be sophisticated, yet grown and sexy. All of those characteristics describe Carol. I know she is going to love the decorations. I made sure that I chose royal blue and white, which represents the second love of her life; her Zeta Phi Beta Sorority Inc. I have included a segment for her sisters to perform a step for her. I'm sure her face is going to light up like a Christmas tree. I am just happy that I can share in such an important event in her life. Hopefully I did a good job and it will meet her approval. When my day comes, I know that she will go all out for me because that is just how she does things, big! That's why it is imperative that everything is special for her.

TISH

Tonight will be my first time hanging with Carol and Lisa since our blow up, and I am so excited! It will also be my first interaction with other people since my release from the hospital. I feel like everyone knows. I know that I have nothing to be ashamed of, but there is a stigma that comes with mental illness. When people know, they treat you very different; and they walk on egg shells around you. I do not want, nor need that type of treatment in my life. I am really happy for Carol and Carl. They have been together a long time and deserve marital bliss. I just hope she treats him right. Let me stop! That is the old Tish talking. I only need to worry about me. For the first time in years, I get to party without watching the clock. I have the smell of freedom and I am never going to be caged again.

LISA

The guests are arriving and bringing gifts. The gift table is already full, so I need to prepare another one. The decorations are gorgeous. Sherry did

a great job. We are waiting on the guest of honor. She is going to make a grand entrance as always. There she is, glowing with happiness! As she enters, everyone claps and cheers for her.

"Hello everyone! Thank you for coming to help me celebrate the most important day of my life. I am so happy to see all of your smiling faces. Now, I am going to have a seat and let the hosts take charge."

"Hi ladies, I am Lisa. Are you enjoying yourselves so far?" The room erupts with applauses and several responses of "yes".

"Great! We have plenty in store for your enjoyment and entertainment. We are going to begin with a fun party featuring Bedroom Kandi."

"Hi ladies. I am Sherry, your co-host for the evening. It is no secret that my brother is eleven years Carol's senior. Therefore in about ten years, she will need a lot of the merchandise presented here tonight." The room erupts with laughter.

"Umm, my honey is going to be still strong at sixty. Watch yourself now!" The room erupts with more laughter and applause!

"Sometimes you don't want to be bothered with a man, but that urge will not leave you alone. These products will change a single woman's life and spice up some relationships!"

Tish comically interrupts Sherry and says, "I am now single. Stop talking and get to presenting the products. We are ready to see what you got!" The other ladies cheer and applaud her outburst, as they all appear ready to have some fun.

"Well, with no further sales pitch, I present to you Tammi Combs. She will tell you all that you need to know about these wonderful products. "I can say my sex life has never been the same!"

"What? Not the Bible Study chic!" I shockingly say.

"Yes, girl! This Bible Study girl has a wild side!"

CAROL

My bridal shower was one for the history books! Everything was well planned and every detail was precise. Lisa knew exactly how I would have wanted things done. It was ladies having fun and learning lessons on how to spice up their love lives. Everyone seemed to have a great time. The grand finale was my sorority sisters singing our sorority hymn and performing a routine just for me. I love all of those ladies, and I know they all love me as well. Carl and I will still be opening gifts come this time next year. The next party is the bachelorette party, and I know everyone will be wild and loose.

TISH

Carol's bridal shower was a grand affair, and I expected nothing less. She was so happy! I enjoyed myself as well, and I spent a lot of money. I probably was Ms. Comb's best customer, as I am planning for a lot of lonely nights. If I don't find a man for a while, I will be just fine. Maybe these toys will curb my urge to jump Fred's bones. I like the bond and the relationship that we have developed. I do not want to ruin it by complicating it with sex. However, he needs to stop walking around here looking so damn fine. It should be against the law for a man to have a six pack like that. He has the audacity to walk around here shirtless. I have never taken a shower so many times in one day.

I am slowly getting my life back to normal. Therapy teaches me to take it one day at a time. My therapist is very pleased with my progress. He wants me to continue to work hard, and he has cleared me to return to work; so I am feeling good about that. I will return the Monday after we return from Niagara Falls. The more I think about it, I may need to change the date to that Tuesday. I am sure that I am going to be very exhausted from that trip.

Sam had the nerve to write me a letter. It came in the mail on yesterday. Part of me wants to read it; however another part of me wants to throw it

away without reading it. My therapist suggested that I throw it away without reading it. If I keep it lying around, curiosity will get the best of me and I will eventually read it. There is a chance that I could relapse if I read it. The new Tish has to make smart choices and choose myself above any and everything else. That means I will shred it. There! The dilemma is over.

Who is ringing my door bell this time of the day? Everyone I know is at work, and my friends and family call before showing up unannounced. Oh wow! Someone sent me some lovely roses. There is a card, too! It reads "Tish, just thinking of you. Hope these flowers make your day!" "Smiley face". "I would like to invite you on a date tonight, Fred." I should have known they were from Fred. He is very thoughtful. How sweet! I have not been on a real date in a long time. Well, there is no time like the present. I am going to call him and accept. What will I wear? I have plenty of new outfits to choose from. The time is now around noon so I have plenty of time to get my hair and nails done for tonight. I am not going all out for him though. This effort is totally for me. I deserve to feel pretty for a change.

FRED

I have decided to take Tish out for a night on the town and she has accepted. I am sure this will be the first real date that she has been on, so I want it to be special. I think it is time for me to step up my game regarding her. I really like her, but I don't know how she feels about me. I know that she trusts me whole heartedly; but I wonder if she thinks of me in a romantic way. I sometimes catch her watching me as I walk through the house in my shorts and shirtless. That could just be hormones. However, I will never know if I don't start somewhere. I am going to play it smooth and see where it takes me. However, I must act carefully because I don't want to do anything that will cause her to relapse. She and I have a lot of things planned to do together over the next month. Maybe the love connection will

happen on its own.

"Hi Tish. My, you look stunning! I see you got a new hairstyle too. It looks great on you!"

"Thanks. And yes, I did. You are going to make me blush. "You look and smell good yourself."

"Thank you."

"So, where are we going?"

"I was thinking dinner and dancing."

"I like the sound of that."

"Dinner is going to be at the Butcher Shop. As for the dancing part, we can be spontaneous on that."

"I suggest Classic Soul for Foursome Thursday."

"We have ourselves a plan."

TISH

Fred is such a gentleman at all times. He opens doors and pulls out chairs for me. We are just friends, but this guy knows how to treat a lady. This is the first time I have experienced any type of chivalry.

"Fred, May I ask you a question?"

"Sure!"

"You are such a great guy. Why haven't someone snatched you up?"

He laughs! "That is a good question. Maybe it's because I have been focused on keeping my life on track. Plus, a lot of women are afraid to date an ex-con."

"Everyman deserves a chance."

"I agree. I am indebted to you for taking a chance on me."

"Are you dating anyone now? You seem to spend all of your time working and taking care of me."

"No, I am not. I am where I want to be for now. Besides, I am very picky. I know what I want."

"I hear you."

"I am a man though, and I do have my eyes on someone special."

"Does she know that you have your eyes on her?"

"No, I don't think she has a clue. What do you think I should do? I haven't said anything because she may not feel the same way; and I am afraid of being turned down."

"I thought only women battled fear of rejection issues."

"Oh no, honey. Men do not like rejection! They just tend to hide it better than women."

"Whoever she is will be a lucky woman!"

"You think so?"

"I know so! If you take care of me the way that you do, and I am just a friend; your lady will be treated like queen."

"Do you think that you will ever open your heart to another man?"

"Yes, I think so. I am a helpless romantic and I believe in love. But next time it has to be right. I don't want to end up back in a mental ward."

"Your relationship with Sam was your first and only. He was a selfish bastard who did not appreciate you. Love is kind and it does not hurt in any form when you are loved by the right person."

"You are right! I just want to make sure that it is love and not lust for me. I want someone to love me for me, and not for what I have or what I can do for them."

"You will find that. It's possible that you may already have it right before your very eyes, but just haven't recognized it yet."

"Hmmm. I think you may be on to something."

"Always keep your past out of your present. Sam is history! The next man will be your future. Just keep that new found confidence that you have. I find it sexy."

"Oh wow! Speaking of sexy, I find your six pack very sexy!"

"Oh! Thank you! I didn't think you even noticed."

"How could I not?"

"Does having my shirt off make you feel uncomfortable?"

"No at all. Actually, it's quite the opposite!"

"Look at us being open and honest with each other."

"Yeah, I guess we are. I really appreciate this date."

"Thank you for accepting. Now, let's hit the club so that I can show you a move or two."

"I would like that. I am especially ready for a slow dance."

"Slow dances are my specialty."

He just doesn't know! I want to slow dance with him all night long. I cannot wait for him to hold me with those big arms. I haven't been held by a man in a long time. So if slow dancing is my way to being held, then he is going to dance with me the entire night on every slow jam. Now that I think about it, I can't recall the last time I slow danced. Tonight has been awesome!

16

LISA

Meagan and Sydney have been with us for two weeks now, and I am pooped. Entertaining two young hyper little girls is exhausting; but I would not trade this moment for anything in the world. I think motherhood is my calling. Mike said that I am doing great, and I concur; although he thinks I should find more creative ways to entertain them besides spending money on outings. However, this is their first visit to our city and I think they should enjoy the best it has to offer for their age group. But tonight, I will honor his wishes. The girls and I are going to bake cookies and cook dinner. We will call it family night at the inn. I am even going to include a couple of movies from the red box to top off the night. I think Mike will be pleased to know that I only spent two dollars for the movies.

Living with Mike the past two weeks has been interesting. Now I know the meaning of the phrase "you never really know someone until you've lived with them". Let's just say that I have much more to learn. I've learned that he is a creature of habit. He sticks to his routines and nothing much ever changes. For example, he eats the same food for breakfast. Turkey bacon, eggs over easy, wheat toast, and orange juice has been his breakfast of choice for twenty-five years. His day begins at five a.m. every day of the year, including weekends and holidays. One downside to that is he is very noisy; and he expects me to wake up and talk to him while he gets dressed for work. I am off for the summer and I want to sleep! I need my beauty rest. Thank God I can adapt easily. This morning, I surprised him by getting up before him and cooking his breakfast just the way he likes it. It was kind of romantic. It gave us a little quality time which is scarce with the girls being here. One advantage to living with Mike is that he keeps me on my toes

about eating healthier and exercising more. I am going to look fabulous in my dress at Carol's wedding. I have lost five pounds and plenty of inches since I moved in. The coke bottle is forming quite nicely.

Tish called me on yesterday. She wants to meet for drinks and wants to know if Carol would come. I told her that I would be there, but Carol most likely will be too busy with her wedding planning. So she will be out of the loop for a while. The truth is there is no way in hell that Carol is going to socialize with Tish. She made that very clear when I talked her into supporting Tish during her illness. Carol does not want Tish to know that she is moving or where she is moving to. It is no secret that Tish has diarrhea of the mouth. Maybe she has changed, but who knows. However, I am willing to try this friendship thing with her once more. I will just keep my grass cut for sure. Since Carol is leaving, I will need someone to have drinks with every now and then; but I will not trust her with any of my secrets.

"Thank you for joining me. I needed this. By the way, I really enjoyed the bridal shower. It made me think about our girls' night out."

"Yeah! We have some stories for the books."

"I wish Carol could have joined us."

"So do I. So, what have you been up to since you got home?"

"I went on my first real date. It's a damn shame that I am just experiencing how a real man treats a woman."

"It's refreshing for you."

"Yes! I am never turning back. I have raised the bar."

"Good for you! I am so proud of you. So, who is the lucky guy?"

"Fred. He is so different. I like him, but I don't know if he will be the one. He has been throwing subtle hints which lead me to think that he wants to be with me. I just play if off. Sometimes, I flirt back. Oh God, the man is fine with a nice six pack!"

"It sounds like you are kind of into him."

"I just don't want the relationship to be built on the whole damsel in distress scenario."

"Take it slow and ask God for guidance. If Fred is the one, God will work it out in due time."

"How are you and Mike doing?"

"We are great! I am living with him for the summer while his girls are visiting. They are so adorable."

"'I'm sorry that I doubted ole Mike."

"Mike is wonderful. We encountered some things that we needed to work through. So, we both went to counseling and we have been stronger ever since."

"So is it safe to assume your wedding bells will be ringing next."

"We are just taking it slow and going with the flow for now."

"I must admit that I am a little disappointed that Carol didn't include me in the wedding party."

"Well hon, what did you expect? If she did not have Carl wrapped around her finger, you could have caused serious damage to their relationship. Or even worse, you could have gotten her hurt if he were a violent type of guy."

"I know! I acted so foolish! I was hurt and miserable and I wanted company in that state. I never meant to betray her. I was not thinking straight, but I have tried to apologize a hundred times."

"She forgives you. She invited you to the wedding and that speaks volumes for Carol. Just give it more time. You have to accept the baby steps with her for now."

"I guess you are right."

"Will Fred be accompanying you to the wedding?"

"Yes, he will."

"I got my eyes on the two of you."

"I volunteered to pay for everything, but he was not having that."

"That is what a real man does. He holds his own. I am glad you now realize that."

"I don't know who raised Sam? He would have wanted me to pay his way and more. By the way, he wrote me a letter."

"What in the hell could he possibly have to say?"

"I don't know. I didn't read it. I shredded it."

"Good for you! I am so proud of you, Tish."

"I refuse to relapse; and I am sure that letter would have sent me backwards. From now on, I am making myself the priority!"

"Let's toast and drink to Tish taking charge of her life and never looking back!"

"Cheers!"

"Tish! This has been great, but I have to get going. I have to do some last minute things for the bachelorette party; plus I have some plans with the girls."

"Okay. Do you need me to do anything?"

"If you want to come over later tonight to help me bag the gifts for the party, you are more than welcome."

"Sure. I would love to."

"Here is Mike's address. Be there at ten tonight."

"Okay, see you then."

"Alright! Later."

CAROL

Carl has already left for Delaware. I stayed behind because I had some unfinished business to handle before departing this great city. Besides, I still have to attend my bachelorette party. We have already sold our home, so I am crashing at Lisa's house while I recuperate from my procedure. That was the second hardest decision I have ever had to make in life. The hardest was when I had to take my mom off of life support. She knew that I could not do

it, so she made the decision for me. I must admit that I never anticipated the need to have an abortion. However, it is not fair to bring a child into a complicated situation. The world is already complicated enough; and I refuse to add to the statistics.

Donovan has been begging to see me. I have been holding him off by using the "I am sick with female issues" excuse. So far it is working. He calls and checks on me several times a day. I'm glad I will finally be able to let this charade go in three days. He keeps inquiring as to when I will be moving in. He said I should be with him at "our house" so that he can take care of me. I managed to convince him that I only feel comfortable being around my bestie, Lisa as I deal with my issues. So far, he has bought my story. I feel bad for having to deceive him, but he left me with few options. More than anything else, I am sad that I had to abort my baby. I have been crying, but I know I must move on. Luckily, moving on has always been one of my strongest qualities.

My bachelorette party kicks off in two days. I have been anticipating the fun and all of the outrageous nonsense that will happen. It will be my last hoorah as a single woman with my girls, and I plan to go out with a bang! Lisa said that she interviewed the male dancers personally. I am going to make it rain. I told her to make sure the male dancer that jumps out of the cake is the sexiest of them all. He will be there for me and only me.

In two weeks, I will be Mrs. Carl Sullivan. I love the sound of that already. I will begin a new career in one month as Dean Carol Sullivan. I have worked very hard to make it to this point in my life and my career. I owe it all to God for giving me the ambition and will power to press on, even when I wanted to give up. God has blessed me, although I don't deserve any of it. I have been lying to Carl, lying to Donovan and cheating on Carl; and he didn't deserve any of that. I have been given another chance to get it right, and I plan to take full advantage of it. My plan is to be the best wife, lover and friend to Carl. We are going to be the old couple that everyone

loves and admires.

Did I just hear the doorbell? Who is that at the door? Lisa did not say that she would be stopping by. Besides, it's her place so she has a key. No one knows that I am here; and everyone who knows Lisa is aware that she is temporarily at Mike's. I am comfortable on this sofa and I don't feel like moving. Whoever it is, they are persistent. I guess I will go to the door and take a peek through the peephole since I can't have any damn peace. Damn!

"I see you! Open the door, Carol!" Like a fool, I open the door.

"Donovan! How did you find this address? I told you that I am recuperating and I do not want to be bothered! DAMN!"

"I am worried about you. I see your house has sold."

"And? What does that have to do with me being under the weather after a procedure?"

"You are supposed to be with me at our house!"

"I told you that I will be there when the doctor releases me from his care. I just want you to leave me the hell alone."

"Forgive me for caring! Where is Lisa? I thought she was taking care of you. Isn't that your reason for staying here with her?"

"She went out. What is with you and your twenty questions?"

"Something doesn't feel right. I can't put my finger on it. You know I will get to the bottom of it. I know you are sick, but you are acting different."

"If your body had gone through what my body has been through, you would act different too. You are a man, so I don't expect for you to understand. You need to leave! You are messing up my high and I need to lay back down."

"I'm leaving, but I will be back to check on you!"

"I suggest you call before you come. Do not show up without calling first! This is not my house. I am visiting."

"See! That attitude you have right now is so not you. I hope your health issue is the only problem there is!"

"Oh, I can assure you of that! I did not want you to see me like this."

"I love you! It does not matter to me. I just want to take care of you and be assured that you are okay."

"Okay. You've seen me. Now you can leave. Call me later!" He kisses me on the cheek.

"You get better. I want my Carol back!"

I slam the door as he walks back to his car. That man is something else. He finds me no matter where I go. That's why I will be leaving the state. His actions just confirmed that the abortion was necessary.

TISH

Life is kind of good. I am back to dating and socializing. Although I am not clear on what is happening between me and Fred; I must admit that I am enjoying the mystique of it all. We flirt with each other regularly, and I have a standing date with him every Thursday. He typically sends me flowers every Monday and places a sweet card on the refrigerator before he leaves for work each Tuesday. He seems like he is in the wooing stage, and it is working. I like being pursued by him. He is definitely a true gentleman which is a little hard to find these days. I met a man the other day at the gas station, and he was a bit of a charmer. He looked good in his navy uniform and he had the sexiest lips. We exchanged phones numbers with each other and he sent me a text this morning to say hello. I guess confidence in a woman is attractive to some men.

Confidence is something that I learned in therapy. Ever since I was a child, I have held my head low. My self-esteem was low due to my weight. I was told by one of my aunts that a man would never want me. I was teased by other children, including my cousins. My uncle molested me at the age of twelve and told me that I might as well have sex with him because he is the only man who will ever want me. I allowed Sam to treat me with disrespect because I never forgot what my uncle said to me. I was happy that he gave

me any attention and wanted to be with me. I became friends with Carol and Lisa because they would always defend me when others teased me. They protected me and looked out for me. Carol would fight for me. She has always been a firecracker. Fred has made me feel worthy for the first time. Adults can really damage children in a way that will affect them for a lifetime. My mom was the only adult whom I felt really loved me as a child.

Carol's bachelorette party is in a couple of days. I went over to help Lisa bag party favorites for the guests. She and I had a great time doing so as we reminisced over our high school and college days. I do not have a single memory in my past that does not include Carol and Lisa. I am lucky to have those chics in my life. Lisa has welcomed me back with open arms; but Carol has welcomed me back with a slight cold shoulder, and that is okay. At least she is finally speaking to me and allowing me to witness one of the greatest moments of her life.

Maybe one day I will have my own great moment. I now know that anything is possible. I have to love myself first before I can love someone else, and I am getting there little by little. That is my reason for taking baby steps with Fred. I have decided to go on a date with the navy man to explore my options. There is no harm in having a meal with someone; at least that is the line that Carol uses. Hell, it got her two wedding proposals!

I have been packing for Niagara Falls. I hear that it is a beautiful place and that it is very romantic. I plan on turning up the heat on Fred during our stay. He has tried several times to turn up the heat on me, but I hit him with the "let's take it slow" line. He respects me enough to accept the terms. When that man kisses me, I seem to melt like ice cream on a hot summer day. Whew! The things that I have in store for him! I hope he is ready! When I ordered Carol's gift for her bachelorette party, I bought a gift for myself; and it will be a treat for Fred. For now, I just want to get laid; but I don't know how to separate my feelings from just having sex. My feelings for him will definitely grow stronger. I think I need to have a conversation

with him regarding this.

Dang! My phone has been blowing up! I have thirty missed calls and I don't recognize this last number that has called me several times. The only way to find out who owns that number is to call it back.

"Hello. Did someone call Tish from this number?"

"Hi. Yes, I did. My name is Beverly White, and I am a social worker at Baptist Women's Hospital. I am calling in regards to your baby girl."

"Ma'am, you have the wrong person. I don't have any children."

"Bianca Jones gave birth to a baby girl and she has given up all of her parental rights to you."

"There has been some sort of misunderstanding or mix up. She asked me to adopt the child a while back, but I told her no."

"That may be so. However, she has left the hospital and the baby is yours.

"You have seventy-two hours to claim her, or we will place her in the custody of the state."

"I will think about it and get back to you."

That damn Sam is gone, but that bastard keeps surfacing in some shape, form or fashion. I really would hate for the baby to go into state custody; but I am just now getting my life back on track. It is impossible for me to care for another life right now. What if it is my last chance of having a child of my own? Oh Lord! Help! I have to call Fred.

"Fred! Guess what?"

"What is wrong?"

"I just received a call from a social worker at Baptist Women's Hospital. She said that Bianca has given up all of her parental rights to her baby and signed them over to me."

"I know you can't be seriously considering it?!"

"Well, she said I have seventy-two hours. If I don't pick her up by then, she will go into state custody. I am a social worker and I know how those kids are treated."

"You told Bianca no! That is not your problem! You have your own sanity to worry about. I will support you no matter what you decide. However, I strongly disapprove. That baby is part of the reason you went over the edge. Remember to choose you!"

"You are right. Thanks for snapping me back to reality."

"That baby will be a daily reminder of Sam and his foolishness."

"I know. Thanks Fred. See you when you get home."

"Okay. See you soon."

I think I will take a little trip to the hospital. I just want to peek at her. I feel like I can do this. I am strong enough to see who she looks like. There is no harm with a little visit.

CAROL

My bachelorette party is in progress. It's my party and I can get as drunk as I want. Lisa has done it again! She made sure that there is a never ending supply of Ciroc in all flavors. Everyone is dancing, eating, drinking, and having lots of fun. We are all anticipating the arrival of the male dancers, which will be the highlight of the night! Lisa said that she saved the best for last. The DJ is on point with the music. This is strictly a grown folk's party and we are doing what grown folks do! I am on round one for drinks. By the time the dancers arrive, I hope I can still stand to enjoy them. I have two hundred dollars worth of one dollar bills, and I am ready to make it rain!

LISA

Carol's bachelorette party is going smoothly as planned. She is having a good time and so is everyone else. We have plenty of food and drinks, so most likely no one will be able to drive home tonight. When I booked this party, I booked two extra suites for those who would be too wasted to drive. I know my friends and associates. When there is free liquor, they drink to

the last drop! The good thing is no one has to work tomorrow. I informed Mike that he and the girls would be on their own tomorrow. I will be recuperating from a major hangover. As a matter of fact, I will be spending the next twenty-four hours after this party at my house with Carol. Where are those male dancers? I am ready to see some sweaty balls.

TISH

I am trying to enjoy myself at this party, but my mind keeps thinking about that poor little baby girl. She is beautiful. Part of me wants to take her home and give her all the love in the world, especially since Bianca trusted me enough to leave her in my care. It would be a shame for her to get abandoned twice. On the other hand, I will get so much criticism from those who love me if I take her in. I have less than forty-eight hours to make a decision. Maybe if I keep drinking this Ciroc, it will give me the courage to go get her and say to hell with what everyone else thinks about it. In the meantime, I am going to get wasted and enjoy all of these masculine hunks that are about to grace us with their presence. Let the foolishness begin! Carol is ready and so is everyone else. Lisa sure knows how to throw a last hoorah. It's time to make it rain! As soon as I sit down on the front row, we hear a knock on the door. When Lisa answers, we see this fine ass man dressed in a fireman's uniform. Actually, it's ten of them, so they must be the dancers. Yasss, honey! The fun is about to begin. Lisa invites them in and makes her way over to introduce them.

CAROL

"Ladies, the wait is over! Carol, take a seat front and center next to Tish" says Lisa. The guests applaud, laugh, scream and whistle.

"You don't have to tell me twice."

"Ladies! Are you ready for some pure adult fun?" The room is loud with horny women ready to tear these men apart, and Tish is the ring leader! She

is more excited that I am.

As Lisa gives us an introductory speech, someone suddenly yells out "Stop stalling! Open the damn door and let them in!"

"I present to some and introduce to others your entertainment for the night; Chocolate, Eternity, Sexy Caramel, Dr. Hung, Mr. Make You Scream and company!"

All of the ladies are going crazy, running wild, and making it rain! I am too tickled at Tish. Mr. Hung is definitely living up to his name! That has to be all of fifteen inches! Oh mercy! He can have all of my dollars! Tish is making it rain and having herself a good time with Mr. Hung as he picks her up and turns her upside down. Lisa is chasing Mr. Chocolate.

"Yeah! Mr. Chocolate! Come on! Bring it here!" Mr. Chocolate obliges Lisa. Caught off guard, Lisa screams, "Oh God! He just picked me up by my thighs and lifted me up to his mouth. His head is buried in my stuff! I wonder if Mike can do that!"

I am laughing so hard at Tish and Lisa! These guys are putting on a great show. The women are thirsty; but damn, these men are fine! I can't seem to choose. Lisa said there is a special one waiting just for me. If it gets any better than this, my heart may not be able to take it. I guess I am a part of the thirsty crew as well. Oh well, I need my thirst quenched.

TISH

Eternity is strong as hell! He just picked me up and put me in a straddle position. Now he is holding onto me tight. I wonder can Fred do me like this! Whew! I love it! He is wearing an Apache Indian Chief costume. If Fred can handle me like that, I would never allow him to leave! I just threw him about fifty ones.

LISA

This party is wild! If we keep this up, hotel management will most likely come and kick us out. Mr. Make-You-Scream is working the room. I am

throwing my girl one hell of a bachelorette party! "Hey! Come back here! You missed me!" These men will make us forget about the men we all have at home. Mr. Make-You-Scream is something serious! He is picking women up and swinging them two at a time! What the hell? They are worth the money and we are enjoying ourselves.

"Ladies, ladies! I know that we all enjoyed that!" The room erupts with women screaming "yeah" and "we want more!"

"Hold on! We have the grand finale which is for the bride to be! After all, this event is for her, right?" Once again the room erupts with screams and applauses.

Then Tish jokingly interrupts and says, "That doesn't mean she has to be the only one who gets to have more fun."

"Hush Tish! You can watch this one, but you can't touch! He is for the bride to be! I present to you, Carol, Mr. Gigolo!"

CAROL

It is real up in here! I may just cheat one more time before I get married. After all, it will be my last bang! Why not? Mr. Gigolo is drop dead gorgeous. He is a red bone, and his long wavy black hair is pulled back into a ponytail. He is about six feet nine inches tall with green eyes, big feet and a big dick! Somebody help me! He is what we call a pretty mofo and he has all the characteristics of the other dancers in one package. "Back the hell up, ladies! This one is all mines!"

As he begins to put on a spectacular show just for me, I am the center of his attention. He came with the works, too. He is feeding me strawberries, and even has whip cream and handcuffs. He is definitely old school! "Eat your heart out ladies!" Damn! He is putting me in positions that I didn't know existed. Shit! He can get it tonight if he wants to! I have condoms in my purse. No! Wait! With all of that between his legs, he might hurt me. I will just dream about this fantasy he is providing.

"Carol, I don't need to ask if you enjoyed the show. However, do you need a shower? I damn sure need one. Lisa sure knows how to bring the entertainment!" Tish says as she dances to the music.

"Hell yeah! Everyone will be talking about this shit for months to come! Thank you, Lisa!"

"You are welcome! I think we should hit up Beale Street."

"No girl! I am too tired and too drunk to stand. I am going to bed."

"Come on!   I know the party animal is not tired. You can't hang anymore, Carol?" Lisa asks.

"Not tonight! I have reached my limit. You girls go ahead and enjoy. I will be fine right here!"

"Come on Tish! We still have time to catch the trolley."

"See you later, Carol. Party pooper!"

"Damn! She is asleep already!"

LISA

It is a good thing that Carol was too passed out to join us on Beale Street. As soon as we got off of the trolley, I saw Donovan's ass. He was questioning me about her. I told him that she is still recuperating and to give her some time and space. Big mouth ass Tish was about to tell him that we left her at the hotel because she was too tired after the party. I had to kick her to make her shut the hell up. He went on and on about her not answering her phone on tonight. I lied and told him that I hid her phone so that she could rest. He demanded that I return her phone as soon as I got back to the house. He claims he needs to hear for himself that she is fine. If he doesn't hear from her by 9:00a.m., he said he will be at the door. He is a damn fool! Now I see why she has to leave and why she is being discreet. That fool was yelling and pointing his finger at us. He is a hot mess!

Two events are now down and there is one more to go. I am not one to brag; but I did that! As maid of honor, my task from now on is to keep Carol

calm. Patricia, the wedding planner, can bring the rest of this home. Tomorrow, I will be leaving with Carol for Delaware, to help drive and help get the new home in order. I am glued to her until after the wedding. I want to take the girls with me. Hopefully, Mike has gotten an answer from Shelia granting me permission to take them.

Being involved in Carol's wedding planning has helped me make a decision regarding Mike's proposal. I have decided to say yes. I plan to give him the answer at the reception. I think that will be the perfect time to make it special. I love being with him and I love being a stepmom to those girls. The right thing to do is make it official. Carol just needs to get ready for a lot of traveling. Both Carol and Tish are going to be maids of honor, but I want Carol to take the lead. Actually, Carol will be the matron of honor because she will be married. Love is in the air! Maybe Tish will soon find love, too.

Carol has agreed to watch the girls, tonight. Mike and I need some alone time before I leave for the next two weeks. I need to remind him of some things; and I just need some good ole TLC! We are having dinner at Ruth Chris' Steakhouse, and a nightcap in the jacuzzi later.

"Hi baby! You're looking sexy as hell and you smell good too!"

"Thank you. I see you missed me last night."

"Yes, I did! I like hanging with my girls; but there is nothing like being held by your strong arms."

"I sure missed you last night. I cuddled with the pillow. Damn! I just thought about that. I will have to cuddle with the pillow for the next week and a half. I won't see you until Niagara Falls! I take it back. You cannot go! Just kidding! I should take off and go with you. I'm sure Carl can use some support. I can help him with the man cave."

"I like that idea. You should really consider it."

"I have plenty of days that I can take. I will check on that tomorrow. I probably won't be able to leave until Wednesday though."

"Just come when you can. I will let Carol know as well. Oh! What did

Shelia say about the girls going with me?"

"She had a thousand questions, but I shut her down. I told her that you take better care of them than I do. Plus, the girls were all hyped up when they talked to her. They told her about all of the fun that they are having and how great you are."

"Awww! I feel so special."

"You are special. I knew that the first day I met and chose you."

"Sure you did. I thought you were alright, too. I only had to whip you into shape."

"Whip is the correct term to use. I was not ready for Kung Fu Lisa!"

"Some men are intimidated by it!"

"Can you blame them?"

"Whatever! I am so glad that you agreed to go to therapy."

"Therapy has saved my life and kept me out of jail! A brother has dealt with some issues in his life."

"Mike, we all have issues whether we are willing to admit it or not."

"I love you for accepting me and helping me cope with my issues."

"Thank you for accepting me and helping with my issues as well. I love you back."

"Do you hear that?" Mike asks.

"What?"

"Peace and quiet! There are no little feet running around, and no loud TV or music. Just quietness."

"I am actually enjoying the noise."

"Yeah right! Tell me anything. It's okay to get tired."

"No Mike, I am serious. I am having the greatest time with them."

"I know you are! The excitement is written all over your face; and they light up with you as well."

"I am just glad they are enjoying their stay. I was thinking about taking them to Toronto's Wonderland while we are in Canada."

"No Lisa! They are taking a trip to Niagara Falls. That is enough!"

"But we will be so close, Mike. Oh come on!"

"I am putting my food down on this one. No!"

"Okay. Party pooper!"

"Enough talk about everything else. Let's enjoy this time alone."

"I am ready for the jacuzzi. We could have skipped dinner."

"Listen at your fast ass!"

"Yeah, but you love it!"

"Indeed I do."

CAROL

Geez! It is 4:00a.m. and I am up packing my car to leave for Delaware. I am so ready for this new journey with Carl. I am leaving my old ways behind, which means no more cheating with any man; no matter how tempting or charming he may be. I am mainly leaving Donovan behind. He is going to flip out when he discovers that I am gone for good.

Once again Donovan showed up at Lisa's place to see me. He blew my phone up during the bachelorette party, and he cornered Lisa and Tish while they were on Beale Street issuing demands and threats. My phone displayed one hundred and one missed calls and fifty text messages. It is really not that serious. He saw me for the last time this morning. I gave him his last passionate kiss which he demanded. I will not lie and say that I will not miss him. However, I will not miss him being clingy and crazy. I no longer have to dance to his beat. As of Monday, I will have a new phone number. If he goes over to Lisa's, she will not be there because she will be in Delaware with me. I really appreciate all that she has been doing for me to help me transition into a new way of life. I am so overwhelmed! With Lisa's help, I will have the house organized in no time. I have one week and one day before we are due in Niagara Falls, and fifteen days before I become Mrs. Sullivan. Life is great!

Carl has been in Delaware for a week now. He said that the only room he has attempted to get in order is the master suite. His idea of getting the room in order is putting up the bed with only sheets for the cover. He mentioned that he has unpacked all of his clothes, and that his side of the closet is finished. So that means Lisa and I, along with the help of her stepdaughters will have a lot of work to do. My Children will arrive sometime later in the week to help as well. I need all hands on deck because there is a lot of house to cover. Lisa has informed me that Mike will also be joining us. Maybe his presence will motivate Carl to contribute more.

It is good to have friends that you can count on and trust with all of your deep, dark secrets. I know that Lisa is that friend to me. Tish still has a lot to learn when it comes to being a genuine friend. I have not shared the news of my moving with her. She is the type that will run her mouth without thinking. If Donovan cornered her, she would tell all and some. I will eventually tell her that I've moved. I just won't share the location. Donovan cannot find me or know where I reside.

"Well Carol, we have crossed the Virginia state line. Do you feel a little relieved now?"

"Yes! I am out of Tennessee and a long way from Donovan. I hated to leave this way, but he pushed me to these extreme measures."

"You should not feel any remorse. He is not, nor has he ever been your priority. He was the boy toy! That is what happens. Boy toys get left behind."

"Yeah, I know. But I need to share a few things with you."

"Oh my! Like what?"

"I continued to have sex with him. Also, he bought a house for us in Arlington. We went furniture shopping and I helped decorate every room."

"Carol! Are you insane? You should never have led him on like that. You know he's crazy!"

"Well there is more."

"Oh God! I think we may need to stop for coffee."

"No! I am in driving mode. Just listen. I need to get this off my chest. For some reason, he had it in his head that I was leaving Carl to come live with him in the new house once our house was sold."

"Where did he get that idea from? Did you tell him that?"

"Hell no! But I didn't exactly correct his thinking either. I just played along up until now. I kept trying to tell him that I was marrying Carl, but he wouldn't accept the truth. Then things began to happen, such as Carl's brake line being cut, his truck was vandalized, and the fool showed up at our house trying to have sex with me. Carl came home and he ran out of the patio door. It was a close call. So I just decided to play his game and appease him until I can get away."

"Carol! He is going to flip out when he discovers that you are gone. Honestly, I don't think he will stop until he finds you. I thought a female vandalized Carl's truck."

"I now believe with all my heart that was Donovan's doing. The crazy thing is I really do love that fool, but I love Carl more. If Carl had not proposed to me, I would have left him for Donovan."

"I know you would have. But let's go back to his antics. He was pulling some dangerous stunts and Carl could have been seriously hurt. "Shoot! Carl would have killed both of you had he caught him in his house."

"Do you remember the day that you went with me to remove him from those hand cuffs?"

"Yes. That was an adventure. You do know that he is going to look for you relentlessly. He knows that we are closer than close, so he will probably begin harassing me. Hell, I may need to move!"

"One more thing. I lied about the type of procedure that I got."

"What have you done?"

"I had an abortion. I went to the doctor for my annual visit and I tested positive for pregnancy. Deep down in my heart, I knew that Donovan was

most likely the father."

Looking stunned, Lisa holds her mouth open for a minute before she utters a word. "Carol! How did you know? It could have been Carl's baby."

"Carl has been shooting blanks for years. The one time that I sleep with Donovan and the condom breaks, I become pregnant. Although I had slept with both men within a four hour time frame, I just could not do that to Carl. I wanted my baby, but I did what I thought needed to be done."

"You poor thing. You have been through some stuff. You are so strong. I would be crazy by now. I probably would be a Tish." We both laugh!

"I made a choice, and what's done is done. I am moving on. My life is about to be awesome and there is no looking back! I am looking to the future. I have been so stressed trying to deal with him, the wedding, the move, and deceiving Carl. It has been exhausting!"

"You have been stressed to infinity."

"Indeed, I have. I finally feel a little sigh of relief."

"If I were you, I would continue to watch my back! Remember, he is a police officer; and he can gain access to a lot of resources if he really wants to find you."

"I know! If he does find me, I will deal with him once and for all."

"I pray that he gets over it and moves on. I hope he finds someone comparable to me, and someone he can love just as much!"

"Your qualities and looks are not all that he loves. You should never have put it on him like that!"

"Girl! You are a mess! I think I will give a picture of him to security in case he finds out when and where the wedding will take place."

"That is a smart move."

There are always consequences for our actions. Sometimes good dick is not worth the hassles that come along with it. I have changed my entire life because of it!

TISH

I have been partying for two weeks with Carol and Lisa. We had a blast, especially at the bachelorette party. I found a good home for Bianca's baby girl. I am just not mentally strong enough to care for such a small precious life. However, she is close enough where I can keep an eye on her and occasionally interact with her. My cousin has been experiencing empty nest syndrome ever since her two children went off to college. She was the perfect candidate to provide a loving home for a beautiful baby girl. She said "yes" before I could even finish explaining the situation. My family can never know that Sam and Bianca are the biological parents. Hopefully, my cousin will be so in love with her to not even care if she ever finds out the truth. As for now, I am the legal guardian. Also, I am the only individual besides the social worker and the attorney who has access to her records. I plan to play a major role in her life and rearing.

Fred and I decided to arrive earlier in Niagara Falls in order to enjoy some of the tourist attractions. It is our first time visiting Canada, and we want to take full advantage of such a beautiful place. God is amazing! This place is breath taking. Niagara Falls is one of God's most amazing creations on this earth. Fred and I have been sitting here staring in amazement at the beauty of the falls from the hotel lobby.

"I could sit here and just stare at this awesome view forever."

"So could I. I have never witnessed anything so beautiful, other than you."

"Ahh thank you Fred. That was sweet of you."

"I am just speaking the truth. Thank you for making it possible to broaden my horizons."

"You are so welcome. I appreciate all that you have made possible for me. It was the least that I could do. Besides, it is no fun traveling alone."

"You know what? I think we should take more trips like this. Let's make a list of places that we would like to visit as soon as this trip is over."

"I like that idea. I actually have a list that Carol, Lisa, and I made some years back. There was a time that we would take an annual girl trip."

"Really?! We can start with what you have and build from there. What happened to make you all stop traveling?"

"Carol and Lisa didn't stop. I chose to stop. It became too expensive for me to travel with them and travel to visit Sam regularly. Basically, I chose Sam over myself as usual."

"He had no idea how great you are!"

"I agree! He would get so angry with me when we would go on our trips, especially if it prevented me from visiting or sending him money. It became too stressful, so I just stopped."

"You placed your life on hold in so many ways for that jerk."

"Honestly, I didn't mind. During that time, I thought I was investing in my future with the man I loved. So much for thinking that our love would last forever."

"You invested in the wrong man."

"Once again, I agree. My friends and family hated him, but I would always defend him. I have lost relationships with family and friends because of him. Luckily, I have been able to rebuild some of those relationships. I was such a fool!"

"No dear, you were not a fool. You were just blinded by love and the power of the penis."

"Ha! Most say the power of the "p" is bad". I guess both can be bad, especially if the heart of one of the individuals involved is corrupt."

"Without a doubt! Are you ready to go for a ride on the Maid of the Mist? There is a lot more to see and experience around these falls."

"Yes! All of this Sam talk is giving me an itch."

Fred grabs my hand and leads the way. Riding on the Maid of the Mist is exhilarating! It takes you very close to the falls. The power of the water that we feel as we sail by is just magnificent! Unfortunately, we both are

now soak and wet; but it was well worth the experience. I was wondering why everyone was purchasing ponchos. Now I know why! I'm just glad I decided to go with Goddess braids as my hairstyle of choice. Otherwise, I would be pissed.

Our hotel has a view of the falls and we can see them while we are having a romantic dinner for two. The falls change colors at night. I think I may retire here. I love water! I can't swim, but I love the peace and calm that water brings.

"Did you enjoy this day?"

"Yes, I did! It is a breath of fresh air to be with someone who enjoys some of the same experiences as I do."

"Tish, I have missed out on so much in life. It is a huge world out here waiting for me to explore. I cannot think of anyone other than you that I would want to experience it with."

"Oh Fred, you say the sweetest things to me. Where were you twenty years ago?"

"Living recklessly and foolishly. I think if we had crossed paths twenty years ago, both of our lives would be so different now. We crossed paths when God saw fit."

"Well, I am glad that God saw to fit to allow our paths to cross at this point in our lives. We are really good for each other."

"We are friends and I cannot wait for us to become lovers. I am not saying that to pressure you. We will not pursue that until you are ready. I am a patient man; and baby, I know you are worth the wait!"

"Let's toast to love and friendship." We clink our glasses together.

"I've been meaning to ask you something. Now that Carol is getting married, how does that make you feel?"

"I am really happy for her! I am a little hurt that I am not a part of the wedding party. And although I understand her reasoning, it still hurts. I appreciate her inviting me though. It gave me an opportunity to visit one of

God's greatest wonders!"

"Yes me too! I will thank her personally at the rehearsal dinner. I'm glad you are talking openly and honestly with me about your true feelings."

"I open my heart to you because you actually listen to me, and I trust you whole heartedly."

"I trust you, too. Carol may be the bride, but you will be the most beautiful girl in the room."

"Thank you, sweetheart! See, you got me all teary-eyed."

"Here! Let me wipe your tears away."

Fred is such a caring, loving man. I am hoping that before we leave this beautiful place, I can give myself to him. I am turned on by him daily, but something keeps holding me back from making love to him. I am going to keep drinking this wine. Maybe this will give me the courage that I need.

Epilogue

CAROL

It's my wedding day! It's my wedding day and we are going to party! Today is my day! Carl and I will say those two magical words "I do". We are leaving out the obey part of the vows because everyone knows that I am a renegade. However, I do the best I can and try to compromise as much as possible. I am going to be the best wife possible.

It has been a long journey to becoming Mrs. Sullivan, and it has not been a cake walk. Our love has survived the test of time. Neither one of us has been a saint. However, we love one another enough to forgive and move on. This day, I am filled with so many emotions. I am sad that my mom is not here to witness my wedding; but I know she is smiling down on me from heaven. Her spirit will be with me as I walk down the aisle. On another note, I am so overwhelmed with joy and happiness until my smile has almost become permanent. I cannot stop smiling. That's just how happy I am. No one or nothing will spoil this day for me. We are in one of the most beautiful places on earth, which is why I chose this location for the most important event of my life.

LISA

God! This place is awesome. I am here to help my bestie get through this day. She does not have to worry or lift a finger because I am making sure that everyone is doing what is required of them. Today is her day; and everyone, including me, is going to cater to her. That beautiful smile she has been displaying for the past two weeks is priceless. The love that she and Carl have for each other is contagious. Being around them for this extended amount of time has made Mike and I want to get the ball rolling on planning

our life together. I don't think I have ever seen Carol this happy. I am so glad that she was able to escape the web that she was in, and be able to experience a magical ending.

Unfortunately, Carol has control issues. She insists on going to the venue to see how it looks for herself. I keep trying to assure her that everything is beautiful, and that her day is going to be perfect. Up until now, I was so confident about my ability to be her maid of honor. I took pictures so that she could have a peek, hoping to satisfy her anxiety. She said that pictures do not give her a satisfactory view.

"Carol! Why are you worried? "Patricia has done a great job."

"I know! I just want to be assured that this day is going smoothly."

"That is why you have me and the wedding planner. Your focus should be on getting ready to walk down that aisle."

"I just want to see!"

"It is not finished! The set up will not be complete until noon."

"The glam squad will be here at noon, so can we go now?"

"Sit down somewhere, relax and trust the people that you have paid to do their jobs. And most of all trust me! Have I ever let you down?"

"No!"

"Just calm down and breathe."

"Whew! Okay. I guess you told me!"

"There is no need for you to get worked up over nothing. Focus on being the most beautiful bride ever."

"I do not have to focus. Beauty is natural for me."

"Now that is the Carol I know!" Suddenly there is a knock at the door. I open the door and see that it is Tish.

"Hey, may I come in?"

"Yes! You made it! Thank you for coming!"

"I would not have missed this for anything. We have been here for a few days. We decided to tour and enjoy the area while we are here."

"Why didn't you call? We have been here since Monday."

"Yeah girl! Why didn't you call?"

"Carol's number no longer works, and I didn't know you were here."

"I am sorry! I thought I texted everyone my new number. I guess I must have missed a few."

"I have been here with Carol for two weeks. I came to help her get settled into her new home."

"New home? What am I missing?"

"Carl and I have relocated."

"Oh wow! You left Memphis?"

"Yes! We decided to start our life together in a fresh new place. "

"Lisa! What are we going to do without her?"

"We are going to do a lot of traveling, skyping, facebooking, google talking, any anything else that is necessary to remain connected."

"Damn! Everything is changing and I am not sure how I feel about it. Please know that I am happy for you; but you are taking me too fast."

"Well honey, I am sorry! Life goes on and it changes daily."

"I know, but that does not mean I have to like it. You are getting married and now you are moving away. I am sure that Lisa will be the next one to tie the knot. As for me, my day may never come."

"Honey, all of our days are coming, including yours! You need to focus on wrapping Fred around your finger. It's obvious that he is crazy about you."

"Have you checked out the package? Have you two sealed the deal?"

"No not really. I mean, I've felt it with my hands, but that is all. I am scared. We have such a lovely relationship, and I am afraid that sex will ruin everything."

"How do you expect to seal the deal without testing the goods?"

"Girl, you better throw that ass in several circles!" We all then share a laugh at Carol's comment.

"I am so serious! You better not let that descent man get away."

"I'm not. I plan to give it to him on this trip. Maybe I will get drunk and get the courage to do it after the reception."

"That will be a good time. There will be plenty of liquor and food. I plan to ride Carl like it's the first and last time!"

"You are crazy, Carol."

"Lisa, you know that you and Mike are going to get busy, too."

"I wish! We have the girls with us, remember?"

"Oh yeah, too bad." says Carol as she and Tish laugh and give each other high fives.

"Oh hush!" Minutes later, there is another knock on the door, and it's the glam squad.

CAROL

The glam squad has arrived and so has the wedding party. Time is winding down! Everything is on schedule and I have let go of my control issues; but only for today. I am just going to try and enjoy this day of pampering and catering. After all, today is my day!

The time is nigh upon us. As I walk down the aisle to Kenny Lattimore's "For You", I take in the scenery of the falls as it flows with all of its majestic power. It is such a beautiful scene. Everyone is waiting on me. My wedding party looks fabulous in their royal blue strapless dresses with long splits, and their silver accessories to complement the attire. The groomsmen are wearing white tuxedos with royal blue bow ties. I will never forget this scene! Our wedding has gone as planned without a hitch!

Carl and I are now spinning around on the dance floor as Mr. and Mrs. Sullivan. Today has been both beautiful and perfect! All of the stress and the events that led up to this moment have truly been worth the joy that I feel right now.

"You look so beautiful Mrs. Sullivan! I let a few tears flow when I saw

you walking down that aisle. You were stunning!"

"Thank you, baby! You were looking handsome and dapper yourself. That salt and pepper hair looks better on you as you age."

"I must say that all the money I spent for this day was well spent."

"Wait a minute! I spent a few dollars, too!"

"The key word is few." We both laugh.

"You know I have expensive taste. I tried to include you as much as possible, but you told me to handle it."

"Baby, I am not complaining. I am just making an observation to say that I am satisfied. I tried to book Kenny Lattimore to sing "For You".

"What happened?"

"That would have broken the bank! I still have to shop when this is all over. Thank you for being considerate. I love you Mrs. Carol Sullivan."

"I love you more Mr. Carl Sullivan."

"Considering the amount of money that we invested into this wedding, the move, and that house, neither of us are going anywhere. We are bonded for life!"

"Agreed! If we get to a place where we cannot get along, the house is big enough that we can live in separate quarters until we work things out. I'll be taking the downstairs."

"No ma'am! You don't get to choose first."

"Oh yeah! I forgot! You allow me to think that I run things." I say as I wink at him.

"After all of these years, you finally get it."

"Whatever man." Deep down inside, I know I chose the right man.

TISH

Carol was so beautiful on today. Her wedding will be the topic of discussion for years to come. Lisa will have to really bring it in order to top this wedding and reception. Fred and I are having so much fun at this

reception. It has turned into an old school party, and I don't want it to end. There is a never ending supply of food and drinks and the bartender is spectacular! Not only can he fix a good drink, he is also pleasing to the eye.

"Easy on the drinks, Tish."

"Oh relax and enjoy the fun."

"I don't think alcohol and your meds work well together."

"I didn't take my meds this morning. Besides, I wanted to see if I could function without them. So far, so good."

"I am just looking out for you."

"I know; but stop worrying about me and live a little. I am fine! As a matter of fact, I am better than ever."

"Ok lady. I believe you. I am taking your word for it."

"Come on! Let's get out of here! I think that it is time for us to take this relationship to the next level."

"Are you sure?"

"I have never been so sure of anything in my life. I want you to make love to me until the sun rises."

"I thought you would never ask!"

LISA

Thank God all of that is over! I am exhausted! I got my bestie down the aisle and to the altar. She looked radiant; and both she and Carl looked so happy! Now, I can get back to focusing on Mike and the girls. Although we still have another month to spend with them, I am going to miss them when they leave to return to Charlotte. However, Mike and I will then be able to get back to our date nights! I miss those nights. Nevertheless, I think I have mastered the science of balancing family life.

It was good seeing old friends and classmates at Carol's wedding. It is certainly true that people change. Most of all, I am elated that me, Carol and Tish are on common ground with our friendship again. Also, we all have

found happiness. As children, the three of us became hopeless romantics and have remained as such throughout our adulthood. I guess the sayings "there is someone for everyone" and "love conquers all" are true!

DONOVAN

A month has passed and I have not heard from nor seen the love of my life. I am living in this huge, lovely home missing her. I know that Carl is to blame for her leaving me without saying a word. They are off the radar right now, but I will find them! I am going to dedicate the remainder of my life and my career to finding her and having my happily ever after with her, by any means necessary!

About the Author

 Carolyn R. Green hails from the city of West Memphis, Arkansas. She received a Bachelor of Science Degree in Mathematical Science from LeMoyne-Owen College in Memphis, Tennessee. She also holds a Master's Degree in Teaching from Grand Canyon University, and a Doctorate Degree in Education Leadership and Administration from Walden University.

She is the mother of two adult children, Toriano Green and Sheneetra Wilson, and the grandmother of two grandsons, Torian and Thomas Green. She currently resides in Nashville, Tennessee.

To order in bulk, or to purchase additional
copies of this book, please contact the publisher:

www.azaidamedia.com
Email: info@azaidamedia.com